Stories for Men...
and Women with spirit

CORNUCOPIA
by Roger Pullen

A Trilogy – Part 1

Includes Chapter 1 of **AZZARO,** part 2 of the trilogy

Published by Tigermoth

CORNUCOPIA

The right of Roger Pullen to be identified as the author
of this work has been asserted by him in accordance with the
Copyright, Designs and Patents Act 1988.

Copyright © Roger Pullen 2009

Cornucopia first published 2009

Cover design by www.design-ig.co.uk

A CIP catalogue record for this book is available from the
British Library

ISBN: 978-0-9562714-0-2

Tigermoth is a division of Royalblue Ltd

www.tigermothbooks.com
tigermothinfo@me.com

Shorts S23 C-Class Flying Boat

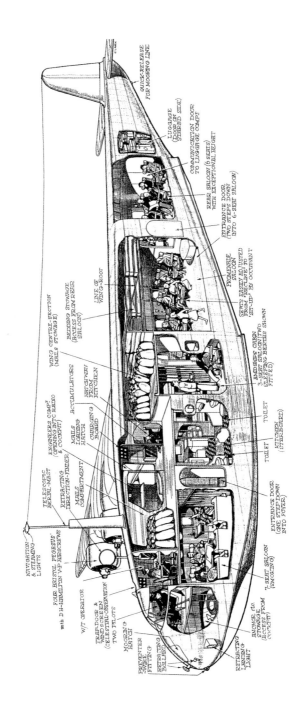

Cutaway by James Clark, in 'The Aeroplane', 4 March 1936

NAVIGATION & STEAMING LIGHTS

FOUR BRISTOL 'PEGASUS' with DH-HAMILTON V-P AIRSCREWS

W/T GENERATOR

TRAP-DOOR & WINDSCREEN (CELESTIAL-OBSERVATION) TWO PILOTS

MOORING HATCH

PREVENTER-WIRE FITTING

RETRACTING LANDING LIGHT

ANCHOR etc. STOWAGE (ACCESS FROM COCKPIT)

RETRACTING BOLLARD

TELESCOPIC AERIAL-MAST

RETRACTING DIRECTION-FINDER

MAILS COMPARTMENT

ENGINEERS COMPt (CONTAINING RADIO & COCKPIT)

ACCUMULATORS

MAILS LOADING HATCH

CHARGING BOARD

HATCHWAY FROM KITCHEN

WING CENTRAL-SECTION (MAILS STOWAGE)

BEDDING STOWAGE (ACCESS FROM REAR SALOON)

LINE OF WING-ROOT

ENTRANCE DOOR (ONE STEP DOWN INTO FOYER)

7-SEAT SALOON (SMOKING)

TOILET

TOILET

KITCHEN (MIDSHIPS)

MIDSHIPS CABIN 3-SEAT SALOON (TWO SLEEPING BERTHS SHOWN FITTED)

SEATS EASILY ADJUSTED FROM RECLINE TO SIT-UP, BY OCCUPANT

PROMENADE SALOON

ENTRANCE DOOR (TWO STEPS DOWN) INTO 6-SEAT SALOON)

REAR SALOON (6 SEATS) WITH EXCEPTIONAL HEIGHT

COMMUNICATION DOOR TO LUGGAGE COMPt

LUGGAGE (DOOR ON STARBED SIDE)

QUICK-RELEASE FOR MOORING LINE

ONE

Twenty knuckles whitened and tightened as they strove to restrain the huge machine. Survival was the priority. Control was fleeting. Stomachs churned with fear. Despite being 1938's finest; the huge four-engine flying boat was in serious trouble, routing north to Rangoon. There had been no respite for three frightening, turbulent hours since the boat had been hit by an unpredicted tropical storm more violent than any in Captain Michael Kelly's extensive flying experience.

Snatched fragments of what lay below appeared briefly as clouds were torn open by the storm. Heavy rain pounded the windscreens and taut aluminium hull of Empress Airways' flying boat Cornucopia as it bucked and heaved downwards through the swirling grey vapour. Brittle shards of lightning stabbed the clouds filling cockpit and cabin with fleeting intense light.

Suddenly, at just eight hundred feet, the roiling grey stratus gave way to a frayed and ripped cloud base racing past just above their heads. They had full sight of the grey-green maelstrom below, liberally daubed with sprawling white breakers.

Irish-Australian by birth, Captain Michael Kelly was a rugged, no-nonsense individual, tanned from years of working in the tropics; a wry smile never far from his slightly lop-sided features. His outwardly easy manner stemmed from his confidence in himself and his ability within his chosen profession. In the aviation world he was known and respected as an exceptional pilot with not a single blemish on his varied flying record. Out of the cockpit it had been a different story whenever he came within arm's length of a spirit bottle. The early-thirties depression years had been a desperate struggle with alcoholism. His father's untimely death left a huge gap in his life; he had worshipped the man and his way of making things clear to him in those rare moments when he was able to devote the time to answering Michael's endless questions. Alcohol helped dull the ache of loss and relaxed the memory.

Time and again he'd pulled back from temptation, fought it and eventually come out stronger. His emotional life remained largely unfulfilled, empty, save for one or two quite unsuitable long-term relationships. His life was spent largely divided between aircraft and the many bars on his routes from here to there. The emptiness had on a few occasions led him again down the slippery slope towards alcohol dependency. After each skirmish with his demons, he came back rationalising it was just an experiment in control; managing to get a grip of himself in time, conscious of its futility. It was the returning realisation that his love affair with booze could stop him flying, and that fact played a bigger part in his resistance than the prospect of an untimely alcohol-induced death. Inside, deep within his soul, he knew the skirmishes were in a sense cries for help – for companionship, for a devoted woman, for love, he supposed. But it had been his love of flying, his justified self-confidence in the air that had got him through the worst of times. And there had been many.

Now, fighting for all their lives, he felt almost powerless for the first time as he marshalled all of his considerable resources to control Cornucopia. He was uncharacteristically thin-lipped, ice blue eyes set hard in a face drained of colour and reaching deep into his reservoir of experience. He spoke sharply, ordering his First Officer and co-pilot Oliver Stoneman.

"Okay, let's try number one, Mr Stoneman. Now!" He ordered

a restart of the silent engine. Rough running and dwindling oil pressure had forced them to shut down the sickly motor just an hour or so into the flight. It was Oliver Stoneman's first flight as a fully qualified first officer – a true baptism of fire, not what he'd anticipated. He glanced across at his skipper, then, rapidly undertook the pre-start checks.

"Primed, prop fine pitch, throttle set, mags on." By rote Stoneman went through the procedures then pressed the No 1 start button.

Glancing momentarily out of the window to his left, Michael Kelly watched as the huge three-bladed metal propeller turned under Stoneman's influence. Jiggling the throttle lever to and fro brought a faint gasp of blue combustion smoke, sucked hungrily from exhaust stubs by the tearing air. Then nothing.

"Again! Keep it pressed till it catches!" Kelly barked. Stoneman reprimed, pressing the button again. Once, twice, the engine caught, turning frantically for a few seconds, promising. It clattered and banged, ejecting long yellow and blue streamers of partially burnt fuel that cast vivid colour and shadows onto the side of the flying boat and through its cabin windows. They willed the engine to live.

"Again, dammit!" His calm had slipped.

Stoneman, increasingly worried, continued pressing until the recalcitrant engine refused all commands. Down to five hundred feet, their height was critical. Kelly made a crucial decision.

"It's going to be an open sea landing; our only choice." It was a bald statement of their only remaining option. Stoneman swallowed hard, acknowledging with a glance and a nod. He thought it might come to this but had hoped against hope for something else. His insides were knotted, throat dry – and he was shaking with the prospect. Despite his limited experience, he knew enough of the near-impossibility of a successful landing in such huge seas.

With only three engines working, they were barely able to maintain height with their heavy load of fuel, passengers, cargo and mail uplifted at Penang just a few hours ago, en route from Singapore to Burma's capital, Rangoon.

Facing rearwards, seated just behind Captain Kelly, baby-faced and slightly built radio operator Herbert Newsome gripped his seat with thin, uniformed legs tautly curled round its metal base. Newsome appeared much younger than his years. At thirty he'd been with Empress since the airline's very beginning. Despite a prodigious appetite, his frame had somehow failed to fill out after a late puberty; his nervous disposition frequently raised questions among Empress crews as to his suitability for a job that required almost continuous backward flying.

Earlier in the day there had been disagreement between Newsome and the Empress station manager at Singapore. Newsome had a reputation for knowing his rights; there had been a number of occasions when crews had been delayed and passengers inconvenienced by his insistence on his rights. Now, barely able to contain his rising fears, he tried to focus on the Morse key under his right hand. All he achieved was varying levels of roaring static through his headphones as the aircraft plunged through the rain and fine spray hurled up from the wild cauldron below. He continued to key their increasingly desperate plight to a seemingly uninterested world.

Somehow his keying was freakishly filtered from the static in the ether by another flying boat, two hundred miles north of their position. It was an Australia-bound Imperial Airways flying boat routing south to Singapore, presently suffering less from the south-easterly storm that was lashing Cornucopia.

The radio operator aboard the Imperial boat transmitted an immediate acknowledgement but in the local conditions it was instantly obliterated by whines and crackles in the airwaves.

However, a ham radio operator at Singapore picked up both transmissions and jotted down both messages. It was, to say the least, unusual, considering atmospheric conditions and the extreme distances.

On board Cornucopia it was evident natural forces far beyond their control would determine their fate. Below the flight deck in the three large and luxurious passenger cabins, Harry Snell, the purser, prepared his five charges for the unscheduled landing with near nonchalance.

"Mrs Gregson, I think you and your daughter would be more comfortable sitting just over here, facing towards the tail. It might be a little bumpy on landing and we don't want you disturbed too much, do we?" Snell moved on, making similar arrangements for his three other passengers. Each was securely bound inside a bulky kapok lifejacket. He murmured comforting platitudes to each of them, concealing his own growing concern, as the job demanded.

Having joined the aircraft at Penang, George Hudson and his raven-haired wife, Lilly, were fixated on each other; their eyes communicated all that was needed above the enveloping roar and turbulence of the three remaining engines struggling to maintain a regular beat.

Returning home to England after seven years of unremitting hard work building a rubber business south-east of Penang, George and Lilly had looked forward to this break. They anticipated the welcome they would receive from loving family and dear friends after their long absence and looked forward to telling of their initial failure and despair, and eventual success. Both man and wife hailed from the colourless mill towns north of Manchester; a region famed for hard graft and a down-to-earth approach to life and its upsets. Despite all their long time in Asia neither had lost their characteristic northern accent. Methodist in religion and their outlook on life, they were tanned, fit and made for each other. Dressed plainly for the long flight home, and both looking a little older than their mid-thirties, they were fulfilled and mature after their hard work and achievement. They soon realised that not even their recent years of struggle and disappointment could have prepared them for the awful trial to come.

Sarah Gregson clung comfortingly to her four-year-old daughter Beth, fearful of how she was going to care for her in the course of the next few hours – or even minutes. During their welcoming on board at Singapore, Cornucopia's all-male crew had gazed in undisguised admiration at her expressive blue eyes and fine blonde hair, underwritten by a wide, full mouth whose smile was totally captivating. When she was introduced to the boat's captain, it was she who instantly captured him; Kelly looked just a second or two too long. He was immediately entranced, and dared to let himself believe the moment of frisson was mutual. Sarah had been supported by dozens of servants, with the result that motherhood and the tropics had not affected her superb complexion and classic English looks. The crew unfailingly noticed her tall, shapely figure as Purser Snell lead her and her young daughter to their seats. Sarah was the envy of most of her husband's circle of Indian Army friends, particularly their wives.

Wealthy in her own right, a product of a long-established

private girl's college on the south coast of England, Sarah moved on effortlessly to a spell at a finishing school near Lausanne. She was a confident, intelligent woman and mother; she and Beth were returning home to the English shires so that the new baby would be brought into a calmer world and climate, devoid of flies, stiff military protocol and one-hundred-per-cent humidity. Now, little Beth, sensing imminent danger and uncomfortable in the bulky kapok lifejacket, gripped her mother's tailored cream linen suit with tiny hands, her big blue eyes appealing for her safe childhood world to return.

Aft, in the boat's smoking saloon, Colonel Deverall was preparing himself. His greying hair added both height and a sense of gravitas to a lean six-and-a-half-foot frame. Ascetic in outlook, today he had chosen to wear his full army uniform with highly polished brown boots, including service revolver and Sam Browne; an unusual and uncomfortable choice for a long flight through the tropics, thought Purser Snell. The Indian Army had been Deverall's life since he was a boy of just sixteen. Unmarried, and not given to small talk, he felt uncomfortable in the close company of women, preferring male society in the Mess, or to be out and active with his troops in the field.

Over the years he'd found a way to manage his emotions carefully, depending upon circumstances. Much decorated for calculated valour, he was, despite his apparent fear of women, frequently the subject of their close attention; he was an enigma as far as they were concerned. But he had discovered a way of rejecting any intimate advances, and had learnt to curtail his imagination to the point of almost eliminating apprehension and fear. As he sat, looking imperious, his cold gaze absorbed the violent scene below from a window in the flying boat's rear smoking saloon.

His immaculately trimmed and greying moustache twitched imperceptibly as the tumult in him rose. There was a clear difference between his situation now and those when he had led men into skirmish and battle. He was in a medium he didn't understand, and was not in control.

During the flight, fussing over his charges, Snell had tried to offer tea or stronger beverages to any who had the stomach. Although a large man, he contrived to glide around the narrow cabins and the confines of his tiny galley in the turbulent conditions with unexpected grace and balance. It was a skill born of his years as a steward on various passenger ships, leaving the sea three years ago as a senior steward with the Pacific & Orient Line for the air and Empress Airways. His continuing purser's activities, and his duty to appear outwardly confident and caring, helped to maintain a sense of normality in an increasingly abnormal situation.

Above, on the flight deck and positioned just behind co-pilot Stoneman, David Rawlinson, Cornucopia's worried navigator, struggled with a handful of doubtful radio navigation fixes provided by the overtaxed Newsome, now crouching over his radio desk, white-faced with traces of vomit on his lips. Rawlinson sat uncomfortably at the small navigation desk, his tall, lightly built frame hunched over his charts. He had become increasingly concerned at their situation. A serious young man, he looked more mature than his mid-twenties; Empress had been his life since his time at Cambridge University, where he managed a First in pure mathematics and a rowing Blue – they'd lost to Oxford the year he'd rowed. Despite high academic achievement, he had made a grave error in rejecting a once-in-a-lifetime opportunity, or so his father had angrily pointed out: to work at a government radio research establishment near Malvern. Instead, he had opted for a chance to travel the world – perhaps sow some wild oats, out from under his father's narrow influence, at least for a while.

The accuracy of Newsome's reported radio bearings was clearly suspect: the position lines drawn by Rawlinson on his navigation charts were much further to the west than their chosen course would dictate.

He cupped his hands round his mouth. "Newsome, can you do another radio fix for me? That last set of bearings doesn't make any sense, its way out to the west." Herbert Newsome swallowed hard and, looking across at Rawlinson, nodded, annoyed.

"It's difficult, the RDF's not working properly; it's this bloody weather!" He stood, holding firmly onto his radio racks while trying to turn the roof-mounted directional aerial that would give a compass bearing onto a distant transmitting station.

"Try one-o-seven degrees for Butterworth," he shouted down from his position, "I'll try for another from somewhere else." But it was still hopeless; the bearings bore no relationship to Rawlinson's estimates of where they were. Accepting that the radio was proving of little value during the storm, he preferred to rely on his own dead-reckoning estimates.

Responding to Kelly's orders, David Rawlinson gave Newsome his own best dead-reckoning position estimate for voice radio transmission to Butterworth, based on increasingly dubious calculations. But as a trained and now very experienced navigator he was loath to admit that they were actually well and truly lost. There had been no sight of land or sea for nearly three hours since shortly after leaving Penang, apart from a brief glimpse of the west coast of Malaya as they climbed heavily into low cloud routing northwards towards Rangoon.

Likewise, there had been no opportunity for wind-drift

calculations, no reliable radio direction bearings, no opportunity for astronomical sights with his sextant – and no indication of what the wind had been doing at the differing heights flown as they tried to find less violent air. He sat for a moment – his professional mind temporarily numb: a first for him. They were lost, he admitted to himself, and they were unable to tell anyone.

Kelly took full control of the heavy machine as the bespectacled Stoneman took a few moments to don his life vest, half standing to make it easier. Despite his keenness on tennis he was a little overweight, which was accentuated by his ruddy complexion. The bulk added by the lifejacket made life more difficult on the cramped flight deck. When he sat down again, his leather-and-canvas seat belt failed to engage fully.

Water was now streaming into the cockpit in small torrents, seeking out every tiny nook in the boat's thin hull as rain threatened to obliterate the scene beyond the pilots' windscreens. Visibility had dwindled to only a few hundred feet and, at times, it proved impossible to see the ocean below. The three remaining engines, all working hard, were overheating with the effort of maintaining their height in the storm's warm air. Kelly reduced engine power by a few revolutions, carefully trimming the aircraft for a slow descent, intending to apply more power once they were again at a height that gave them full view of the ocean.

His stomach hit his Adam's apple. Fearful, Stoneman glanced up from the instrument panel. The aircraft had either sunk rapidly into an air pocket, or was being physically thrust seawards by a violent downburst of air. His eyes caught sight of the vertical-speed indicator in front of him. Its needle showed a descent of over five hundred feet per minute. They were seconds from disastrous, uncontrolled contact with the water. Already reacting, Kelly thrust the three throttle levers fully forwards, pulling back firmly on the control wheel.

Stoneman glanced expectantly across at his captain as the clawing propellers laboured to produce every last ounce of thrust. Crew and passengers were pressed by mounting gravitational force into their seats, or down onto the floor, in the case of the valiant Snell, struggling manfully in the galley to secure some provisions for their coming ordeal.

Momentarily the aircraft appeared to climb almost vertically, so it seemed to those passengers with the presence of mind to consider the matter. Below, in the forward saloon, Sarah Gregson let out a brief cry as disorientation caught her unawares. Further aft, tense white fingers gripped the polished wood and leather armrest as Deverall closed his eyes, trying to shut the whole awful business out.

Kelly and Stoneman spent a few moments loudly talking through a plan of action for the imminent and dangerous open-sea landing. Kelly knew that no crew had previously managed to land a 'C' class boat and survive in such awful conditions. The seeming normality of their near-routine pre-landing checks was a temporary diversion from what must follow. But the die was now firmly cast; the three remaining engines were complaining overtly, number two – the port side inner – nudging the red line on its temperature gauge, and suffering from slowly falling oil pressure. To accomplish any sort of survivable landing they needed all remaining engine power to control the speed and attitude of Cornucopia during what was certain to be her final critical approach and landing. Further dallying might bring other engine failures, possibly without warning, and potential loss of control.

From a hundred and fifty feet the seas looked daunting. Their size precluded the conventional smooth-water landing, normally done into wind. Such a course would leave Cornucopia leaping from crest to crest like a flat stone thrown across a pond; skimming and skipping until, forward energy spent, she would plunge headlong into the front wall of an advancing wave. Instead, they would be forced to land cross-wind, along the line of heavy breakers, aiming to touch down and stay down on the top of a moving wave's boiling white crest; at least until the aircraft had lost sufficient way. With the aircraft levelled off, Kelly turned slightly in his seat, shouting to the radio operator.

"Newsome, go below and warn Snell and the passengers that we shall be landing very shortly; make sure they are all properly braced."

Immediately Newsome left his radio desk, white-faced and anxious. Clinging to anything solid, he staggered below to warn Purser Snell of their chosen course of action.

On his way back to the flight deck, despite his fear and unremitting nausea, Newsome took the initiative to release an overhead escape hatch positioned in the roof at the rear of the flight-deck compartment. He gave no thought to the mail and heavy boxes of bullion he'd glimpsed being discreetly stowed in the aircraft's secure mail compartment, just behind his racks of heavy radio equipment.

Kelly banked the aircraft gently to the left, ceasing the turn as they flew parallel to the line of breaking seas now barely a hundred feet below. He set the aircraft up for a three-engine landing in the violently snatching crosswind. It would be a difficult manoeuvre with the port outer engine hanging silently unproductive on the wing. Tightening his canvas seat harness once again, he ran his tongue over dry lips, preparing for the most crucial landing in his seventeen-year flying career.

Descending, the two pilots were able to assess the horrifying magnificence of individual seas as they swept unchecked towards and underneath them from their right. It was only too clear that, to maximise their chances of survival, they must touch down on a wave's crest – not into its following trough where the next wave face would overwhelm them immediately and probably fatally.

Stoneman fought an almost irresistible urge to push forwards the throttle levers again, giving the three tired engines power, and to pull back firmly on the control wheel, putting space between them, and the cruelly beckoning ocean. But his faith in Kelly, and a recognition that the remaining engines could not now be relied upon, helped to restrain the impulse. Despite Kelly's undoubted skill, luck had a major role to play in the next few seconds. They estimated the height from wave trough to surging crest at twenty-five, perhaps thirty feet. It was a long way to fall at speed, if their timing and positioning were even slightly wrong.

"Good luck," mouthed Kelly, glancing briefly across at the white-faced Stoneman, and keeping the right, windward wing down, while the aircraft crabbed sideways uncomfortably, tracking parallel to the line of heavily breaking seas now just feet below. Carefully co-ordinated, Kelly pulled gently back on the control wheel, holding on a little left rudder, the right wing still held down. Closing the throttles, the aircraft settled into an attitude near appropriate for a landing in the extreme conditions. Tension on the flight deck, and in the cabins below, was palpable. For a few seconds the only sounds came from three softly idling engines and the buffeting, whining wind.

Michael Kelly's landing in such conditions reflected years

of experience, his mastery and dedication to his profession. Beautifully timed and controlled, the boat's long elegant hull kissed the top of a rolling crest. For few moments Cornucopia ploughed, die-like, along the top of a foaming breaker before settling down the wave's dip-slope, into a trough of temporarily smooth water. Off to their right, a new wave approached, its menace heightened by their position deep in the trough, cutting off much of the pale grey daylight.

Caught by the approaching wave, the starboard wing float faltered in its stable sea skimming. The float, submerged by a cascading wall of water, was torn off by huge wrenching side loads. The now-unsupported wing struck the sea. The approaching crest was on it in a trice. Cornucopia, still running at nearly forty knots, swung violently around to the right, into the approaching wave's near-vertical face. Everything came to a sudden, shuddering halt as they plunged into the moving green mass.

Ocean poured solidly through the cockpit windscreen frames, which only minutes before had been filled with protective laminated glass. The impact with the wall of water also caused the fuselage to split almost evenly along the centre line of the cockpit roof, ten feet aft of the missing windscreens.

Oliver Stoneman's failure to refasten his seat belt properly after donning his lifejacket caused him to be forcibly ejected by the boat's sudden and dramatic deceleration. He left unrehearsed, through the remains of the windscreen frames, into the temporarily green and airless world ahead. Fortunately, he met the imploding windscreens on his way out. They ruptured his chest, giving him little time to consider the loss of his shiny black shoes and new spectacles as he left the boat by such an unconventional route.

Newsome was now headless; ragged and violent decapitation

inflicted by the mass of heavy radio equipment breaking free from its mountings. It had exploded forwards, into his face and chest as the aircraft halted abruptly in the face of the wave. Blood shot briefly in rhythmic session across the cockpit floor before his heart succumbed to trauma. His head was nowhere to be seen, and the Morse key remained crushed in the claw of his bloodied fingers.

Navigator Rawlinson knew that he must have been terribly hurt. He was aware, despite the volume of water on the flight deck, of a great deal of blood on his body, on his bedraggled navigation charts, and in the water surging past him on its way down to the lower deck. Fumbling in panic, he found his seat-belt buckle. Releasing himself, he was surprised to find his body was intact, undamaged, as far as he could tell. Through the openings in the nose of the aircraft he could see a new seascape preparing to pour itself into the cockpit.

Turning fearfully, he struck out blindly for the rear of the flight deck towards the hatch that the luckless Newsome had opened. Reaching up to climb out and onto the roof, Rawlinson heard what he thought was a seabird cry piteously. It wasn't until he was clinging precariously to the outside of the hatch surround that he realised he must be wrong. Any sane bird would be walking very carefully in this weather. Lying belly-down on the slippery aircraft roof, firmly gripping the rim of the hatchway, he looked down and forward towards the flight deck. He saw an arm move. Captain Kelly was still strapped into his seat and apparently shouting.

"God's teeth," hissed Rawlinson, as he clambered down into the aircraft, his limbs suddenly independent, defying logic, this was not a space to be entering again. He found himself staring down at his captain. He was obviously mentally alert but unable to get out. As the aircraft had rolled and slewed sharply around to the right into the wave's vertical face, the centre console and the captain's instrument panel had shifted rearwards and to the left. Combined, they had trapped Kelly firmly by the legs. The briefly airborne and shattered windscreens had inexplicably missed him, passing to his left before hitting poor Newsome and his radios, before continuing in free flight.

Looking more closely, Rawlinson then saw something that made his horrified mind freeze. From where he crouched, it appeared that Kelly had no right leg below the knee. Equipment behind the instrument panel, the forward cockpit floor and the torn and broken metal skin of the aircraft's nose had smashed up and into the area where his right leg had been but surprisingly, Rawlinson noted, there was very little blood; no doubt washed away by the sea, he reasoned.

Below, in the passenger cabins, they had watched the approach to the enormous seas from the windows with fearful fascination. In the comfort of leather seats, and mahogany cabin facings, and with the dregs of afternoon tea still in china cups, the certainty of an imminent dangerous landing was difficult to believe or comprehend. Strapped securely by Snell into the few rear-facing seats, they heard as well as felt the aircraft hull contact the water – it seemed normal, little different to the experience they had all known during previous landings along the aircraft's route. Then, as the aircraft began to settle comfortably onto the full length of its hull, and a sense of naive relief began to envelope them, the aircraft dipped sharply nose-down, rolling rapidly to the right, hurling loose items across the cabins.

Lilly Hudson distinctly heard the sound of smashing crockery in the galley in the three minutes before she succumbed to uncontrollable blood loss from a ripped femoral-artery wound in her upper thigh. As the aircraft had rolled sharply, then hit the giant breaker, its thin hull and cabin floor, over which she sat with her husband, was penetrated by shards of torn aluminium, dragging up wire stays, struts and brackets. The remains of the wrenched and disconnected starboard wing float, together with supporting structure, were driven sideways and upwards through the aircraft hull at speed, like a barbed skewer through lard.

Water bubbling noisily up through breaches in the hull began to fill the lower cabins rapidly. There was momentary panic. Sarah Gregson saw Snell unstrap and grab Beth as he quickly motioned her and George Hudson towards the galley, and the narrow stairway up to the flight deck. Hudson, in denial as to the gravity of his dying wife's injuries, tried to carry her limp, soaked body with him. Blood streamed from her torn blue-and-turquoise batik-print dress. Snell, seeing his efforts, assumed an outwardly impassive role, firmly taking the unfortunate woman from George Hudson's grasp, laying her with as much propriety as circumstances allowed onto one of the submerging leather-bound seats. He intended to return immediately, once his other, more able-bodied charges were safe.

Hudson looked on, not comprehending, numb from events, before complying unquestioningly with Snell's politely bellowed instructions to get up the stairs in the galley and to take young Beth with him. Quickly turning to follow Beth and Hudson into the tiny galley and up the narrow stairs down which water was pouring in a pink torrent, Sarah Gregson glimpsed Colonel Deverall.

Still in the aftmost cabin, Deverall was still not in control and fought to contain the unexpected apprehension and fear that were now engulfing his senses. This was new – an experience beyond his reckoning. He had belatedly discovered that he couldn't deal with it. Pausing for breath, brushing his hair back tidily with both hands, he straightened his tie, looking about for his uniform hat. Water was now tugging at his thighs as he gazed about the cabin. It lay on a rapidly submerging table across the aisle; he lunged for it, pulling its dripping and shapeless form from the consuming water. At that moment the cabin lights failed and what little illumination there was grew a deepening shade of green.

Standing erect, stock-still, Colonel Deverall held his breath, and braced himself against a seat, staring around the darkening cabin and at the rapidly rising water. It was just too much. His right hand fell automatically to his belt. Unclipping the holster, he withdrew the service .45-calibre revolver. With no second thoughts he raised the weapon to his temple, pulling the trigger. He had omitted to release the revolver's safety catch, something he would never have done on active service. The lurching aircraft caused him to lose his balance, as he fell he released his hold and the weapon fell into the rising water. Regaining his balance and now totally soaked, Deverall drew himself up and struck out through the promenade saloon, unseeing, past the finally expiring Lilly Hudson, for the galley stairway, in response to Snell's waving arms and shouts.

Snell chivvied his charges up the stairs to the rear of the flight deck and eventually, and with some difficulty, out of the open hatch onto the fuselage roof. Deverall emerged a few seconds later, still clutching his hat.

The scene was devastating, the contrast unimaginable. Wind and seas were combined in a fantastic co-operation that threatened to sweep them all off their wet and slippery perch. Most of the fuselage was under water; the wings endeavoured to support the impoverished aircraft in a highly stressing, liquid medium, for which original design calculations had never been considered. Waterlogged, Cornucopia emitted loud groans; grinding noises could be heard from her contorted and straining structure as she fought to survive the remorseless blows being struck at her every few seconds. Her engines ticked and hissed as saltwater cooled their overheated cylinders for the final time. The aircraft's huge rudder and fin kept her nose into the wind, and unfortunately for Kelly, trapped in the cockpit, head-on to the enormous breaking seas.

"Where's everyone else?" shouted Sarah Gregson, her words ripped away by the storm even as they were uttered. Harry Snell had also expected to see some of the crew on top, or perhaps on the flight deck.

Rawlinson had seen them climb through the hatch from his forward position next to the trapped Kelly; he'd been shouting to no avail until the girl Beth caught an instant of his cry. Pointing, she attracted the attention of Snell and Deverall, the latter mentally dismissing the child's actions as a manifestation of the fear they all felt, convinced the aircraft would founder in the next few minutes. Snell had been below again and found the injured Lilly Hudson dead. He was trying to drag the heavy mail sack of provisions gathered from the galley up and through the top escape hatch, alone.

Almost succeeding, he glanced down and forward into the darkened flight deck; it suddenly lightened as a new breaker reflected its phosphorescence into the small space. There he saw Rawlinson staggering back towards him, his mouth opening and closing with no sound above the wind's roar. Harry Snell let himself slide back into the aircraft just as another wave swept into the breached cockpit. Water sluiced past him, falling down the stairway to the flooded cabins below, carrying all manner of detritus in its wake. Newsome's torso, still attached to his broken seat, rolled as the aircraft gyrated. Snell was stunned at the ferocity of the injury inflicted on their radio operator and the damage to the forward section of the aircraft.

Lunging, Rawlinson managed to grab Snell just as he was about to be battered against the empty radio racks; the aircraft's motion was unpredictable and quick.

"The captain's badly injured. I need help to free him, he's trapped by...." Rawlinson didn't finish as another breaker surged heavily up and through the broken cockpit windows. Snell could now see the physical effect the aircraft's final shuddering impact with the sea had had on his captain.

"Leave me, get yourselves out of here before she sinks!" Michael Kelly was banging his fist on the control wheel for emphasis. Instinctively, Snell and Rawlinson took hold of the remains of the centre throttle console and pulled. It shifted only a few inches but enough for Snell to see for the first time the real plight of the trapped man. Kelly slumped back into his seat; shock was taking hold, aided by the cool water constantly flooding through the empty windscreen frames and broken bow of the wrecked flying boat.

Touching Rawlinson's arm, Snell got his attention, pointing rearwards before stumbling aft to the aircraft's central mail stowage. He tried to open it but the doors had been distorted by the impact. Eventually one of the plywood doors gave in to blows from a fire axe stowed nearby. Inside, Snell tugged and pulled the mailbags about, well aware that if the boat were to take its final plunge at this point he stood little chance of surfacing alive. He found what he was looking for, carrying it forwards. It was a large folded tarpaulin used by boat crews to protect the bulging mailbags as they were being ferried by launch from shore to the aircraft during the tropical rainy season or English drizzle. Rawlinson looked at him askance.

"We have to stop some of the water coming through the windscreens if we can!" Snell bellowed at the now-comprehending Rawlinson. Together they unfurled the tarpaulin, losing control of it now and again in the howling gale blowing through the flight deck. With a mix of severed electrical cables collected from around the cockpit and some ropes already attached, they lashed it as best they could across the inside of the windscreen frames.

It was not ideal but the effect was immediate: relative calm descended on the small space, most of the incoming water being deflected downwards into the flooded forward mooring compartment below. Kelly looked waxen in the beam of the small flashlight Rawlinson held.

"My God, we have to get him out of there!"

Snell nodded, not quite sure what to do next. He made his way back to the hatch and climbed partway through.

"Any of you have first-aid experience?" he shouted, hands cupped round his mouth.

Sarah Gregson, catching the words, turned to face the howling wind and mouthed an exaggerated 'Yes' at Snell. She was attempting to protect her sodden daughter from the worst of the sea and wind. The child was shivering almost uncontrollably despite the warm ambient temperature. Shock and fear were having their effect on both her and her mother.

Sarah released her locked arm from around the aircraft's radio mast and, holding her child firmly with the other, shimmied on her shapely derrière aft towards the open hatch. Snell backed down the short ladder and, with some misgivings, Sarah passed Beth down to him. Regardless of the state of Kelly and his need for medical help, Sarah Gregson also knew too well that survival time on top of the wind- and torrent-swept fuselage was likely to be short for Beth. Deverall and Hudson sat with their legs dangling through the hatch, holding onto its broad rim with determined grips. They could not be persuaded to come back inside, beyond the storm's blast.

Sarah was aghast at the sight of Newsome and turned rapidly to shield Beth's eyes from the gruesome scene. Rawlinson, seeing the move, wrenched the shattered chair unceremoniously from its pivot with Newsome's inert form still seated, pushing it with difficulty out of immediate sight under the mangled wreckage of the radio desk. A brief discussion followed, then Sarah lay on the wet cockpit floor and inched her way under the partially repositioned central console to inspect Michael Kelly's injuries at close quarters. Her superbly tailored cream linen suit was soaked with brine, oil and blood.

Kelly's right leg had been partially severed some four or five inches below the knee; that much she could easily see. The remains of the lower leg and foot with an immaculately polished but soaked black shoe in place lay oddly, almost at right angles to his leg in among the smashed rudder pedals and torn cockpit floor. Standing up, she took Kelly's pulse and peered into his half-closed eyes. The pupils were now heavily dilated. Moving away from the injured captain, she intimated,

"I need to cut off the shattered and trapped part of his leg. We can't possibly free him with his foot attached, it's hopelessly entangled in the wreckage down there." Her training as a nurse under her surgeon father's tutelage had been long ago and had not prepared her for such an eventuality, even under perfect conditions.

"First we need to remove everything else that's holding him and I need to get a tourniquet around his upper leg before...." She felt a little light-headed but surprisingly calm. Then her daughter's safety became her focus again. "Beth, I'm here," she called, as she stumbled back towards the hatchway, reaching arms outstretched for her first-born. Snell had wrapped the little girl in the only dry blanket he could find among the masses carried on board – some of which were mistakenly but fortuitously located high up in the dry centre mail stowage at the rear of the flight deck.

Sarah hugged the child briefly, thinking how incongruous the unhappy little face appeared surrounded by the huge, unwieldy lifejacket and blanket. Beth was both frightened and emotionally all-in. Snell nodded to Sarah, signifying that he would now take full charge of the child while Sarah assumed responsibility for Michael Kelly's release and immediate well being.

Cornucopia heaved sluggishly in the water, her response to the charging seas ponderous as the water stabilised at a level just below the main flight-deck floor. The sea continued to flow through the space but emptied itself through the gaping hole in her bow and the scuppers formed by the short stairwell, down to the flooded galley and cabins below. Snell sat the child just inside the mail stowage then, turning, looking up at Hudson and the colonel. The latter sat implacable, back to the wind-blown spray and rain, his eyes firmly shut. Hudson faced him across the opening, staring into wind and rain, eyes wide open and red-raw, his face contorted in a mixture of distress and the shock of abandonment. Snell was very concerned for them. He tried persuading them both to come down into the shelter of the flight deck. They refused and stayed put, gripping the hatch frame with whitened hands.

Cornucopia somehow contrived to survive, rising and falling with the serried ranks of marching waves. Her portside wing float now also appeared to have broken away. Snell could see the remains of its cables and support struts from one of the flight-deck portholes as the craft wearily raised her heavy span clear of the water from time to time.

"It's a bloody miracle," Kelly mumbled, as Sarah and Rawlinson returned. They had found a simple first-aid kit by the mail-loading hatch. Rawlinson carried a piece of radio electrical flex for use as tourniquet.

"What's a miracle, Skipper?" asked Rawlinson, allowing himself some familiarity.

"This boat. She still floats after all we did to sink her."

"The landing was extraordinary, Captain, under the circumstances." He wanted to ask Kelly about Stoneman but gave it a second thought, deciding that this was perhaps not the time.

"It's amazing, I've never known a 'C' Class boat to survive this long in conditions much less severe," Kelly said, his eyes now bright again after his earlier lapse. "Bill Gordon lost his 'C' landing in a bloody harbour on near-smooth water!"

It was true; those inside the aircraft had temporarily forgotten the possibility of the aircraft suddenly submerging beneath one of the rolling seas, never rising. Sarah tried to remember her training as she assessed Kelly's state and position. She asked Rawlinson to see if he could find another dry blanket to cover him. While he was away on his errand she looked again at the leg with the aid of the navigator's small torch.

"I'm going to have to do a little local surgery to get you out of there," she said, looking up at him from the cockpit floor.

He looked down at her, grimacing.

"I trust you have a competent anaesthetist in attendance, and full facilities?" His voice strained but the wry smile was almost there. She forced a smile briefly back at him; at least he knew the implications of her proposed approach. Rawlinson did his best to wrap the damp blanket around his captain, muttering soothingly to the trapped man.

"Did Newsome manage to get off a distress call?" Kelly barked, pushing the enthusiastic Rawlinson's arm away.

"I gave him my best estimates of our position but I don't think he was having much success in transmitting. The weather...."

Kelly nodded, he had expected as much with the weather as it was. He thought they were probably well off track.

Sarah managed to wind some electrical flex twice around Kelly's right leg a few inches above the knee after tearing off the leg of his immaculately creased khaki uniform trousers. Together they loosened his still-secure seat belt and pulled the cable tight around his leg before tying it off with a screwdriver from the flight-deck tool kit in place. The screwdriver was to act as the lever for further tightening the improvised tourniquet before the final amputation procedure began. They retightened his seat belt and harness as securely as possible. He was not to move while cutting was in progress. Michael did not complain but sat slumped and motionless; he was back in shock.

What was she going to use to cut the leg, and what if both bones were not entirely severed, thought Sarah? This was a problem she began to quickly contemplate. There was nothing suitable to hand that met her needs. "The galley, there must be some knives in the galley," the thought flashed through her mind. Leaving Kelly temporarily in Rawlinson's care, she made her way back through the pitching boat to Snell, still trying to persuade George Hudson that he would be much better off inside the aircraft. Beth lay curled in a tense ball just inside the open hatch of the upper mail compartment. Sarah briefly smiled at her and brushed the child's wet hair away from her face, attempting a cuddle.

"Mr Snell," she raised her voice, "are there any sharp knives in the galley?"

He looked at her initially with surprise then understood her needs.

"There are, Ma'am, but the galley is under water and...."

He did not need to express his concerns about descending the submerged stairs into the darkened and flooded galley.

Hudson either slipped or deliberately jumped through the hatch onto the flight-deck floor. He looked at them both, not really comprehending.

"My wife ...." He did not finish the statement.

"Mr Hudson, Sir," said Snell, pulling the unfortunate man upright from where he had fallen. "You're safe now, Sir, come and sit over here, out of the wind." Snell knew too well that safety was a relative term in their current position. Hudson moved unsteadily against the pitching of the aircraft, peering forwards towards the cockpit.

"What's happened, why's the captain still up there?" He pointed vaguely.

"He's badly injured, Mr Hudson; we're trying to help him ... remove him from his seat."

Hudson grunted, nodded and sat down heavily, his back against the navigation table now folded down against the fuselage side. Eyes closed, he slumped slightly sideways. Sarah hoped against hope that he could not see the remains of Newsome thrust under the buckled radio desk; it would probably be too much for the shattered man. She and the purser quietly resumed their talk about knives and the dangers of going below to retrieve them with so much rubbish floating about. The subject would not go away. They looked around the areas accessible to them and found nothing else that would prove more suitable.

George Hudson woke suddenly, struggled upright and began removing his soaked jacket and trousers. The purser and Sarah looked at him, assuming he was undressing because they were wet and uncomfortable.

"If you need knives, I'll fetch some. Tell me where they are."

Clad only in shirt and shorts, Hudson moved towards the galley stairs, apparently having overheard the debate a few feet from him.

"You can't go down there, Mr Hudson!" Sarah cried, grasping at his arm and looking into the distraught man's face.

"I have to, I haven't said goodbye." Brushing her arm brusquely aside, he stepped onto the first tread, preparing to descend, swaying with the pitching and rolling of the stricken aircraft.

"I can't let you do this, Mr Hudson. It's my responsibility, I know the layout of the galley, I will fetch whatever Mrs Gregson needs." Purser Snell prepared himself.

"No! Tell me where to find them, I'll fetch the knives!"

The look on the distraught man's face brooked no argument and the pitch of his voice confirmed his intention. For the right or wrong reasons he was going to descend into the airless, flooded cabins. Snell described quickly where the drawer containing the galley knives could be found. Gradually making his way down the stairs, he grabbed some air before his head disappeared under the swirling, scum-laden water.

David Rawlinson joined Sarah and Snell and the three stood staring down at where the water sloshed in ragged wavelets at the upper rungs of the galley stairs. Twenty, thirty, forty seconds passed. Rawlinson moved closer to the stairwell as he undid the now-tarnished buttons of his uniform jacket. Suddenly, Hudson appeared, having shot to the surface in a welter of splashing and gasping. In his hand was a selection of knives, which he threw onto the deck beside the group, then turning and without a word, gasped and plunged back down into the water-filled stairwell. Purser Snell collected his knives together, drying them ineffectively on the remains of his dirt-streaked white jacket.

"Hope these will do the job, Ma'am," he said, "he's managed to get hold of a good selection."

They looked again down at the galley. It was possible to gain a distorted view of the area immediately around the galley stairs; translucent, rippling green light made its way through the galley window from the surface.

"He's not there," Rawlinson exclaimed, kneeling to gain a better view below. It was true: by kneeling down and looking further into the galley space it should have been possible to see any movement.

"Where the hell is he, then? I'd better go down and make sure he's not caught up on something."

Below, George Hudson had made his way aft from the galley through the midship cabin, which was completely full of water, and into the promenade saloon. Unused to this sort of activity, his lungs were beginning to demand relief. Where was she? Despite the shock at seeing his wife fatally wounded in such cruel fashion, he remembered exactly where the purser had gently laid her. His lungs increasingly protesting, he cast around desperately for his Lilly. Increasingly worried, he ventured underwater into the rear saloon: there she was, relaxing in the cabin aisle. While he wanted to be with her both in body and now in spirit, he needed oxygen immediately. As he turned to make his way forward again he noticed wavelets breaking against the cabin rear bulkhead above him. This interaction of water and air needed no explanation and he surfaced into an air pocket.

He had not been into the rear cabin during their journey. Looking around, he saw a large shelf clear of the surging water above the main saloon entrance door. The space appeared to be full of blankets and other bedding, enough for a full complement of sixteen sleeping passengers. In fact, he realised, it was the area for bedding stowage during daytime flying. In any event he knew that they rarely flew at night. He climbed up, out of the water, managing to crawl into the space, water streaming off him and running in small waterfalls from the shelf into the waterlogged cabin below. Most of the bedding and the mattresses were soaked; he leaned back against them to catch his breath. He just knew had to bring her up here and make her comfortable.

Rawlinson turned right out of the submerged galley and, swimming forwards, entered the flooded smoking saloon. He was aware of a strong current hindering his progress. On entering the saloon the reason was obvious. Damage to the aircraft's bow extended down into the nose-mooring compartment. Water pressure on impact with the wave had forced some of the saloon's forward bulkhead panel rearwards, allowing him to see through and beyond the mooring compartment, to the ocean. Lungs aching, he took advantage of the current and swam back to the galley stairs, rushing up the short flight to the air beyond. He took

a few moments, then said, "He's not there, he's not gone forward."
They looked at him as he prepared himself for another dive.

"No, don't go, Sir! He could be anywhere, we don't want you in
trouble as well." Snell was uncharacteristically alarmed.

"I think he's right, he might be anywhere .... we don't know
what could have happened to him down there." Sarah caught
Rawlinson's arm as he prepared to step down into the stairwell.

David Rawlinson had never considered himself heroic or even
mildly brave but felt that, as the senior crewmember still able to
act, he had his responsibilities. Gathering his breath, he prepared
himself mentally for the plunge. The aircraft suddenly pitched
violently up then sharply down, as though swooping steeply
through a liquid sky. Dull, worrying thuds and rumbling noises
came from the void below them. The storm was slowly abating
but as the wind lessened, the seas, relieved from its pressure,
began to rise into chaotic peaks and ravines, at times creating
steeper, even more formidable walls of water. It was one such
freak breaker that had passed under them, causing the sickening
swooping movement, catching them all off balance.

Turning as best he could, Michael Kelly called out, "What's
happening, where are you?" Rawlinson and Sarah struggled
back to the cockpit just as the last water-intake had drained off.
Changing his mind, Rawlinson rationalised that his captain was
the priority now. George Hudson may be trapped, even dead:
although terribly injured, at least Michael Kelly was breathing.
They reassured him by their presence and began preparations
for releasing his leg.

"Here, Sir, you might find this useful." Purser Snell thrust
a bottle of brandy at Rawlinson. "It might help the skipper to
relax, and perhaps help sterilise the knives?" Snell had rescued

the brandy from the galley during his pre-landing gathering of supplies.

"Oh, well done, Mr Snell!" Sarah snatched the bottle from Rawlinson and removed the cork top. Then she did something not entirely congruent with her genteel upbringing. Placing the bottle firmly to her lips, she swallowed a large slug of its contents. Kelly watched her.

"Steady on, girl," he gasped, trying to reach up and relieve her of the brandy.

"I guess if you need some, I need it more!" She gave him the bottle, then quickly took it from him, remembering.

"Before you have a drink, just let me just check that you have no other abdominal injuries." She felt around his chest and upper trunk as best she could. "Any pain here?" she said, pressing on his stomach and liver.

"No, girl, but my right foot is giving me bloody hell," he grunted, through clenched teeth. Sarah studied him carefully then gave him the bottle, warning, "Only a few mouthfuls now," while briefly wagging a stern finger. Unspoken, they all noticed that the water in the cockpit appeared to have risen slightly and was not now draining away completely.

"We need to get a move on – it may not be tenable in here much longer." Rawlinson spoke as calmly as he could, but could not entirely conceal the anxiety born of the responsibility he had inherited for his captain and the rest of his charges. Sarah could not put off the inevitable. Releasing the tightened tourniquet, she prepared to reposition it slightly higher on Kelly's right thigh. Looking down, she anticipated a flow of blood from the hideous wound. It bled a little, but not as much as she had anticipated, considering its seriousness.

"There's something odd here," she thought, as she looked carefully at the wound again, lying on her right side holding the torch to shine along the smashed limb. Then she noticed the front edge of the seat and the broken instrument panel had somehow moved together and had formed an almost perfect tourniquet, cutting off all but rudimentary circulation to the leg.

"So, blood loss may have been minimal," she surmised, as she got up, nodding to Rawlinson.

"Okay, let's get on with it." Kneeling beside Michael Kelly. "Your leg and foot are trapped, as you know. We can't remove them from the smashed metalwork so I'm going to have to do a bit of cutting to get you out. It may hurt a bit," she added, as an afterthought. Kelly looked at her pointedly. He took another very long swig from the firmly gripped brandy bottle. She could see him mentally summoning his reserves as she got up, taking the half-empty bottle from him.

"Do it, but be quick," he said. 'Oh God, don't let me scream out,' he worried silently. Sarah took the brandy, dousing the knives and a piece of linen torn from her skirt.

Steeling herself, she lay again on the wet cockpit floor holding the dimming torch in her mouth. Gently, she wiped the area around the part-severed leg with the brandy-soaked cloth. Kelly made no move; his hands gripped the armrests of the seat until his fingers were white with the effort. Looking carefully, Sarah determined that the tibia was broken completely. The break was jagged but she could perhaps deal with that later. Selecting a serrated and pointed knife, she focused and started to cut quickly and resolutely at tissue and flesh. As she did so, the partially severed leg began to sag away a little from below the knee. Through muscle she cut, blood vessels, more tissue and flesh. Incongruously at this point she found herself thinking he had quite a well-shaped leg, if a little hairy. Then she came to the fibula. Through the severed tissue she could see it was cracked but not completely severed. She would have to saw through it, but with what? Taking the torch from her mouth, she gestured to Rawlinson and he bent towards her.

The scene reminded him of a butcher's shop; raw meat, red and bloody, on display. Sarah's hands and arms were sticky with blood and fragments of what looked to him to be flesh and tissue. He gulped.

"How's he taking it?" she whispered, looking up. Kneeling, Rawlinson spoke into her ear.

"He seems to be asleep, or maybe unconscious; he was groaning and struggling earlier but then seemed to just collapse. How long are you going to be?" There was deep concern in his voice as he watched his captain's pallid face and closed eyes.

"I have to cut the fibula. It's not completely severed. What can I use? I need a saw or something"

Rawlinson gestured to her not to move, and then disappeared rapidly to the rear of the flight deck. Michael Kelly suddenly lurched upright in the chair, tense, his eyes wide open, pain etched indelibly on his face, teeth clenched hard. Sarah made to stand, grabbing for his hand, to comfort him. Relaxing slightly, he looked up at her, his eyes appealing for some relief from the excruciating pain. She leant over, taking his head tenderly in her arms, taking care not to let him see her bloodied hands. There was nothing, absolutely nothing she could do to relieve his pain. He slumped again into precious unconsciousness. David Rawlinson shouted aft.

"Mr Snell! Do you know if the engineer's tool kit was left on board at Singapore?" Snell stood and, cupping his hands around his mouth, responded.

"If it is, Sir, it will be in the accumulator box behind you."

Rawlinson turned and wrenched the lid off the large wooden box fixed at the aft end of the flight deck. Inside, rows of heavy lead-acid batteries sat, normally enough to turn the starter motors for the four Pegasus engines, and more. To one side lay a fitter's tool bag, carried to cope with possible maintenance problems en route. Rawlinson tugged the grease-stained canvas bag out of the box, upending it and spilling the contents onto the wet floor. As he had anticipated, there was a large metalworker's hacksaw lying among spanners and screwdrivers. Moving quickly back to Sarah, he cleaned its blade with his brine-soaked handkerchief, following up with a generous dousing in brandy, and passed it to her. She looked at it, grimaced and took it from him. These were not the Lysol-clean operating conditions she recalled from her hospital nursing days.

The saw was large, the space small and the torchlight waning. Using only minimum pressure, she pushed the saw to and fro, two or three inches per stroke, until, finally, the damaged lower limb separated completely. She grunted with the effort of holding such an awkward position while trying to avoid dripping blood, still gripping the torch in her mouth. Finally, exhausted by the effort and her concerns, she pulled herself up from the floor, water running off her right side. Tearing off a large piece of her silk underskirt and soaking it in brandy, she lay once again, cleaning the open wound then covering it with the protective, brandy-drenched silk bandage. Finally satisfied, she spoke.

"He's free. Let's get him out of the seat and somewhere where I can deal with him more easily."

As instructed, Rawlinson moved and retightened the tourniquet around the leg. They undid the seat belt and checked that Kelly, now limp and comatose, was actually disconnected from anything that might impede their efforts. His breathing was shallow but steady. Rawlinson then levered the broken instrument panel upwards with the aircraft's boat-hook, which had somehow floated up from the forward mooring compartment, jamming it securely in place with two soaked copies of the Admiralty's 1938 Astronomical Sun Sight Tables. Snell, meanwhile, prepared an area in the flight-deck mail stowage where Kelly could be laid in relative comfort. Beth watched his efforts with increasing interest, even attempting to help a little, her small hands arranging the blankets. Neither Rawlinson nor the purser were big men, and Kelly weighed the best part of fourteen stone, even without half of his right leg.

The disarranged seas continued to make the boat pitch unpredictably and the group debated how best to move Kelly the twelve feet or so to the sanctuary of the mail stowage. Space in the shattered cockpit was limited. Most of their ideas failed to meet Sarah's criteria of security for Kelly and the need for minimum shock to his lower abdomen and limb. She looked at the pallor of the captain; there was no pink flush to any part of his exposed flesh. She knew the brandy would not have helped his situation, but what else was she supposed to do with no medicinal alternatives?

Rawlinson took the initiative and stood, knees bent, side-on to Michael Kelly. He inched his fingers, then hands, under Kelly's thighs and around his back. Timing his lift with the pitch of the vessel, he straightened, holding his limp captain like a huge baby against his chest. Rawlinson held his breath with the effort. Kelly moaned continually as Snell steadied the navigator on the left side as he turned to face rearwards, at which point Sarah took up a steadying position on Rawlinson's right. Shuffling together in the confined space towards the rear, they carefully manoeuvred the patient past obstructions and laid him onto the rough bed of assorted blankets Snell had prepared. Rawlinson sat gasping for breath for some minutes after his effort.

Below, George Hudson came out of his reverie, remembering with a terrible sense of loss where he was. He could see her now, slowly dancing in time with the water's surging. Lowering himself from the bedding stowage, he slipped back into the water. It seemed colder now, and the light from the submerged cabin windows was less bright. He breathed in deeply and swam down to Lilly. She gazed at him with open eyes, her faint smile steady and evocative of those days of warm sun and hard work. He pulled her to him, his arms around her back, and kicked for the surface. He thought for a moment and planned what he would do to get her out of this wet, cruel environment. Gripping her dress at the shoulders, he managed with one hand and his feet to regain his position on the bedding stowage shelf again. Kneeling down with both hands under her arms, he raised her carefully onto the platform. He tenderly excused his clumsiness, whispering,

"Forgive me, my love."

He lay back, physically drained. She was beside him, and in the cabin's twilight he looked at her. She was gone: his whole being suddenly collapsed and he cried tears of sorrow and longing. Gone, was this what was planned? Had they joined together to be so wretchedly and brutally torn apart at their moment of success? What sort of bloody God was this? Self-pity was not in Hudson's nature but the past few hours had barely given him time to return to rationality.

He gently removed her wet clothes, intending to dry them somewhere; why and where, he had not considered. He saw her wound again and asked how God or anyone could have been so vindictive as to inflict such trauma on such a wonderful and innocent woman. And they were childless. Sobbing, he turned and, kneeling, pushed and pulled among the thin mattresses and bedding behind him until eventually he found a dry set. Making a space, he laid her out, covering her carefully, placing pillows under her head. He kissed her face and her hands, telling her repeatedly that he loved her; and then he removed her wedding and engagement rings. It was done for the moment but he would come for her again.

Sitting at the rear of the flight deck, Sarah was still recovering from her exertions under the captain's seat. As Hudson broke surface in the galley stairwell she jumped and let out an involuntary yelp.

He staggered up and onto the flight deck, breathing in deep gasps. Holding onto the radio racks for support, he was bent over, still fighting for breath when she saw the gold and silver jewelled rings drop from his grasp and roll towards her. She bent down to retrieve them. As she reached up to pass them back, she looked into his face. He had come to terms for the moment with his tragedy.

Outside, it was darker, the seas quietening, their wind-driven energy almost spent. Sarah looked at her charges. Kelly lay semi-comatose but obviously in considerable pain. How long would the effects of the brandy last, she wondered? How long would he last? It occurred to her that he must have the constitution of an ox as she had cleaned the amputation in the dim torch-light, tying-off blood vessels with silk thread drawn from her underskirt, and managing to sew the untidy flaps of skin over the end of the wound. His pulse was steady and surprisingly strong but she knew her handiwork would have to be revisited by a professional, if they ever got out of this situation.

Beth was now fast asleep. Some colour had returned to the youngster's face following Snell's ministrations. Sarah looked around for somewhere to sit and saw Deverall clamber awkwardly down from his position above the hatch. There was a fleeting, embarrassed smile as he slumped down onto the floor, which was now beginning to dry out in places. Grabbing the blanket they had used to protect Kelly while he had been trapped in his seat, she covered the soundly sleeping Deverall. Rawlinson was already asleep as the tropical night quickly enveloped the remote and damaged Cornucopia. Snell suggested he take first watch, standing in the hatchway. Sarah lay curled around her daughter within easy reach of Kelly. She was now very hungry but sleep proved irresistible.

TWO

The Imperial Airways flying boat that had intercepted Cornucopia's desperate wireless signal landed safely four hours and forty-five minutes late at Singapore. The 'C' Class machine had put down for a while, moored near George Town, Penang Island's capital to avoid the worst of the storm that had now swept out into the Bay of Bengal. From there the radio operator had telegraphed Imperial's station manager, Claude Pardoe, in Singapore of the signal's content, and the timing.

Pardoe had been in aviation all his working life. A studious young man, he had been taken on as an engineering apprentice at the expanding de Havilland works at Hatfield, north of London. As mail and passenger services grew to the British Empire and its dominions, the requirement for competent aircraft engineers had developed rapidly. He was in the right place at the right time; a young man with a sound record of work and supervision.

A fellow de Havilland apprentice had introduced Pardoe to the chief engineer of Imperial Airways, coincidentally his uncle, during one of the growing number of flying displays taking place at north London's Hendon aerodrome. The Royal Air Force was showing off as usual and there was great excitement at the growing mix of new aircraft being flown and displayed – both civil and military. Later, following refreshment in a crowded beer tent and a useful and frank exchange of ideas, the chief engineer asked Pardoe to contact him by telephone the following Tuesday. Pardoe spent the next two days considering the matter and telephoned. He joined Imperial one month later, and within three months was sent to Singapore as the airline's station manager.

Imperial Airways, benefiting from government support as its chosen instrument of international aviation, did not take kindly to the competitive private venture operations of Empress Airways, particularly as Empress had chosen exactly the same type of aircraft for its competing services. Despite this, there had been some local co-operation between the two airlines. Only two days before, Imperial engineering staff had helped sort out some instrument problems on the now-missing Empress aircraft. Claude Pardoe and Empress pilot Oliver Stoneman had also become firm friends during the latter's recent posting to Singapore.

Regardless of commercial competition, Claude knew it was his duty was to facilitate the rescue of a downed civil aircraft if at all possible, and he was concerned for his friend Oliver. He picked up the telephone and wound the handle. The operator was instructed to connect him with the station manager for Empress Airways at their base on the other side of Singapore Island, near Keppel harbour.

After Cornucopia had left Singapore for Penang that morning, Empress Airways had no scheduled flying-boat service through Singapore until the following Tuesday – a southbound boat from Rangoon bound for Batavia and eventually onwards to Darwin. Empress's station manager, Cyril Porter had, as usual in this situation, taken the opportunity for a long weekend, and crossed the Johore Strait by regular ferry into Malaya, intending to visit friends who managed a pineapple plantation near Kempas.

A young local deputy manager manned the Empress offices: Lee Chi Kwan, a thin, nervous man with pale white skin, only a shade or two darker than his crisp white shirt. Speaking on the telephone, he confirmed to Pardoe that Cornucopia had left

Singapore early that morning on schedule for Rangoon with a stop at Penang for fuel, mails and a couple of additional passengers. Penang had subsequently telegraphed the aircraft's departure details to them in Singapore. He also mentioned that they would normally have had some further confirmation of their progress until finally Cornucopia was out of radio range. However, they were not unduly concerned when contact was lost just fifteen minutes after the aircraft had left Penang. Atmospheric conditions frequently made both Morse and voice radio reception difficult in the tropics.

No, they had not been advised of Cornucopia's distress calls and yes, Pardoe's call was the first intimation they had had that something was amiss. Yes, he would attempt to contact Mr Porter but it would be difficult, as he was known to be going away for a long weekend to friends across the strait. But he would try to reach them through the local district officer, who, he understood, had a telephone. In Empress' s outer office the one-sided conversation between Lee and Imperial's Pardoe was listened to with growing interest by Lee's brother-in-law, who had come to share some tea with the young deputy manager, helping to while away the boring hours of his inactive weekend duty. It all seemed rather pointless with no aircraft due. They had been discussing the problems of competing with Imperial Airways, with its assured government subsidy, and Empress's need to maintain a regular schedule as a private airline to ensure passenger and mails brought the revenues needed for their continued survival.

Lee had been less than discreet in boasting to his overweight and perspiring brother-in-law that Empress was now carrying occasional secret cargoes of gold bullion to England from Australia and Hong Kong, to help fund military expansion in the face of growing international unease over Germany's increasingly belligerent posturing. The contract for its carriage was a valuable one for Empress providing they could maintain a reliable and secure service. Lee wrote down the latitude and longitude coordinates given by the Imperial Airways radio operator from the message broadcast by Newsome, onto his desk pad.

Realising that Lee was inexperienced, Pardoe considered the situation, wondering why the Empress aircraft had left Penang when even the Singapore meteorological service had warned of possible serious weather disturbances on the route north to Burma's capital city. Perhaps the crew had thought that they could out-fly the approaching storm. He decided to contact the duty officers at the Royal Air Force aerodrome at Tengah, and at the Changi naval base on the east side of the island. His call to the Royal Navy drew a blank. The duty operations officer advised him that the larger part of the navy's Far East Fleet was engaged in an exercise with the Royal Australian Navy in the Timor Sea, it was not scheduled to return to Singapore for two or three weeks, depending on how the exercise went. Those ships of the fleet remaining in Singapore were either undergoing repair or bunkering, or ordered to remain in port on standby for any military emergency.

"Sorry, old man, sympathise with your situation but no can do," the naval commander apologised with undue bonhomie. "Typical of the navy," muttered Pardoe, unkindly. Wing Commander Don Chivers at Tengah airfield was more positive.

"I've just had a word with my opposite number down at navy HQ – Fleet Air Arm actually – they can provide an amphibian aircraft to help look for the Empress boat from early tomorrow morning – if we can supply one of our own RAF crews. That's

OK with us but it does sound to me as though the position report for their ditching is rather suspect."

Pardoe agreed, thanking the wing commander for his assistance and confirmed that he would be in touch with any new information that might come to hand before the aircraft took off on its search at 07.00 hours next day. Finally, a Fleet Air Arm Walrus amphibian, manned by a combined air force and naval crew, would first have to fly to Penang to refuel before commencing any search out into the Bay of Bengal, there being no other suitable RAF machine based in Singapore.

Lee's brother-in-law finished his tea, continuing to chat about family for a few minutes before taking his leave of the Empress offices. Before mounting his bicycle he quickly wrote down the position coordinates he had memorised from Lee's desk pad onto the cover of a cigarette packet with a stub of pencil. He then joined the Saturday evening throng of bicycles, rickshaws and cars into town. Forty minutes later he leant the heavy black bicycle against the wall of a large, secluded house in a muddy, puddled lane just off Orchard Road. It served as a form of the Japanese trading office; he knocked on the tradesman's door at the rear of the darkened nondescript building.

❖ ❖ ❖

Well before joining the Swire Company in 1936, Harold Penrose had been interested in radio. He had been fascinated by the apparent magic of distant contact through the ether via electromagnetic waves while at school. Later, at university, he'd frequently missed lectures while fabricating some new radio kit, or new idea of his own. His university degree in economics was not of the best, and he was like many young men who failed to meet high family expectations, and found themselves on a ship bound for some distant part of the Empire, all undertaken with the aid of introductions from well meaning relatives. The intention was for them to 'make something of themselves' before returning to England. That, at least, was the theory.

Hong Kong was Penrose's destination. He would work as a junior trade officer within the hugely influential Swire Company. He was lucky in his position and could have progressed upwards with a little more application. But he somehow failed to assimilate what was expected of him both at work, and as importantly, in his social life.

A string of affairs with the wives of some of the colony's most influential expatriates began to affect his timekeeping and work in general; he had also gained something of a reputation as a cad. Considered by most young ladies as handsome, he was square-jawed, tall and well built with a shock of red hair and a ready boyish smile to enchant both eligible daughters – and their frequently bored and often desperate mothers. He was useful with a cricket bat and had developed a justifiable reputation as a fast spin bowler, regularly decimating opposing batsmen in matches with the army, navy and air force, as well as other trading houses.

Being caught in flagrante with the wife of the senior naval officer in Hong Kong in the cricket club house very late one evening – following a closely fought needle match that afternoon – had finally brought Harold Penrose to the premature conclusion of his career with Swire's. A very frosty meeting in a humid, sun-soaked room with the head of his department, and the company secretary, late the following afternoon, led to Harold being given a boat ticket home and a small sum of money to tide him over but, more importantly, to ensure his further discretion. He was given no references.

Later, that evening, he contrived a farewell meeting with the naval lady concerned in her luxurious house around the island coast at Thunder Bay, during the course of which, he impregnated her. Her husband was briefly absent from the colony on naval business. She promised undying love for him and to follow him home to England as soon as possible. He never heard from her again despite tentative messages sent through a trusted intermediary.

His route aboard the SS Chagos had taken him slowly south through the Philippine archipelago, skirting Java, then to Singapore. Bored with the turgid company on board, he left the ship at Singapore intending to catch a later vessel to England. He intended to spend a little time capitalising on his charms with both local and expatriate ladies. On more than one occasion he had become too deeply embroiled; time just slipped by. He was also penniless. The hedonistic lifestyle he had adopted, including a short period of residence at the Raffles Hotel, soon reduced his sparse resources – including those realised from the sale of his boat ticket to a deserting and homesick civil servant – to virtually nothing. But he still had some of his personal effects, including his radios; time on his hands had helped to reawaken his interest in their potential.

Testing a radio set he had newly constructed from the remains of others and casually monitoring the airwaves one wet and stormy morning in his small room at the very top of a run down local hotel, he picked up Newsome's very faint, static-laden Morse message. Something, intuition possibly, made him write it down – along with the more readable Imperial reply. The thought occurred to him that it might be worth doing some investigation. With little else to do he braved the incessant warm rain and went down to the Inter-Services library later that afternoon.

Pulling out the largest atlas he could find he sat quietly at a sizeable teak table under tall windows, and turned up the pages devoted to The Bay of Bengal and Andaman Basin. With scribbled note in hand, he plotted Newsome's transmitted position report, noting its location. With some tracing paper from the young and rather flirty female librarian he carefully made a copy of the map and the reported position. Replacing the atlas, he left the library with a purposeful step. The young librarian watched him go, disappointed; now the rain had finally stopped, steam rose from the rapidly drying roads as the late afternoon sun burst through.

During his all too brief time at Swire's he learnt something of bullion shipments from Hong Kong, and elsewhere, as part of the British government's borrowings from the Empire and its colonies to meet its needs for rapid rearmament. Secretly, Swire's had been partially responsible for the logistics in locating, assembling and securing bullion for dispatch to England, undertaken now by both boat and air. With such an exotic commodity the matter soon turned into an open secret within Swire's. Initially south-west from Hong Kong, then following the coast of Indo-China, the air route eventually connected with the now firmly established 'Kangaroo Route' at Darwin in northern Australia. From Darwin the direction home took in Batavia, Singapore, Penang and Rangoon before turning west across the Indian sub-continent, across the Middle East and Mediterranean until finally heading north from Marseille, across France and over the English Channel.

Harold Penrose was acting on a hunch, nothing more, he knew too well. He had no idea whether the lost aircraft was carrying bullion – despite it being an open secret, detailed information within Swire's as to just how often transfers of gold were being made to the motherland was impossible to find out at his level. But he did know from what little had come his way on the company grapevine, that both regular shipping and now air transport was being used in an effort to minimise delays, and to reduce the risk of loss of a very large consignment in a single, dedicated shipment. He surmised that as far as air was concerned, only two British airlines were covering the route: Imperial Airways and Empress Airways – and that one or possibly both were being used. The problem was how to find out.

Penrose went directly from the Inter-Services library back to his hotel room, avoiding the puddles left by the morning's precipitation. Here he rooted around in a large sea trunk that contained what remained of his possessions, finally pulling out a crumpled business suit, one he had often worn at Swire's. It had begun to accumulate a delicate green mould in places, a problem for unused and unprotected clothes in tropical high humidity.

Calling the hotel owner's thin and harried wife, he arranged for the suit to be cleaned, pressed and made presentable within the next two hours.

In the hallway of the hotel, sat on a heavy marble-topped table, was a venerable telephone. He used it to make appointments with both Imperial Airways and Empress Airways station managers to discuss the secure shipping of some highly confidential documents and artefacts to England. In particular he wanted to be assured that they were capable of handling such valuable items, and to learn something of their expertise in these matters.

❖ ❖ ❖

Lee's brother-in-law, Ng See Wok, was led into a sparsely furnished, poorly lit and windowless room. The senior trade officer would see him on completion of his evening appointments. He sat, or occasionally walked, about the stifling small room for nearly two hours, with only some faded sepia photographs of the Japanese homeland for company. His every move was followed by the searching eyes of the Emperor gazing down at him from an ornately framed portrait above a locked glass-fronted bookcase containing books with indecipherable titles. The trade officer's meetings were pure pleasure, and he made a mental note to invite the younger of the two Singaporean girls to his anniversary celebrations in two weeks' time. His colleagues would be impressed with his choice, he was sure. He may even share her.

Ng was bounced from his reveries as Colonel Kiichi Hyami of the Imperial Japanese Army, de facto Consular Trade Officer, strutted into the room through the heavy door held open by a rather downtrodden and impossibly thin manservant. The servant was signalled to leave immediately. Once the door had closed Ng was invited to sit while Colonel Hyami ignored his proffered and insincere greetings.

Small, even by Japanese standards, the colonel saw himself as a strong and decisive leader. He'd shown his metal in Manchuria and had benefited materially from his no-nonsense containment of local resistance in that now-occupied and oppressed Chinese province. He was now the youngest colonel in the Imperial Army and his appointment to Singapore reflected future opportunities for him and his nation. He looked with disdain at Ng in his grubby and stained white shirt, half-length black trousers and the torn broken sandals encasing dirty feet.

"Colonel, I have some news that I should like to share with you." Ng started the dialogue with ingratiating overtones.

"No doubt you have a motive for wishing to share your news with me at this very inconvenient hour and without an appointment?" The tone was unmistakable, full of irony. The girls were waiting.

"But Colonel, since my assistance with information over British fleet supplies, I believed we had an understanding. Was the information not worth the small amount asked?"

"The information you supplied could hardly be described as crucial to our liberation plans for Asia!"

Ng looked at the diminutive colonel trying not to expose the detestation he felt for this uncaring example of military elitism and arrogance. Although in civilian clothes, the pressed and starched shirt and trousers had militaristic overtones, together with his highly polished brown boots. They provided an outward cloak of power to this man's strutting. Ng had little time for the British and Dutch as colonial administrations but wondered momentarily whether the Japanese would prove any better. But money is money, he thought, wherever it may come from.

"I have some very important information this time. It is very valuable information and could have great benefits for you and Japan's plans for liberating Asia. Perhaps ... satisfying your need for raw materials like oil, bauxite and chrome? It could become less of a problem with this information."

Hyami stopped pacing and looked at Ng trying to determine whether this wretched local was being fanciful, worth the time and trouble – he had certainly taken a fancy to the youngest of the Singaporean girls still in his rooms upstairs. He was, however, well aware of Japan's problems in gaining sufficient raw materials for developing the scale of military equipment that would be needed to relieve its Asian neighbours from the curse of British and Dutch colonial oppression. He also knew of the problems that Japan was experiencing in making payment for key materials.

Japan's expedition into Manchuria and mainland China had received a bad press; many suppliers of matériel were less than keen to be seen supporting the cruel Imperial dynasty, which was being regularly accused of all sorts of atrocities. Purchase by proxy had been resorted to in some instances; it helped disguise the final destination but payment had usually to be made in gold or some other acceptable but hard-to-obtain currency. Japanese currency had become unacceptable to many traders and nations.

"And what exactly is this incredibly important piece of information that will alter our fortunes?" The sarcasm continued.

"I have been made aware that regular consignments of gold are being dispatched through Singapore by air and sea, and, it is very likely that one consignment has been, shall we say, misplaced. However, its probable loss is even now being recognised and no doubt steps will be taken quickly to find it again."

"How is it possible that you should have been chosen to be made aware of such a consignment? What do mean, 'misplaced'? How much gold is there? Where is it now? Who else knows about this?" Hyami barked the string of questions out, as he would have done to his troops.

"The information is from an impeccable and highly reliable source, I assure you," Ng said with some defiance as he explained very briefly how he had come by it. "I know where it is, Colonel, but it will require recovering. That shouldn't present too much of a problem for such a resourceful nation as yours, should it Colonel?"

Again Ng allowed himself a little more leeway in dealing with Hyami. He also failed to mention that if bullion was being carried by Cornucopia, it was probably lying on the sea-bed even as they spoke. In any event the local Straits Times newspaper would probably run the story tomorrow.

Hyami sat at a small black-lacquered desk and looked at Ng for a full minute; he decided to ignore the Singaporean's disrespectful attitude. To Ng it seemed ages; he had time to appreciate the adjective 'inscrutable'. The room was gloomy and oppressive; Ng wished they could conclude an arrangement quickly so that he could leave.

Hyami finally broke the silence, "What have you in mind, Ng san?" Ng was not taken in by the cunning of Hyami's sudden civility.

"If I tell you the amount of gold misplaced and its location, I should need my commission in advance. I will require three per cent of the value of gold at its present price in the Singapore market."

"You are expecting us to take a lot on trust, Ng san. You still have not told me how much gold there is, or even where?"

Ng decided that there was nothing to be lost in indicating the amount that he had learnt was a typical consignment from his brother-in-law.

"The gold is, I understand, worth over two million dollars." He whispered the amount reflecting the enormity of the sum involved for someone of Ng's standing.

Hyami stared at him; he too was silently impressed with the amount. Two million dollars would oil the wheels of Japan's war machine quite adequately for a while.

"I see," he too was whispering now. "If I believe your story, how do we set about collecting it?"

The distrust was total and mutual. They were both greedy in their own way; further steps might be difficult.

"If you are interested in recovering the gold you will have to move quickly. It is located some way from Singapore." Ng had decided to encourage the colonel to make clear his intentions.

"And, if we decide to move quickly, where exactly do we move to?" The colonel was still experiencing some difficulty in dealing civilly with this local, who refused to react as one of his cowed subordinates, and who, for the moment, had the upper hand.

"I am prepared to tell you that we should first need to go to Penang."

"It would seem that you intend to be a part of this recovery?"

"Of course, Colonel, I too have much at stake but I will still require at least half of my commission before we go further." Ng had begun to compromise.

The colonel considered the matter. Even half of three per cent of two million dollars was a lot of money to raise from the trade office's immediate resources. The fact that Ng was prepared to be a part of the recovery suggested that his story, so far, was worth risking some time and resources. Japan could certainly use the gold, and in particular what it could buy.

"You will return here at five tomorrow morning and I will have an answer for you."

Hyami failed to mention that he would have to take instruction from Tokyo over the matter. It was close to eleven o'clock in the evening before Ng left the trading office the way he had entered. Two whimpering local girls also left a few minutes later by the same door. Hyami had a busy night ahead.

❖ ❖ ❖

Harold Penrose had meetings in turn with Pardoe at Imperial Airways and Lee at Empress that evening. Pardoe indicated that Imperial was quite capable of undertaking the safe and secure transportation of important documents and artefacts; indeed, they were, after all, entrusted to carry His Majesty's mails. If Penrose wished to accompany his cargo, there would be no problem; the Imperial boats usually carried some sixteen or so passengers and a prompt booking would confirm his place, and that of his cargo. Notwithstanding his earlier concern for the lost Empress flying boat, he casually mentioned to Penrose that Imperial's reliability and safety record was usually very good and had he heard that Empress might have lost one of their aircraft en route to Rangoon earlier in the day – and that he understood a search was getting under way tomorrow. Penrose feigned surprise.

Lee could not dispute Penrose's opening remarks concerning the possible loss of Cornucopia. But where had he learnt it from so quickly, he wondered. Lee made the point that, like Imperial, they too were entrusted with carrying His Majesty's mails on occasions, and that at present information about Cornucopia was sketchy and she may have just landed on the sea until the storm blew out.

They both knew the naivety of the statement considering the ferocity of the storm that had swept over Singapore on its way north-west. Penrose carefully encouraged Lee to elaborate more on the Empress service and, leaving the unfortunate circumstances surrounding Cornucopia aside, what guarantees of service could Empress provide in carrying important documents and artefacts to England? Lee made clear that Empress may require a little notice of intended shipment owing to weight limitations on board – and due to current freight and mail contracts. It may restrict the availability of service at short notice. Penrose decided to play a wild card to entice further information – indicating that he would be prepared to pay a premium for the service, even if it meant carrying less than their normal complement of sixteen passengers – to accommodate his fictional cargo.

"But with our present commitments we rarely are able to carry more than three or four passengers from Darwin to Poole," Lee said. Penrose understood that Poole harbour was the English Channel port terminus for their route from northern Australia. More importantly he believed that in all probability Cornucopia was carrying some bullion on its flights. Imperial's more numerous flight frequencies, he reasoned, probably meant that they were carrying the lion's share of mails up and down the aptly named Kangaroo Route. Empress would be left to carry surpluses at peak times such as at Christmas.

Harold now suspected that Empress could at present only accommodate four passengers in an aircraft designed to carry anywhere between sixteen and twenty-one, plus only occasional mail. It suggested that something else was making up the aircraft's maximum take-off weight. It was not mail, he was certain – it was the wrong time of year. It had to be something whose value to volume must be very high, after all, he considered; there was little room for large and bulky cargoes in the Empire flying boats – after passengers and their often-copious baggage. Penrose thanked Lee for his assistance and carefully took his leave, his mind racing. So it was just possible that Cornucopia was carrying bullion – a high-value consignment could be quite small. What, he asked himself, had happened to the aircraft following its position report of over twenty-four hours ago? Had it survived the landing? Were they safe with the bullion?

For an hour or so he turned the matter over in his mind; tomorrow the morning papers would be full of the story of the lost flying boat, but few would be privy to detailed knowledge of its cargo manifest. Penrose decided on the basis of what he knew now, and what he could reasonably surmise, that he needed to get to Penang, or even further north up the coast towards the Siam border without delay. During his discussions with Lee, the Empress deputy station manager had passed on some information gained from Pardoe indicating that the Royal Air Force were intending to send a borrowed naval search aircraft to Penang at daylight on the morrow. It was to his mind a further imperative to get north as quickly as possible that very night.

The question was how? A boat would take far too long; by car the distance and the rudimentary road between Singapore and Penang would be slow and fraught with difficulties, and neither Imperial nor Empress had a flying service available, in any event they didn't usually fly their commercial passenger services at night.

But the only way to get north that very night was by flying, somehow. He considered; then quickly brushed from his mind a wild thought of him stealing an aeroplane from the local flying club. He knew nothing of flying, even less of navigation. But he did know someone who did. Cecilia Grosvenor-Ffoulkes was the daughter of a high-ranking army officer, and was also a member of the local Singapore Flying Club.

Ceci, as she preferred to be called, had learnt to fly in England at the London Aero Club, a seventeenth birthday present from her mother, who had also learnt to fly at the same club, before giving birth to Ceci and her older sister. Ceci's father, a rather unbending, dyed-in-the-wool military man, didn't believe in young ladies, or mature ones for that matter, undertaking such dangerous male-dominated activities. His attitude may have been a somewhat coloured by his then-young wife's indiscretions, with her even younger ex-RFC flying instructor.

Ceci, in her early twenties was not the normal genteel product of a wealthy and privileged family. She had gained her pilot's licence in a remarkable seventeen hours, only taking eight hours to go solo. As her experience had grown she had flown further and further afield including one or two trips to France and Belgium; her mother worried – her father was happily unaware. On her father's posting to Singapore to take up an appointment as deputy commander of the garrison there, Ceci flew her small de Havilland Gypsy Moth biplane in stages across Europe and around the Mediterranean to Alexandria to meet up with her parents' ship, later continuing on board with them. The Gypsy Moth, carefully dismantled by the local RAF detachment, was crated and sent on to Singapore by cargo ship, some weeks later. Over recent months Ceci had been flying her newly assembled aeroplane around the local Singapore area, and on one or two occasions to a small airstrip at a family friend's plantation near Keluang in Malaya.

Harold had first met Ceci at a polo match late one afternoon, some months after he had stepped off the ship in Singapore. She was riding-in one of the mounts following the match, and was a natural on a horse. From Harold's perspective, she was a very desirable target. Beautiful in a tomboyish sort of way, long strong legs, pale blue eyes, a wide mouth set in a round face, always laughing, intelligent, certainly wilful and very confident; and with an energy he had rarely encountered in his amorous past. He contrived to meet her and they had quickly struck up a very steamy relationship within a very short space of time.

It was Ceci's older, rather prudish sister Eliza, who had brought matters to her parents' attention after bursting into Ceci's bedroom early one morning, to announce plans for a picnic that same afternoon. Ceci and Harold were in the bath together; there was a great deal of water on the floor. It required but little imagination, even for a young woman of Eliza's prudish persuasion.

Ceci's father, a heavy-set man beset with early stages of gout, was white-faced with quiet rage. He had warned off Penrose in terms that should not be ignored. Now and again he caught sight of her at various Singapore society functions that he had managed to gatecrash, but apart from fleeting looks, matters appeared to be well and truly over. Ceci now had a new, approved beau – a seemingly emotionless and rather mature squadron leader pilot in the Royal Air Force with a good fighting record in France. Penrose noted that whatever the situation Squadron Leader Wills was always immaculately attired, whether in uniform or 'civvies'. He could not tell if Ceci was happy, though.

He arrived silently at the Grosvenor-Ffoulkes home. The waning moon provided just sufficient light. Did she still have the same bedroom, he wondered? He knew the layout of the large house intimately, but could not risk entering, there would almost certainly be servants awake and on guard. Most of the window shutters were closed but one or two were just ajar. To his joy he saw that the shutters at Ceci's bedroom windows were partly open. He watched for a few minutes. He was right; there was a night-watchman in the grounds of the house. Picking his moment, and taking a chance when the moon sailed briefly behind a cloud, he ran across the darkened and carefully manicured lawn and stood on the wide terrace beneath Ceci's balcony.

She awoke to something falling onto her bed. It was probably just one of the small indigenous lizards that lived about the house harmlessly walking the walls but rarely falling. It crossed her mind that it might also be something more threatening. She quickly got to her feet; with the bedside light on she was puzzled at the stones and pieces of earth lying on the light counterpane. More stones came through the window and she stepped to the half-open shutters to better see what was causing this nocturnal phenomenon.

He saw a movement.

"Ceci," whispered Penrose as loudly as he dared. She looked down between the balcony balustrades from behind her partly open shutters and saw the unmistakable outline of her past lover, looking up, towards her.

"Harold – are you mad? If my father finds you here he'll have you shot," she said in an incredibly loud whisper – normal speech would have had less impact.

"I know, but I have to talk to you." Ceci thought for a moment.

"This had better be good," she muttered to herself, turning from the window and pulling on a light cotton bathrobe. She came to him from around the side of the house, running to him barefoot across the lawn and into the dark shadows by the garden wall encased in bougainvillea.

"Well?" she said, smiling at him. He picked up the smile in the dark, her teeth glinting in the available light. Holding her, he realised that she was totally naked beneath her robe, and she smelt delicious; was it Gardenia? Harold Penrose outlined the story to her in a few minutes. In the dark she sensed him waiting for her reply to his ludicrous plan.

"You are mad! Of course, we must do it, it sounds great fun." He went to hug her but she pulled away.

"I have never flown at night; we can't start until there's at least some light." She introduced an element of practicality, but he did not care.

"Okay, but get dressed now and lets get down to the aerodrome and prepare so that we can leave as soon as possible." Returning twenty minutes later she was dressed in riding breeches and a cotton blouse with her flying jacket slung over her arm together with a white cotton helmet and a very small travel bag. Again she smelt wonderfully of soap.

Once he was safely strapped into the front cockpit, Ceci primed the engine and swung the propeller of the machine. It started after five attempts, clearly unimpressed at being woken so early. Completing her final checks as a crimson dawn pushed against the eastern horizon, she taxied to face the lightest of breezes. As she opened the throttle, the Gypsy engine delivered full power; rolling forwards, then stick slightly forward, its tail rising; they were airborne within seconds. The flying-club watchman saw them leave, not understanding why anyone should undertake such a dangerous form of travel – particularly so early in the morning. As they flew over the calm Johore Strait, separating Singapore Island from the Malay mainland, a few minutes later, they saw activity below them around an amphibian aeroplane on the water. It was being prepared for flight, and to search for Cornucopia. Looking up, the naval ground crews and the two search pilots were surprised to see a small blue-and-silver biplane, at such an hour in the morning – climbing and heading roughly north-west across the strait, towards the Malay jungle.

Colonel Hyami and Ng boarded the chartered Douglas DC-2 twin-engine aircraft two hours later, along with two other Japanese trade officials. Agreement had been reached with Tokyo overnight and approval given to undertake recovery of any gold by whatever means, providing, that no link with Japan or its representatives could be established in the event that something went awry. Ng had had to concede more information than he had planned before agreeing a deal with Hyami. He had given the latitude of Cornucopia's position report but still retained the longitudinal information safely and he had accepted the equivalent of just one thousand pounds Sterling in local currency as an advance on his future commission. This was deposited with his ageing mother on their way to the airfield. By seven o'clock that morning three aircraft were heading north towards Penang.

THREE

Colonel Deverall was on watch as the upper limb of the sun broke through the low cloud clinging wistfully to the horizon; he had recovered his composure during the night. During his four hours of broken sleep the seas had subsided into a long oily swell and a certain confidence in a safe recovery from their situation began to develop in him.

The coming daylight allowed him to better realise Cornucopia's situation; she was lower in the water particularly towards the nose. He pondered what was actually keeping her afloat. Not very mechanically minded, he knew enough to guess that the partially empty fuel tanks were probably providing some buoyancy. Additionally, and unknown to him, buoyancy also came from air trapped in the rearmost cabin and tail section, including the aft luggage stowage.

He stepped down carefully through the hatch from his position on top of the aircraft, onto the flight deck. Water was now slopping gently from side to side as the boat gently reacted to the long swell. The woman and her child were asleep wrapped in blankets alongside the captain in the dry mail stowage. Purser Snell was snoring gently, his head hung uncomfortably forward onto his chest as he semi-reclined on a mail sack, keeping him clear of the wet floor, his back against the fuselage side. Rawlinson had moved his position during the night and finally returned to sleep in the captain's seat, his feet resting on the instrument panel coaming, below the empty windscreen frames. With no appreciable wind the aircraft would not lay head to the swell but despite that the position had proved fairly comfortable.

Rawlinson stirred as he heard someone moving at the aft end of the flight deck. It was cool now and his khaki uniform felt damp. His long limbs were stiff, both from the fixed position in which he had spent the last few hours in rewarding suspended animation, and from the coolness. He swung his legs down and around until he was sitting sideways in the seat. His now-dirty khaki cotton uniform smelt of brine and other odours he was unable to identify, none of them very pleasant. Standing, he turned to walk back to where the others lay in various states of slumber, and then his eyes fell on the remains of poor Newsome, still jammed under the bent radio racks, only properly visible from the cockpit.

Newsome's fate had been avoided as a subject for discussion before sleep had collectively overtaken their exhaustion the previous evening. Now, disposal of his remains was an issue requiring some urgent attention. Normal daytime temperatures would soon encourage decomposition and its associated odours in the small potential oven that comprised the flight deck, with its aluminium roof, sides and decking.

"I'm so sorry I didn't pull my weight yesterday ... unforgivable, I know." Colonel Deverall was both embarrassed and contrite as he looked at where Rawlinson's gaze was fixed. David Rawlinson shook his head and smiled.

"We had better make arrangements for his burial at sea as soon as possible," Deverall continued. Rawlinson nodded; they both knelt down to establish how difficult it would be to remove Newsome from his position, now firmly caught under the distorted radio racks. It would not be pleasant but they both agreed that his removal, and a Christian-like sea burial, should be effected before the sun grew much higher.

Rawlinson left Deverall carefully manoeuvring Newsome from his temporary morgue in preparation for a suitable and short ceremony. Stepping quietly and gently over his captain, the woman and girl, he found two blankets in which to wrap the headless corpse. As he searched among the mailbags for something to tie the blankets around the body, he came across a series of sturdy wooden boxes in the centre-section mail hold, there seemed to be dozens of them. He had no idea what they contained, not normally being party to the cargo manifest, or the aircraft weight and balance calculations prior to flight. Within Empress Airways the aircraft captain was totally responsible for all mail and cargo documentation. In the poor light available in the confined space he tried to decipher the stencilled lettering on top of the nearest box. The name of a Hong Kong bank unfamiliar to him appeared in Cantonese script, together with a series of reference letters and numbers. The final boldly stencilled line stated clearly in English: 'Ingots 4. Gold (Au) – 24 carat. 768 ounces. Property of HM Treasury – LONDON'.

Rawlinson sat back on his heels trying to make sense of what he had just read. They were carrying gold! And by the number of boxes concealed within the mailbags, and possibly elsewhere on the aircraft, a very substantial amount. Goodness knows how much it all weighed; no wonder passenger numbers had been so few on some flights over the last couple of months. It might explain why the Cornucopia had had trouble maintaining height on three engines. Pulling the mailbags and remaining blankets back around the boxes to cover their location, he left the compartment quietly with two blankets and some thin twine he had usefully discovered in the empty tool bag.

Colonel Deverall was no stranger to violent death. He had seen it often enough in the course of his military duties; in Rawlinson's absence he had managed to free Newsome from his entrapment under the radio rack, releasing his seat belt, which was blackened with dried blood. Rigor mortis had already set in; the body remained in a partly seated posture even when finally removed from the seat. Between them Deverall and Rawlinson struggled to secure the blankets around the hapless headless corpse. This accomplished, they then carried it with as much reverence as circumstances allowed to the hatchway, watched by an awakened Snell. He rose as they struggled in silence to lift the inert and bent remains through the top hatch. Giving the benefit of his ample strength, he pushed the body upwards from below while the other two men pulled from above. It proved difficult; the hatch was not large and Newsome's body was not only literally dead weight but also configured into a sort of stiff 'S'.

Deverall quickly took charge of the burial arrangements. With the remains of the radio operator's seat they weighted the body. Standing a little precariously on the slightly pitching port wing they muttered the Lord's Prayer together and Deverall spoke what he could recall of the military burial service. Together they pushed nearly all of the late Herbert Newsome over the trailing edge of the wing; he sank swiftly into the depths. Nobody mentioned the whereabouts of the departed's head.

As they made their way back to the hatch opening they stopped and looked at the seascape around them. Now, well after sunrise, they could see distant cloud begin to bubble up.

"Probably from land, but how far away it is, is impossible to tell. It could be twenty miles, it could be fifty miles, it's so difficult from this level at sea," Rawlinson commented expertly as they began to discuss their next steps.

A key concern for all was the state of Cornucopia. She was slowly getting lower in the water, they had to find a way of at least preserving what buoyancy she had, or if possible find a way of increasing it. They were all silently certain that she would not survive another pounding in heavy seas. Rawlinson pointed out tears in the aluminium fairings around her wing roots where tremendous stresses had been placed on the structure. By stepping outboard of the engines on the wing, they were also able to see forward, externally, to the catastrophic damage done by the final impact of the aircraft's nose with the sea.

Snell suggested that they throw overboard everything that they could reach that was of no use to them in an effort to lighten the boat. As they lowered themselves back down onto the wet flight deck they became aware of heavy breathing and moaning from the centre mail stowage area. Sarah was trying to calm Michael Kelly, tormented with pain and now fully conscious. The brandy bottle lay empty beside him; he'd consumed its remaining contents in the night to stave off the reality of the savage surgery recently undertaken.

The girl Beth stood in the compartment's half-light looking at this grown man crying, desperate, his back arched in painful tension, hands grasping and crushing the light aluminium formers that supported the compartment's wooden sides. Her mother continued to placate the poor man, holding him tenderly, wiping his brow.

Turning, she spoke sharply, "Have you no more brandy, Mr Snell?" Snell went to the sack he had rescued and carefully withdrew a further small bottle.

"I'm sorry, Mrs Gregson, it is the last, and it's not full either." The bottle was uncorked and thrust at Kelly's lips. He sucked at it, grabbing its neck with the energy of a man clinging to it for some sort of salvation from pain. Sarah Gregson was too aware that this was hardly an approved medical solution. As he began to relax a little, she gave some thought as to what could be done to ease his pain, based perhaps, on a more empirical medical approach. Resources on board were scarce.

Rawlinson and Deverall climbed back on top of the aircraft; below Snell and the now-wakened Hudson formed a chain gang and began lifting loose items and mailbags to throw into the sea, in an attempt to lighten the aircraft. After some minutes or so of labouring they uncovered the wooden boxes seen earlier by Rawlinson in the compartment, where at the moment Sarah Gregson was attempting to comfort her frightened daughter – and the pain-wracked Michael Kelly.

It seemed a good point at which to stop for a rudimentary breakfast, which Snell prepared with a certain amount of style, despite the circumstances. He had managed to keep most of the contents of his rations sack dry if a little crushed, and sitting or standing around the navigation table, they satisfied themselves on some rather salty, stale bread rolls, canned preserves and porridge oats mixed with tepid fresh water. It was their first meal in almost twenty-four hours, and they plundered the sack more than they ought. Michael Kelly ate nothing but clung painfully to the small brandy bottle. There remained pitifully little in it.

Little was said about the bullion lying boxed a few feet from where they ate their meal. It was almost an embarrassment; they intuitively seemed to understand that it would not be following the mailbags over the side. At least, not immediately.

Rawlinson found the aircraft's chronometer lying in its splintered teak box under the first officer's seat. It was seriously damaged; it must have broken loose in the final violence of the landing. The only other timepieces on board were those worn by the surviving passengers and crew. He needed an accurate chronometer with which to calculate their position in combination with the aircraft sextant, and the daily sun sight tables now contained in wet Admiralty nautical almanacs, presently propping up the left-hand instrument panel.

Like the chronometer, the aircraft's sextant was sat within a stout wooden box that was fixed securely to the cockpit structure. It appeared to have safely survived the landing impact with the heavy seas; the box was undamaged. From his damp charts he knew that the marks and lines drawn there the previous day could hardly be relied upon. He noted the time of each wristwatch still working, Deverall's, Hudson's and Snell's had all succumbed to seawater. Taking the mean time from his own, Michael Kelly's and Sarah Gregson's watch – together with the watch recovered from Newsome before burial, he began to calculate their position from a series of sextant sights, and the pages of tables in the Admiralty almanac. He would have to accept that pinpoint accuracy would not be a feature of his final calculations – but he made as many allowances as he thought prudent to reach some sort of conclusion.

He could not believe it. The position line showed them to be on a line of longitude that didn't accord in any way with what he believed to be their location. He went through the process a further four times with small adjustments; on each occasion he ended up with a similar result. He would have to wait until midday local time before he could establish a line of latitude from a further sun sight with the sextant. Where the two position lines crossed would be their roughly calculated position based on some fairly dubious timepieces and a sextant that may have had its mirrors jolted slightly out of alignment during their landing. Rawlinson decided to say nothing about his fears until he had had an opportunity to take a new sun sight at midday.

Meanwhile, the rest of the men looked for items to throw overboard in their continuing effort to lighten the boat. The four huge lead-acid batteries were removed with considerable difficulty from their stowage on the flight deck, and eventually followed the mailbags and other assorted paraphernalia into the sea. At the end of their sweaty efforts, Cornucopia was riding a little higher in the water, but by only a paltry few inches.

The temperature inside the aircraft had risen steadily as the morning progressed. Cool seawater lapping against the hull sides helped to contain the rise but soon they all sought a place on top of the hull, underneath a rudimentary shelter put together by George Hudson and the colonel. They had managed to tie the tarpaulin, originally erected in the cockpit, onto the radio aerial and the boat-hook, forming a crude tent. Out of direct sunlight it proved a cooler location in the welcome, slight breeze. Michael Kelly remained below, inside the roasting hull, tossing and sweating in a stupor of heat, pain and alcohol.

Approaching midday, Rawlinson again assumed his navigator's responsibilities – taking a series of sun shots with the sextant to determine the star's absolute zenith, while Deverall noted the times. As earlier in the day, he checked and rechecked his calculations. Plotting their position on the chart he tried to think out their implications.

The storm, it seemed, had swept them way out to the west of the Nicobar and Andaman chain of islands, well into the Bay of Bengal. Their early morning observation of clouds beginning to build to the east and to the north of sunrise probably meant that the land lying underneath them was one or some of the five hundred or so islands that made up the two island groups that stretched roughly north–south. It was not the Malay mainland, as he had logically hoped. They were hundreds of miles off their prescribed track from Penang to Rangoon, and certainly many hundreds of miles from his in-flight estimated dead-reckoning position. He was conscious that it was this position that the recently deceased Newsome had transmitted in their final radio distress calls. Assuming that the transmission had been heard, and acted on, any search would be in completely the wrong place: well to the east of the Nicobar Islands chain. He made the situation clear to Cornucopia's survivors.

"We are a long way from our reported position, far, far to the west; I think it unlikely that any search will look for us this far off track. They will assume after searching for a time that we sank with loss of all life. We remain afloat, but for how long I cannot predict. If we meet any further bad weather we cannot, unfortunately, assume that the aircraft will survive another battering." He was blunt: "I think we shall have to be responsible for our own salvation. First, we need to assess our food and water supplies, and what we may be able to retrieve from the galley, it means rationing, I'm afraid. Second, we need to prepare some form of rescue signal in case we see a ship. Thirdly, we have to find more ways of improving this poor old boat's buoyancy."

There was some feeble clapping from the mail stowage compartment. Michael Kelly was sufficiently compos mentis to take in his navigator's impromptu speech and applauded the effort. Sarah held Michael's head in her lap for a while, mopping his face and neck; perspiration was pouring off him, from both the heat in the enclosed compartment and the fever that was building in him. Regularly inspecting the wound she saw no sign of early infection but took the precaution of cleaning it lightly with some of the remaining, precious, brandy. He jerked violently as she carefully touched the raw spirit on his wound. Her concerns began to extend to where she could obtain clean dressings for the wound and she mentioned this to Rawlinson.

With the contents of the engineer's tool kit, Deverall and Hudson worked to remove all accessible engine cowlings and threw them into the sea, save one. Its dish-like shape was filled with mail, some blankets and pieces of stripped-out electrical cable. It would serve as a smoke-signalling device in case they spotted a ship. Removal of some of the wing's small upper inspection panels with their available tools gave them access to the fuel tank fillers inside. With care and using the stripped outer casing of electrical cables to make a tube, they managed to siphon off some of the fuel into the sea, aiming to provide additional buoyancy. The petrol fumes were heavy, powerful and dangerous; Deverall insisted that no one undertook any activity that might lead to a conflagration. It took hours for the fuel to siphon out of the tanks, through the thin makeshift pipes, into the sea; the survivors sat as far upwind as they could to avoid the worst of the sickly, heavy vapours.

Purser Snell laid the remaining provisions onto the navigation table; not much remained after their extended, but necessary, breakfast. However, he knew there was still some tinned food in the galley – they always carried spare supplies in case they were held up somewhere owing to weather. But his main concern was for water. The aircraft's fresh water tank was positioned in the galley, and there were also some bottles of soda water located in the waterlogged compartment. Someone would have to go below and try to locate them.

"There is another way we could lose some weight," said George Hudson looking expectantly around the group gathered, standing at the late and rather sparse lunch table. Rawlinson anticipated a comment concerning the boxes of bullion.

"We could empty the baggage compartments." Hudson recalled looking back and seeing the rearmost compartment in the aircraft when their baggage was loaded at Penang. He had also seen the door to the same compartment during his last dive to rescue his beloved Lilly. The others looked at him waiting.

"I can go down and bring the bags up if you like?"

"But you can't expect to dive and bring cases and portmanteau all the way from the rear baggage compartment up here to the flight deck. It's a long way underwater; I think you're asking for trouble." Deverall admired the man's pluck but thought the idea a little beyond their capabilities.

"I could do it with some help!" Hudson proclaimed. He outlined his idea. He would use the air he'd discovered in the rear saloon to breathe as he passed bags from the aft baggage compartment to someone else positioned in the mid-section lounge where there was another much smaller pocket of trapped air. They could then swim the short distance to the galley stairs and push them, or pull them up to be grabbed by someone on the flight deck. In any event, he could go to see his Lilly again. But he didn't mention this. Rawlinson considered the matter. It seemed just plausible; they just needed a volunteer to help poor Hudson. It would have to be him.

"Okay," he said, "it's worth a go," and he began to strip off ready for the plunge. Sarah Gregson insisted he tie a rope around himself in case something went wrong, or perhaps one of the bags proved be too heavy.

Hudson and Rawlinson stepped down into the water-filled galley. Together they moved to the rear of the aircraft, Hudson showed Rawlinson the air trapped in the rear saloon. They paused to gain their breath; it was then that the navigator saw the corpse lying on the stowage shelf.

"You can't really leave her there, George." In the interests of sensitivity he didn't expand on reasons why the body should be quickly buried at sea. Even this far into the aircraft with a good deal of water to keep the temperature down, the warmth in the enclosed space was noticeable. George Hudson looked at the other man. It was too bizarre, grotesque, he thought, groping around in a sinking aircraft with his dead wife lying just two feet from his face.

"Later," he said firmly, looking away.

Turning from the makeshift catafalque, he moved, head just above water, to the rear of the cabin, took a great intake of breath and sank beneath the surface. His hands soon found the luggage locker door and its handle; with a struggle he wrenched it open. It was dark inside and like the rear cabin there was a lot of air trapped in the top of the stowage. Moving quickly his hands closed over a piece of baggage and he pulled it clear, allowing it to arc slowly out and into the water, in the rear cabin aisle. He repeated this twice more, all the while, grabbing lungs of air from within the roof of the baggage compartment. Rawlinson climbed onto the shelf and looked in the dim light at Lilly Hudson. He'd taken a lot of trouble to care for his dead wife. She smiled slightly with her eyes closed as if remembering some private pleasure. Plain she may have dressed but nevertheless, she was a handsome woman.

"What a tragedy," he murmured.

Hudson resurfaced and saw Rawlinson looking at his departed wife. Rawlinson's expression even in the half-light was evident to George Hudson; it was one of sorrow.

"No one is to blame," Hudson said clearly. "I just don't understand why it had to be Lilly. I can't let her go just yet."

David Rawlinson, exhausted and tense, bit his lip, and swallowed hard.

"When you're ready, George, when you're ready," he uttered with difficulty, holding the man's arm firmly, reinforcing his understanding of Hudson's plight. Together they arranged a system for clearing what they could from the rear baggage compartment. In breathless relays they passed cases and bags forwards with the colonel pulling them up sodden and dripping onto the flight deck with a rope. There were fourteen bags in all, some quite large and two or three very heavy. They also raided all the cupboards and stowages in the galley, retrieving anything consumable or that might be of possible use.

Each of the assembled group identified their bag or case and opened it, water oozing from the soaked contents. Five pieces of baggage remained standing, untouched, seeping mute testimony to what had befallen some of their complement on their innocent flight to Rangoon. Those with bags tipped the contents out and started to spread sodden clothes and a few personal treasures around the small flight deck hoping the gentle breeze through the space would help to dry them out. Rawlinson inspected the Empress destination labels on the five remaining pieces. One small one was Newsome's, one belonged to Michael Kelly, one to Oliver Stoneman and the two large matching cases belonged to George and Lilly Hudson.

A sudden tearing sound caused those lost in thought or activity to look up. Sarah Gregson was ripping up her beautiful silk and cotton skirts and blouses for amputation dressings. She hung the expensive broad strips from the roof of the flight deck and they blew gently in the breeze. Rawlinson spoke.

"The reason we've collected the cases from the luggage stowage is because we need to reduce weight on the aircraft. I know it's difficult but I must ask you all to take a few vital or precious items and let the colonel and I put the rest into the sea."

Silently, they all retrieved a few items, picking through the contents carefully: clothing, washing accoutrements and one or two irreplaceable keepsakes. There proved to be some useful additions including two electric torches, which, once dried out, might be made to work, a sizeable sewing kit, another small first-aid kit – and a small travel atlas. George Hudson took one of the two leather-bound cases that he and his wife had packed so carefully together and turned the brass combination lock allowing him to open the heavy lid. He pulled out one or two items of clothing – they appeared to be almost dry – and a framed photograph of the pair of them on the balcony of their plantation home. She looked fit and tanned, and they were both laughing, looking more alive than they ever had. It had been taken on the afternoon that they had learnt that they had won a long-term contract to supply raw latex from their rubber plantation to a major commodity broker in Singapore. It was the afternoon that Lilly had told her husband that she was pregnant. It was barely four weeks ago.

Hudson wrapped the dry unblemished photograph in the few clothes he had retrieved, shut and secured the lid of his case and pushed them both up through the roof hatch into the hands of Colonel Deverall. The others followed suit, Sarah acting for Michael Kelly. Soon all the cases and bags were assembled on top.

One by one they were pushed off the wing and into the sea each leaving a long wake of bubbles as they majestically descended into the infinite blue, with the exception of George and Lilly Hudson's. Their two cases ascended from their initial plunge in the calm water and floated slowly away. They could still be seen drifting, semi-submerged, to the north-west two hours later.

Cornucopia appeared to be riding a little higher in the smooth, glassy sea. Water now only just reached the top step leading down into the sunken galley. Snell managed to retrieve the few remaining soda water bottles from the galley, and devised a way of extracting the fresh water from the galley water tank using pieces of rubber oil pipes cut from one of the engines. The water tasted odd but it was better than nothing. During the late afternoon they sat quietly with their thoughts, mournful at their losses, anxious for the future but still pleased to be alive. Beth spent some time splashing her little legs in the warm sea, pretending to fish with some string and a bent safety pin found by her mother in the sewing kit. That is until Rawlinson warned Sarah Gregson of the potential for sharks in these tropical waters.

As the sun settled on the western horizon, they prepared for a second night at sea. A simple meal of canned fruit and the two remaining stale bread rolls divided among them served as supper. They lay where it proved comfortable; at least the flight deck floor was now dry and some of the bedding retrieved from around accessible areas of the aircraft proved to have largely dried out in the sun. Sarah attended to Michael, redressing his wound with her new bandages. Holding his head tenderly she encouraged him to take some water and four aspirin that she'd managed to dry out in the sun, knowing full well they were little better than placebos in his painful state. Lying head in her lap, staring up at the roof of the small compartment he held on to Sarah's hand, his grip and eyes communicating when waves of pain overtook his ability to absorb them. Each time she held him tight.

Deverall volunteered for the first night watch; he sat in the opening of the top hatch gazing at the fast-emerging stars. About two and a half hours into his lonely watch he saw something; in the distance, he could see a light moving. Was it a star coming above the north-west horizon, was it a boat or was it just wishful imagination? Watching the location intently his experience told him that at night he stood a better chance of seeing his object by not looking directly at it. Whatever it was, it was moving slowly from left to right, how far away he was unable to tell, but possibly some miles, he guessed. Was it worth waking Rawlinson to show him? He stood on the aircraft roof to gain a better view and started to tap out an SOS distress signal on the one torch that could be persuaded to work.

Suddenly he lost sight of whatever it was, its small light suddenly extinguished. Still looking hopefully twenty minutes later, he realised that whatever it was had now gone.

He sat down again, the silence broken occasionally by the sea gently kissing the underside of the useless wings and the occasional groan or sleeping snort from below him. He dozed, occasionally looking around the horizon but there was nothing to be seen save the stars. He missed the faint wake of a motorised vessel as it passed slowly by, a mile distant, downwind.

At about four in the morning they were all awoken by heavy thuds and banging seemingly coming from all parts of the boat as she lifted and swayed in the short sea that had now risen in tune with a stiff south-easterly breeze. Purser Snell had been on watch and the shock of the initial noise caused him to fall through the hatch.

FOUR

Ceci's Gypsy Moth had an airborne duration of about four hours. For flying around England and the Continent she'd had fitted an additional fuel tank allowing another ten gallons to be carried forward, in the front cockpit, where Penrose sat in admiration, if a little cool in the early morning air at two thousand feet. The additional gallons gave them a useful range of about three hundred or so nautical miles in still air; with the wind from the south-east they were gaining an additional fifteen miles for every hour from its favourable direction.

The warming land caused the Moth to bump and shake in growing thermals rising from the thick variegated jungle over which their course took them. Ceci tried to minimise the thermalling effect by climbing into cooler air but the growing number of clouds peppering the sky as the morning progressed thwarted her plan. Levelling off at four thousand feet she gave some thought to where she might land to refuel. Her experience of flying around Singapore was normally within a radius of one hour, about sixty miles or so. The island of Singapore and the tip of the Malay Peninsula provided a variety of easily recognised local landmarks by which to navigate from the air.

As they progressed further north, her familiar landmarks soon disappeared and she was left to fly a compass course hoping to pick up some salient features on the ground at prescribed times during their flight. Her pre-flight preparation had been a little scant, her only navigation charts being old RAF ones given to her by her new squadron leader fiancé. She had decided to route northerly up-country to Kuala Lumpur, avoiding the Gentian Highlands to the north and east of that city, and, having refuelled and taken a light lunch, proceed up the Malay coast to a small airfield at Butterworth, lying on the mainland opposite the island of Penang. The distance to 'KL', as it was locally known, was about two hundred miles direct and with help from a south-easterly tailwind she anticipated covering this in about two and a half hours.

An hour later saw the River Muar below, engorged; as it carried the past days storm water to the sea. Far to their left, despite the slight haze, they could see the featureless ocean in the distance; ahead and slightly to the right lay the shadow of the Gentian Highlands. Penrose half turned in the cramped forward cockpit gave and gave her the thumbs-up; she smiled warmly at him from behind a pair of oversize aviator's goggles. This rogue in front of her was an invitation to indulge her wild side again she thought deliciously. She was looking forward to it. The RAF could wait, for the moment.

Barely three hours after leaving Singapore, Ceci expertly executed a perfect three-point landing on the grass airstrip at Kuala Lumpur's horse race course. Taxiing towards the grandstand she was relieved at how easy the flight had been. They had the aircraft fully refuelled while enjoying a welcome mid-morning snack with hot tea. Ceci telegraphed her mother to the effect that she had gone flying up-country and would be back by the weekend. That should suffice to reassure them she hoped. Harold Penrose watched this girl, so full of confidence and style, despite her rather masculine garb. Had he really lost her to some service type? He mulled the matter over for a few minutes while waiting for her to return from the ladies washroom in the club house.

Checking the weather with the local Met man, Ceci was concerned at a prediction of reducing visibility due to heat haze the further north they went, with visibility barely half a mile at Penang according to telegraphed reports. She knew the problem, having experienced the vicissitudes of English and continental weather in her past flying, but felt confident that if they stuck to the coastline they would eventually come across Penang Island with its highly visible central hill, topped by a tea room.

They checked around the Gypsy Moth, its dark blue fuselage and silver doped wings shimmering in the mid-morning sun. Penrose climbed into the front cockpit and strapped himself in. Ceci answered the ground-crew starter's call until finally, "Magnetos on – contact!" Despite being still warm, the Gypsy engine burst into life, the propeller giving a welcome blast of lukewarm air to its crew. Oil pressure at thirty-five pounds, Ceci waved away the chocks and blipped the engine as she turned towards the grass airstrip. Lined up with the prevailing breeze, a last check that all was well and she gently pushed the throttle lever forwards, applying a little left rudder to counter the usual aircraft swing from the propeller's torque. The small machine rushed tail-up down the sward of rich, damp green and was airborne within seconds easily clearing the grandstand. In the warm air they climbed slowly north-westwards away from Kuala Lumpur towards the beckoning coastline some miles distant. Penrose was becoming excited at the prospect of reaching Butterworth and Penang by mid-afternoon.

❖ ❖ ❖

As the Gypsy Moth banked gently on its way north-west, a brightly polished aluminium, twin-engine airliner turned onto final approach for the racecourse runway at Kuala Lumpur.

Before the engines had finally clattered to a halt, Colonel Hyami and two other Japanese men stepped from the DC-2, followed by two pale Europeans, the latter wearing uniform with badges of rank: its captain and first officer. Hyami demanded that they have the machine refuelled. This despite the fact that the almost-new aircraft could hardly have used much during its seventy-minute flight from Singapore. Ng remained on board watching the colonel throw his weight around like some diminutive sumo wrestler, his cropped hair allowing perspiration to run freely down his forehead and neck.

The local ground crew rushed about and within twenty minutes the aircraft's twin engines were turning over again, tanks brim-full. Hyami had made use of his time on the ground, briefly meeting with a local Japanese trade officer who had been following the plight of Cornucopia as best he could through news and weather reports, and monitoring the local airport radio transmissions. In the light of his news, Hyami decided to order the two Dutch charter pilots to fly well out to sea from KL, and then to route roughly north, midway between the Malay coastline and the Nicobar and Andaman islands chain out to the west.

Synchronised, the two engines purred as the DC-2 cruised at three thousand feet with all on board watching the sea below. They knew that the chances of seeing Cornucopia were slim even if she was afloat but Hyami was insistent that all should keep a good lookout. His 'face' in Tokyo was crucial – and he intended to maintain his reputation with his overseers regardless.

❖ ❖ ❖

Squadron Leader Harvey Wills had tried to contact his fiancée at her parents' home from the RAF Mess, before leaving for the naval seaplane base. He was pleased that the navy had agreed to loan the air force one of their Supermarine Walrus amphibian aircraft for the search, it would certainly prove more useful if they found any survivors adrift on the sea than a conventional land plane. A servant had answered the phone after some time and advised the squadron leader that 'Miss Cecilia' had left home for the airfield very early that morning with another young gentleman and that her parents were still asleep. Harvey Wills was nonplussed. Why would Ceci go to fly at this ungodly hour – and with another man? He knew she was keen on flying, but at this hour? Odd, he pondered, as he climbed into the cockpit of the borrowed Walrus biplane and strapped in with his crewman, a fresh-faced Fleet Air Arm pilot, Sub-Lieutenant David Kildonan.

Water streamed from the hull of the venerable Walrus as it left its creamy wake in the strait between Singapore and the Malay mainland. Once airborne, they followed the Malay coastline, sweeping slowly round to the north, Wills lost in thought as Kildonan handled the machine. They had advised RAF and naval operations that they would commence a search once past Penang and make their best speed to that destination initially.

❖ ❖ ❖

Ceci now turned north flying along the Malay coastline about a half-mile offshore. As predicted, haze was causing lower-level visibility to deteriorate steadily; she estimated they still had about an hour's flying before reaching the mainland airstrip at Butterworth; it should be easy to locate opposite Penang Island. Descending gently to a thousand feet, closing the coastline slowly they continued northwards. Ahead and above them she caught fleeting sight of something flash brightly in the sky. The DC-2 banked steeply to the right as it too closed the coast, the afternoon sun reflecting off its highly polished under surfaces.

Colonel Hyami sat behind the DC-2's two Dutch pilots pondering his next move. The Dutchmen could not be allowed to understand their true reasons in trying to locate the lost Cornucopia. He knew enough of westerners to realise that the captain and his co-pilot were already a little suspicious of their Japanese clients, in particular their interest in a lost British flying boat. The story they had presented, that Ng was a senior local official in the colonial administration and had a relative on board the lost aircraft, would not stand up to serious scrutiny, he was too aware. Fortunately natural language barriers helped to maintain the story, and the crew's interest in earning from the aircraft charter helped to inhibit any serious questions. Hyami had paid cash in advance for the charter. It had been a precautionary move to bring his two Japanese compatriots; they were both conscientious trade administrators – perhaps more importantly they were also experienced pilots from the Imperial Japanese Navy.

❖ ❖ ❖

Ceci scribbled a brief message on a piece of paper and passed it forwards to Penrose, there being no other way of communicating with her front-seat passenger in the tiny aeroplane. 'Look for airstrip opp. Penang Island, 20 mins.' Penrose acknowledged the abbreviated message with a half-turned nod of the head. Looking out to starboard he could see the blurred sand and jungle coastline through the heat haze. Twenty minutes passed and they could just see the coastline, continuing to trend away north towards the Siamese border and far beyond. Ceci reduced engine power and the Gypsy Moth started slow descent towards the sea and jungle-fringed coast.

Nothing, there was nothing she could recognise from her

inadequate charts. Their fuel situation was not critical for the moment but they needed to determine exactly where they were. There was little point in continuing further north if they had missed the airstrip in the murky visibility, she knew. If they had passed the airfield unseen, any distance further north she went would mean twice the distance to return – then they may have a fuel problem. They flew onwards for a further ten minutes and still nothing that resembled the island with its central hill and George Town at its north-eastern end appeared.

Banking to the left she turned the Gypsy Moth out to sea intending to fly back down the coast on a reciprocal of her original compass heading. As they banked the engine coughed once, and then continued to run normally. Ceci looked up at the crude float gauge on the fuel tank; it showed about one-third full. Flying with one hand, she used the large Vickers hand pump located in her cockpit to transfer fuel from the aircraft's front tank up and into the top tank mounted centrally between the two upper wings. The coast slowly emerged from the haze with greater clarity, she rolled out of the turn to head roughly south with the steaming land now on her left. Her efforts in flying, navigating and now pumping fuel had allowed her concentration to falter; they had lost some height and were down to only five hundred feet.

The engine coughed again causing the small aircraft to shake, it picked up, running normally then started to cough fitfully for a few seconds before stopping altogether. Like most owners of light aircraft, Ceci thought it was at times like this that having an electric starter motor would be an absolute boon. Now the only sound was the wind soughing softly through the flying wires. Penrose tried to turn to see what was going on but Ceci was too busy carrying out her forced landing drills, something she'd had to do once before in England, followed then by a successful forced landing in a stubble field somewhere south of Oxford.

Here, there were no stubble fields. With less than five hundred feet in hand and just a few brief seconds – jungle or the narrow sandy beaches were her only options. The stationary propeller stood erect, testimony to their predicament. Gliding down at sixty miles per hour, Ceci had only one real choice: the narrow sandy beach. Banking the aircraft with extreme care, she lined the silent Gypsy Moth up with a strip of sand seemingly barely wider than the near-thirty-foot span of her wings. Harold Penrose instinctively pulled his harness tighter, crouching down and watching the beach rushing up to meet them. Ceci noticed in the last few feet that the beach was littered with small outcrops of rock submerged in the sand. She quickly adjusted her approach aiming to land nearer the small waves breaking on the shore rather than the overhanging trees. Bleeding-off speed, she allowed the aircraft to float a few feet above the beach, gently pulling back on the control stick. By luck, or perhaps careful judgement, the tail-skid contacted the moist sand first bringing the main wheels into prompt contact with the ground. Working the rudder bar furiously she tried to control the Moth as it fought to ground-loop, and bury its nose or wingtip in the sand.

They stopped. The Gypsy Moth stood facing the fringing jungle, right way up, preceded on the beach by three contorted tracks through the sand. She switched off both magnetos and pulled the fuel cock to off, unstrapped, and got down from her position and sat slightly shaking on the sand.

Penrose sat beside her.

"Well done, old thing, thought we'd had it for a moment."

Ceci looked up at him, he had no idea how concerned she

had been or what a miracle it was that they were both down and unharmed. The bonus was that the aeroplane was in one piece. But how they were going to get it out of here was a question she had not fully posed to herself yet. She looked at him, a small tear in the corner of each eye.

"Thanks, Harold. I thought it was touch and go for moment, especially when I saw those bloody rocks in the sand at the last minute. Landing off to one side on the firmer wet sand, I think, helped to keep us upright. If the main wheels had dug in to the soft dry stuff we would have been on our nose in no time; it wouldn't have done us a lot of good either."

She laughed nervously; he put his arm encouragingly around her shoulder.

"I must say, you were very cool, Ceci. I'm very impressed." She looked up at him again, basking in his admiration, and then pecked him on the cheek. They sat for few moments allowing pulses to slow then started to carefully inspect the machine. Ceci lifted the engine cowlings looking for obvious reasons for the engine's demise. There were none externally.

"It seemed to be a fuel problem from the way it spluttered and banged before giving up on us," suggested Penrose.

"Could be," she said locating the fuel filter and undoing the knurled nut that secured it to its housing. On removal and looking inside, they found particles of all sorts of debris – including the remains of an insect, and some water.

"Obviously they don't take the same sort of care over fuel contamination at KL as we do at the flying club," she announced.

They spent time cleaning out the fuel filter and blowing through the pipes going from fuel tanks to the engine's carburettor.

Satisfied, they put things back together again, then, dragged the aeroplane back along the beach with the intention of starting her and attempting a take-off run along the wet sand. It was hot work lifting the machine by its tail and dragging it four hundred yards along the beach with its cloying surface. At the end Ceci was glowing gently; Penrose was wet from the effort.

Leaning, panting against the trunk of a palm, he looked through his perspiration.

"Sorry, Ceci, I have to cool off." So saying, he began to disrobe. They had known each other's bodies intimately in the past; he felt little inhibition in stripping off before her in this remote spot, then running thankfully towards the water.

After splashing about for a few minutes he felt something brush past his thighs. 'My God, sharks', the idea shot through his mind and he started to swim frantically for the shore. She burst up through the surface in front of him relaxed and giggling with mischief.

"Ceci, you ..." She pulled him down into the warm water and he realised that she too was completely naked. He put his arms around her playfully; Ceci wrapped her legs around him. They stayed like this drifting in the waters surge until out of breath they came coughing to the surface. She smiled at him as they splashed their way through the shallowing water. On the beach she turned and held him, looking up into his face. "I'm glad you called, Harry," she smiled. He kissed her gently.

The sun was well past its zenith but it was still very warm in its dwindling rays. He picked her up and carried her to the shadows caused by the overhanging trees fringing the deserted beach. They lay together kissing and touching; it seemed they still knew each other so well. He entered her gently; she gasped with the pleasure of his movements. They lay for a moment, still enjoying the sensation of coupling after so long. Holding her, he gave vent to his passion; she arched and cried joyously as he climaxed.

Still the engine would not start and it was beginning to get dark. Their stretch of coast was isolated and curved slightly out to sea but they were able to see a faint light to the north in the deepening twilight. Lost and feeling rather hungry, they decided that it looked near enough to walk and set out along the beach. Stumbling along in the dusk, tripping over rocks, getting wet where the jungle left no room to walk on the beach, they eventually reached a small group of broken, derelict huts, a spluttering paraffin lamp and now a large beach fire over which a group of fishermen were cooking a meal. The smell was tangible a mile away and drove them onwards.

The fishermen were startled by the arrival of two Europeans stumbling into their small pool of light, out of the surrounding darkness. Ceci spoke to them, reassured them; her very limited command of their native tongue enabled her to barely describe their situation and more importantly to ask to share their food if possible. The fish grilled over the open fire was delicious, accompanied with rice and vegetables including delicious small onions. She managed to glean that one of their small group was away for the night visiting relatives; he, it seemed, spoke some English, and would be back at daylight in time for them to sail.

Penrose and Ceci slept under the stars in each other's arms, just within the glow of the campfire. In the grey light of approaching dawn movement in the little camp awakened them. Water was put to boil and the fire replenished with driftwood. A new face greeted them.

"Hello, my name is Krishnan; my crew tell me you have some

problem with flying machine. I am not expert in this, only fishing and trading." The brown weathered face was wide and open, dark, almost black eyes alight, his black hair glossy in the half-light. Penrose elaborated on their problem but it made no difference to the stocky Malay in front of them.

"Where are we?" asked Ceci, "Where is Penang?"

Krishnan turned and pointed south.

"About ten miles," he suggested.

"Can you take us to Penang in your boat, we can pay you?" Ceci thought that they needed professional mechanical help to get the aircraft off the beach and Penang may be able to help in that respect. Krishnan thought for a moment.

"It is not possible for me to go to Penang now, it is too dangerous. We do not only fish, we are trading as well and we have some problems there."

For Ceci the penny dropped after a moment, it struck her – they dabbled in smuggling as well.

"We are from Camorta; it is an island to the west," he pointed seawards, "part of Nicobar Islands." Neither Ceci nor Penrose had heard of the place. Ceci pulled out the crumpled chart she had stuffed into a bag with a few other key possessions before they had left the aircraft the previous evening. They looked but could not identify anything bearing the name of Krishnan's island. A brown hand interrupted their muttering and pondering over the chart with a wavering forefinger pointing to a very small island in the Nicobar group, a chain that extended northwards to the Andamans.

"It is here," he said pointing roughly a third of the way up a group of islands that were spread over six hundred miles north-south, about three hundred and fifty miles offshore and roughly parallel to the Malay mainland.

"These are the Nicobar and Andaman islands," he said.

"So you are not Malay?" Said Penrose enlightened.

Krishnan explained that his father was ethnic Malay but his mother was from the Nicobars and was actually Indian. He was one of four sons, two of whom lived with his infirm father not far from this beach.

"My brothers may be able to help you, they have a much larger boat than I have – it has an engine and sails and is used for trading as well as fishing. They are not here at the moment but will return perhaps today or tomorrow."

Harold Penrose was becoming increasingly concerned at the delay in progressing with their search for Cornucopia.

"Let's go back to the aircraft and see if we can finally persuade it to start," he said anxiously. Krishnan agreed to take them back along the coast as far as aircraft in his fishing boat – it should prove quicker than walking. They waited impatiently while the group finished their breakfast of rice, fish and tea, slowly gathering their things together and preparing the small craft for sea.

A light but slowly rising onshore breeze made short work of the journey back to the aircraft. They disembarked into the surf and said their goodbyes to Krishnan and his crew, Ceci pressing a large wad of local currency in his hand. He looked at it, his eyes widened. It was more than his fishing would earn in a month. He thanked her profusely, holding her hand firmly saying that if they needed help again that he could be contacted at the small village about half a mile inland from where they had found them last night. The boat was pushed off and was soon riding the small waves back to their beach camp. Harold and Ceci waved, watching the small craft until it was hull-down in the growing swells further offshore.

"Perhaps we should have asked them to wait until we knew whether the engine would actually start," remarked Ceci.

"They were keen to be on their way I sensed," replied Penrose.

Together they quickly inspected the blue-and-silver machine. It had come to no harm during the night; few if any people would frequent this part of the coast, especially at night. With the engine cowlings open they again cleaned the fuel lines, checked spark plugs and their high-tension leads, turned the engine over by hand pulling on the wooden propeller, checking that there was equal compression in each cylinder. Ceci fussed about, wiping oil from the inside of the cowlings and generally looking for the possible cause of their engine failure yesterday. 'Yesterday,' she thought to herself. My, what a lot had happened to her since yesterday.

She showed Penrose how to start the engine, swinging the propeller by hand. He soon grasped the technique – at least enough to prevent him being chopped up in its whirling arc. Ceci switched on the fuel and primed the carburettor. Clambering into the rear cockpit she opened the throttle a fraction. Penrose pulled the propeller over six times, sucking in the volatile air-and-petrol mixture.

"Mags on!" cried Ceci. Both sets of magneto switches were flipped up; they would allow a vital spark-free passage through wires that would ignite the dormant mixture in the engine's cylinders. Penrose placed his right hand as far up the propeller blade as possible and pulled it down as hard as he could, moving both sideways and backwards as he did so, endeavouring to remain outside the propeller's disc.

Apparently keen to make up for its past poor behaviour, the

Gypsy engine fired immediately. A puff of blue smoke and it ticked away comfortably at eight hundred revolutions per minute. Ceci waved a laughing thumbs-up; Harold Penrose did an exuberant jig in the sand before climbing into the front cockpit, but not before planting a kiss on his lover's oil-smeared nose.

So far so good, thought Ceci, now to get it off the beach without mishap. She allowed the engine to warm while fastening her seat harness and then quickly carried out her pre take-off checks. The aircraft was now positioned on soft dry sand; she taxied gently forwards onto wet firmer sand left by the slowly receding tide.

"Here goes," she shouted, pushing the throttle lever fully forwards. The aircraft paused momentarily in the rutted sand, then moved down the beach, speed building rapidly as the tail came up. At forty-eight miles per hour Ceci pulled very gently back on the stick. The Gypsy Moth left the impromptu yellowish runway and tracked out over the sparkling blue-turquoise sea in a gentle climbing turn to the left, the richly green and wet vegetation contrasting with the strand of pale yellow bordering the ocean. Visibility was perfect.

Twenty minutes later they had landed on the mainland airstrip at Butterworth, which served both the island of Penang and the mainland's interior. Parking the aircraft, they walked slowly in the damp heat towards the little cluster of brick and wooden buildings that served as offices. Inside, the small operations room was packed full of people: the airport manager and his assistant, the local Empress Airways agent, a meteorologist, pipe in mouth, three Japanese, two Dutch pilots, and the two service pilots; all were smoking, talking, drinking coffee and gesturing around a table covered with charts.

Ceci noticed a khaki RAF uniform immediately she entered

and could not believe her eyes when standing, with his back to her, she recognised Harvey Wills, her fiancé. Ducking quickly out of the small room she managed to get out of the building unseen. If she were seen to be with Harold at this place there would be hell to pay, both with Harvey and her parents. Harold caught up with her.

"It's okay, I saw him as well, you'll have to go to ground until he's gone." She nodded.

"Supposing he sees the Gypsy when he comes out?"

"I think he is one of the crew that the RAF intended to send from Singapore to look for Cornucopia. They must have moored the amphibian down by the Penang ferry point instead of landing it here. If I go back in I can distract him, he'll be surprised to see me here, and you can move the Gypsy around the side of that small hangar so that he doesn't see it."

"He's not going to be over the moon to see you with or without me." Ceci bit her lip. She didn't like this situation. She knew she was in the wrong in actively condoning the re-establishment of their relationship – but there were times when her wilful nature would not be curbed.

"Ceci! Did you hear what I said?" She looked at him and nodded. Walking quickly back to the aircraft she lifted the tail and with the aircraft balanced on its two main wheels pulled it slowly behind the nearby hangar. It was energy-sapping work in the heat. Penrose entered the small operations room again.

"and with the strength of the south-easterly wind as it was I don't think they had a chance to put her down safely with the seas that would have been running. However, if she did survive, and as I say I doubt it, she would have been blown well out to the west as she routed northwards. She reported by radio that she was climbing through low cloud and turbulence just half an hour after leaving here. Nothing was reported after that. The Imperial boat coming down from Rangoon heard a very faint transmission that would have been about two hours after she left us, it gave the position I have marked here on the chart." The speaker pointed to an isolated X. "If you want my opinion, they hadn't a clue where they were and you can't rely on that." The Met man, tall and authoritative, tossed his pencil onto the chart and stood back to light his pipe – billows of blue aromatic smoke enveloping the small room. Until two years previously he'd been a radio operator with Queensland & Northern Territories Air Services until a burst eardrum had curtailed his flying for good. He was very confident of his analysis.

There was a brief period of quiet. The DC-2 crew and their three passengers walked outside to discuss their next move. The two service pilots pulled out their charts and began drawing possible position lines based on known wind strengths locally and the time that Cornucopia had been in the air since leaving Penang based on the timing of Cornucopia's distress signal. Harvey Wills turned, conscious that someone was standing behind him. His eyes widened.

"Penrose! What in God's name are you doing here?!" he said with certain disdain in his tone.

"Oh, just visiting some friends in George Town before going back to Blighty." He tried to sound as nonchalant as possible.

"Are you looking for the crashed flying boat then?" He asked with feigned innocence.

"Yes, we are going to look for the Empress Airways flying boat. We're going to be based here for a few days, nobody seems to have too much idea where she may be but we shall attempt to narrow it down, assuming she is still afloat. I don't know why I'm telling you all this. I can't see what it's got to do with you Penrose. Excuse me, will you, I have work to do." He gathered together his papers and instruments and was about to push past Harold followed by the young naval pilot.

Penrose nodded and leaned over to get a better view of their chart on the table. Someone had pencilled a large cross on a piece of remote ocean. He'd spent a good deal of time looking at the tracing he had made at Singapore's Inter-Services library and memorised the position in relation to adjacent coastlines. It was the same position.

"So you don't think that is where she is, then?" he said.

"It's always possible but we don't know how long she remained airborne after their weak distress signal, nor do we know how strong the wind was out there," Wills said, pointing in the general direction of the sea.

"The wind tends to be stronger out at sea as there are no obstructions to slow it down as there are on land. Also, the wind varies in direction depending on your height; we don't have that information in any detail."

"So what will you do, then?" replied Penrose. Squadron Leader Wills looked at him pointedly.

"Well, we'll calculate a number of options based on the information we do have and then go looking. Our Dutch friends will do the same, so we might have some chance of locating Cornucopia or, at least, signs of wreckage."

Harold left the building, deliberately ambling slowly towards the small wooden hangar, while the two service pilots got into a car and were driven back to the harbour and their Walrus. He told Ceci what he had heard and seen.

"Are you sure you want to go on with this, Ceci? It could be a lost cause and we're running a real risk of Harvey seeing you and me together. Your father will mobilise the whole of the Singapore garrison if he finds out we're together again."

"I know ... but we've come this far, so perhaps we should persevere for a bit. Why don't we wait here for a day or so and see how the other two crews get on. We don't have the range to fly directly to the position marked on your chart. We would have to fly up the coast, refuel somewhere then strike out to the west over the sea to the marked position. The others will already have been there by this evening or tomorrow morning and may report back whether they have found her. Anyway, I wouldn't want the engine to die on us again, especially if we're well offshore."

Harold agreed and walked back to the little group of huts and engaged the Empress agent in conversation. He learned something of the Dutch, Japanese, and in particular Ng's interest in Cornucopia. The local Empress agent said that he was a little surprised at Ng's involvement as he was unaware of there being any Singapore Chinese passengers on board Cornucopia; these flights were almost exclusively the preserve of wealthy expatriates. They shared some tea and Penrose talked of his new interest in aeroplanes and asked if the agent would mind if he visited the airfield from time to time while in Penang. The agent appreciated his interest and took him on a tour of the limited airfield facilities. Harold Penrose had worked his charm again, and when they parted he and the agent were as thick as thieves.

Ceci, in the meantime, had been supervising the refuelling of the Gypsy Moth. On this occasion she took precautions, using a chamois leather spread out in the filler funnel to filter out water and any other detritus that might be in the forty-gallon drums of aviation spirit carried on the back of the small, ancient refuelling lorry. As the lorry finally bumped away over the uneven surface of the airfield on solid rubber tyres, Penrose came back to her.

They watched the shiny DC-2 turn to line up into wind. After a minute or so, the two radial engines growled and the aircraft moved down the grass strip tail-up and into the air, climbing on a north-westerly heading. An hour later the Walrus amphibian lifted from the sheltered waters between Penang Island and the mainland and, having climbed clear, turned onto a heading of three five zero degrees – almost due north.

Carrying their few possessions, Ceci and Harold caught a lift with the Met man down to the island ferry, which took them over to Penang and its capital George Town. They found a small, freshly painted hotel managed by an efficient Indian from Gujarat, and settled down on the clean linen sheets. The ornate overhead fan creaked but created a welcome, cooling draught as they stared up.

"But Harold, it's nearly lunchtime ..." Her protests were less than convincing and she succumbed finally with passion and delight. They bathed and went down for afternoon tea at four o'clock. They were both famished after the day's events and their more recent stimulating exercise.

The Dutch crew and their Japanese charterers returned to Butterworth later that afternoon. It turned out that they had found absolutely nothing. One of the Japanese in the party seemed to be in a particularly bad frame of mind, scolding the Chinese member of their team.

The joint RAF and navy crew had flown up the coast, forty miles offshore, past the Siam–Burma border searching endlessly for a needle in a haystack, so it seemed. They remained at the Burmese coastal town of Kawthaung overnight, some 370 miles north of Penang, intending to fly further west the next day in a square-search pattern over the ocean as they routed back, southwards, towards Penang and eventually Singapore. They had experienced problems in finding suitable fuel for the Walrus, but managed, with the district administrator's help, to buy some at a premium using the imprest account Wills had obtained before leaving Singapore.

The next day the routine was much the same – acres of dark ocean with only small fishing vessels or an occasional dhow providing brief visual relief on the slumbering sea. At one point they thought they saw an aircraft squirt a burst of reflected sunlight from its polished skin in the far distance, perhaps the DC-2 conducting its own independent search? The Walrus crew were increasingly frustrated that their aircraft was not fitted with the new type of powerful American radios now becoming available. If it had been, they would have been able to co-ordinate their search efforts to much better effect with the other aircraft.

After three days, despite a lack of communication, both search aircraft had scoured the seas along and around the probable track of the missing flying boat, until they concluded that Cornucopia had broken up on landing and had probably sunk with her crew and passengers. The two aircraft landed back at Penang and Butterworth within an hour of each other during the early evening. The crews were exhausted, looking forward to a bath, dinner and an early night before their return to Singapore the next day.

Hearing the approaching engine noises, Penrose was there when the two crews finally came in to report and compare notes. The small, aggressive Japanese man barked incomprehensible streams of apparent invective at the Singaporean. He was accompanied by the two Dutch crewmen, who seemed slightly embarrassed. Penrose soon heard that they had had no joy, except that one of the Dutch pilots reported seeing something like a wing float or possibly a wheel bobbing about in the gentle swell. They were not able to identify it positively even from fifty feet above the sea's surface as they flew over it, barely above stalling speed. They had made a note of its position, however, some two hundred miles west of Phuket. Penrose looked over the assembled shoulders as they all studied the chart again. He noted the spotted object's supposed position: it was much closer to the Nicobar Island chain than to either the Malay or Burmese coast.

The next day the borrowed navy Walrus and the DC-2 left early in the morning for their respective bases in Singapore. Penrose and Ceci arrived at Butterworth around mid-morning, intending to prepare the Gypsy Moth for their return flight via Kuala Lumpur. They had a chat with the Empress agent and inevitably discussion entailed tea and the talk turned to the situation with Cornucopia. At this point the Met man joined them.

"I've been looking in more detail at our wind recordings for that day," he said, pulling out a neatly compiled chart showing time and wind speed at regular intervals.

"We have to record this information and telegraph it to Singapore and Rangoon each day. It's supposed to help them with their forecasting. I often wonder if they ever use it. Anyway, it seems to me that the air force and the Dutch have not calculated enough effect from the wind when considering their search areas."

"What do you mean, are they looking in the wrong place?" they asked, almost in unison.

"Well, I reckon that the Empress boat was blown much further west than they all thought possible. The last regular position report we had from them, half an hour after they left, indicated that they were climbing through cloud at five thousand feet. They normally reckon to cruise at somewhere between one and three thousand feet, depending on the weather. If, as we know, they were experiencing bad weather, they may have been tempted to climb much higher hoping to break clear of it."

"And, if they had, they would have experienced even greater wind speeds the higher they went, and the wind direction would also have changed!" burst in Ceci, remembering her early meteorological flying training lectures and the physics of weather systems in the northern hemisphere.

"You're right, young lady! Flying over the sea would have compounded the problem because there is no slowing effect from the land – creating a drag on the wind, slowing it down if you like," responded the Empress agent.

"So what you're saying is that the machine could have been pushed by the wind much further to the west than anybody has ever considered. It seems strange that the RAF didn't spot that."

"Well, you have to understand that in this situation there are all manner of possibilities. The RAF and Royal Navy tend to see themselves as the experts ... standard procedures and all that. Anyway, it's very difficult to tell them anything."

They continued to chat about Cornucopia and other matters until they all realised that time had slipped by and that perhaps a return to Singapore tomorrow would be a better plan. Ceci and Harry thanked the Empress agent for his tea and advice, and made their way back to the hotel that they had paid and left earlier that morning. Their old room was clean and waiting.

That evening, as they were strolling arm-in-arm about the small streets of shop-houses in George Town they ran unexpectedly into

Krishnan. They were surprised to meet him there – after all he had said about it being dangerous for him – but he made it clear that he was in George Town for only one day as he needed to collect money that was long owed to the family. They all sat with tea under the small thatch of a street vendor's canopy.

"How's your father?" asked Ceci. Krishnan explained that he was now much better but wanted to go back to his wife on Camorta. "My brothers are considering taking him and his belongings in their boat in the next few days. You must have managed to get your flying machine from the beach, I think?"

"Yes," they smiled, "the engine started first swing." He smiled with them. "My brother has told me a story of a big flying machine that is now missing. At first I was concerned for you but then I thought your machine is not so big!"

Again they shared laughter.

"No, but it is a mystery. There have been two aircraft searching the ocean between here and the last position they reported but without sighting even any wreckage," said Harold Penrose. Krishnan was silent for a few minutes. Then he spoke, quietly.

"Perhaps they look in the wrong place?"

"What do you mean? They spent just about three days, covered thousands of square miles and found almost nothing, except possibly a wing float or wheel, even that couldn't be positively identified. Anyway, it wasn't too far from your Andaman Islands, much too far to the west, I would have thought?" Penrose waved his empty tea glass about as he spoke.

Krishnan told them that the storm of a few days ago was very unusual, with little warning and with unseasonable strength. Also, he added, there had been a great deal of thunder and lightning. "It is possible," he said, "that the wind could have driven them far to the west, perhaps as far as the Nicobar and Andaman islands." Ceci and Penrose stopped to think.

"But it must be well over 300 miles, perhaps more; the wind would have to have to have blown at speeds over a hundred miles an hour to have got them that far in the time available." Krishnan looked at them.

"What is your interest in this machine? Why do you enquire and discuss its fortune?" An interesting use of words under the circumstances, thought Penrose.

"Oh, we happened to know some of those on board," Ceci replied, in the past tense, without thinking. Krishnan looked on knowingly and then spoke.

"On his return to Camorta my brother told me a strange story. He said his crew had had a fearful experience some two or three nights earlier while fishing well to the west of Car Nicobar Island. He says the crew called him from his sleep as they had seen a great shark with a huge fin, eerily white in the night. The eyes of the shark flashed, so they told him! He wanted to go and see what they had seen but they begged him not to go, but to return to Camorta immediately." Ceci and Penrose looked at each other, not quite knowing where the story was going but suspecting there was some relevance to their previous discussion about Cornucopia. Krishnan continued:

"When I leave you on the beach with your machine and we are some way from shore, I look back. All I can see above the waves is the silver fin on the back of your machine as you are lifting it to move the machine, the other blue colour and shapes cannot be seen. To me, for a small moment, I think then that it looks very much like a shark's fin." He got up, leaving them to draw some conclusions from his analogy.

"I will be here tomorrow morning for breakfast; perhaps we can share it together?" They stood up, but too late, he was suddenly gone among the shadows. A rotund Chinese-Malay man at an adjacent stall left a few moments after, walking quickly to the local telegraph office. Ceci looked at Penrose.

"Krishnan knows something, doesn't he?" Penrose wasn't sure, but he nodded.

Back at the hotel, Ceci's attempts to entice him into bed were proving difficult. She had surprised herself with her uninhibited and predatory nature; she had never before behaved like this with Harvey, on those rare occasions when they were sufficiently alone at her parents' home for her to try. Her sighs and posturing wearing little more than a newly bought and strategically placed silk shawl left him, apparently cold, sitting in the room's only chair with his traced map, a pencil and a piece of paper covered with figures.

Harold suddenly spoke, "Yes, he knows something, alright, or at least suspects that his brother's crew may have seen the ditched Cornucopia. Let's think about it. If the aircraft had survived the crash, and it's a big if, it would probably be damaged. Okay? So, it might be only just afloat, perhaps just showing its fin and rudder above the sea. The Empress aircraft are basically white and it could look like a huge fish, or shark, as Krishnan said, floating just above the water. To an uneducated fisherman it may appear to be something quite horrifying."

"Harry, it doesn't explain how they could have got to the other side of the Nicobar Islands in the time. It's probably four hundred or more miles from where it was supposed to have been." Her ardour had cooled a little and she was beginning to enter into the spirit of advocate. Harold Penrose stood up and walked about the small bedroom.

"There is one thing that could explain it. They could have flown directly there – the combined speed of the aircraft and a tailwind of, say, only forty miles an hour would have given them plenty of time if they were all going in the same direction. It would mean a speed over the ground, well, ocean actually, of something like 220 miles an hour. More than ample speed to cover four hundred-odd miles in less than three hours."

Ceci pondered for a moment.

"Why would they fly almost at right angles to their proper course to Rangoon, towards the west instead of north?"

"Simple, young lady." He grabbed her wrists and sat her down on the bed to explain.

"There was a lot of thunderstorm activity, lots of lightning banging around according to Krishnan. If they were within the influence of an electric storm of that intensity, particularly within the storm clouds, it could have easily upset the sensitivity of the aircraft compasses; deflected them one way or the other, perhaps permanently. They would appear from the compass to be steering a course of north but were actually flying say, to the west, and of course with no visual reference points, land and so on, inside the storm clouds, how would they know?"

She thought back to her basic flying training and what she had been taught about compasses and weather – he may be right.

"It assumes that what was seen by Krishnan's brother's crew was Cornucopia and not some figment of their fertile imagination." He agreed with her, but said that no sign of floating wreckage or aircraft after three days or so, with two aircraft searching, and the apparent sighting by the fishing crew of something that might possibly resemble an aircraft on the water, could mean his compass theory may be worth considering. Anyway, he felt that Krishnan was aware of something similar.

"Can we fly to the Nicobars tomorrow?"

"Don't be ridiculous, Harold; it's too far for my poor little Moth. We'll talk to Krishnan in the morning, he may have some ideas, and perhaps his brother could take us in his boat?"

"Mmm ... perhaps now ... I could sample this wonderful body you have been propositioning me with most of the evening."

"Harold Penrose, how dare you suggest I am even capable of propositioning!" she giggled, pulling him down onto her reawakening body.

FIVE

Rawlinson was up and on top of Cornucopia's fuselage in seconds. What was that banging and crashing into the frail sides of their craft? Taking the torch from Purser Snell he walked gingerly out onto the rolling port wing. It was there, long and glistening, plunging in the swell. Goodness, what was it? There were others and they were huge. Then he saw. The aircraft was being battered by a horde of teak logs energised by the waves. The colonel joined him.

"Must have been the deck cargo off a ship; probably lost them overboard in the same storm that did for us."

Rawlinson and the other three able-bodied men spent the rest of the night fending off the massive logs, which threatened to ram and puncture Cornucopia's thin aluminium skin. By morning they were utterly exhausted, and there was little to eat or drink for breakfast.

"If we could find a way of controlling the damn things," suggested the colonel, "we could push them under the wings. They may provide some additional and useful buoyancy."

Later that morning, while Rawlinson, Snell and the colonel pushed and pulled the huge logs about in the water, risking serious injury from the massive timbers, Sarah kept watch for sharks. Through good timing and co-ordination they managed, eventually, to jam two logs on either side of Cornucopia, lying parallel to the fuselage between the inner and outer engines. The logs would now provide some additional floatation for the aircraft if the weather should worsen, Rawlinson hoped. During the rest of the day they were forced to fend off other stray logs but were pleased to find coconuts also floating among the timber, and eagerly fished them out. The milk was extracted by Snell and decanted into empty soda water bottles, which he kept cool by plunging them into seawater, and the husks and meat were dried in the sun atop the fuselage guarded by Beth.

During the afternoon a welcoming cool breeze got up from the south-west, gradually developing into a brisk wind. The sea began to sport white horses as Cornucopia started to roll viciously in the confused and developing swell, but the carefully positioned logs, now lashed crudely under the wings, helped to reduce the violence of the motion. Deverall noticed that they were now moving through the ocean towards the east; glancing up from his study of a piece of floating seaweed that confirmed their eastward drift, he saw a dim, greyish shadow on the far horizon. Watching it carefully for some minutes, he determined that it was something tangible, not a cloud or a deeper blob of haze.

Leaving his position atop Cornucopia's fuselage he moved unhurriedly down to the flight deck, where he found Rawlinson in earnest conversation with Sarah Gregson. They were discussing the condition of their erstwhile captain, lying feverishly wrapped in blankets within the centre mail stowage compartment.

Deverall, waiting for a brief interlude in their conversation, commented, almost offhand, "I think we may be approaching some land. There is definitely something solid on the horizon to the east, I'm pretty sure it's not my imagination."

They both looked at him questioningly as they got up and climbed up and out onto the aircraft's roof.

"Look there, it's still where I saw it a few minutes ago, it must be land."

David Rawlinson and Sarah followed Deverall's gaze and pointing finger. There did appear to be something there, something tangible that could possibly be land. Rawlinson continued looking for some minutes.

"If it is land then it's definitely not Malaya," he said, with some certainty. "If my calculations are correct then it must be somewhere in the Nicobar or Andaman island groups."

They took it in turns to watch all afternoon, hoping that what was as yet a smudge on the horizon was in fact somewhere more solid. They all wanted to get off this ruptured craft, and back to a more normal and predictable existence. Sarah Gregson had more reason than most: she was concerned for her young daughter, Beth, for the condition of her patient Captain Kelly, and for her own physical state, being nearly three months pregnant. Fortunately she had not been affected by the morning sickness that had afflicted her when pregnant with Beth. Long may it continue, she prayed.

Beth proved to be a prime example of how children can adapt if they feel secure, despite outlandish and sometimes dangerous circumstances. She spent time playing with a few toys rescued from their baggage before it had been pushed overboard; both Deverall and Snell turned out to be good storytellers and kept her amused, with the other survivors, for hours. But the problem for all of them was the diminishing water and food supplies.

Hudson took the initiative next morning and shinned up the tail fin with a length of ripped-out control wire. He secured the cable to the fin top, and then he and Snell pulled, with difficulty, the large tarpaulin, which had served them well as shelter from storm and sun, intending to set the flailing cloth as a sail. It would enhance their progress downwind towards whatever land lay there.

After experimenting with different settings they managed to fix the sail so that it would pull them roughly in the wind's direction.

"Perhaps more importantly, it helps to stabilise the boat in these growing swells – it's taking out the more violent rolling in this confused sea. What sort of navigation lights do we exhibit for an aircraft under sail?" Rawlinson joked.

Below, Sarah was carefully peeling the dressings off Michael Kelly's shortened right leg. As she neared the core of the dressing she was increasingly concerned at the amount of blood evident. But of infinitely more worry was the evidence of pus and infection. With all the dressings removed, the smell was unmistakable. His wound had become infected over the last twelve hours or so; it had begun to exude a yellowish fluid along with blood. The rough surgical area was red and angry; the skin taut where her improvised stitching caught it. She was at a loss as to what to do with the few resources to hand. Kelly lay between pain and unconsciousness. She spoke with Snell. "Is there any possibility that there is still some alcohol down in the galley?"

"I don't think so, Ma'am, but I'll have another look if you wish." He really did not feel inclined to go down into his sunken kitchen again but if there was a good reason, then he was nevertheless prepared to try.

"There might be something down there that might be of use, if I can find it, if it hasn't been affected by sea water." He went on, "I sometimes suffer from serious headaches, migraines, they call them. Not very often but they can be quite unbearable and debilitating. The company doctor prescribed some tablets but they didn't seem to make a lot of difference. You know what these quacks are like. So, the Empress station manager in Singapore, Mr Porter, recommended that I go to see a Chinese doctor friend of his, which I did eventually. He gave me some sort of herbal tablets he had concocted; I honestly didn't think they would be much good. Anyway, I had to use them once and, believe it or not, they worked, pretty well too."

"So where are they now, Mr Snell?"

"Down in the galley. I always kept them handy, in a bottle in the glasses cabinet. The bottle has a screw top; the sea might not have got in."

Not keen to administer any drug or quack potion that came to hand, she had but few choices now, she was well aware.

"Okay, let's see if we can get them – and any more alcohol." Snell stripped quickly down to his shorts and Rawlinson tied a mooring rope in a loop around his waist. Gulping, the purser stepped down into the water.

He worked quickly in his familiar galley. The medicines he had pinned his faith on finding lay within the cabinet as he had described. Then, up to the surface, bottle clutched securely in his hand. Sarah Gregson inspected the dripping bottle. Any label it may have had was gone.

Down he went again, pulling open all the cupboards and drawers in the tiny galley, frantically seeking any remains of the stock of passenger refreshments he had so carefully stowed while in Singapore. Nothing. Then he remembered. Tucked away in a small cupboard in the forward smoking lounge was a bottle of aqua vitae left from a previous trip by a Danish pastor on his way to take up a missionary appointment in Siam. The poor man had clearly put up a 'black' with his bishop and had been posted abroad to repent at his leisure. Short of breath, Snell rose back into the warm air of the flight deck and recounted the memory to the others.

Sitting ready to descend again, breathing deeply in preparation, he caught sight of a movement in the water below him, not actually in the galley, but moving quickly past the galley entrance, towards the ruptured aircraft nose. He kept watching but saw nothing further. A trick of the light in water, he thought. Grabbing a new lungful of air, he quickly sank again into the flooded galley space, passing through its door to the right, intending to swim into the forward smoking lounge.

It came at him in a flash. He struck out instinctively in self-preservation, his frantic efforts slowed by the viscosity of the water. His hands struck the abrasive skin of the shark's flanks; it didn't hurt but he was aware fleetingly of his blood mingling in the water. The shark turned violently in the restricted space, attempting to swim clear through the broken aircraft nose. But the exit hole was too small. Excited now by the smell of fresh blood and Snell's terrified thrashing movements, it turned its eye hungrily onto the increasingly breathless man, lying prostrate at the bottom of the cabin.

Snell needed air, now, desperately. But regardless, he pulled himself further under the seats, as far as possible from the symmetrical rows of razor teeth in the huge jaws. The rope around his middle wasn't helping his situation; it kept catching on the many protuberances in the cabin. Suddenly, the shark veered away from its attack, shooting across the cabin space. It had gone for something. As it turned, Snell saw something in its mouth – something horrifying, grotesque. Staring from the grip of the shark's vile jaws was a crushed human head. It was Newsome's. Face showing, without expression, the sockets eyeless. It was carried, trophy-like, out of the cabin towards the rear, tiny pieces of skin and brain tissue left jiggling in the wake of disturbed water.

Leaving his own trail of air bubbles behind him, Snell followed at a respectful distance until, reaching the galley, he shot to the surface. He couldn't speak. He couldn't stop shaking; gasping for breath. Eyes wide. Neither sitting nor standing could he control the tremors. It was a good ten minutes before he could speak coherently.

"I'm sorry; the Aquavit is still down there as far as I know but don't, please don't ask me to fetch it ... there's a bloody great shark down there." They looked at him, stunned. For a few seconds nobody spoke.

"Mr Snell, you've had a very lucky escape, it seems." Deverall put an arm around the shaking man's shoulders as they sat on the galley stair. "Don't worry about the bloody booze. After what you've just been through, we'll sort something out." They undid the rope from around him. But the bloody booze was important; they all knew it. The infection in Kelly's leg had to be fought – any alcohol may help to contain it.

They now suspected that somewhere below the waterline, the hull of Cornucopia had been breached sufficiently for a six-foot shark, by Snell's account, to gain entry into the crippled boat. Damage done the previous night by the pounding logs may have created a sizeable hole in the hull. To go down again was clearly a risk: where there was one shark there were probably more, they agreed. The three other men decided a further effort to recover the alcohol was worth it only if all three went down to keep watch and to search.

Deverall collected the boat-hook from its lashing on the fuselage roof and then he, Rawlinson and Hudson went slowly and nervously below. Hudson clung to the submerged galley door frame, staying on guard in the passage between the galley space and forward smoking cabin. The other two swam cautiously into the forward saloon, to the small locker mounted on the forward bulkhead. There inside was a bottle. Rawlinson peered briefly in the half-light at its contents; it seemed almost full. Hudson led them quickly back to the bottom of the galley stairs, remaining on watch while they mounted the steps in haste. He took one look aft before following them. In the underwater murk, the whitish underside of a shark could be seen shaking and thrashing at something in the rearmost cabin. Lilly Hudson was not receiving a Christian burial.

He was out of air and rushed up the stairs to breathe. As he surfaced he struggled to gasp out: "It's there, it's taking her!" He grabbed the boat-hook from Deverall and turned to retrace his upward flight. Then, he was stopped dead in his tracks by Deverall, who caught him very firmly by the arm.

"What is happening, George?" His tone was authoritative, demanding, Hudson should stop and explain despite his abhorrence at what was taking place below them. He struggled to articulate what he had seen.

"The shark ... it's Lilly, my Lilly. My God help her!" It was a cry of true sorrow. Deverall and Rawlinson pulled the distraught man gently up from the stairwell.

"George, George ... I don't think there is anything you can do for her now." Deverall's statement invited no discussion. He held the man's shaking hands in his; it was a remarkable act of understanding and firm leadership, thought David Rawlinson. They were quiet together except for Hudson's breathing, just standing together. Then the tension went from Hudson's shoulders; he began to relax and after a few minutes gently released himself from Deverall's hold. He wiped his tears, swallowing hard.

"You're right, thank you," he whispered. "I don't think there was very much I could have done. It was horrible ... my Lilly." His chest heaved in suppressed sobs as he staggered forward to be alone in the cockpit.

Sarah took the high-proof spirit from Rawlinson and set about cleaning Kelly's wound. She carefully released some of the pressure by piercing the skin with a sterilised knifepoint. A flood of pus, blood and other infected matter rushed out, she swabbed it away carefully. It was therapeutic, seeing the evil mess exiting the small incisions she made. Kelly shouted with rage at the pain, banging on the sides of the small space and making Beth cry out with fright. As the pressure subsided he felt the pain subside a little. It was still acute but just bearable. Sarah took a justifiable risk and gave Kelly twice the dose of Chinese pills recommended to Purser Snell, and a large slug of the spirit. Within fifteen minutes he was asleep.

It had been a fearful and tension-filled day; they were all very tired. Snell prepared another simple meal of canned fruit and coconut meat, to be washed down with a few ounces of the remaining, now-brackish, water. Beth drank some coconut milk, wrinkling her nose up at the new taste; her mother insisted. As dusk settled, the wind began to fade. The makeshift sail flapped in desultory fashion until it became annoying and Deverall lowered it for the night. They all looked eastwards hoping to see the land they now knew was there, but visibility was poor in the evening dusk. It was quiet as darkness fell, except for the lapping of water against the stationary hull and the occasional clunk as one of the teak logs rubbed itself against the wings in the swell.

❖ ❖ ❖

Twelve miles downwind of where Cornucopia lay rocking gently, the crew of a small fishing boat had difficulty hauling two large travel cases over the side of their frail vessel. Once on board they noticed with interest the Empress labels attached but were unable to read the indelible English script on them. Early the next morning, on reaching their island, and after unloading their catch, they spent time with other villagers hilariously trying on the western clothes they found, almost dry, inside. The papers they found in the trunks blew across the beach.

Chandra Patel picked up some of the blowing papers as she walked along the beach late that afternoon and noticed that they were in English. She spoke little English although she had spent a little time working for the district officer near her home village some years ago. Some of the papers, she understood, were letters to 'Dear Lilly and George,' and were signed, 'With love and affection, Aunt Madge' in somewhere called Alderley in Cheshire, England. Others appeared to be legal documents concerning a trust for a child. She hadn't a clue what a trust was but collected as many papers as she could, intending to show them to one of her sons on their return from visiting their father. Perhaps they would bring the old man with them; it would be good to see her husband again.

SIX

Colonel Hyami left the overheated aircraft at Tengah airfield in Singapore still an angry man. During the flight from Penang to Singapore the unfortunate Ng had been berated endlessly. Hyami still had some faith in Ng's story concerning Cornucopia but had increasing doubts about the efficacy of its position reports, and had begun to doubt the likelihood that the aircraft had actually been carrying bullion. Ng was instructed to obtain more facts from his brother-in-law, or indeed anyone else who may have vital information, provided, Hyami made clear, that no Japanese connections were made.

That afternoon Ng again made his way to the Empress offices, where he found not only his brother-in-law but also the Empress station manager, Cyril Porter, a florid-faced man with a large stomach held vaguely in place by a slowly failing trouser belt. Perspiring profusely under an open-necked, greying white shirt, Porter was increasingly concerned at the lack of positive information concerning Cornucopia from the RAF or the navy. His absence in Malaya over the weekend of her disappearance had not won him any plaudits from London HQ. The Empress board in London pestered him daily with telegraphed questions about the aircraft, its passengers and seemingly more importantly, its cargo.

Porter had been trying to answer these questions over the past few days but nothing satisfactory had emerged from the reports submitted by the RAF after the Walrus's return and the comments from Squadron Leader Wills.

Ng waited while preparations for the departure of another Empress flying boat were completed. Eleven passengers were boarded with a small load of empire mail, the next scheduled stop being Penang, where four more passengers were to be uplifted together with a further small quantity of mails. Once the aircraft was airborne, Porter telegraphed Penang with departure details and the passenger manifest. He had been on duty since four o'clock that morning dealing with the departure of a Darwin-bound boat and was feeling both tired and under pressure in the heat and humidity. At times he hated Singapore's constant high humidity: it brought on his prickly heat rash. Leaving his second-in-command in charge, he resolved to go home, bathe, have an early night and take up the challenge of responding to his London directors the next day.

Ng settled down with tea and asked Lee how things were at home with his sister and the young children. Gradually he steered the subject onto the fate of Cornucopia.

"We still have no real information about what happened to her. The search has been unsuccessful so far," said Lee, in response to some gentle prodding.

"I heard that the RAF had been looking in the wrong place," Ng offered. "I was overhearing a conversation and it was suggested that the flying boat was well off course when it was lost." Ng had to be careful not to expose how much he knew. Lee must not discover that he had already been involved in the search with Hyami and the Dutch DC-2.

Lee sighed, "Who knows? I don't suppose she will be found now. It is a big problem. Mr Porter is having telegrams every day now asking for news and we have none to give."

"But why do they keep asking this? They know that the aeroplane cannot be found after the searches. Why do they keep asking?" Ng was hoping to get further confirmation from his sister's husband that the aircraft was carrying gold. Lee's earlier indiscretion had only alluded to Empress's involvement in carrying bullion.

"I believe, from things said by Mr Porter, that the directors in London are being held responsible for the cargo on board." Ng looked at Lee pointedly.

"But surely the lives on board are more important for these Europeans? The cargo will surely be insured, is that not your practice? Why should this be a problem for them, and what is the cargo anyway?"

"Yes, but some cargoes are very expensive to insure and recently the directors do not want anyone to be aware of what is on board, even insurance agents," said Lee, hesitantly.

"So, was Cornucopia carrying gold?" Ng shot the question quickly at Lee. Lee stopped and looked at his brother-in-law. He tried to make his expression neutral, non-committal, avoiding eye contact. He failed. Ng was now absolutely sure that Cornucopia had been carrying bullion. There was nothing in writing, nothing tangible to support the fact but he now knew, beyond any doubt.

"It is strange that the flying boat should not have left any wreckage when it crashed. As you say, there was a last, faint radio call giving a location; there might have been some wreckage in the area?" Ng decided to press on with his agenda. "I wonder why the people I overheard suggested that the aircraft was a long way off course."

"Mr Porter too has been saying this. From our station manager in Penang he has received information about the weather over the day of Cornucopia's schedule to Rangoon. The wind was very strong from the south and east. He says the aircraft could be anywhere between here and the Nicobar Islands, perhaps well out to the west, perhaps even into the Bay of Bengal. There was much lightning; it may have struck the aeroplane causing it to catch fire."

Ng nodded, helped himself to more tea and started to discuss the prospects of Lee's further promotion in the light of Mr Porter's problems, and how the two families would celebrate the next Chinese New Year.

Early next morning, in the marketplace at Serangoon, a small town in the central north-west of Singapore Island, Ng and Hyami met and discussed the prospects for retrieving any gold, sitting in the back of the colonel's black car. Ng expressed his firm conviction that the aircraft was carrying gold and cited his latest discussion with his brother-in-law. He supported his comments with the newspaper reports that there were only five passengers on board when Cornucopia left Penang that morning, including a child. Whereas, he emphasised, normally Empress and Imperial Airways carried around sixteen passengers. Indeed, it was well known that there were long waiting lists of passengers waiting to fly either to England or to Australia; carrying only five seemed odd with demand so high. He took the opportunity to discuss the question of the aircraft's final position report with Hyami again. He elaborated on the doubts expressed by the Met man in Penang and station manager Porter, after receipt of more detailed hourly weather reports sent by the Penang station manager for the day Cornucopia was lost.

Hyami absorbed Ng's report in silence and sat quietly observing the early-morning bustle in the crowded market.

"You will come to the trade office tomorrow evening at ten." Hyami's driver opened the door of the car and Ng was quickly ushered out among the market stalls, which were alive with people, livestock and brightly coloured vegetables and goods. The large, black car manoeuvred slowly round the noisy and cluttered market and left for the Japanese Trade Office by way of Tengah airfield.

❖ ❖ ❖

Krishnan was sitting, tea glass in hand, at the roadside stall they had visited the previous evening. His simple breakfast eaten, he shook hands with Harold and Ceci as they sat on the bamboo-framed stools scattered around the tea vendor's stall. While taking tea and noodles Penrose opened the conversation.

"We've been doing some thinking about what you said last night. We have a theory that may tie in with some of the ideas you mentioned." He went on to explain how an intense electrical storm could affect the compasses on Cornucopia. How she could have inadvertently flown to the west while believing she was heading north. The sighting of a large 'shark' by one of Krishnan's brother's fishing crew may actually not be so far-fetched. If the aircraft had survived a ditching in the stormy sea, it may well look like a huge, semi-submerged fish with dorsal fin erect, particularly at night. He extended his earlier thinking as the thought crossed his mind that the flashing eyes were possibly a flashing torch, signalling for help to the fishing boat. Krishnan nodded quickly at their excited comments.

"I think you should consider a search with your aeroplane to the west of our islands." They both sat quiet for a moment, realising that this idea presented a more complex picture, a long way from home.

"How would we get our aircraft to the Nicobar and Andamans? We can't fly there; it's too far for the amount of fuel we can carry safely. It must be over four hundred miles from here. Do you have airfields there?" Ceci asked.

"There is a small government airfield at Port Blair on the main island of South Andaman, but you seem able to land almost anywhere, even on a beach," he said, laughing.

"That's true up to a point," she agreed, smiling. Penrose had been looking at a map of the region unfolded on his lap as he sipped his tea.

"Can't we fly via Sumatra? Look, we could fly to Medan, then on to Banda Aceh here at its most northerly point, and then across here, to Great Nicobar then Little Nicobar and finally to Camorta?" His finger traced a curving route from Penang, north-west across Sumatra to Camorta, the little island Krishnan called home.

"I have been warned not to fly in Sumatra; it's supposed to be quite dangerous in places. We would be in trouble if the engine conked-out somewhere over the jungle, it's not like here." Ceci did not relish the prospect of flying over large tracts of totally uninhabited, jungle-filled territory.

"Perhaps there is another way, but first I must ask you something." Krishnan looked at them before proceeding. They both nodded, looking at him expectantly.

"You are taking a lot of trouble to find this lost aeroplane. Why is that? Who is on board that matters so much to you? You speak of relatives or friends on board, but you do not seem to me to be much upset or concerned. There must be something else that interests you greatly for you to spend so much time looking? I think you English have a saying like looking for pin in hayfield."

"It's a needle, actually ... in a haystack," said Harold, playing for time, and smiling as only the English can when caught out by a pertinent question.

"Okay, there is a good reason why we are so interested and I'm prepared to tell you more when we get to Camorta. How can we get there quickly with the Gypsy Moth?" Krishnan thought for a moment.

"First I need to speak with my brothers. Can I speak with you again later today? May I come to your hotel?" They both nodded. Krishnan got up, shook hands and quickly left, leaving them to pay the street vendor for all their breakfasts. Ceci said, "Is it a good idea to involve him? We don't know much about him, Harry."

"No we don't ... but I think he can be trusted, up to a point. Anyway, we don't have too many other choices, do we? I have a feeling that, from the deductions we have made, plus Krishnan's comments, information from the Met man at the airfield and so on, Cornucopia could be on, or the other side of, the Nicobar Islands, perhaps even still afloat."

They walked back to the hotel after Ceci had extended her limited travel wardrobe from one of the small shop-houses lining the streets of George Town. She looked quite fetching in the long, colourful batik print cotton saris she had bought. Penrose thought that they made her look very feminine, and were a welcome a foil to the rather masculine flying garb she had been wearing over the past few days. The brightly printed, and in some cases almost sheer, cotton clothes prompted a private fashion show when they got back to their hotel room. Harold became bored with the proceedings and pulled the tempting Ceci onto the bed, where with just a little encouragement he ravished her; at least that's how she subsequently described the following forty minutes, with a wicked smile.

❖ ❖ ❖

Ng met Hyami at ten o'clock that evening. He was surprised to be told that, apart from the RAF and themselves, there had been a third aircraft looking for Cornucopia.

"My agent at George Town has telegraphed me with some information he overheard between two Europeans and an Indian or Malay man. It seems they have an interest in your lost Empress machine. The European's name is Penrose and he appears to be with his wife or possibly his mistress. They are staying at a small hotel in George Town. My agent says they met the Indian or Malay man twice, once last night, when he was able to overhear most of what they were saying, and he also saw them together again this morning." Ng looked at Hyami with a worried frown.

"Do you know this man Penrose? What aircraft does he have?" Hyami had reverted to type, barking out his questions in his high-pitched tone.

"This is fresh news to me, Colonel. What did your agent say they had been discussing?"

"It seems that they have a view not dissimilar to the one I have formed myself concerning the location of the Empress aircraft. It could well have been off-course owing to thunderstorm electrical activity affecting the compasses. I have managed to discuss this technical matter briefly with our Dutch pilots and they say that it can happen. It is a possibility that the aeroplane is either on or somewhere to the west of, the Nicobar and Andaman islands. In fact, well over four hundred miles off course!" Hyami sat back in his chair and looked at Ng, waiting for his reaction. After a minute or so he went on.

"If you know something of this it would be wise to tell me now. I should perhaps mention that I have arranged to take into safe custody the money we left with your mother. It would be unfortunate if it was mislaid while we are away." Hyami was smiling but there was no humour in it.

"While we are away?" responded Ng, with a trace of worry. "You mean we are going to the Nicobar Islands to look for the aircraft?" Hyami rose from his chair and moved towards the stout door.

"Yes, indeed, in two days. In the meantime I have decided that you will be our guest here at the Trade Office; make yourself comfortable but please, do not make any attempt to leave the building. That would be most unfortunate. Sleep well, Ng san, I will have some supper brought to you shortly." The door closed and the turning click of the key in the huge, crude iron lock signified capture to the depressed and angry Ng.

❖ ❖ ❖

Penrose spent some time trying to calculate how much bullion there might be aboard Cornucopia.

"If they can carry sixteen passengers, and they were only carrying four and a child, that means that possibly the equivalent weight of, say, ten passengers, and their baggage, may have been made up in gold."

"Goodness! If each passenger with their portmanteau weighed, lets see, about fifteen stone, then that's about 150 stones or ..." Ceci grabbed a piece of paper from Penrose and multiplied 150 by fourteen pounds. "That's 2,100 pounds of gold! Or, even more unbelievable," she was excitedly scribbling numbers on her piece of paper, "33,600 ounces!" she said, casting the piece of paper on which her rough calculations had been scribbled across the bed towards Penrose.

"My God, Ceci, I can't believe that they would ship so much of the precious stuff in one aircraft, it's far too risky. We must have made a mistake in our assumptions."

"How much is 2,100 pounds of gold worth, Harry?"

"I don't know, darling. We need to contact a bank or dealer to see what today's rate is per ounce, but I seem to remember it being around thirty-four dollars an ounce when I was with Swire's." She took her paper again and rapidly carried out the multiplication.

"Goodness, Harold!" she exclaimed, "It's well over a million dollars."

He looked at her and swallowed.

"But we're assuming that she is carrying the equivalent of ten passengers and baggage. It may be far less."

Their simple but logically derived calculations were considerably underestimated, but they were not in a position to know. Cornucopia's load sheet, now besmudged and floating gently in the Bay of Bengal, had clearly indicated to its captain and the Empress loading agent alone that she was overloaded, carrying 5,400 pounds of gold in total, valued at just under three million dollars. Such a sum was indeed a fortune in 1938 as both Kelly and the agent would know. It was also a final desperate shipment from the Empire and Colonies, and inexplicably broke all the rules about risking very large shipments to loss. In addition the four-engine machine was carrying a near-full fuel load, its five passengers, their baggage and an unusually large quantity of mail, plus crew. It was unprecedented and dangerous, but considered by the authorities very necessary.

Suddenly there was a quiet knock on their door. Penrose opened it a crack to see Krishnan standing outside.

"Come in," he beckoned, pulling the door fully open. Krishnan raised his fingers to his lips, half-turning to look behind him down the short corridor of the hotel's first floor. He then stepped quickly inside, and gently closed the door.

"You might have given me some warning, Harold." Ceci was standing with only a towel wrapped around her. It was not a very large towel.

"Please forgive me," Krishnan said, embarrassed, and began to back away towards the door and out of the room.

"Don't apologise, please. Harold sometimes forgets his manners and the situation," she smiled, enjoying the way the poor man was torn between wanting to look and turning away to protect her modesty, out of simple good manners.

Ceci moved into the bathroom and dressed. Krishnan explained to Penrose that he had had feelings of being followed to the hotel from his temporary lodging on the outskirts of George Town, near the island ferry point.

"I have a number of enemies here in Penang – people whom my brothers and I have somehow upset with our trading. It may be my imagination, but we should be careful where we speak."

They finally decided to stay in the hotel room to discuss matters concerning Cornucopia. Krishnan explained that his brothers intended to take their father to Camorta in their boat the following day. He was concerned about Ceci's aeroplane: it was too large, he didn't see how they could take it, the wings would not fit across even the wide beam of their boat. Ceci, listening from the small bathroom, surprised them both by saying that the wings on a Gypsy Moth were designed to be folded so that the overall width of the aircraft was only about eleven feet.

"But we don't have tools to undertake all this engineering, Ceci," Harold remarked, sighing.

"We don't need anything, Harold. It's just a question of pulling out four large pins and folding the four wings back, parallel to the fuselage – it takes only a few minutes. I've done it often enough when there's been too little space in the hangar." Harold was both amazed and shocked.

"You mean I have been flying in a machine where the wings could fold at any moment!?"

"You silly boy," she laughed, fondly. Krishnan was intrigued that this woman should speak to her man so disrespectfully – they are a strange race, these Europeans, he considered.

They established a plan whereby Ceci would fly her aeroplane back up the coast the following morning, to the place where they had landed on the beach after their engine failure, and would then meet Krishnan. Krishnan's brothers would fuel and provision their boat, including some drums of petrol for the aircraft, and bring it into the shore so that, with the aid of some planks lashed together, the Gypsy Moth, with wings folded, could be wheeled safely on board.

Krishnan's father would then be brought aboard and they would set out for the Nicobar Islands. Krishnan said that, depending on the wind and weather, it would take about two to three days, perhaps less if the wind was favourable, and they could set the sail as well as use the engine. On a previous voyage they had managed to maintain eight or nine knots for hours on end with the wind behind them and the engine running.

The next morning, Ceci left Butterworth and managed to land the Gypsy Moth safely onto the wet sand, where the receding tide had left more room on 'their' beach, without mishap. Krishnan's brothers carefully brought their vessel as close to the shore as possible; then with numerous planks, and most of the local village population, they safely deposited the aeroplane, undamaged, with wings folded, onto the deck of the heavily constructed wooden vessel. It didn't leave a great deal of room for anything else; the huge, loose-footed sail would have to be carefully adjusted to clear the aircraft if it was to be used. Penrose inspected the large pins that secured the wings for flight.

"I will make a point of inspecting this aircraft more closely before we fly again," he said.

You are a fuss." Ceci grinned.

The same agent who had reported their conversations to Hyami observed their morning's exertions. He paid the local driver well to drive as fast as possible back along the ten miles, south to Penang, and the telegraph office.

❖ ❖ ❖

Cyril Porter was distinctly fed up. Why did London constantly demand more information? Had he not telegraphed all the information he had available? What was he supposed to do – make it up? The search had found nothing; did they now expect him to row around the ocean himself? Lee suggested, after his reading of the Met report for the day Cornucopia was lost, that they should ask the RAF to carry out another search further to the west, perhaps even as far as, or beyond, the Nicobar and Andaman islands. Porter considered the idea; Cornucopia had been lost for almost a week with no news. Was there really any point in pursuing yet another search? It would be one way of keeping London off his back for a few days – the odds at this late hour were against anything being found, but perhaps he should initiate some new action, if only to demonstrate that he was doing something.

The RAF wing commander listened to Porter's thoughts, and was especially interested to hear the Met man's theories, which, he agreed, may have some merit. He requested a copy of the hourly meteorological report for the fateful day, but said he wanted to discuss the viability of such an operation, in light of all of their other commitments, with Harvey Wills when he returned from a short detachment up-country. The wing commander said he would be in touch, possibly late the following day. Porter put the receiver down and quickly wrote out a telegram to Sir Claude Vickers, Chairman of the Empress board, outlining his intentions concerning a further search for the flying boat up to four hundred miles west of her last reported position.

"Perhaps they will leave us alone for a day or so after that," he remarked to the young deputy manager, as he handed him the completed form to take to the local telegraph office.

❖ ❖ ❖

With everything secure, Krishnan's elderly father was brought from the village on a litter to the beach and carried through the small breakers to the boat. A bed of sorts was made up in the rudimentary shelter that doubled as a steering cabin and he was able to watch proceedings with ease from his slightly elevated vantage point. Both Ceci and Harold took a liking to the frail man with his penetrating eyes who, while now weak in body, had clearly not lost his powers of perception.

Finally the vessel was ready for sea and they set off heading west. The wind was onshore, the result of the normal sea breeze that developed as the land warmed under the sun's rays during the morning. The humid air coming in from the sea took the place of warmer air rising above the jungle, eventually setting up a choppy sea that caused the small ship to pitch sharply through the short waves, covering all those forward of the single mast with a welcome, cooling spray. The engine pounded regularly deep in the bowels of the hold; its vibrating energy could be felt throughout the boat's solid wooden hull and deck. There was a holiday atmosphere aboard and the crew laughed and joked as they went about their duties. Krishnan and his father smiled together, the old man glad to be at sea again after so long. Ceci and Penrose sat on a mat by the folded wings of the aircraft enjoying the movement, and the sparkling, gin-clear water.

❖ ❖ ❖

Hyami received the agent's telegraphed report about four hours after Krishnan and his brothers had left the beach. It was additional evidence that confirmed his own theories: that Cornucopia was indeed some considerable way off course, and far from its own reported position. It also told him who the mysterious crew were and the type of aircraft they were flying. He telephoned the Dutch charter company at Tengah airfield to say that he wanted to leave as early as possible for Port Blair. Unfortunately, so the elderly Australian secretary said, the aircraft was away until the following evening. Hyami fumed with frustration. He spoke at length with Tokyo that evening, bringing his superior at the War Ministry up to date with his plans and proposals and getting approval for further efforts.

That evening the wing commander phoned Porter at his home. Cyril Porter was lying sweating on a couch on the veranda of his rented house, unable to sleep because of another attack of prickly heat – the overhead fan barely stirred the sticky air. Answering the phone he recognised the clipped tones of the RAF station commander.

"I've spoken with Squadron Leader Wills. He says that it may possibly be worth taking a look towards the west, possibly as far as the Nicobar Islands and Port Blair in the Andamans. He will leave early morning the day after tomorrow, using the navy's old Walrus again. He can't leave any earlier as she has to have some scheduled work done on the engine." Porter thanked him and prepared another short telegram for London – just to keep them sweet.

SEVEN

The Dutch crew, it had been agreed, were to be paid a bounty for an unusual night flight to Port Blair, in the Andaman Islands. As well as the Dutch flight crew, their passenger complement again included Hyami, his two Japanese trade officials and Ng, who was watched constantly on their way from the house to Tengah airfield.

He was quickly and carefully boarded onto the aircraft by one of Hyami's trade officials, who sat with him while the two Dutch pilots did their external aircraft checks and the necessary paperwork was completed. The Dutchmen had no idea that Ng was in essence a prisoner. Hyami now reckoned that, although Ng no longer possessed any advantageous information about the location of Cornucopia, he was very aware of Japanese involvement in the search. The Singaporean could present him with unwelcome complications if left to himself in Singapore. Ng watched the two pilots board and walk up the narrow aisle to the cockpit. Hyami left his seat to talk to them briefly, then returned to his position seated just behind the two pilots. As he turned to speak to one of his Japanese associates, Ng noticed the dull blue-metallic gleam of a heavy pistol tucked into a neat holster, half-concealed beneath his military-style bush jacket. Clearly Hyami had a motive for carrying such a weapon, and Ng's imagination easily managed to conjure up a few possible scenarios.

Ng suddenly felt it important that he leave the aircraft before it took off. He too recognised that his value to Hyami had diminished to almost zero: the game being played now was a new one that took little account of his need to participate. With the engines running, the crew started to taxi towards the far end of the darkened grass airstrip with the aid of the aircraft's landing lights and illumination from headlights of two cars pointing in the direction of take-off. Hyami and the other members of his party were perhaps a little too relaxed about security once the aircraft door had been closed and they were moving.

Surreptitiously Ng undid the clasp of his rudimentary seat belt and positioned himself so that he could see the door-opening mechanism. The poor light in the partially darkened cabin did not help but at least it also made it difficult for the Japanese to see what he was up to. He turned slightly so that his legs were now partly in the aircraft aisle, his right hand on the nose of the armrest ready to pull himself up quickly in his bid to reach the aircraft door before his guards could restrain him. He intended to jump from the aircraft and run into the darkness beyond the aircraft lights – and keep running.

He felt the DC-2 slow and start to turn. The aircraft brakes were applied and the aircraft bobbed slightly as it came to a halt. For a minute nothing happened, then the right engine was opened up, ready for power and magneto checks.

He was up and running, at the door in less than two seconds, his hand on the chrome handle, turning. The handle had a catch to prevent its inadvertent opening in flight. The opening mechanism was not immediately obvious to the near-frantic Ng. He fumbled for a moment – pulling and pushing anything and everything. Suddenly, the door moved outwards. By pure chance he had struck on the opening sequence and made ready to leap down onto the grass.

The crack came a split second after the bullet had entered the left side of Ng's neck. The blow threw him sideways around the frame of the door, pushing it open into the bellowing wind from the starboard engine running at full power. Ng was blown to the rear. His hand moved instinctively up to clutch at his torn throat and he struck the tailplane, falling to the ground, his lifeblood pulsing from the wound into the warm, grass-covered soil.

Hyami heard the pistol shot. Looking round, he could see the taller of the two trade officials preparing to fire again. But Ng had already disappeared through the door, which was now closing under the fierce pressure from the revving engine. Henrik van der Valk, the Dutch captain, heard a shrill noise as the starboard engine was running at full power. He waited a few seconds, studying the assorted engine gauges in front of him. Nothing wrong there, he noted, pulling the right-hand throttle lever back to slow running.

Looking briefly across at his co-pilot, he sensed something going on. When he turned around fully he was shocked to see one of his Japanese charterers on his feet at the door with pistol in hand appearing to fire indiscriminately out of the opening into the darkness. The Singaporean, he quickly noticed, was now missing. Hyami, face contorted in anger, was facing the pilot and pulling a pistol from under his jacket. He thrust the barrel of the weapon painfully into the nape of van der Valk's neck, pushing his head harshly forwards.

"Take off, take off!" he screamed. Van der Valk, face half-buried in the instrument panel, tried to turn with hands half-raised.

"We shall go nowhere with your gun pushed into my captain's neck." The young co-pilot looked Hyami straight in the eye, his stance aggressive, defiance pouring from his glare in the glow of the instrument lights.

It was a heroic but wasted performance. Hyami was used to futile gestures and had no truck with them, as many deceased Chinese citizens could vouch. He fired just once. From less than three feet the effect was both accurate and final. The young pilot jerked upwards, then fell lifeless across the central throttle pedestal, blood dripping onto the controls and down into their mechanisms. The other Japanese trade official pulled the scarcely dead airman from the cockpit, down the cabin aisle, and tossed the him out of the door. Van der Valk was directed in turn by Hyami, still holding his gun, into the passenger cabin and made to sit in one of the vacant seats.

The two trade officials then took their places in the cockpit, spent a few minutes familiarising themselves with key controls, then opened up both engines as they lined up with the still-lit airstrip. Within a few seconds they were airborne. From the small control building nothing of these events had been seen or heard in the dark shadows beyond the cars' and aircraft's lights. The next morning two bodies were found lying only a few feet apart at the end of the airstrip. It became obvious that Ng had lived for a while after being shot but without immediate first-aid he died from blood loss; the brave but foolish young pilot had been shot clean through the heart. The local Empress Airways agent called the government district officer and the police, who, after spending some time at the scene, finally concluded that the deaths had something to do with the departure of the DC-2 late the previous evening. The Empress agent thought it obvious. A telegraph alert was issued to all district officers giving the registration numbers of all aircraft that had left the airfield that evening – there had been only two. They also gave the names of the pilots, including the Dutch captain. The names of other passengers on board were not known.

❖ ❖ ❖

The small boat ploughed a westward course towards the Nicobar chain of islands. The regularly pounding single-cylinder engine, assisted by a now-brisk, south-easterly breeze, meant that they were managing to make nearly ten knots at times, surfing off some larger waves. The rolling motion was quite violent and Harold Penrose hung exhausted, head down over the vessel's side, 'communicating with the fishes', wishing he could just step back onto dry land for even a few minutes. Ceci had no such problems and spent time with Krishnan's father in the small cabin learning something about life on the paradise islands, as the Nicobar and Andaman islands were sometimes known. During their first night at sea, in the early hours, they briefly saw faint coloured navigation lights in the sky and heard an aircraft to the north of them, its course diverging slightly from their own. It was very unusual to see an aircraft in this part of the world flying at night. Ceci mentioned the fact to Penrose during one of his brief periods of remission from being ill. She said the noise was similar to the beat of a twin-engine aircraft, possibly two Wright Cyclone engines. It could be the DC-2 they had both seen at Penang as part of the search team a week ago, she suggested. It was, she knew, the only aircraft of its type in the region. Penrose was too taken up with the constant motion of the vessel to take much heed of Ceci's deduction.

On the evening of the second day they saw, silhouetted black against the sunset, the distant image of land. By early morning some detail of the Nicobar Islands could be made out but they were still some way offshore. The wind that had assisted their passage westward so far had slowly veered to the west overnight. The motion of the vessel changed. It was now plugging into a short, steep sea, the wind catching sheets of spray and casting them to leeward as they crashed westwards. The crew became concerned for the Gypsy Moth as its windage, even in its folded form, threatened to destabilise the rolling craft. They furled the huge sail, unable to set it as they were now heading directly into wind, and the engine took the strain of progressing the small ship, its crew and unique cargo towards Camorta.

Harold's condition changed for the better with the alteration of motion and he held Ceci to him as he leaned, pallid under his tan, against the crude cabin structure. They watched the detail of Great Nicobar Island unfold, fascinated. As they drew closer the waves calmed in the lee of the land, and their progress improved. By early evening they were moving smoothly along the sheltered coast under engine power, all hands looking forward to seeing friends and family again. Harold wondered what they would find once ashore. Had this all been a big mistake? 'No,' he decided, 'I have Ceci back.' They had taken advantage of the voyage time to discuss the Cornucopia situation, and agreed with Krishnan and his brothers that they would be landed with the aircraft onto an island other than Camorta. The island they spoke of had broader beaches and would prove more viable than those on their home island, which was only a short sailing distance away. Such a move would also help to ensure that their activities were less likely to be seen by the other citizens of Camorta.

❖ ❖ ❖

The Walrus was wheeled out from the hangar, down the slipway and gently launched into the water. She had had care and attention from the naval fitters and riggers and was now ready for any task presented to her and her mixed-service crew. Squadron Leader Harvey Wills was becoming increasingly concerned for his fiancée: she had now been gone for well over ten days. Her parents had been in touch and he had visited them at home the previous evening. Between them they had managed to telephone all the friends she might possibly visited in her aeroplane. The report by the aero-club night-watchman that she had left with an unknown man early in the morning cast an increasingly mysterious shadow over her apparent disappearance. Harold Penrose's name arose as a possible suspect but was discounted, despite Wills reporting seeing him in Penang and at the airfield.

After long discussion and many difficult-to-connect telephone calls, her parents had begun to suspect something terrible had happened to Cecilia and her Gypsy Moth. Could she have had trouble with the aeroplane and have been forced down into the jungle, or worse, the sea? As the evening proceeded the mood became increasingly glum. Wills said he would get messages to all government district officers in the south of the Malay peninsula asking for information about the aircraft and crew, and whether they had refuelled at any local airstrips. Cecilia's original message had been sent from Kuala Lumpur well over a week ago, and they also knew that her intended destination from KL that day had been Penang. They also knew that the aircraft had arrived at Penang a day later than expected and had left for an undisclosed destination almost four days ago. Cecilia's reputation for undertaking seemingly hair-brained ideas on the spur of the moment was well known, but she had one saving grace. She had always contacted her parents regularly to keep them abreast of her latest adventure. But information from airfield authorities was not the same as direct communication from Cecilia herself. The question was, who was the man she had flown away with that morning? Wills remarked again that he had met Harold Penrose at Penang during the course of his search.

Brigadier Grosvenor-Ffoulkes's ears pricked up this time.

"You say you met this Penrose fella at Penang while you were there?" Wills nodded. "Don't you think it a little more than coincidence that this wretched man should be there at exactly the time that Cecilia was supposed to be there?" Wills knew what the brigadier was thinking and cast his mind back to his meetings with Penrose.

"He said he was visiting friends before returning to England, and I got the impression that he would be there only a few days. I saw no sign of Ceci while I was there."

"That bloody man has inveigled his way into my daughter's affections again, I'm damn sure of it. That girl has disobeyed me for the last time and I will not have it!" The brigadier's blood was up, and he was a man who would not countenance disobedience at any time, from anyone. His nose was bright red.

"Richard, we can't be sure that you're right. There may well be a more straightforward explanation." Ceci's mother spoke calmly. Wills was affronted at the suggestion that his intended had left with another man, and that man in particular.

❖ ❖ ❖

The DC-2 landed at Port Blair. No one was expecting it and the aircraft touched down guided by only its landing lights. Finding the landing field in darkness was a considerable achievement in itself for the Japanese crew. The aircraft taxied to what appeared to be an unlit administrative building and a small wooden hangar, and was met by a night-watchman with a feeble lamp. The poor man was half-asleep as Hyami jumped from the cabin and started issuing him with orders. There was no telephone service at the airfield and no transport could be summoned so late at night to take them into Port Blair. The crew made themselves as comfortable as they could in the aircraft, Captain van der Valk tied with his hands behind him to the frame of an aircraft seat. The position positively discouraged sleep and recent events ensured that his mind spent much of the remainder of the night considering his position.

The seat frames on the DC-2 were early models formed from steel tube and metal plate with a cover and cushions pulled over. The edge of the seat below the thin cushion was made of pressed metal and fortunately the quality of this detail was not of the best. Van der Valk soon noticed that as he tried to relax into his seat, his bound wrists came into contact with the sharp metal edges at the back of the seat frame. He was able to move his position slowly so that he could carefully rub his bindings an inch or two along the seat's rough cutting edge. He had absolutely no idea how thick the rope was, but he had little else to do over the next three or four hours and worked at moving his wrists along the blade-like surface, cutting himself frequently in the process. His hands soon became sticky with blood, his efforts often interrupted by movement elsewhere in the cabin. One of the Japanese pilots fidgeted almost constantly and Hyami on more than one occasion shouted at him to stop it. Their colleague snored with increasing volume until he awoke, shifted and settled to start the process again.

Finally, van der Valk felt the rope suddenly slacken. He carefully pulled one hand free and around to his front, flexing his hand to get the blood circulating again. Nobody had seen or guessed what he had been up to. Between him and the aircraft door to the rear slept Hyami and one of the pilots, the latter with his feet stretched out across the narrow aisle. How could he get away without being hit by a well-aimed gunshot? Having witnessed the deaths of two innocent men within the last few hours, he had no doubt that his own survival figured well down the list of priorities for Hyami, his one-time charter client.

In fact, all things considered, he could not fathom any reason why they should keep him alive, but he still had his own search agenda to complete. The row of seats he was sitting in was adjacent to a side hatch that led out onto the port wing. It was there for engineers to gain access to the top of the engine and other external areas of the aircraft. The hatch could also be used as an escape point in the event of a forced landing, being quickly operated by a red-painted handle at its forward edge.

He rehearsed his proposed escape carefully in his mind: 'Edge slowly towards the hatch to my left, raise my right hand until it's on the lever, pull the lever towards me while with my left hand pushing the hatch outwards with all my strength. Then, dive through the hole, over the leading edge of the wing.' This last point he considered important for two reasons: one, they would likely expect him to go for the rear, trailing, edge because it was nearer the ground, and two, because it would give him a clear run away from the hangar towards the darkness of the airstrip and thick surrounding vegetation.

Mental rehearsals over, he began to move his body and reach with his left hand gingerly towards the hatch. The younger of the two Japanese pilots started snoring again. Anticipating a reaction from Hyami behind him, he waited, and sure enough, a few moments later Hyami was on his feet berating and slapping the sleeping crewman. Twenty minutes went by and all seemed quiet in the cabin again, although he was fearful of turning around fully to ascertain whether Hyami and the other crewman were asleep.

Again, he made his first moves. Incredibly, nobody said or did anything except sleep. With a firm grasp on the lever, adrenaline coursing, he jerked it up with energy born of flight. It moved with a loud crash. He pushed with all his strength against the window. Stuck momentarily, the hatch then shot out of the hole and he with it onto the wing. His captors were wide awake. In the chaos, guttural expletives were spat out and boots scraped hastily on the metal aircraft floor. The first shot smashed into the framework of the hatch. The second took the heel off his left shoe.

Outside on the wing, he tried to maintain the momentum of flight over its leading edge, tearing his shirt, and with it some of the skin from his left side, on protruding parts of the engine cowling. He had a brief moment to notice that the cowlings were still warm from their recent flight. The next couple of bullets ricocheted off the top of the cowling and the wing's stressed skin, back into the fuselage side. They shot across the space under the cabin floor, passing between pipes and cables. One exited, fully spent, on the starboard side. The remaining dying bullet spun through the space and just clipped a fuel pipe, without severing it.

As he fell, head-first, from the wing's leading edge, his hands hit the ground first, followed by his right shoulder. He felt and heard a sharp crack from his left forearm as it broke under the impact of his weight and speed of descent. Adrenalin had carried him this far, and it was only when he stood up and ran beneath the nose of the DC-2 and out from under its shelter on the starboard side, along the line of the wing, that the pain flooded in. Frantically, he staggered out and was quickly enveloped by the beckoning darkness.

Hyami had been first out onto the port wing, in time to see van der Valk run under the aircraft's nose toward the starboard side. A few more shots were expressed to no effect; he had got away. The local night-watchman came from his rough bed in a crude lean-to against the hangar wall. He was now shouting at the three men standing on the aircraft wing. Not understanding his utterances they knew enough to realise that the old, sun-wizened man had seen enough to implicate them in attempted murder.

Hyami passed rapidly back through the hatch into the aircraft, jumping from the main door down onto the grass. He walked purposefully towards the old man in the broken shadows. The man continued to shout as he approached, asking for an explanation in his own language, his hands gesturing. Hyami brought his right hand, gripping the heavy pistol, around from behind his back.

The watchman saw the move, and even in the shadows he suddenly realised the extreme danger he was in. Turning, he tried to run towards the hangar, looking for shelter in its dark, looming mass. Hyami fired once. The round hit the man in the right shoulder. It exited his chest, dragging tissue and bone in its wake, blood jetting ahead as he staggered. The bullet's powerful impact propelled him briefly faster into the shadows, where he finally collapsed against the corrugated hangar wall with his head resting in the coarse dry vegetation growing there. His breathing was laboured, interspersed with harsh and fitful coughing. Straining around, he looked up, eyes wide in horror. Hyami strode closer, until he stood over his quarry. He fired twice at the helpless man as he lay looking up into the muzzle of the weapon. The report echoed against the hangar wall, rebounding loudly out into the night.

❖ ❖ ❖

The boat carrying Ceci's Gypsy Moth, still securely lashed in place, surged in the breaking surf making it difficult for the crew to control its irregular rolling motion. It was early morning; the sun rising in the east brushed a faint, peach-toned light onto some high cirrus clouds. The receding tide had left the beach ridged and damp; the crew struggled to moor the vessel securely so that they could offload the aeroplane. In this remote spot there were no wooden planks to ease its passage, except for the two stout teak logs flattened on one side that they had brought with them. With care they pushed and pulled the delicate machine to the starboard bow, where they had lashed the two precious logs.

Managing, eventually, to put the aircraft's two main wheels on the log's flat sides, they slowly let her roll down the makeshift ramp until the wheels were resting on the submerged beach. With the tail held high they gently pulled the aircraft backwards, up and onto the beach's dry surface. Ceci was concerned at the effect the salt water would have on the aircraft's fabric-and-wood construction, not least the wheels and their bearings. Krishnan brought a little fresh water from the boat and they attempted to wash down the affected areas, removing as much of the damaging salt water as possible.

The sun was now well up as they prepared breakfast. Harold surveyed the scene. Krishnan and his father had chosen the disembarkation point well, he mused. The beach was deserted, well away from any habitation, sloping only gently down to the sea. It was quite broad with the tide out. There were also some breaks in the bordering trees with their rich dark foliage, under which the aircraft could be manoeuvred to protect it from the sun and possible prying airborne eyes. However, they only had enough fuel in cans for the Gypsy Moth for about six hours' flying. Krishnan said he would try to bring some additional petrol when he returned the next day. In the meantime, Ceci decided it might be an idea to try a flight off the beach without Harold on board, to practise a few landings before the sand fully dried out, and to familiarise herself with the local landmarks.

After breakfast, taken on board the boat, the crew got ready to leave for their island and village. Harold carried Ceci through the shallow water and they waved Krishnan, his father and the happy crew a thankful goodbye. They'd helped to pull the aircraft to the downwind end of the beach. Ceci and Harold turned her around and carefully prepared her for flight. Penrose was not keen on Ceci flying without him, but understood the need to keep the aircraft as light as possible for these initial practice take-offs and landings in their new location. With the engine primed, he pulled the propeller over six times, as he had been shown, and when everything was ready they flipped up the two pairs of magneto switches. The engine was loath to fire, and it took some time in the sun's warming rays, but eventually it was busily ticking over.

Ceci opened up the throttle as she tested the surface of the beach, seeing how the aeroplane would react in the now-fast-drying sand. Not an ideal surface she was too aware, but her successful attempts in Malaya had given her an expectation of conditions. Taxiing as near to the surf as possible to gain benefit from firmer wet sand, she opened up the engine to 2,200 revolutions, glancing finally at the oil pressure, now at fifty pounds per square inch. After an initial lurch the aircraft gained speed, the tail, responding to Ceci's gentle touch forwards on the stick, was soon up, and the small blue-and-silver biplane left the beach, clearing the one-hundred-foot trees at the far end of the beach by a good thirty feet.

Banking slightly right, she allowed the aircraft to continue climbing, parallel to the land until, at fifteen hundred feet, she throttled back and flew level while she surveyed the local area and seascape. Just offshore she could see Krishnan's boat moving quickly through the clear, turquoise water. Now and again the sea would sparkle where the breeze caught a small wave, causing it to break. She dived, flying low over the boat, and the crew waved excitedly in response to her wing-waggling. Then, climbing again, she spent a few more minutes taking in the local landmarks for future reference before turning back towards their new beach airfield.

Her landing was not of the best. The aircraft took control from her as she lowered its tail onto the beach. It slewed around to the right in a ground-loop, heading for the sea. Penrose watched in horror. The tail began to rise again as the aircraft continued swinging violently. He could see in an instant the possibility of the propeller striking the sand, shattering into dozens of misshapen wooden lumps. Holding the control stick hard back and over to the right, she kicked the rudder full left trying to stop the Moth's careering towards the surf. The steering tail-skid found no grip in the loose sand. The aircraft continued to gyrate, the starboard wings now beginning to lift, threatening to flick the aircraft over her nose and onto its back. Suddenly it was all over. The tip of the port wing struck the ground and the aircraft spun around it to a halt.

Penrose ran to where the aircraft had stopped. There was a cloud of fine sand in the air being blown away by the still-turning engine. He pulled the magneto switches to 'off' and climbed onto the wing of the aircraft. Ceci had a small trickle of blood running down her forehead from a cut just below the hairline where she had hit it on the cockpit coaming. She looked shocked. Penrose undid her straps and helped her down.

"That's how not to do it!" She was angry with herself and frowning darkly as she walked shakily over to the damaged wingtip. The fabric was torn and there were some broken pieces in the delicate wooden structure that lay within, but at least it was clear that the propeller had not actually hit the ground.

"It doesn't look too bad," said Penrose confidently, prodding the silver-doped fabric on the wingtip. But inside, a closer look showed that a number of the wooden ribs were either broken or cracked at the wing's leading edge. Ceci swore; her rarely used family-bred army vocabulary was useful at times like this. The damage was beyond their resources to repair and they would have to wait until Krishnan returned to see if he or his family connections could help. Penrose took the small first-aid kit from the aircraft's rear luggage locker and set about cleaning up Ceci's cut head. She sat quietly, on the verge of tears, furious with herself as he tended her wound with uncharacteristic tenderness. Alone, he struggled to pull the aeroplane through the cloying sand into the shade at the verges of the beach. They both lay under the wings listening to the waves breaking regularly and gently on the shore. Ceci slept while Penrose watched her.

EIGHT

Sarah Gregson had taken the opportunity to bathe herself and Beth, and to dress in something less formal for their imposed cruise aboard the Cornucopia. Her generosity in making dressings for Captain Kelly from her limited wardrobe meant that her skirts were now well above the knee-line and might perhaps be more appropriate for a dance hall specialising in the Charleston. She was an accomplished exponent of the dance, which had caused a little upset at recent social events in India. Her legs were long and lithe, and their increasing exposure gave the men on board a welcome distraction from their plight. Kelly, now recovering to some degree, realised that he must be over the worst when his interest in her ministrations started to focus more on her superb, tanned limbs than on his appalling injury. Sarah was aware of the effect she was having. She enjoyed it.

David Rawlinson scanned the horizon regularly. Sometimes they could see the shadowy outline of land in the far distance: at other times there was nothing but seemingly endless ocean. He suspected that they were just drifting to and fro in the ocean currents, sometimes nearer to the land, sometimes out of sight. The weather had been kind so far and they had benefited from some order to their enforced journey over recent days. Snell had managed to rustle up two very basic meals a day from their fast-depleting rations. The word 'meal', as he said, was possibly an over-generous description of dried coconut, grilled fish cooked rapidly over a petrol fire in the upturned engine cowling, and the last remaining cans of fruit. They had managed to catch a little fresh water in the suspended tarpaulin on the few occasions that it had rained, usually at night. The storytelling had expanded from tales suitable for little Beth to more adult literature, usually in the late evenings after she had gone to bed.

Hudson recounted his experiences with Lilly from their early days in Malaya and it seemed to be cathartic for him. Snell recalled his time on passenger ships and had them in stitches with the more intimate goings-on that occurred at all levels of shipboard society. So time passed but it was becoming increasingly boring, with anxiety never far away.

Kelly was carefully brought out of his makeshift sick bay when conditions allowed, gently lifted and secured onto the roof of the aircraft so that he could benefit from a change of scenery, and to allow the air and sun to get to his wound. Sarah insisted that he leave the dressings off on these occasions but gave him a cloth with which to shoo away the few flies foolish enough to be so far out over the ocean, encouraged, perhaps, by fresh blood. As it was, the aircraft was still too far from land to suffer from their attentions too much.

By mid-afternoon the line of clouds out to the west had lowered and turned into a palette of greys with streaks of charcoal passing through them here and there. They became ragged and torn, and the wind began to rise as the cloud cover extended slowly over the aircraft. Worried, Rawlinson ordered everyone below. They tied the tarpaulin tightly over the outside of the exposed front cockpit windows and did their best to prepare for the worst, conscious of Rawlinson's earlier comments about the dangers of encountering another serious storm. He made sure the kapok lifejackets, now dry, were kept close at hand and that they had done everything they could to be ready for the approaching threat.

The seas increased steadily as the late afternoon passed, their colour changing to match the mood of the lowering sky until Cornucopia was again complaining noisily about the new stresses to her sorely tried structure. Water began entering the flight-deck area again as seas were pushed into the aircraft's broken nose, but the tarpaulins covering the cockpit windows from the outside kept most of the water out.

As the evening developed, the motion on board became increasingly violent. Thunder bellowed occasionally from the clouds racing by, and cracks of lightning jagged their frantic way across the sky. One of the huge teak logs became loosened from its position under the wings and for a while posed a serious danger as it drifted close to the aircraft. Kelly, watchful, was propped up on some mailbags at the rear of the flight deck, murmuring his concerns to Rawlinson at the possibility of a lightning strike. They were the only objects above the sea for many miles around and it was a possibility – they had seen lightning strike the sea to the west more than once during the afternoon. The wind was driving them eastwards; on one of his regular lookouts from the open hatch David Rawlinson could see that the hard-pressed flying boat was shedding a turbulent wake in the white breakers as she was propelled downwind by the storm. The night was spectacular from the hatchway, and nerve-racking. Beth cried and clung again to her mother, sitting in the centre-section mail stowage. Snell and the colonel took over the watch and came down for occasional relief drenched in spray and rain from their exposed position atop the fuselage.

At around three-thirty in the morning Cornucopia was eventually struck by lightning, and again two or three minutes later. A bolt of incandescent energy shot through the thin aluminium panels in the aft fuselage, leaving small, blackened holes where it had entered and exited.

The second strike hit the port wing and passed through the near-empty fuel tanks, now almost full of buoyant but ignitable vapour. The top skin of the wing erupted in an orange-and-blue flash, the force thrusting the wing down into the sea; water surged into the petalled void. Deverall, on watch, was momentarily blinded by the flash, and then saw a gaping rent in the wing's surface. Already Cornucopia was listing towards the damaged wing. He slid off the aircraft roof and across onto the wing. Clinging to the uncovered inner engine, he made his way outboard to the hissing and distorted metal. The skin had curled up as if some subterranean monster had burst up from the depths, forcing it to open, like so many blackened petals, around the gaping hole.

Deverall caught hold of the aluminium 'petals' forcing them down in an effort to fill some of the void to prevent more water from entering. He had some success but in the process cut his hands on their lethally sharp edges. Hudson joined him; he had had the presence of mind to bring two blankets, which he and the colonel managed to jam into the cracks between the flattened shards of metal. Every now and then a sea swept powerfully across the surface of the wing, now barely above water. Hudson made his way back to the fuselage and stood in the top-deck hatch waiting for Deverall to follow.

Suddenly, soundlessly, it was on him. The stealthy, menacing, mass of water caught Deverall off guard, lifting him bodily from the wing's surface. It carried him into the ocean ahead of the drifting aircraft. Finally surfacing as the wing passed over him, he saw Cornucopia's tail just a few feet away, the water surging in and out of the now open passenger door. He flailed his bloodied hands, trying to swim across the short, turbulent stretch of water, but was unable to grasp the doorframe as the aircraft swept inexorably past. Inexplicably, it struck Deverall at that moment that this may have been where the shark had got into the flooded passenger decks to take Lilly Hudson's cadaver. Thrashing frantically in the water, he could not reach the tailplane as it was pushed past above his head by the wind and driving waves.

'So, this is it, then, how it will end.' He felt weak, being constantly being drawn under the water then rising clear, to see Cornucopia driving on, further away from him. David Rawlinson had come up through the hatch when he had heard Hudson's warning cry of alarm, following his pointing arm to the barely visible head of Deverall as they passed him in the rush of waves.

He slid down the slippery fuselage and, as his grip failed on its wet surface, dived over the side landing a few feet ahead of the failing colonel. David Rawlinson's other interest apart from flying, rowing, beautiful women and a good party, was swimming. He had swum for his school and college, and always took advantage of any swimming opportunity that arose, particularly if it involved the opposite sex. This was one opportunity, however, that he might have foregone, given a choice, but the spur-of-the-moment decision didn't allow that luxury.

He grabbed, just once, and caught Deverall, placing him in the classic drowning-swimmer position and kicking furiously with his legs and swimming with his free arm, pulling the spluttering man with him. His efforts were magnificent but quite outclassed by the strength of the seas. Cornucopia was racing further away from them.

Snell stood transfixed – what now? Almost automatically, he

grabbed two of the lifejackets from beside the hatch and tried to throw them upwind towards the swimmers. The wind lulled for a moment, and by luck rather than judgement, one of the jackets almost struck Deverall in the face as he surfaced, now weaker, for the umpteenth time, its straps catching around his head. Rawlinson, treading water, tied it around the tiring man and looked back at the aircraft. Caution to the winds; Hudson had somehow reached the tail and snatched the line they had used for hauling up their makeshift sail. Coiling it, he prayed earnestly for help in throwing it accurately to the stricken pair. He threw hopefully, allowing for the wind. It was a once-only shot; the line fell a few feet from Rawlinson, who had to leave Deverall's side to retrieve it. In the heaving water Deverall's head soon disappeared from Rawlinson's view. Hudson waved and signalled the colonel's position from his precarious vantage point atop the tailplane. Rawlinson, now very tired, swam clumsily over to Deverall and tied the line around the poor man's upper body and under his arms, just as the slack in the rope tightened. Hudson took the strain. At each lift of Cornucopia he very gently pulled the slack. Rawlinson helped as he could by swimming but he was now utterly exhausted.

Finally, hauled inelegantly back on board, Deverall was lowered through the top hatch, shivering from shock and exertion. Rawlinson slumped onto the floor next to him, equally spent. It had been a close call; both men had shown what they were made of, and had survived as a result of their courage and Rawlinson's life-saving skills – there had been no panic. Sarah bandaged the nasty cuts to Deverall's hands and gave him two of Snell's now-famous Chinese pills. Snell looked out of the hatch and there were a number of sharks circling the boat. The blood from the colonel's cuts had been a clear invitation to visit, despite the sea state. Rawlinson and the colonel were back aboard not a moment too soon. Snell shivered and put the idea to the back of his mind.

Cornucopia, now listing, continued her accelerating drift downwind in the last few hours before dawn. There was no sunrise, but a grey light, gradually gaining strength, started to filter below to the sodden flight deck. Nobody but Beth had had more than an hour or so of real sleep. Rawlinson climbed the short ladder through the top hatch and peered downwind. No mistaking it, it was land, just a few miles to leeward, and even from this distance he could see the very tops of trees bending in the wind and now and again a fine mist blown skywards from waves breaking heavily on shore. Interestingly, he noted, their likely destination island appeared to be unlike others within his range of view. They were all low-lying; the island they were likely to contact had a central peak with a sort of flat top, like an extinct volcano, covered on its sides and peak with thick jungle.

Kelly was awake and discussed the situation with his second-in-command and surrogate eyes, David Rawlinson. They would be washed ashore within the next couple of hours or so, that was clear to Rawlinson. Cornucopia might disintegrate completely if the seas were steep and breaking onto a shoreline that may be sand or rocks – they had no idea. With a child on board, and a crippled captain, courses of action were limited. They could do nothing to stop the flying boat's drift and had to have at least some contingency plans, depending on what they found at the last minute as they approached the shore. Kelly made it clear that he would stay with the aircraft, come what may.

An hour passed. They were less than a mile from shore. The thunderous surf could be easily seen and heard pounding above the wind's roar. Everyone put on lifejackets and Kelly's injured leg was wrapped securely with a spare kapok lifejacket. Rawlinson stared, increasingly worried, at the approaching shoreline backed by steep hinterland. The boat began to heave more violently in the increasingly steeper waves as they moved into shoaling water. As the waves approached the shallows he noticed that the distance from crest to crest was becoming markedly reduced, and this was more than made up for by their increasing height from trough to crest.

When they were close in and Rawlinson looked back, he could see that many of the approaching waves were near vertical before teetering then plunging, white and furious. Cornucopia shuddered in her stride as her long keel struck the sea-bed, then swept on again, forced forwards by the huge energy hounding her to the shore. They could now see, to their relief, that the shoreline immediately to leeward appeared to be clear of rocky outcrops, and that the waves were breaking heavily onto a sandy shore in a small, near-circular bay. Again, and with increasing frequency, the boat seemed to trip briefly as she hit the sea-bed in the troughs of the steepening swells.

The wind increased as Cornucopia was driven on until, suddenly, she stopped sharply, heeling over, pivoting around her embedded keel, presenting her beam to the breaking seas. The thundering noise of waves smashing onto her hull was frightening; tons of water were crashing against the once-taut aluminium skin. The tortured metal screamed and snapped as each massive sea pounded her with continuous, devastating blows. On board, they exchanged apprehensive looks, with faces whiter than they had been since Cornucopia's final landing. It was clear to everyone that their contingency plan to swim to the shore would be fraught with danger, particularly for little Beth and Captain Kelly.

Every so often a larger wave would lift the boat clear of the sea-bed again, accelerating her violently shoreward, until one massive breaker struck just as she was rolling to recover from the previous pounding. The noise was deafening; the aircraft jerked violently as though being thrown like a bath toy. Water poured in through a wing root into what had been the safe and secure centre mail stowage. The devastating seas had finally amputated the port wing. Kelly fell sideways, landing on his protected stump, roaring unheard with pain, inaudible above the storm's din. Seawater flooded the compartment. Sarah tried pulling her patient clear of the falling water in the chaotic confined space. It proved too much for her. Screaming for help, she held firmly onto her daughter. Beth risked being pulled out of the stowage as each wave sucked noisily back.

Then, a brief interlude: a few seconds of comparative quiet. Hudson stood up, looking out of one of the smashed flight-deck windows. It seemed unbelievable. A truly huge and menacing sea was sweeping silently towards them, dark olive-green, climbing higher into the sky as it approached. The broken wing, with one engine still attached, was caught up by its towering crest.

"Hold on!" was all he had time to shout before it struck.

The wing, skittering down the wave's face, was smashed forcefully against the hull, breaking through the thin skin in several places and causing terrible rents. The engine broke free and sank below the water. Relieved of the weight of her wings and engines, Cornucopia was lifted bodily from the sea-bed and thrown further up the beach, her port side crushed as she landed half in and half out of the hungrily sucking surf. A huge following sea tried to draw her back into the ocean's maw, to play the game again, but it was no match for its truly gigantic predecessor. Cornucopia was firmly beached.

Finally becalmed, the emotionally and physically drained occupants looked about them, wet and frightened. Snell pulled the clinging Kelly from the broken stowage compartment, carrying him like a baby through the knee-deep, dragging surf, up the beach. Kelly was almost unconscious. Sarah Gregson, aided by the colonel, carried her wide-eyed, wet and shivering daughter onto the deserted sandy shore, the sea constantly attacking her legs, trying to pull her back. Hudson cast around, looking at the shattering damage done to the flying boat before he too struck out through the boiling water for the comparative safety of land, just avoiding the two hefty logs that had once helped to support Cornucopia. David Rawlinson checked that no one remained on board and followed his passengers and crew. He had time to note that there were dozens of the wooden bullion boxes scattered around inside the destroyed hull, some broken open with their contents glistening in the half-light. Cornucopia was carrying forty-eight boxes, he now knew. From the security of the beach he looked around at their circumstances. To their backs appeared to be impenetrable jungle, in front the sea angry, voracious and white. The word 'shipwrecked' crossed his mind.

NINE

Krishnan returned by boat mid-morning clutching a sheaf of papers that he had been given by one of his home islanders. The woman had said that they had come from a floating box that one of the island's fishing boats had retrieved from the sea some nights earlier. The papers had apparently blown around when they had opened the box, and the younger people had been dressing up in the western clothes they had found inside. Ceci and Penrose looked at the papers; they were a mix of personal correspondence and business papers. The name Hudson appeared prominently on many of them.

"I wonder," said Ceci, "I wonder if the box they found came from Cornucopia? I seem to remember the name Hudson from the passenger list." They continued to look through the papers, forgetting, for the moment, the problem of repairing the Gypsy Moth.

Then it was virtually confirmed. Penrose found a letter from a woman, an aunt it seemed, in England addressed to 'George and Lil Hudson'. The letter expressed envy at their intention to take a flying boat back to England when they visited in three months. 'What a wonderful experience, I look forward to hearing all about your trip on the Empress flying boat.' The dates tallied.

"It must be luggage from Cornucopia," said Ceci. Penrose nodded in agreement.

Krishnan explained roughly where the boxes – there were two – had been picked up. The location was to the west of the Nicobar chain of islands.

"Were there no other signs of Cornucopia? No wreckage ... nothing at all?" asked Harold, looking again through the papers. The answer was no, but Harold suspected that there may be a link between the rescued boxes and the sighting of a 'huge white shark with flashing eyes' at night by his brother's crew, mentioned by Krishnan earlier.

"I think it would be wise to fly your aeroplane around the islands to see if you are able to see a sign of the big flying boat. You might see pieces, even bodies." Krishnan was as keen as they were to progress matters, although he was still unsure of the reasons for their search – aside from any possible survivors.

"We have a problem on that front," explained Ceci, pointing to the damaged wing. "I fouled up my landing yesterday and managed to catch the wing in the sand when the Gypsy ground-looped." They inspected the wingtip together. Krishnan said that he had a good ship's carpenter in the village that should be able to repair the wooden ribs and stringers with local hardwood, but he didn't see how they could finish the fabric covering.

"Perhaps you have some cotton fabric and some paint?" Ceci thought that sticking or sewing some cotton or linen over the damaged fabric using paint as glue could effect a temporary repair. Krishnan said he would bring what he could find tomorrow, together with his carpenter. In the meantime he unloaded some food, matches, fresh water, and a roll of oil-cloth with which to make a simple shelter. They waved him goodbye as he sailed back to Camorta in a strong breeze, the hull of his fishing boat disappearing completely in the swells, leaving the sail apparently disembodied above the water.

The crew of the Gypsy Moth spent some time building and sorting out their sleeping shelter and arranging the secure storage of their provisions. They then both stripped off and went swimming with après swim as before. There was a difference this time: Ceci was in control.

❖ ❖ ❖

The Dutch pilot had managed to lose himself completely in the green depths of jungle during his desperate night escape from Hyami and his murderous crew. It was early afternoon before he stumbled wearily out of the humid under- and overgrowth, coming across a woman nursing a small child as she sat outside a tiny hut by the sea. Two small fishing boats were drawn up below the huts on the beach. The pain in his arm was becoming intense and he was hoping for some help. The woman seemed petrified and ran inside the hut, pulling a crude sackcloth door across its entrance, screaming unintelligibly. He tried unsuccessfully to calm her from outside. Looking around, he saw no one else around the collection of rude huts and shelters. He walked slowly down the shelving beach to one of the boats drawn up untidily on the shore, and sat on its gunwale to inspect his arm again.

The arm was black and blue in places and needed treatment and support, he knew too well. The pain came in waves and left him feeling nauseous. In the boat was some thin fishing twine; with this and some choice lengths of driftwood he effected a crude splint to support the limb. It took time. Having the use of only one hand, and the extreme pain of any movement or touching of his arm, slowed his efforts. When he had finished he found that the crude splint gave some relief and he slumped down onto the sand, his back against the shaded hull of the boat. His escape and need to keep moving all night meant that he was now in extreme need of sleep. Overhead, the sun shone from a hard, pale sky and the air was stifling despite a desultory breeze. Making himself as comfortable as possible, he tried to sleep, but his painful arm allowed him only fitful dozing.

After a few hours he suddenly jerked awake, somehow conscious that he was being watched. The screaming woman, now quiet, was watching him from the top of the beach dressed in a shapeless bag of pale green, a small, nut-brown and naked boy standing behind her. Holding his arm protectively, he looked up and affected a smile; she slowly returned the expression unconvincingly, then, gingerly came down towards him, the boy's tiny hand in hers. Standing a few feet from him, she stopped and spoke something he was unable to comprehend. Then, gathering all her courage, she came right up to him, kneeling and pointing to his arm, her small, beady black eyes communicating avidly.

He was unable to understand any of her near-constant high-pitched chattering but her concerns for his broken limb was obvious. She gestured to take hold of it and he nodded. Still kneeling, she very gently undid the crude bindings and cradled the damaged arm in hers, looking at it carefully. She spoke sharply to the boy, who ran up the beach to the huts, scampering back seconds later with a square of grubby cotton in bright blue. She quickly made a sling around his neck with the cloth and rested the fractured arm in it. He winced as she manipulated the arm, and the little boy frowned at his gasps. Then, helping him to his feet, she guided him up the beach into her hut, where it was blessedly cool. He sat on the only rickety chair, and she, standing at a small lop-sided table set against one wall of the accommodation, began a long process of mixing various herbs and plants together in a large clay pot, occasionally getting the boy to fetch some missing ingredient from the luxuriant plants and shrubs outside. The wounded pilot watched, less exhausted now, and fascinated despite the relentless pain. Finally, the gooey, pungent mess was spread lavishly onto a piece of whitish muslin and wrapped painlessly around the injured limb. After a few minutes the wound felt warm and for the first time he enjoyed some relief from its constant deep ache.

Outside, she lit a fire in the lee of the hut and began preparing some food: fish with small vegetables and fruits garnered from a patch of sandy garden and from the surrounding jungle. More confident now, she glanced up at him as she worked, nodding and smiling shyly at him from time to time, making the odd comment. The boy, he judged, about four years old, watched him quietly from behind his mother, his large brown eyes sparkling above a perfect set of even white teeth. They played a simple game, the boy hiding behind his mother's brightly coloured apron, peeping out with a big grin, van der Valk feigning surprise.

After the meal, which she gently fed him, the woman took him to another empty hut nearby and gestured that he should lie on the crude wooden-framed bed inside. With difficulty, but gratefully, he did so, and feeling much better, he fell asleep, no doubt aided by the bitter potion she had lastly mixed for him to drink.

❖ ❖ ❖

Hyami instructed his two acolytes to collect the bundle of humanity he had murdered the previous evening and load it into the aircraft. They would dispose of the evidence unceremoniously from the air at some opportune moment. As the small airfield came to life in the early morning they were able to refuel the aircraft and prepare it for flight. The younger of the two Imperial Navy pilots inspected the two holes in the fuselage and then climbed inside, under the cabin floor, to inspect for damage. He found nothing untoward, expressing their luck to Hyami.

Nobody at the airfield commented on their late-evening arrival, or at the apparently missing night-watchman. The crew later made their way, walking, into Port Blair and checked into the only guest-house in the small community. Hyami visited the local telegraph office for messages. There was one from his agent in Penang to the effect that two bodies had been reported found on the airfield. It said that the local police and the district officer were keen to speak with the Dutch captain of the DC-2 and had circulated his details to other airfields in Malaya. It also mentioned the fact that the RAF and navy were intending a second aerial search, to the west of the Nicobar and Andaman Island chains.

The Japanese pilots were woken from an afternoon nap by the sound of an aircraft circling the small town. It was the naval Walrus loaned to the RAF for a second and wider search for the Cornucopia.

❖ ❖ ❖

The carpenter Krishnan brought was a very tall, very thin and wizened man, with only one brown eye peering out from under large, bushy eyebrows. His gnarled, brown fingers gently investigated the damage to the Moth's wingtip, prodding and manipulating the delicate ribs, while he grunted and nodded knowingly. Eventually he stepped back, uttering a few incomprehensible words to Krishnan.

"It will take a few hours, but he says there is no real damage and it will be possible to repair it simply with the bits of timber and tools he has brought," Krishnan smiled at Ceci. They were relieved.

After turning the aircraft around so that the offending wing was under the shade of the fringing trees, the carpenter started work removing broken pieces of rib and frame. He then matched these to the timber he had brought with him in a small sack, which appeared to be some sort of local hardwood. Carefully he manufactured the new rib noses and centre sections. Working fast, he was soon lighting a fire to boil up a concoction to glue the repair together. By mid-afternoon he seemed to have finished. They inspected his work: it was perfect but not yet complete. From his bag he pulled in triumph a small piece of linen and a large needle with some sort of thread. Krishnan grinned at their surprise.

"I told him about the fabric and he has brought a piece of linen with him. It was given by one of his many daughters. I'm sorry it is not silver but we have a little blue paint as well to keep out the rain." He spent time cutting and sewing the linen to fit the damaged area, making sure it was tight and wrinkle-free. It was as though he had been doing it all his life, Ceci watched admiringly. Finally, he painted the thread-tautened fabric with his blue paint: it matched neither the dark blue of the fuselage nor the silver wings but was nevertheless a very serviceable job under the circumstances.

Packing his few simple tools away, he stood back looking at his handicraft, smiling and nodding. Ceci noticed that he barely filled the simple clothes he was wearing.

"How much do we owe this joinery genius?" asked Ceci, smiling gratefully. The man uttered a few words in a conspiratorial way, his head to one side.

"He says he does not want to be paid. He says he would be eternally grateful to have a short ride in your aeroplane." Ceci looked at the carpenter.

"But of course," she exclaimed, "but we must also pay him!"

Krishnan laughed, and the carpenter smiled.

"He only wants a ride in your aeroplane. Nothing else, he's quite sure."

So it was agreed, she would test the Gypsy Moth the next morning when the locally made glue was dry; if it was all okay, she would fly him around the island. The carpenter beamed with delight and shook Ceci's and Penrose's hands vigorously, grinning broadly, his long, sensitive fingers gripping firmly. His status in his home village would be elevated by leaps and bounds, having flown in an aeroplane.

Early the next morning, Krishnan, the carpenter and the boat's crew came ashore from their vessel, anchored just off the beach. They pulled the beautifully repaired Gypsy Moth to one end of the strand of sand and waited half an hour for the tide to retire so that Ceci could make use of the firmer, damp sand. An hour later the aircraft was started and Ceci was soon airborne, flying carefully around the local area. Fifteen minutes later she returned, lining up with the wet foreshore, and managed to put the Gypsy down without mishap. With the engine still ticking over, she hopped from the cockpit and checked over the repaired wing. It was perfect. The carpenter, now excited, was guided and strapped securely into the front cockpit, his face a permanent grin through a pair of oversize goggles.

Once they were airborne, he gazed about, amazed at the experience and clearly loving every moment. They flew around the island and buzzed Krishnan's boat, which was moored against the beach. After some minutes Ceci again lined up, this time with a wider beach, as the tide had retreated further, and slowly approached the impromptu runway. Although there was now more room, a rising onshore breeze meant that there was now a difficult crosswind to contend with in addition to a loose and drying landing surface. She made a low pass over the beach, not intending to land but to gauge how much the wind would affect her final approach. It proved to be gusty and turbulent where the wind, blowing off the ocean, met the shore with its boundary of jungle. The little aircraft bumped and shook in the skittish conditions. The carpenter loved it, waving wildly as they passed, just a few feet up, along the beach. Worried, Ceci turned out to sea and flew in a long circuit, preparing for another landing approach. By taking a longer approach than she would normally, she was able to adjust her speed and the aircraft's attitude in plenty of time. The engine was just ticking over as the Gypsy Moth gradually descended towards the sand. Penrose was aware of the possible problems that could arise and watched Ceci and her carpenter with concern.

Now they were in the turbulent zone just above the tall trees that dominated both ends of the beach. Suddenly the Moth dropped into an air pocket. Ceci opened the throttle and the engine responded, lifting the frail aircraft's nose. The undercarriage struts struck the topmost branches of the trees, carrying some of the waving fronds away. Clear of the trees, Ceci again closed the throttle fully and continued her descent from about a hundred feet. Managing to anticipate almost every move of the aircraft, Ceci brought the Gypsy Moth to within a couple of feet of the sand. The touchdown was firm and without bounce. Countering the crosswind with the rudder and skid, she maintained a straight course along the beach until all the energy was gone from the aircraft and it stopped two-thirds of the way along the shore. Turning carefully through the wind, she taxied back to the waiting group at the end of their sandy airstrip.

The carpenter, safety straps now off, was standing up in the front cockpit as the aircraft came to a halt. He was wildly applauding everyone and everything. With the engine stopped, they both got down from the aircraft. Everyone was smiling and laughing as they had strong tea, brewed over a campfire. The carpenter was beside himself with pride.

"When do you intend searching for the lost aeroplane?" asked Krishnan. Ceci and Penrose told him that they proposed to start looking that afternoon. They manipulated a heavy drum of petrol from the boat up the beach and into the shade of the trees. Krishnan gave them a bucket; they would have to dispense the fuel into it and then pour it through a funnel and chamois cloth to strain it into the aircraft's two tanks. It would not be easy but they would manage.

❖ ❖ ❖

Harvey Wills was surprised to see the American-built, Dutch-registered DC-2 on the airfield as he flew over Port Blair before landing the Walrus on the water near the beach. Later he briefly met its now-all-Japanese crew, whom he recognised from the discussions in Penang. They were staying at the only guest-house in town. With excessive politeness they cagily greeted each other with a certain sense of mistrust. Wills surmised that they could only be here on the same quest. However, the difference was that he had not been informed about the possibility of bullion being on board the missing Cornucopia. The Japanese had left their simple lodgings for the airfield in the early afternoon. Once airborne, the DC-2 over flew the small group of huts before turning back, climbing steeply to the south, crossing Rutland Island then the narrow stretch of water forming the Duncan Passage towards Little Andaman Island and the eighty-mile-wide Ten Degree Channel, dividing the northern Andaman Island chain from the

Nicobars. The renewed search for Cornucopia had begun again with determination. Wills wondered why the Japanese were so keen to help in the search. Interestingly, they did not appear to have the two Dutch crew members with them this time, nor even the Singaporean, who was, he understood, looking for a relative he'd understood had been lost with Cornucopia.

❖ ❖ ❖

Penrose held the barrel of fuel at a suitable angle while Ceci held the bucket under its short spout, collecting two gallons of fuel each time. It was hot, fume-laden work but they accomplished the task, with a little supportive cursing. Eventually filling both tanks, they carried twenty-nine gallons on board in total. Penrose checked the engine oil level; it was okay but they would have to ask Krishnan if he could somehow obtain a few pints of good-quality motor oil for the Gypsy Moth's engine.

Ceci was now well practised, and they were soon airborne and at a thousand feet cruising around the small island where their base was now established. The islands lay scattered in haphazard fashion but did form a discernable chain of low-lying stepping-stones from south to north. Close by, to the north, lay Camorta, where Krishnan and his family lived, and beyond, ninety miles or so further on, Car Nicobar Island, the most northerly of the Nicobar group marking the southern limit of the Ten Degree Channel. They flew watching the seas below them, carefully taking the opportunity to circle the island of Tillanchong on the way, which lay to the east of the direct route to Car Nicobar, but Penrose thought it worth investigating in case Cornucopia had ended up there. Nothing, absolutely nothing – it felt as if they really were 'looking for a pin in a hayfield', as Krishnan had said.

The DC-2 had made two search sweeps out in the western approaches of the Ten Degree Channel, during the course of which they disposed of the night-watchman's body, heaving it casually out of the rear door at three thousand feet, watching it fall like a heavy bundle of flapping rags, until it finally splashed into the sea. Hyami smiled grimly from the open door. They were now aiming to turn over Car Nicobar Island in preparation for a search going north across the Ten Degree Channel back to Port Blair. The co-pilot saw it first, off to his right, a small aircraft also flying roughly due north as they approached Car Nicobar from the west.

The blue and silver biplane was about two thousand feet below them. It was an odd place to find such a small aircraft. The co-pilot turned and beckoned Hyami to look out of his window as he pointed downwards. Hyami became excited; it must be the biplane that his agent had said he had seen shipped aboard a large trading schooner from a beach north of Penang. It must be the man and woman who, he knew, from earlier intelligence, were also seeking the lost flying boat. He ordered the crew to stalk the small aircraft to see where it went. The Gypsy Moth flew on, oblivious to the watchers overhead, until finally it turned in a wide semi-circle over the channel and headed south again. The DC-2, running short of fuel, had to abandon its Gypsy-stalking, much to Hyami's annoyance, and returned to Port Blair. Frustrated, the Japanese colonel would have loved to find out where the small aircraft was operating from; their own charts showed no other airfields within the two long chains of islands apart from the basic facilities at Port Blair.

❖ ❖ ❖

Harvey Wills went through his pre-flight inspection with care.

They would be flying the borrowed Fleet Air Arm Walrus over an empty seascape and he was keen not to become another 'missing' statistic. His naval co-pilot was already seated in the amphibian's right-hand seat as Wills came aboard. The co-pilot passed Wills a signal. It was a routine message received by the navy asking all ships and aircraft to watch out for the Dutch-registered, polished-aluminium DC-2, and advising that its crew were required for questioning about an incident at Penang. The co-pilot had been given the message just as they were leaving Singapore, and in their hurry to get airborne had stuffed the flimsy white signal sheet into his flight bag. He had come across it while looking out a navigation chart.

Wills glanced quickly at the signal as they prepared to start the aircraft's single radial engine mounted high up behind them, between the machine's two main-planes. He knew that the aircraft in question was the one he had seen as they had arrived over Port Blair, its crew, the Japanese, they had met in the guest-house. He made a mental note to telegraph Singapore at the end of this search patrol. Once they were airborne, clear of the islands, Wills and his crewman initiated a classic square search out to the west of the island chain into the Bay of Bengal. Their search pattern was based on a combination of RAF procedures, intuition, experience and the wind-speed records carefully kept by the Met man at Penang.

The flying was monotonous, droning over the slumbering ocean, its surface dappled with cumulus shadows. Twice they alighted on the sea, having seen something that might have been wreckage, but in one case it proved to be nothing more than a group of drifting teak logs; in the other it turned out to be a travel bag.

They had managed to retrieve the bag after some careful

manoeuvring, the co-pilot risking a dunking as he leaned down to retrieve it with the boat-hook. It was made of white canvas with leather handles, and was partially split so that most of the contents were gone. One or two small molluscs had attached themselves to this mobile island, which suggested that the bag had not been in the water too long. There had been a label attached to one handle but that too had gone, only the reinforcing eyelet and string remaining. Inside, Wills found a pair of rolled-up white socks, one worn tennis shoe, size nine, and page two of a sodden letter with blurred, indelible handwriting that in one barely decipherable sentence made some reference to the 'need to meet as soon as possible to arrange the discreet transfer of funds to London after completion of the agreed contact'. There were no clues to the identity of the writer or the intended recipient. For the Walrus crew it provided nothing of any real value and they continued their search until bad light dictated a return to Port Blair.

After their almost uneventful flight and landings they left the aircraft, stiff and tired, carrying their flight equipment, together with the canvas bag and its contents recovered from the ocean. They understood from the port manager that the DC-2 had returned during the afternoon but had quickly refuelled and taken off again within the hour. Where it was bound he was unaware. Wills telegraphed the information gleaned about the DC-2 to Singapore together with such details as they had from the recovered tennis bag; he had done his duty.

❖ ❖ ❖

Airborne again, Hyami and the Japanese pilots flew back south towards the Ten Degree Channel; having crossed it, they flew steadily onwards at four thousand feet, the crew scanning each of the Nicobar Islands for a possible landing ground. They saw the fishing village on Camorta and the activity around a large boat moored in the surf just off its narrow beach. Onwards they flew until they were overhead a small island; the pilots had been attracted to some odd marks carved into a wide tidal beach on its eastern side. Hyami was called from his position looking from a window at the rear of the cabin and shown the marks as the aircraft was banked around to give him a better view. He dismissed the marks, saying they were probably tracks made by natives dragging boats along the beach. But even as he uttered his ill-considered verdict he realised that it was unusual.

Why would boats be dragged along a beach? First, surely boats would be dragged up or down a beach from or into the sea? Secondly, and oddly, there was no sign of a fishing village or settlement, absolutely nothing; the island was fairly remote and deserted, its beaches surrounded by thick masses of impenetrable green. The aircraft continued turning out to sea and then Hyami gave instructions for the crew to make a low pass along the beach, a hundred yards or so offshore so that they could get a better look at the marks. Banking steeply around, the pilots lined up with the beach allowing the aircraft to settle at about a hundred feet above the water, reducing speed to facilitate Hyami's observation of the shoreline.

Penrose had heard it first and watched the polished-silver aeroplane turning out to sea. They had just finished refuelling the Gypsy Moth in the shade of overhanging trees. Ceci jumped down from screwing the filler cap back onto the top tank and stood in the shade watching the glinting aircraft manoeuvring around, then towards them. Momentarily, as it turned very low it was out of their sight, then, with a burst of noise, it shot across their field of view, barely above the surf, faces peering directly at them from its cockpit and cabin windows. Pulling up steeply, it banked left and made another swoop along the beach, even lower this time, the noise of its engines frightening the birds from the surrounding trees. Suddenly it was gone.

In the quiet that followed, Ceci and Penrose realised that their private location had been discovered. They also knew why the DC-2 was there.

Hyami sat quietly at the rear of the twelve-seat cabin turning ideas over in his mind. The marks in the sand were very odd. What could they be? There was nothing obvious on the shore that could have produced them. Suddenly he became aware of a pungent smell: fumes – it was petrol. He sniffed about the cabin then walked forward and spoke to the two pilots. The captain nodded, unstrapped and, leaving his seat, stepped aft with Hyami, sniffing at the cabin air, looking for the source of the worrying vapours. He agreed with Hyami's diagnosis, and with some urgency unscrewed and lifted a small hatch in the cabin aisle giving limited access to the under floor area. As soon as the hatch lid was raised a much stronger smell of petrol hit them both. The hatch was too small to allow a man to pass through to determine more. The pilot's expression was one of great concern. He realised that they were sitting inside a potential bomb that could erupt at any moment; a spark was all that was required. Sitting down again, he set about switching off all unnecessary electrical circuits, itself a risky business with the possibility of sparks.

The two pilots quickly discussed the problem and possible cause; they finally suspected that the bullets that had been fired and ricocheted at Port Blair had caused a weakness in one or some of the cross-flow fuel pipes. The pipes supplied petrol from wing fuel tanks on one side of the aircraft to the engine on the opposite side. With normal in-flight vibration, one or more pipes may have cracked or failed in some way, allowing raw fuel to leak into the aircraft belly space, which could now sloshing about below them. They had to find somewhere to land – very quickly.

TEN

The following morning, the wind had died down but the seas were still retained much of their surging white energy. Cornucopia's survivors sat surveying the material carnage on the shore. The aircraft's broken remains lay scattered, the hull partly on its side like a huge carcass, stranded and gutted. The description was a cliché, thought Sarah, but totally apt.

A broken wing lay about two hundred yards away, its stump a mass of torn aluminium, wires and cables, like ligaments from a sundered limb. In the water lay one of the engines, its contorted propeller blades pointing all ways, the water sucking as it covered and uncovered the finned cylinders. There was no obvious sign of the other wing and engines.

The warming sun had begun to stir movement within the group, huddled together under the shelter of the trees bordering their castaway's camp. David Rawlinson stood up and slowly stretched. He walked towards the broken aeroplane. Inside was puddled chaos. Water lay in pools on the shattered floor and side of the hull; splintered boxes of bullion lay scattered and smashed. He picked an ingot up and turned it over, intrigued by its precious simplicity. 'You can't eat it, you can't drink it and it won't bring help but it's probably the reason we're now stuck here.' He moved around the hulk looking at the destruction. In the cockpit the port side had been stove in as though by a giant hammer. Little remained that was recognisable. The instrument panel that had trapped Captain Kelly lay broken, hanging face-down supported by pipes and wires. He pulled at it out of curiosity. Then he noticed.

Behind the wrecked panel, attached to the magnetic compass case, was an odd-shaped lump of something. It looked out of place and he studied it for a moment, then he touched and pulled at it. With some resistance it came away. It was a large magnet that had been placed on the compass mounting, hidden behind the instrument panel. As a navigator, he was only too aware of the effect an external magnetic field could have on a compass. Stepping over debris, he looked up and across at the starboard-side instrument panel, which was still in place. Sliding his hands carefully up and behind it, he located the matching compass-mounting point for the co-pilot's position. It had no similarly large magnet attached to the mounting like the one found attached to the captain's compass. Though tired, he realised that there had been an attempt to sabotage the aircraft's crucial directional instrument. He did not know why, but he was astute enough to realise that somebody must have had a plan for such an action. Could it have anything to do with the fact that Cornucopia was carrying a large amount of gold? He did not need any convincing.

Sarah set about changing Michael Kelly's dressings. It appeared that the salt water had had no harmful effects on the wound, which was beginning to heal quite well, after her regular twice-daily cleaning and change of dressings. It had ensured that no new infection could gain a hold in the surgical area. There was some blood evident on the remains of one of her silk-skirt bandages but it seemed to be as a result of him falling on his right stump when the aircraft hit the beach. Kelly half-raised himself to watch Sarah fondly, and then looking about, saw David Rawlinson returning from the wreck of the aircraft. He beckoned to him.

They talked about the situation. What about their location?

Had Rawlinson any idea on which island they had finally ended up? They needed to collect the bullion and store it somewhere, and finally, they should collect wood for a signal fire. Rawlinson considered and gave his best answers, and discreetly told Kelly of the magnet he had found in the cockpit attached to the captain's compass. Kelly took the rough iron magnet from him, turning it over in his hands. It appeared to him to be a piece off of a broken armature such as one would find in a large electricity-generating dynamo fitted to a car or aeroplane.

Snell, meanwhile, was retrieving what little food and water remained in Cornucopia's hull. Hudson and Deverall had been for a short exploratory walk along the beach and a little way into the island's immediate interior. On their return they were able to report that they had found a freshwater stream running off a rock face, forming a small waterfall. There were also some types of fruit on various trees that may prove edible. Beth ran joyfully about on the beach, pleased to be out of the confines of the wrecked aircraft. But she made it clear that she was keen to have something to eat, it was a long time since their last meal the previous afternoon. Purser Snell got to work.

Having reported the local situation to Rawlinson and Kelly, Deverall walked down to the aircraft and stepped inside through the gaping hole in the nose. Like Rawlinson, he was shocked at the scale of the damage done and wondered how they had survived at all, much less unhurt. His bare foot stubbed painfully on something in one of the shallow pools of water lying in the wrecked cabins. Looking down, swearing quietly to himself quietly, he saw his service revolver: he'd dropped it all those days ago after Cornucopia had finally settled onto the boiling ocean. Picking it up, he noticed it had taken on a rusty patina but was otherwise undamaged. Cleaning it off on the tail of his shirt, he continued his investigation of the wreck.

Hearing of the fresh water supply a short distance away and feeling much better, Michael Kelly wondered if he should take advantage and have a wash. Having spent his recent days sweating and swearing in the confines of Cornucopia's centre-section mail stowage compartment, he felt a freshwater cleansing would do him good, both from a hygiene standpoint – and as a way of helping to purge those terrible, pain-wracked days from his mind. Sarah volunteered to help Michael to the water and found a piece of stout driftwood, which Snell simply fashioned into a crude form of crutch to place under his arm. Once fully upright, he felt immediately light-headed. Clinging firmly to Sarah as she put her arm around his back, he placed his left arm over her shoulders. Together they hobbled slowly and carefully up the beach, watched by the others.

The water ran gently off the face of rock and into a small pool set back into the surrounding greenery about two hundred yards in from the beach. The run-off was far from a torrent but there was just enough to achieve a reasonable cooling and cleansing shower. From the pool the water then meandered in a number of small sandy tributaries through the rich mix of sand and soil down to the sea. Clearly the water run-off was a result of the heavy storm rain of the previous day and Kelly doubted they could rely on there being water available all the time. Still light-headed and feeling distinctly frail, Michael lowered himself cautiously and painfully, with Sarah's help, down onto a convenient moss-covered rock and gathered his breath. He was still very weak from the crude operation and his subsequent enforced lack of activity, made no more bearable by his concern for Cornucopia and its valuable cargo of people and bullion.

They sat for a moment under the shady green canopy, which was occasionally pierced by brilliant shafts of sunlight that made the running water sparkle. They were both struck by the magical nature of the place. It was the complete antithesis of recent days.

"If you don't mind, Michael, I should like to have a quick shower first, then I'll help you," she said, very matter-of-factly. He looked at her and nodded. She must know what she's doing, I can't move from here on my own. With irrational modesty in view of what was to follow, Sarah stepped behind some thick variegated bushes and undressed, emerging, beautifully naked, onto a small stage of sunlight. Kelly did not quite know what to do. He felt unusually awkward. Should he attempt to turn away with all due modesty or, it struck him, was this a deliberate act to somehow entertain him? He was unsure of himself for the first time in a long time.

A renegade beam shone into his eyes as he looked at her. He was aware of her smiling gently at him but her image was slightly blurred as she moved into the sparkling water. It was exciting; her tanned body and blonde hair submerged under the waterfall, and then as she emerged, sparks of sunlight reflecting the myriad drops of water on her skin. This was a very private performance, he knew. But why? He was engulfed by chaotic emotions. Despite his weakened condition, his body was responding predictably to the beautiful vision under the water. His mind was racing. It was bizarre; he was confused and wanting. 'My God, what if one of the others comes here now?' The thought crossed his mind.

She came towards him, naked and smiling. He looked at her face, into her huge blue eyes. This was no sordid act. There was, he realised, something very sincere in her complete exposure. She undid the remaining buttons on his ripped shirt and slipped it off over his shoulders and down his arms. Delicately, she removed his cut-about trousers, together with the bandage dressings.

When he was naked, she placed the driftwood crutch under his arm and helped him to the waterfall. The feeling of her naked skin against him as they stumbled the few yards threw all other thoughts from his mind. Taking the remaining sliver of her soap, she began to lather him. Now he had a legitimate reason to hold her. She pulled him gently under the water to wash away the soap. When he was free from lather, she helped him back to his boulder and dried him slowly, taking care of his wound.

"Michael, how does your leg feel now?" She asked, slowly, but he sensed that it was not the real question in her mind.

"It's very sore but bearable," he said quietly. "Sarah," he faltered, "Why?"

She said nothing, just looked at him, trying to understand her own emotions and the situation she had partly engineered. She couldn't. She sat close to him, her gaze shifting between his eyes and the ground.

"Michael, over recent days ... in fact ... possibly, ever since I boarded Cornucopia, I've been attracted to you. I can't explain it. It's very much more than being attracted to the uniform – what's left of it," she smiled. "I've watched you, and how you've coped with the situation, the perfect landing, your courage during and after my attempts at surgery and your concern for all of us despite your condition. It's all heightened my feelings for you. Michael, I think I'm in love with you. I can't possibly explain it rationally, I'm already married, and I know it shouldn't be, but that's how I feel." Tears were welling in her eyes.

Michael sat stunned. He had had no idea, or had he? He was

flattered, completely out of his depth, his mind unable to function logically. He had rarely, if ever, felt such powerful emotions about another person. A beautiful, extraordinary, woman like this, expressing love for him; it was amazing. How had it happened? As he tried to comprehend it, all of the tension and trauma of recent days – the crash, their time adrift, his injury and the fact that Sarah had probably saved his life – suddenly overwhelmed him. He found long-forgotten tears stinging his eyes and overflowing down his face. He turned, swallowing hard, biting his lip, trying to conceal it, but she saw and wept happily with him, covering his face with her hair, tenderly holding his head in her hands. They didn't speak, but kissed gently, lips just touching. The others saw them return. Something had changed between Michael and Sarah.

Deverall joined them, interested in the magnetic lump David Rawlinson had found, and showed them his gun, recovered from Cornucopia. Under the circumstances Kelly felt that the weapon should be under his control. With no use for it, the colonel said he would clean it – it was, after all, army property – and then agreed to give it to Kelly for safekeeping. Kelly asked for all the bullion to be collected from the aircraft and placed in a shallow pit, dug with some difficulty in the sand among the roots of the trees bordering the beach. Kelly knew that forty-eight boxes had been loaded, each containing four ingots, and he wondered at the missing four boxes. Perhaps, as the boat had struggled towards the shore, they had been lost through holes in the damaged hull. Or perhaps one of the party had decided to secure their financial future if and when they were rescued. The sandy hole was covered; Kelly thought that perhaps he now needed to watch his party with more care.

They all sat up within a few seconds of each other, woken from their late-afternoon siesta. The distant noise of aircraft engines disturbed the sultry quiet. Snell rushed to light the bonfire that they had prepared for such an eventuality, the sighting of a passing ship, but he realised, even as he stood up, that he was probably too late. The aircraft, now very low, appeared to be moving quite slowly across their island's interior, apparently descending, the engines almost indistinct against the background hum of the jungle. Then it was gone. David Rawlinson had the presence of mind to determine and note down a bearing from their position towards where the aircraft was last seen, using the first officer's retrieved and now demagnetised aircraft compass.

His earlier attempts to ascertain their position, which island they had been cast onto, had been thwarted by the lack of a working timepiece. The disappearance of the boat's sextant in the final lunge to the beach, and the loss of the vital nautical almanacs, had made celestial calculations impossible. They discussed the situation: if an aircraft was so close, perhaps they were near to human habitation. It may be worth someone trying to walk towards where they had seen the aircraft descending, towards the high, jungle-covered plateau above them. It was now late in the afternoon and everyone later agreed over a simple fish supper that the colonel and Purser Snell should try to find where the aircraft had landed, if indeed it had.

The colonel spent the evening cleaning his pistol using a little oil scavenged from one of the engine oil tanks on the remaining piece of starboard wing. He had just six rounds for the weapon and wondered if they would work if needed. They intended to carry the pistol with them on their expedition as protection from any wild animals they might meet. Snell prepared a few rations and filled some bottles from the dwindling waterfall. Hudson had been playing with Beth, teaching her how to swim in the gentle surf and how to fish. They'd had some success, catching four fair-sized fish using coconut flesh as bait attached to twine and a crude hook fashioned from thin wire found among Cornucopia's torn wing root. They were unable to identify the fish, but they looked tempting and Snell prepared them for cooking.

As the twilight turned quickly into a deep tropical indigo, they sat around their small fire of driftwood, finishing their simple supper. Sarah was telling her daughter a bedtime story before wrapping her in a dry blanket and laying her on a platform of branches and leaves. Beth, pleased that it was her own bed, said it was a lovely one, and was soon asleep. Michael Kelly sat upright, his back against a tree, tired – he'd been practising walking with his new crutch. Sarah leaned on his shoulder, uninhibited. The others appeared to be asleep in varying positions around the dying fire.

"I was stunned by you this afternoon. I'd never realised such feelings could exist." Michael whispered, squeezing her shoulder gently.

Sarah looked up at him, the fire casting a ruddy glow over half his face.

"It's true. I've never felt about anybody the way I feel about you, not even in the early days with Malcolm, my husband. What's so strange is that, apart from me helping with your injuries, we haven't really been together in any intimate way." She paused, and then said, "Do you think you could love me, Michael?"

There was a long silence while he gathered the words together.

"If what I feel for you right now, that I want to protect you and care for you, come what may, is love, then yes, I love you more than my own life." It occurred to him that he had never made such a statement before in his life. She looked at him longingly and held onto his strong hands, finally falling asleep on his chest. His leg throbbed painfully but he would bear it.

By the time they awoke, preparations were well under way for the expedition. Snell and Deverall were ready to leave, with a small bag of provisions sufficient for a full day, including water, the loaded pistol, some dried-out paper and a pencil in case they wanted to map their route or leave a message somewhere. They also took the largest knife they could find from Snell's salvaged collection. They came to Michael to say goodbye. He managed to get up, leaning heavily on Sarah, shake their hands and, wishing them luck, said that if they had a problem they were to fire two shots in quick succession. What he was going to do if that happened he was far from sure.

The remaining five, including Beth, playing happily in a sandy pool, watched them enter the jungle and disappear; now and again they could hear the rustle of foliage and the squawking of disturbed birds as the two of them pushed their way upwards into the island's high interior. Soon they were gone and Hudson decided to walk a mile or so along the beach in both directions to see if there was anything that could help them.

Sarah cleaned Michael's wound, leaving the dressings off for a while to help it dry in the sun. He looked at his foreshortened limb. 'I'm a cripple.' It struck him, shocking. 'My God, what am I going to do if we get out of this?' Rawlinson turned from gazing out to sea and, looking down at the reduced limb, read his mind.

"Don't worry, Skipper, I know a chap in Blighty who crashed a Rapide. They had to take both his legs off, one above the knee. Now he's the chief pilot at Western Airways, happy, confident and a bloody good pilot, and he's managed two beautiful kids," he winked.

"Thanks, David, you've done a first-class job while I've been out of it. Pity, I don't think Sir Claude is going to be too impressed with what's happened to his aeroplane, his passengers and crew, or the bloody cargo," he pointed to where the bullion was now buried.

"Sir Claude isn't our problem at the moment; we can deal with him later."

Standing, David Rawlinson pulled the remains of his uniform cap further down to shield his eyes.

"She obviously has strong feelings for you, Skipper," he said before striding off to inspect the aircraft again. Sarah picked up Beth, who was covered in sand from her excavations for yet another sandcastle, and carried her, laughing and giggling, towards the break in the trees and the hidden waterfall. It was shower time.

Kelly watched them, the little girl now skipping around her beautiful mother, kicking up little spurts of sand. Sarah seemed to have a spring in her step as she teased her young daughter with a long palm frond, their relaxed laughter tinkling along the beach.

So Rawlinson has noticed something. How am I going to tell her ... and him, and the rest of them? It's not going to be easy; I've misled them. Cornucopia was grossly overweight with all the bullion on board, but he'd agreed despite the risks. The prospect of his financial reward had overcome his normal prudence where flying was concerned. He lay back and closed his eyes.

ELEVEN

Hyami anxiously watched the two pilots as they prepared urgently but calmly for an emergency landing. The petrol fumes were now very noticeable in the confined cockpit, even with the side screens open. Ahead and about two hundred feet below was a patch of scrubland, roughly rectangular, atop a plateau in the centre of the island. It was the only place available if they were to have a chance of survival, they all knew that. The Japanese captain turned briefly, telling Hyami to sit down in his seat and pull the straps very tight. It was an instruction from the aircraft's captain to a passenger; the niceties of face or rank were of no consequence in their literally volatile situation. The captain uttered a short order; the co-pilot took action immediately. Both throttles and mixture levers were pulled to 'close' and fuel cocks turned to 'off'. With flaps down, all electrical equipment was isolated and the DC-2 instantly became a high-speed, heavy glider heading for a landing, on what, they weren't sure.

The size of the shrubs and unevenness of the ground became increasingly evident as they flared for a touchdown well above a normal powered-approach speed. The captain allowed the two main wheels to touch gently down first. Their rumbling along the ground was immediately accompanied by shocks and bumps as the aircraft tore through the coarse shrubbery in their path. A cloud of dust followed. It billowed high into the air behind, increasing measurably as the tailwheel came down to land. The captain was good, very good, his experience as an aircraft-carrier pilot left him anticipating each lurch and bounce that the aircraft made as it gradually slowed in its headlong rush. Following them, unseen, was a pale trail of petrol soaking the ground and greenery as they plunged on. Suddenly it was over. The machine stopped, a veil of dust settling over it.

Hyami blinked and looked forward. The crew were sitting listless and exhausted. He noticed that the backs of their shirts were wet. The smell of fuel was now even stronger as he moved to the rear of the cabin and, opening the door, jumped down into knee-high grasses and shrubs. Hot air rushed into the aircraft, carrying clouds of the dust they had stirred during landing. Looking under the belly, he could see a thin trickle of clear fluid pouring onto the ground. The fumes shimmered in the sunlight before melting into the hot, humid air. The captain and first officer joined Hyami under the aircraft's belly looking at the steady stream of fuel. Taking a screwdriver from a small toolkit, the first officer undid twenty-four machine screws that held a sizeable belly-access panel in place. It took a long time: as the panel became free, so fuel tended to pour out in an increasing stream. They were all coughing and choking. With the panel off they tried to peer inside to locate the root of the problem but it proved too dark. Nothing could be seen inside the belly space against the bright sunlight outside. They left the problem until the next morning hoping that the vapours would clear from around and within the aircraft overnight.

After another night sleeping in cramped aircraft seats they inspected the underside of the DC-2. Fuel was now dripping only slowly from the open panel. The fumes outside had almost cleared with a soft breeze. The first officer went back into the cockpit and collected a torch. With the potential for a spark from its switch, it would be too dangerous to use it within the aircraft's fume-laden belly but they may be able to shine its beam from the outside into the dark space and pinpoint the problem area. Their earlier supposition proved to be correct: one of the cross-flow fuel pipes had partially fractured where it entered a complex joint with one of the main engine fuel feed pipes. Hyami's free shooting at Port Blair was the probable cause, and he was keen to see it remedied with no fuss or repercussions. They had few tools and certainly none that would match the sizes of the large union nuts that locked the pipes together. They did, however, find a roll of thick electrical insulating tape in the co-pilot's flight bag and thought that this, together with some torn strips of cloth, could be used to effect a temporary, near-leak-resistant, repair, at least until they got back to Port Blair.

After wasting most of the morning, Hyami ordered the first officer to climb inside the hot aircraft belly to lash up a temporary repair to the offending pipe, while he held the torch from the outside. The aircraft captain objected, saying that the space was still too fume-filled and unsafe for his co-pilot colleague to enter. Hyami, now beginning to reach the end of his tether, moved to withdraw his pistol, insisting that the young pilot enter the belly to undertake the repair. It was an order from a superior officer. The captain and his co-pilot were unarmed, having seen no reason to carry their sidearm on a search flight. The young pilot looked pained at his captain who looked away pointedly, ashamed.

Inside the belly space it was impossible to breathe properly, the heavy fumes causing choking and gagging. Working for thirty or forty seconds the young pilot would then throw himself towards the open hatch gasping in air, much of which was also enveloped in petrol vapours. He did this ten or twelve times then, finally, indicating that he was almost finished, took a deep breath and returned to the pipes. Forty seconds went by, fifty, a minute. Hyami and the aircraft captain became agitated, though not perhaps for the same reasons. After a minute and a half, the captain pushed past Hyami and climbed up into the small space. A few feet inside he saw the legs of the co-pilot, who was lying on the floor. He grabbed them, trying not to breathe the all-pervading petrol fumes, pulling the limp man to the opening. Jumping down and grabbing a few fresher breaths, he pulled the inert form out, carrying it into the shade of some nearby young trees.

The young pilot was breathing but only just. Working furiously for a few fraught minutes, the captain tried valiantly to resuscitate his flying partner. The stricken young man opened his eyes and looked for a few seconds at Hyami, standing over him. He muttered a few words and died. The captain continued to kneel for a while beside the dead man, still pumping his chest, feeling uncharacteristic grief in this situation. Hyami walked away, concerned that he now only had one pilot on whom to rely. It occurred to him that it was fortunate that the DC-2 could be flown by just one pilot.

❖ ❖ ❖

Van der Valk awoke, still feeling a little light-headed but definitely better, in the rude hut where the woman had insisted he lay quietly to recover. There was noise outside, a babble of voices, some excited. The curtain to the shelter was pulled slowly back and a wide face with big eyes looked around the opening.

"Please forgive, I thought you might be still asleep," the man said in accented English. "My sister-in-law has taken care of your arm, I see. How is it feeling now?"

"Thanks. It seems okay, but what time is it?" His voice croaked.

"Now it is late afternoon. Very lucky you arrived yesterday as we have come today to take my sister-in-law and her young son back to our island. Fishing here is only good for a few months. Henrik van der Valk slowly raised himself from the simple bed and sat up, holding his hand out. They shook hands; the young Indian had a strong grip.

"How do you do?"

"Tell me, what has happened to you? We rarely see Europeans on this island apart from the district officer now and again. What are you doing here, and how did you manage to injure your arm that way? My sister-in-law says you were very tired when you arrived. In fact, you have been asleep for almost a whole day." Van der Valk's mind was befuddled. He thought slowly, and then spoke carefully.

"I am here looking at plants and insects, I am studying the possibility of making medicines from your island's natural flora and fauna. I was climbing a tree and fell, breaking my arm, then spent some time wandering about looking for help. Your sister-in-law has taken care of me and I am very grateful. Please tell her."

He had deliberately lied. Before taking up flying as a career he had trained in Holland as a chemist and some years ago had actually undertaken a series of field trips in South America looking for promising source plants. It was a plausible answer based on real experience for his recent activities. He rationalised that telling this local he was working for the Japanese, searching for a lost aeroplane in abnormal circumstances may be viewed as incredible. It was easier to present less dramatic, more plausible reasons for his arrival. He slowly got up, staggering slightly and went outside, screwing up his eyes in the bright sunlight. The Indian's sister-in-law was there with her fisherman husband and, it seemed, her entire extended family, all talking and helping to pack her few possessions, ready to load onto the boat bobbing a few yards from the shore.

"Would it be possible to come with you? I should welcome the chance to see another island as part of my field research." There was some discussion among the group.

"Of course, if you wish. It is no problem for us. We live on a small island called Camorta. We have family there – but where are your things?" Krishnan smiled, holding out his arm.

"I must have lost them when I was wandering around lost yesterday. Don't worry about them, I'll come with you and get a few things later."

Krishnan wondered, but nodded helpfully, and helped Henrik van der Valk across the surf and into the boat. Twenty minutes later they were under way, motor-sailing south in the late afternoon sun with a gentle breeze from the south-east.

❖ ❖ ❖

Deverall had been watching the silver aircraft from deep within the trees since early afternoon and saw three men under the aircraft's belly. What they were up to was not clear. He had seen one of the men, the smallest, threaten to draw his pistol, and he saw the odd events that followed, through Cornucopia's damaged binoculars. The aircraft sat at the far end of a patch of rough shrub-strewn ground measuring about quarter of a mile by a mile. Instinctively he knew that it would be unwise to approach the oriental-looking men. He whispered to Snell what he had seen. The purser was lying back, tired, against a tree, a few yards away. The trek from the coast to the centre of the island had been draining on them both but Deverall's military background and fitness had equipped him better for the heat and humidity. Snell was exhausted and limp after the near-five-hour uphill struggle. They had already drunk over half of their water rations and there appeared to be little prospect of them getting more until they returned to the beach where Cornucopia's remains lay scattered.

"The crew of the aircraft might be Japanese. One of them is either very ill or even very dead. In any event one of them seems too quick on the draw with his pistol. They're just sitting under the wing of the aircraft now, not even talking. I can't understand why a Dutch-registered aircraft should have a Japanese crew. What the hell are they doing here?"

Snell shrugged his shoulders. It was about all he could manage at present. Leaving Snell to regain his strength, Deverall decided to circle around the aircraft under the cover of the surrounding trees and thick undergrowth. As he was about to move off, he saw just two men get into the aircraft, the door closing behind them, then, moments later, heard the aircraft's engines start. Snell got up and joined Deverall looking down the strip of land at the aircraft and the cloud of dust billowing out behind it. The DC-2 lumbered over the uneven ground, slowly turning amid the shrubs and stunted bushes that dotted the landing area, looking distinctly alien in such raw surroundings. It began to taxi directly towards their hiding place, lurching and occasionally turning to avoid a particularly large piece of outcrop of greenery.

The sun, sinking behind the two hiding men, reflected off its windscreens, making it impossible to see into the cockpit, to see the faces of the crew. Deverall and Snell slowly backed further into the undergrowth, watching the aircraft's slow, laboured approach. About fifty yards from their position barely concealed in the trees, the silver machine stopped, then turned quite sharply with a burst of engine power propelling it around to face down the strip of scrubland, into the light breeze.

Hyami peered from his position in the right-hand seat, previously occupied by the younger of the two Japanese navy pilots. The aircraft lurched round. He looked at the fringing jungle, watching that the starboard wingtip cleared the trees in the turn. As he did so he looked straight at where Deverall and Snell were sheltering. It must be his imagination. He thought he had fleetingly seen two white faces looking at them, but he knew that this island had no inhabitants. He was tired; perhaps the petrol fumes were affecting his brain and eyes. The engines were run up, hurling wind, loose plants and even small rocks at where Snell and Deverall stood sheltering behind bending tree trunks. When the engines had slowed to tick-over, the brakes were released, the hiss of pneumatics signifying a pending departure. With engines bellowing, the aircraft waddled down the same stretch of strip they had torn up on arrival, eventually becoming airborne, and turning slightly right as it climbed, heading north, towards Port Blair.

Their course required a partial circumnavigation of the island before settling on a northerly heading. Hyami looked down on the jungle and beaches below. A near-disaster, but he'd managed to save the situation and was pleased with the outcome from what could so easily have been a disaster. What, after all, was one man's life against the needs of the homeland, he rationalised ... and his saving of face.

They were just straightening up from a turn when he saw it. The image formed instantly and indelibly on his mind's eye. The lost white flying boat was lying broken on a beach just below them. He was in no doubt. He reached across, grabbing the pilot by his arm, with the other hand pointing downwards in violent gesticulation. "There, there, below us!"

On the beach below, Rawlinson and Kelly watched the silver DC-2 turn above them before appearing to descend slightly, then setting off towards the north. Instinctively, they waved, as any survivors would, looking to be rescued. Disappointed, they watched as the aircraft flew away, the rich note of its radial engines steadily fading.

Deverall and Snell made their way to where the aircraft had been standing when they had arrived earlier that afternoon. After a few hundred yards they came across a body: a Japanese man lying partly hidden under a large bush. He was wearing a sort of uniform with no badges of rank. Already the body was beginning to attract flies and insects that rose, buzzing, as the two men tried to search the man's pockets. There was nothing on him, not a single scrap of paper or anything to identify him. It was clear that whoever was flying the DC-2 did not want the man's death associated with them. They searched around the area and, on finding nothing, began the long fight back through the jungle to the beach and the remains of Cornucopia. The next morning they described what they had seen to the other survivors, who were surprised and worried. Why had the crew of the aircraft not acknowledged them or made any attempt to help them?

❖ ❖ ❖

Van der Valk, sitting comfortably on the boat's broad rail talking with Krishnan, saw the setting sun reflect off the side of his aircraft. Krishnan caught the look and tried to make a connection; just what it was, he was not sure, but there was something.

TWELVE

It was almost dark as the DC-2 landed again at Port Blair's grass airfield. Harvey Wills saw it taxi rapidly towards the hangar and walked quickly through the gathering dusk in that direction. Arriving just as the aircraft door was pushed open, he watched one of the Japanese passengers he had briefly met at Penang climb stiffly down the short ladder. Wills nodded acknowledgement, unsure if the Japanese man spoke English. Hyami followed and stood looking at Wills. Wills waited for the Dutch crew to disembark but no one came.

"You are flying the aircraft yourself?" asked Wills, a little surprised, after a minute or two. Hyami smiled.

"We have chartered the aircraft from the owners. My colleague here is a highly qualified pilot."

Wills was aware that the aircraft and its Dutch crew were being sought by the Malay authorities and wondered if he should raise the matter. They were within Indian jurisdiction now, but it was still part of the Empire. However, it was the Dutch crew that the signal had indicated were being sought. Wills was unsure of his ground.

"I am surprised to meet you again, here of all places, I had understood that there were some problems at Penang and that this aircraft was impounded along with the Dutch crew." It was not quite the truth but seemed a reasonably diplomatic approach to the subject of murder. Hyami stood staring and thinking.

"I think you must be mistaken, Sir. Our Dutch friends have allowed my pilot to charter and fly the aircraft after a thorough checkout in Singapore. There are no problems, as far as I am aware."

"Oh ... perhaps I have misunderstood matters. Please forgive me. Tell me, what are you doing in such a remote place – are you still searching for the lost Empress machine?"

Hyami uttered a terse order to the Japanese pilot, who promptly got back into the aircraft. They could hear his boots clattering up the metal aircraft floor towards the cockpit. Down on the left-hand side of the captain's seat was a canvas pocket that was normally used to hold maps and charts. In it was a large-calibre Japanese automatic weapon, black and brutal.

Wills waited until the noise abated, looking askance at Hyami.

"We have some fuel problems and I need to make arrangements with the local mechanic to have it looked at, so if you will forgive me, Sir, I must deal with matters right away."

He turned sharply and strode across the dusty earth towards the dim glow coming from the part-open hangar door, disappearing inside. Wills was too aware that Hyami had deliberately avoided his question. This was no misunderstanding of language: Hyami spoke very good English, it seemed. The Japanese pilot, watching from the cockpit window, slipped the safety catch back to 'on' and put the heavy weapon back into its canvas stowage. He then followed Colonel Hyami into the hangar, glancing slyly back at Wills from time to time.

Hyami agreed to pay the mechanic a bounty if he managed to repair the fuel-pipe damage in the belly of the aircraft and have it ready for flight by first light the next day. Arrangements were being made to tow the aircraft nearer to the small, ramshackle hangar as Wills took the opportunity of walking around this modern machine. It was the first time he had had the chance to inspect an all-metal American monoplane with a stressed skin. Such innovation, he thought, as, out of the corner of his eye, he saw two small puncture holes in the lower port fuselage side, just forward and below the wing's leading edge. It was difficult to see much in the semi-darkness. He touched them, and they were bullet holes, he was sure, from his military experience.

So, he questioned, why should this aircraft have two bullet holes in such an unusual place? He walked around to the starboard side out of curiosity, to see if the bullets had exited there. There was just a single exit hole. He thought that the second bullet's energy had probably been dissipated somewhere within the fuselage, possibly damaging some internal components or structure, perhaps even the fuel pipes that Hyami had referred to.

As he turned to walk back to the small airfield administration hut, his eyes fell on the main undercarriage. A beam of weak light emerging from the partly open hangar door fell just short of the wheel but he could see that the wheel well and main undercarriage leg were covered in dust and small pieces of vegetation. He knew the signs from air force exercises when they were forced to use unprepared airstrips. The service riggers were always complaining about having to clear and clean out grass, leaves and small branches caught on aircraft undercarriages during such exercises. 'So Mr Hyami has been out in the boon docks with this aircraft, has he? The question is, where and why?' Wills considered, and moved back into the shadows as the hangar doors were pushed aside to allow a small tractor to emerge. The aircraft was pushed partway into the hanger, nose first.

❖ ❖ ❖

Ceci and Harold awoke to the rising sun piercing the nooks

and crannies of their small bivouac. It was already quite warm though barely seven o'clock. Ceci rushed naked into the gently breaking waves a few feet from their camp, splashing and laughing at Penrose, who was still standing, half-asleep, against the shelter. Eventually she taunted him to the point where a gentle revenge was fully justified. Rushing, he plunged beneath the water and swam towards her. She glanced around in expectation, waiting for his surprise. Grabbing her by both legs, he pulled her down, making her squeal in a fusion of fright and glee. As they surfaced they heard the sound of a powerful aero engine, its pulsating beat growing louder. They stood waist-deep in water holding each other, watching and waiting for the aircraft to show itself through the early haze.

Harvey Wills started to descend the Walrus as they approached the islands that made up the lower group of Nicobars. His plan had been a very early start from Port Blair aiming to search the westernmost coasts of the chain's islands in case Cornucopia had managed to ditch near to one of them. If they had no luck there, he would institute a square search in the sea areas out to the west of the island chain, perhaps as far as a hundred miles, then they would do a more detailed aerial search of other islands.

"An aircraft, this early in the morning?" Ceci asked, watching.

The two of them saw the Walrus just as its crew saw them. It banked sharply away from the beach out to sea and then returned slowly, only a few feet above the water. Ceci knew it had to be Harvey. Who else would be flying a military seaplane out here? He had, after all, been flying it when she almost ran into him in the small room at the airport offices at Penang.

"It must be Harvey, Harold!" She shouted above the engine roar and pulled him down under the water as the aircraft ran along the shoreline. Penrose understood instantly and swam under water towards the beach, with Ceci in pursuit. As they surfaced, coughing and breathless, the Walrus was at the far end of the beach turning again out to sea. They both ran as fast as possible up the sand and into the sheltering trees. From their hiding place they watched Squadron Leader Harvey Wills pilot the Walrus in a sweeping left turn with full power reverberating from its single pusher engine. It swept along the beach, the two pilots looking for the two swimmers they had seen earlier. In the Walrus cockpit Wills smiled and his young navy co-pilot was laughing uproariously. They had caught two natives swimming nude in the water and were going back for a second, closer look. They were disappointed; the two, a man and a woman, they thought, had disappeared while the aircraft had been in the turn. The low eastern sun did not help matters. The crew's focus on the shoreline water and swimmers had left the Gypsy Moth's location unobserved as their aircraft completed its second run, pulling up to continue its coastal search further south.

Ceci and Harold, still naked, waited tensely for the aircraft to return, but the drone of its engine slowly faded as the Walrus flew away around the island. Having eaten and dressed quickly, they pulled the camouflage branches and broad palm leaves from the Gypsy Moth, Penrose lifting it by the tail, pulling it fully from its cover onto the beach. Ceci completed her external checks while Penrose climbed aboard, ready to activate the throttle and magneto switches as, this time, Ceci swung the wooden propeller. With the engine running, Ceci settled into the small rear cockpit and fastened her seat straps.

She tapped Harold on the shoulder and he turned slightly, thumbs up, indicating he was ready. Lining up on the narrow strip of sand, Ceci slowly pushed the throttle lever purposefully forwards, the Gypsy engine responding, and soon the small aircraft was moving along the beach. Bringing the tail up quickly, she juggled the rudder pedals to and fro countering the propeller's torque and the ruts and bumps in the beach's gently sloping surface. Just as she reached flying speed the aircraft lurched to the right, its wheels momentarily cutting through the waves that broke onto the shelving sand. Once safely airborne, they headed north to investigate some of the other local islands they had not covered during their previous search flight. Harold had been warned to keep a good lookout, not only on the ground, but now also in the air, for the silver DC-2.

Visibility was beautifully clear as they flew northwards at a few hundred feet between the islands of Katchall and Camorta, above the occasionally white-speckled azure-blue sea. As they passed Camorta they could see the village where Krishnan and his brothers lived. There were now two vessels moored just beyond the surf line, bobbing in the light swell – one much larger than the other. They continued northwards, Penrose looking up occasionally, watching the skies for the DC-2. Ahead and slightly remote lay an island set in a neat lace collar of surf breaking lethargically onto golden sandy beaches, its surface entirely covered with dense jungle except for a small flattish area atop the island's central plateau. Ceci decided to do a circuit of the island just to be certain that nothing would be missed. Turning and banking left, she began an anti-clockwise search of its coastline. The eastern side was clear of anything remotely interesting; the jungle came almost down to the sea for much of the coastline here. Around the northern end of the island they flew very low, a hundred feet from the sea's surface.

The sun reflected harshly off the sea's surface, the resulting glare making it quite tiring to continually watch the passing scenery. They had been airborne for just about half an hour and were now turning south, along the island's west coast, climbing slowly at the same time. It had not taken long; Ceci could now see the southern end of the island from where they had begun their circumnavigation. As they approached their starting point she opened up the engine and began to climb, intending to double back on their course and look at another island further to the west.

The unexpected turbulence struck them forcibly. It flicked the Gypsy Moth almost onto its back, the nose pointing heavenwards. They were aware of a very loud roar, being tossed around, at the mercy of invisible hands in unstable air.

Ceci instinctively pulled the control stick backwards, hoping to gain some speed and avoid an inverted stall. The Gypsy engine was performing at maximum revolutions. The biplane slowly turned over the top of a loop, inverted. It plunged towards the sea only a few hundred feet below. Penrose could do nothing. He stared down at the sea and beach. It rapidly filled his field of vision, the propeller turning rapidly a few feet in front of him. Now they were almost vertical. Speed was building fast. Ceci slammed the throttle closed, continuing to pull back on the control stick.

Penrose saw the wreck of Cornucopia just as the Gypsy Moth began to claw back from its horrifying vertical plunge. There it was, scattered on the beach, immediately below, in a small bay. He had even time to notice some people standing on the beach. They stood frozen, faces upturned, some with hands cupped to their mouths. Ceci recovered her composure less than fifty feet above the water. She and Penrose were still unsure what had caused such an upset. The watchers on the shore had been amazed to see the DC-2 fly directly across the top of the tiny Moth, clearing it by only a few feet before opening up its two powerful Wright Cyclone engines as it had pulled upwards.

The ensuing rush of turning air caused by its wake had created a vortex of energy. It hit the lightly built Gypsy Moth causing just what Hyami and his pilot had intended. But they were hoping for a more catastrophic outcome. Looking up, Penrose saw the DC-2 turning towards them from seaward, a half mile or so away, its propellers two solid discs as their blades reflected the bright sunlight. It was coming straight towards them. He turned slightly, pointing emphatically. She had already seen it, manoeuvring to avoid another attempt on their lives. Ceci had been very frightened and disorientated before: now she was very angry, and extremely calm.

Turning to face the DC-2, she opened the throttle fully, pointing her small aircraft directly at the shining twin. This was madness, she knew, but the other pilot must be mad too. The time it took to cover the distance between them was a few seconds. Penrose was unsure whether to pray or turn and remonstrate with Ceci. There was no time for either. Their combined approach speed was a little short of two hundred and sixty knots. The DC-2 rapidly filled the small windscreen in front of Penrose. His eyes were forcibly closed just before the Moth, engine roaring, pulled up and very sharply to the right. The Japanese pilot, Hyami beside him, stared open-mouthed as the small blue-and-silver aircraft swept up and across their windscreens. It was barely yards away it seemed. The DC-2's control yoke was immediately hard forward, the control wheel to the right. In a fraught avoiding move, the DC-2 swept down towards the sea, its engines thundering angrily. She had been reckless in the extreme. She was no aerobatic pilot, she knew, and the realisation hit her like a sledgehammer that her moment of pure anger had needlessly risked Harold's life and her own.

The Japanese pilot was an expert at aerobatics, but not in a heavy passenger aircraft. Closing the aircraft's twin throttles, he pulled back on the control yoke firmly, but he was already too low. Changing his mind, he opened up both engines to full power, kicking on right rudder, with the control wheel over to the right. The aircraft stood instantly on its wingtip and pivoted around before quickly levelling off, flying seemingly inches above the sea out of the small bay where Cornucopia was now beached.

Particular features of the shallow bay where Cornucopia lay were low, sandy and shrub-filled promontories, running seawards at both ends. On the northerly promontory there were some rather stunted wind-blown trees, with just one exception. An upright, solid specimen grew proud and tall, a full flush of dark green crown at its head. The Japanese pilot's attention had been focused on recovering the aircraft after their near-collision with the Gypsy Moth; he had failed to notice precisely which direction they were taking. Hyami, less preoccupied with flying, saw the promontory, with its tall specimen tree, squarely in the centre of his windscreen as they rushed across the surface of the bay, so close that the vortices created by the propellers caused small white tornadoes on its flat surface.

Hyami panicked, screaming and pointing at the rapidly approaching tree. Instinctively the pilot hauled back on the control wheel and the aircraft climbed crazily upwards at an impossible angle. Then, engines snarling at maximum revolutions, the DC-2 levelled off and shot out to sea and was gone.

Ceci watched, heart in mouth, the antics of the DC-2 before it swept off. Turning towards the beach where Cornucopia lay, she slowed the engine and allowed the Moth to descend towards the group of survivors gathered on the shore. The beach was littered with debris from Cornucopia. Ceci and Harold both waved as they flew along the shoreline before climbing to avoid the big tree on the promontory. Circling, with her heart still pounding, Ceci managed somehow to write a crude note, stuffing it into the finger of a leather flying glove – she never wore them anyway – and threw it forcibly at the small group as she passed overhead for the final time. David Rawlinson ran the few hundred yards to where the glove had landed and pulled out the note plugged into one of its fingers. 'Back tomorrow, don't worry. Ceci,' it read.

THIRTEEN

Ceci and Harold flew back to their camp by way of Krishnan's village, circling overhead and waggling the wings. They hoped that they had given the impression of a need to meet but there were now no boats moored nearby. She made a faultless landing on their beach and together they pulled the Moth up and under the tree camouflage, all the while discussing the dangerous behaviour of the Dutch pilots in the DC-2. Ceci was both proud of and angry about her actions.

The sun had almost set but the temperature was agreeable. The air had a warm silky feel to it as they undressed for a swim before supper and bed. In the water they had their customary water fight, which led eventually to a gentler form of jousting.

As they were preparing to leave the water, Ceci glanced up and out to sea; the sun was just sinking below the horizon. She was surprised to see a craft entering the southern end of the bay that embraced their beach. It showed no lights and it was difficult to recognise any detail in the enclosing dusk. However, the shape was becoming familiar, as almost silently, the boat closed on them in the water, before Krishnan shouted a greeting. Ceci was nonplussed; here she was, naked under the clear water with a boat full of young fishermen ready to gawp at her as she tried to escape to some form of modesty on the beach, thirty yards away. With water up to her shoulders, she greeted Krishnan and his crew amicably enough, hoping that the lengthening shadows would provide some cover for her naked form in the crystal water. A European with his arm held in a sling smiled gently down at them.

Krishnan manoeuvred and anchored the boat just off the beach opposite their campsite. Understanding her dilemma, he tactfully managed to occupy the attention of his crew as Ceci, with Harold's help, crept unseen from the water to their small shelter, where she was able to dry and dress in privacy. Again, she was surprised how excited she was at her near-nakedness in the company of so many young male strangers. As they emerged together onto the beach there was much activity a few yards from the tide line as Krishnan and his men tended the new fire, over which they were arranging various heavy, smoke-stained pans in preparation for cooking. The European walked shyly towards them as they stood in front of the fire, his arm slung across his chest.

"Hello, my name is Henrik van der Valk. I am a researcher with a Dutch pharmaceutical company. Krishnan and his brothers have given me an opportunity to see new islands for additional sources of botanical material for my research. It's nice to meet you."

Ceci smiled and carefully shook his free hand. 'He's quite handsome in a lean sort of way,' she considered, 'Pity he's lying.' Both she and Harold recognised the Dutchman, with his apparently broken arm. He had been in the operations building at Penang with the Japanese, and obviously did not recognise them, in particular Ceci, who had had to keep a low profile in view of Harvey Wills's unexpected presence there. She and Harold exchanged quizzical glances, both wondering silently who was flying the DC-2 if the Dutchman was here.

Krishnan ambled around the fire, which was now blazing, and joined them. They spent some time in general chat until the campfire meal was ready. While they were sitting on boxes and logs around the crackling flames with the boat's crew, Harold managed to isolate himself with Krishnan. He told him all about their recent experiences, of the dangerous activities of the DC-2, and the fact that they had at last sighted what they believed to be Cornucopia. Krishnan's jaw dropped at the last piece of news.

"Where is she? Will you tell me now why you have spent so much time seeking her?" he asked, in a hoarse whisper. "Are there passengers with her?" Penrose ignored the questions for the moment, and directed some questions of his own.

"How did you meet Henrik van der Valk, Krishnan?"

"My sister-in-law found Henrik. He came to my brother's fishing huts on South Andaman. He told her he had been wandering lost for some time, and was very tired when my sister-in-law looked after him. She cared for his broken arm, and later he asked to accompany us when they all returned here to Camorta at the end of the fishing season. He asked to come with us to visit you this evening. Why do you ask, do you know something of this man?"

Harold thought for a moment, then told what he knew of the Dutchman and his compatriot co-pilot, and his Japanese passengers. The DC-2 crew, whoever they were, must also know where Cornucopia now lay and possibly even knew that she may have been carrying bullion.

"When you are saying bullion, you are meaning gold?"

"Yes, Krishnan, that's exactly what I mean; it's why we've spent so much time looking for Cornucopia."

"It is a valuable prize, Mr Harold, and I think you will need some help to collect it?" Krishnan looked at Penrose pointedly, clearly expecting some definitive response.

"I promised you that we would tell you our reasons for looking for the lost Empress aircraft if and when we reached Camorta.

We have, and now you know the reason. You've helped us so far and we shall certainly need your help to reach the aircraft, its crew and cargo. Can we rely on you?"

"But of course, Harold. We just need to agree a percentage for myself, my crew and parents."

It was only at this point that Penrose fully realised the import of finding Cornucopia and any bullion she might have been carrying. The reality was translating into something very different from the almost adolescent game he and Ceci had been playing until this afternoon. If Cornucopia was actually carrying over a million dollars worth of bullion, what were they going to do with it? It could only belong to the British government and they were unlikely to let it be taken by a few opportunist fortune-seekers like themselves. The arms of the Empire were mighty long, and even in this remote area, news would eventually come out about the aircraft and its passengers. The rightful owners of the gold would want to know where it was and want it back. He had also been overcome with an unexpected feeling of patriotism. He knew why the gold was en route to England from his Swire days. He began to feel it was a duty to ensure it went to its rightful owners. The implications could be vital to his homeland.

Krishnan watched him as he struggled with the conflicting issues that now suddenly came flooding into his mind. He needed time to think, and to talk to Ceci. Standing up, leaving his meal virtually untouched, he patted Krishnan on the arm and walked off down the beach, into the dusk alone. Ceci had been watching them. She got up and followed as he walked along the surf's edge, letting the water catch his feet as each wavelet was spent.

"Harold, what's wrong?" He continued his walk, oblivious to the worried calls after him. Then he stopped, facing the ocean, and stood looking out at the slumbering, powerful, mass. Becoming aware of her and still looking out to sea, he spoke.

"Ceci, if Cornucopia was carrying gold and it's as much as we estimated, what exactly are we going to do with it, assuming we can recover it?" She looked at him, saying nothing. He went on.

"There are survivors. If any of the crew is alive then they will have responsibility for its safekeeping and presumably its return to the appropriate authorities."

"Perhaps there will be a reward for its safe return?" she said. He thought for a moment.

"What size of reward would be made for its recovery, I wonder?"

They walked further along the beach, the fine sand squeaking beneath their bare feet. By now, darkness was almost complete apart from a few early stars, and as they turned they could see Krishnan's fire still burning brightly in the distance.

They began to earnestly consider and discuss what to do next. First, who now knew the whereabouts of Cornucopia? Other than themselves, there was Krishnan, the crew of the DC-2 and, of course, the survivors, who probably did not know exactly where they were anyway. Ceci and Harold did not know either whether Harvey Wills, who had unknowingly caught them swimming together naked, had found Cornucopia as he flew around the islands. However, they did know with absolute certainty that his purpose in being there was to search for the lost aircraft, probably at the request and expense of the government and Empress Airways.

If they managed to find somewhere to land the Gypsy Moth on the island near the broken hulk and its survivors, they could fly them out, one by one, to Krishnan's village on Camorta tomorrow;

they could at least be cared for there. But what of any gold? It too could be flown out as cargo in the front cockpit, little by little, but as an increasing number of people became aware of its existence there would no doubt be problems. Alternatively, perhaps it would be best to trust Krishnan and use his boat to go to the beach where Cornucopia lay, collect the survivors and any gold and to return direct to Penang or Singapore. Could Krishnan be trusted, faced with such a fortune in his hands, they wondered?

Penrose's early dreams of keeping any recovered gold for himself and living a high life of leisure and style were fast evaporating. It seemed increasingly unrealistic as he thought matters through with Ceci. However, if there was a reward for recovery of the bullion, perhaps that would be the next best option, he pondered. They returned to the now-sleeping camp, undecided as to what to do. Krishnan watched them from his simple bed of palm leaves. The night was beautiful and around ten-thirty the moon rose in the east and cruised silently in silver elegance across a cloudless heaven. Penrose and Ceci watched its course, unable to sleep until the early hours, exhausted.

The morning started just after six o'clock, when two dented tin cups of scalding-hot tea were pushed unceremoniously into their confused hands. The sun, very low on the eastern horizon, was struggling as a bank of low cloud moved quickly towards it, pushed by an increasing wind from the west and the Bay of Bengal.

They gathered themselves together and watched the activity, sitting by the dying remains of last night's fire, cups in hand.

"We have some problem with the boat's engine. It will not start," said Krishnan, annoyed; Henrik van der Valk stood at his side, his good hand dirty with oil and grease. Ceci and Harold asked if there was anything they could do. There was nothing.

Van der Valk volunteered to go back to the boat to see if he could help the crew. He walked back to the surf's edge and waded out to the bobbing vessel, holding his injured arm up clear of the water. Penrose stood up, assessing the beach and sea: the weather was definitely changing for the worse, and they had promised to revisit the survivors today. He and Ceci downed a quick breakfast of more tea and a few slices of fresh mangoes while the wind continued to increase in strength, gusting strongly from time to time and blowing sand across the beach. Waves were beginning to crash heavily as they approached the shelving shoreline.

A few yards off, Krishnan's boat pulled taut against the single crude anchor as the crew tried to resuscitate the ancient engine in the vessel's bilge. Every so often one of the labouring crewmen would turn the starter handle for a few minutes, his head bobbing up and down above the ship's gunwale as he tried unsuccessfully to evoke life in the lazy block of iron. Their concerns increased at the growing size of the breakers now marching resolutely to shore. Their relentless progress caused the boat to snatch violently at times at the thin and worn links in the anchor chain as each swell surged powerfully underneath the straining vessel. Then, finally, there was a puff of black smoke from the tall, wobbly exhaust stack as the bobbing winder cranked the engine over for the umpteenth time, after yet more engine adjustments, and invocations to various gods and spirits. The engine settled into a regular beat and the vessel motored upwind and offshore, taking the strain from the anchor chain.

Ceci, Krishnan and Harold watched the unfolding drama from the surf's edge, open-mouthed. They saw the crew pull the anchor, its chain and thin warp aboard as the boat edged further out towards safety. They heard the blown shout from the bow crewman signalling that the ground tackle was clear and saw the increasing smoke from the exhaust stack as the throttle was opened and the boat moved out into deeper water. The crew were intending to anchor using two anchors, away from the breaking swells. About half a mile out, where steeper swells began to form as the ocean met the shelving shore, the engine suddenly stopped. The boat began to drift shoreward, uncontrolled.

From the beach they could see two crewmen and the one-armed van der Valk rushing to pull up the bottom boards covering the engine in the vessel's deep bilge. As they lifted them clear, acrid clouds of black smoke were swept to leeward, and then no more. It seemed as if some vital component had overheated and failed; the briefly seen smoke evidence of its demise.

Action on deck became increasing frenetic as they all struggled forward on the pitching deck, pulling at the anchor chain, attempting to unravel the cat's-cradle of chain and rope that had been carelessly deposited on deck just a few moments earlier. Seconds later, a few fathoms of thin chain were cast over the bow. It sank vertically towards the sea-bed. The chain, or at least a large part of it, was still tangled, which prevented its full scope being deployed. Now in deeper water, the anchor's tines failed to dig into the sea-bed. Unable to arrest the vessel's increasing shoreward drift, the crew panicked.

Krishnan could see disaster looming. He ran and plunged, cup in hand, into the sea, swimming strongly out towards the boat, which was now being thrust mercilessly by wind and waves towards the shore. He was a powerful swimmer but in the growing waves it took some minutes of real effort before he was being pulled clumsily, over the gunwale, by his worried crew.

Ceci and Harold watched, breathless, as Krishnan took charge, but all of his experience and expertise was futile. As the vessel closed on the shore, the steepening swells began to affect its stability as it eventually swung broadside to them. The inevitable happened. Within a hundred yards of where the two watchers stood, the craft suddenly rolled over in the steep, heavily breaking surf. Krishnan and crew jumped clear as the final roll began. They all surfaced, spluttering and coughing, struggling through the departing wave's suction. Their energy was sapped by physical effort and fear. Ceci took charge, leaping into the water, followed by Harold, and between them they pulled the three shocked sailors and the wincing Dutchman up the beach. Ceci settled the shivering crew around the fire, now enlivened by Harold and the increasing wind, and put a pan of water over it to boil for tea.

Harold sat with Krishnan and put a hand on his shoulder as they watched the sea play cat-and-mouse with the shallow-draught fishing boat. The wind was now blowing very hard. The seas had built strongly accompanied by the repetitive sounds of planks bursting as the long hull was lifted and pounded on the submerged beach. Before long, evidence of serious fractures became visible and items of clothing, cooking pans and other effects were soon drifting in the surf, drawn from the breached hull by the hungry water. Harold and Krishnan desperately grabbed what they could, making a small pile of recovered items. But the boat was finished, or soon would be. Turning, they trudged up the beach and joined the shocked crew and Ceci sitting silently, stunned by the rapidity of events.

Krishnan sat glumly on the sand, his knees up, and his chin resting on them.

"What are we going to do? What will my brothers say at the loss of our boat? How will we all get back to Camorta?" He sighed, in desperation.

"Don't worry about that now; at least you're all safe. We still have the Gypsy Moth. We'll find a way." Ceci patted his shoulder encouragingly. Later, while the boat crew searched among the flotsam on the beach for items worth retrieving, Harold and Ceci set about further securing the aircraft in the increasingly stormy weather. A discussion developed about what to do next as the grey overcast started shedding spots of rain that soon grew to a solid torrent. It rained on into the evening, ceasing only as darkness fell. Everyone clustered around the smouldering fire.

Krishnan thought that the beaches on Camorta were perhaps not suitable for landing an aeroplane. It was agreed, however, that he would fly with Ceci the next morning, first to drop a further note to Cornucopia's survivors advising of the situation, and then to fly to Krishnan's village to determine whether he was right about the lack of landing places. They prepared another note to drop on the village with a message to his brothers asking for help, with their location identified. The brothers owned a much larger trading vessel that could be used to rescue the crew when they returned from their extended fishing and trading voyage. The problem for them was that Krishnan did not know exactly when this would be. He wanted to add a few lines about Cornucopia and its location but this was vetoed by Harold; he was not keen to divulge this sort of information until he absolutely had to.

Soon the sky was completely black, the wind gusting across the beach and blowing new life into the glowing fire embers. The crew were soon asleep, stretched out on the damp sand under a sail supported by three sheets strategically tied to some conveniently positioned young trees. It flapped and tore noisily in the blustery conditions. Ceci and Harold sat for a few minutes then retired to their more permanent shelter within the tree line, where they flopped down onto the makeshift bed and were soon asleep.

FOURTEEN

Colonel Hyami took some time to recover from the hair-raising moments a few feet above the final resting place of Cornucopia. He sat staring blankly out of the windscreens as the aircraft droned north towards Port Blair. His Japanese captain now sat alert, but calm, occasionally adjusting the throttle settings or the aircraft's trim as they flew with the setting sun's deepening crimson rays penetrating the cockpit from the left-side windows, filling the small space with an unnatural light.

Hyami finally spoke. He had been thinking deeply, weighing up the situation, and realised that now they needed to take some action to capture the prize and transport it to some secure point, from where it could be dispatched to their homeland. He turned his gaze from beyond the windscreen and looked across at his pilot's profile, stark against the red glow.

"How much fuel do we have?" he barked.

The captain looked at the aircraft's fuel gauges and thought for a moment, doing some quick mental calculations. Hyami stared at the dark profile, unable to see the expression on his face.

"We have about four hours at normal cruise, enough to get us to Penang within two and a half to three hours, depending on wind direction and strength."

Hyami slumped back in his seat, turned and gazed unseeing out of the windscreens again. He guessed that the authorities at Penang would be interested to talk to him about the discovery of the bodies of Ng and the young Dutch co-pilot after their unusual night-time departure. There may also be questions pending about a missing night-watchman from the airfield at Port Blair and what had happened to the escaping Dutch captain van der Valk, he supposed.

Unusually, he spoke just loudly enough for his captain to hear above the engines' gentle rumble.

"We cannot go to back to Port Blair. Neither can we go to Penang – they may be waiting for us." The captain slowly turned and looked at Hyami, waiting for some new instruction but Hyami was again looking out at the run of shadow-filled islands below them. Out to the west the late sun was sinking into a dark mass of cloud hanging just above the sea's surface. The aircraft continued northwards, droning on through the deepening twilight. Hyami knew the prize could only be acquired through some bold action, but there were only two of them, and they did not have the luxury of enough fuel to allow them to collect others to help them.

"Turn around and land back on their island again." The instruction was succinct, not open to misinterpretation. The pilot again turned and looked across at Hyami, his face expressionless. His eyes engaged Hyami's for a few penetrating seconds and then, turning the control wheel gently to the right and watching the instruments and the darkening horizon, he steadied onto a southerly course. The shadows were rapidly lengthening below, each darkening island defined by a necklace of fluorescent surf as night began to settle. Both Hyami and his pilot knew the risks attached to Hyami's arbitrary order, and he felt inwardly uneasy with his decision, but it would be their only chance.

As they approached the island they descended carefully towards the sea, keen to minimise any announcement of their approach to Cornucopia's survivors. The captain curved out to sea, towards the east, intending to approach the island from the opposite side to where they had seen Cornucopia's beached wreckage. It was becoming increasingly difficult to see the detail of the land below them and both were concerned to land the machine as soon as possible, before all daylight had gone. Finally, the aircraft was suitably positioned to make an approach to the rough, shrub-strewn landing strip where they had left the body of the young Japanese co-pilot, days earlier.

With only a hundred feet to go the captain switched on two powerful landing lights positioned in the aircraft's wings. They illuminated the ground with bright yellow light, creating stark shadows in the folds of the ground – and beyond the capture of their beams. Unlike previously, when they were in a panic to get to earth before the aircraft erupted in ignited petrol fumes, the engines were kept slowly turning, providing increased control during the difficult landing. With full flap extended and the propellers set to fine pitch, the engines grumbled gently as they felt their way down towards the unlikely and hazardous landing strip. With the aircraft on the point of stalling they touched down heavily, main wheels first, the undercarriage struts compressing fully to absorb the penetrating shock. Once they were firmly in contact, the tail was lowered and firm braking applied to slow their swaying and lurching rush. Hyami shouted, even as they continued to slow.

"Switch off everything now!" The pilot understood in a second. He switched off the two pairs of magneto switches above his head, and the engines, immediately drained of sparking energy, faltered and wound quickly to a halt while the aircraft continued to trundle like a rushing elephant through the plateau's unevenly scattered flora. Quick fingers soon disengaged all the other key switches; the aircraft stopped completely without life, dark and silent, except for a regular ticking sound from within the engine cowls as the motors cooled. They opened the cockpit side-screens and sat quietly, listening. It had started to rain and the wind was strengthening.

On the beach Cornucopia's survivors heard the sound of an aircraft in the distance, hoping and assuming it was part of the rescue and failed to register that its fading engine noise was as a result of it landing on their island again, and not the machine's departure from their island's vicinity.

"I should think we can expect a rescue in the next few days with all this air activity," announced Rawlinson, smiling broadly.

"I do hope so," mused Sarah. "We must get Michael proper medical care as soon as possible. I don't want any complications with his wound now." She looked across at Michael anxiously; Beth too had noticed that Mummy was somehow changed.

Snell relit their campfire and they all sat within its glow under a strategically hung tarpaulin out of the rain, patiently awaiting the results of his culinary experimentation: the smells were titillating all their taste buds despite the smoke. During the afternoon, before the sighting of the Gypsy Moth and the shiny DC-2 and their strange aerial jousting match, Snell and the colonel had explored further along the island's coast. They had discovered wild papaya fruits and scores of coconuts, both on the ground and high up in the trees. Heavily laden, they returned to camp with their booty. David Rawlinson had also had some success in fishing off the low headland at the end of the beach, its single upright tree casting some thin but valuable shade as he sat looking out to sea. He managed to bring home three fair-sized fish that he and the others were unable to identify. They looked good enough to eat, all agreed.

Kelly was thinking about that afternoon's events, which took his mind off the continuous ache from his missing leg and foot. Possible rescue was both a relief and a worry and he pondered further the strange behaviour of the two aircraft that had found them. He was genuinely surprised to see a Gypsy Moth in such a remote location. With its limited range, how on earth had it got there, he puzzled, and come to that, where on earth was it getting its fuel from? He was unaware of any of the type in this part of the world, although he knew that one or two were based at the Singapore Aero Club. The metal monoplane, he agreed with his navigator, was probably American, a Douglas DC-2. They were a relatively new type, certainly in this part of the world. He had briefly noted that it had Dutch registration letters on the underside of its highly polished wings. That was less of a surprise to him – the Dutch had large colonial interests in the region, particularly Java – but what was inexplicable was the way the two apparent rescue aircraft had seemed intent on carrying out an aerobatic display for their benefit as they flashed over the bay and beach.

After dinner, all sat quietly looking at the glowing embers of their dying fire, imaginations working, except for the colonel. He had found the small, sodden atlas that had been taken from one of the suitcases, before they were ditched in the sea on their second day afloat. It was now dry, if somewhat warped. In the flickering light he studied the page showing the Indian Ocean and the continents bordering its huge expanse. The Andaman and Nicobar islands were shown on a larger scale in a box at the bottom of the page, but beyond there was nothing but endless sea before reaching Antarctica's wastes. Despite the improved scale it was difficult to make out each individual island, most of which were unnamed. He wanted to get an idea of exactly where they were but it was proving difficult. He walked around the fire to where Rawlinson was peering through half-closed eyelids at the diminishing glow. He knelt down,

"David, I've been trying to assess where we might be on this map. The scale's not too good and I wondered if any of your larger charts survived the beaching?"

Rawlinson looked up with a start at the colonel's silhouette.

"Sorry, I was drifting off after Mr Snell's superb alfresco dinner. What was it you asked?" David Rawlinson sat up, looking at the small pages in Deverall's hands.

"Ah, yes, I see what you mean. It is a bit small, isn't it? We could be on any one of these islands, I suppose. If I remember correctly, there are over five hundred islands in the two groups. God knows where we've ended up. Unfortunately my charts are all lost; I never managed to find even one after our beaching."

They pored over the small map, trying to gauge where they might be. They noticed the location of Port Blair and agreed that in all probability that was where the rescue effort was probably being co-ordinated from. Discussing their first sighting of land from Cornucopia, Rawlinson remarked that the clouds that they had seen had probably bubbled up from the humid land masses under them. They had tended to stretch northwards, away from their seaward position, suggesting that the bulk of the island chain's mass was to the north of them.

"So, if that were the case, and it's pretty flimsy evidence, we may be somewhere in this southerly group of islands," said Rawlinson, his finger circling a clutch of twenty or so dots and smudges on the water-stained map. They both sat back and thought about it briefly until sleep overcame them.

❖ ❖ ❖

Hyami and his pilot sat for almost an hour waiting to see if there would be any reaction to their noisy landing. As the time passed, the noise of the jungle gradually resumed to a low crescendo as their presence was accepted, and for a while the rain pattered noisily onto the aluminium skin of the aircraft. After the rain stopped, they stirred, carefully leaving the aircraft, both armed with heavy-calibre pistols and a torch. Hyami and the captain split up and went in separate directions, intending to reconnoitre their immediate surroundings. Individually they stumbled away from the aircraft in the near-dark towards the perimeter of the makeshift landing area, occasionally falling over larger tussocks of undergrowth or broken branches.

Suddenly the captain uttered a deep groan. Hyami heard him rushing through the flora mumbling, breathing heavily. In the dark the pilot had tripped over the decomposing remains of his erstwhile co-pilot, which were subject to the attention of various creatures anxious to partake of well-ripened meat and tissue evident in the torchlight. A host of flies accompanied the horror of the moment, still laying and gorging on the almost unidentifiable cadaver, dark in the tropical night.

Both men reached the door of the aircraft at the same time, the pilot clearly disgusted and shocked by his discovery and experience, only wishing to get into the cabin, away from the mix of horror and pity he felt for his dead young colleague. Hyami climbed the short metal ladder into the fuselage and pulled the door closed, he switched on the light over the entrance area, its feeble glow illuminating the white, shocked Japanese pilot. He had managed to drop his gun in his wild rush back to the safety of the aircraft, and Hyami quietly scolded him as he sat shaking in one of the passenger seats, the same one Ng had occupied before his fatal escape attempt.

They spent an uncomfortable night in the aircraft, and slept little. As early-morning grey turned yellow with the rising sun over the surrounding trees, they slowly ate the small amount of cold rice remaining from the previous day's lunch, washed down with brackish warm water from the aircraft's near depleted galley tank.

Hyami stood on the top step of the aircraft ladder and surveyed the surrounding area. He could see that they had landed along the same path as their previous, fraught visit. From the direction of the landing run he knew in which direction Cornucopia lay, broken on a beach to the west side of the island. How far it actually was he had no real idea, but that was not his key consideration for the present. First they had to find the lost gun and second, they must formulate some plan for taking the gold, assuming it was still recoverable. Hyami sat in the doorway of the aircraft thinking of how to accomplish the latter, with minimum risk to himself.

The pilot had finally fallen asleep and was snoring gently, his head relaxed, lolling out into the aircraft aisle. Hyami noticed his shirt and trousers were stained and badly torn in places, no doubt from his panicked run through the wet undergrowth in the dark. Moving up through the narrow aisle, he entered the cockpit and on finding some charts there, wrote a note indicating that when he awoke the pilot was to retrace his steps from the previous night and find his pistol, then to remain with the aircraft. In the meantime, Hyami was going to investigate the location of the broken Cornucopia on the beach, find out how many survivors there were, and if possible, locate the gold bullion – without attracting attention.

Taking a half-full water bottle and checking his pistol, he pulled on his kepi, moving towards the tree line bordering the plateau. The going was difficult, with dense masses of greenery struggling for light beneath the high canopy of the trees. He seriously wished he had a machete, or even a bayonet. Below the canopy the temperature rose steadily, and so did the humidity, a result of the sun's relentless climb into a near-cloudless sky. Sweating profusely and cursing silently, Hyami was driven by a need to accomplish his plan, to maintain face with his superiors at Imperial Army HQ in Tokyo.

❖ ❖ ❖

Ceci struggled with the huge drum of petrol, rolling it towards the Gypsy Moth. Her progress was slowed by the drum's constant digging into the beach's soft sand as it tried to change direction of its own volition. Harold woke late. A good deal of the early hours he had spent pondering their situation, wondering how best to arrive at a solution that would ensure they gained something from recovering the bullion, assuming it was still in or around the flying boat. More important for him now was the retention of Ceci's affection for him. He dearly hoped it was something a lot more than just affection and friendship from her – he suspected strongly it probably was. In any event, he knew now that he was genuinely in love with her, despite her being officially engaged to another.

Dressing quickly, he heard Ceci talking loudly to someone and moved out of their crude shelter under the palms to see who. She was gently cursing the barrel of fuel, which lay on its side, and trying to lift it upright so that she could insert the simple hand pump into its top. The barrel contained about thirty-five gallons of petrol, weighed some two hundred and fifty pounds, and was proving very awkward for her to lift upright on her own.

He watched her struggling for a while, a smile slowly forming on his lips. Suddenly the barrel sat up as she heaved all of her eight and a half stone at it. As it did so, she was taken by surprise, falling back in the sand with a dull thump. Penrose laughed out loud. Surprised, she turned to look at him.

"Harold Penrose, you bastard! How long have you been watching me struggle?" She shouted, her eyes flashing with a mixture of annoyance and fun.

"Ceci, you were doing so well, I thought I'd leave you to it," he laughed and walked towards her, helping her off the sand and into his arms. She stayed a moment, enjoying the feeling, then pulled away in mock anger.

"Well, you can jolly well fill both bloody tanks on your own. Here, take the pump and get on with it!" She threw the small pump at him and strode back to their shelter, kicking the sand deliberately, and smiling happily to herself. Fully fuelled with twenty-nine gallons of their rapidly depleting petrol supply, the Gypsy Moth was ready for anything. Krishnan's crew had helped with the pumping and were now trying to coax some life from a small paraffin stove they had rescued from their broken craft.

❖ ❖ ❖

In Singapore, things were different for Ceci's parents. Their concern for their daughter had now escalated from annoyance at her unthinking lack of contact to real worry that something untoward had happened to their daughter. Their woes were intensified by a report in a local newspaper that had somehow heard of the young woman's disappearance so shortly after the reported loss of Cornucopia. Two aircraft had gone missing in the space of a few days and the local press were in heaven. Reports were also reaching Singapore about the finding of an unidentified aircraft wheel, lodged, it was said, in some rocks on a beach off the Malay coast. Ceci's father put his arm around his wife's trembling shoulder, an uncharacteristic gesture.

"Don't be too concerned, dear. I'm sure she'll be in touch soon. You know how impetuous she can be at times. I've a feeling that that wretched man Penrose has something to do with this. God help him if that is the case." He was just managing to contain his anger.

"Calm down, Charles. We don't know anything at the moment. I just pray she's safe somewhere. When is Harvey going to be back from his search?"

He said nothing as they sat quietly together for a few moments. Then Ceci's mother rose from the sofa and walked towards the open terrace windows. Turning back towards the morning cool of the room, she looked at her husband, who was still sitting. His face was down and his shoulders unusually hunched. He looked up at her briefly and a beam of sunlight streaming through the window shone onto tears that were welling up in his eyes. He was as near to crying as he had ever been since he was a boy of six, left after an unemotional farewell, at his first boarding school.

They heard the phone ring and then a servant came in to say that the Singapore garrison commander sent his compliments and had requested a meeting at HQ in forty-five minutes. Nodding, Charles rose from the sofa and crossed towards the door, then, turning, walked back to his wife and kissed her gently on the mouth before leaving the house. His wife touched his hand lightly; it was a long time since her husband had made any physical move towards her. From the shade of the large, tiled hallway, she watched him climb into the khaki staff car, conscious of sickly fumes from its exhaust as the driver gunned it up the long drive, which was overhung with a variety of exotic cultivated plants. Her feelings were a curious emotional mix as she briefly touched her lips with her fingers.

❖ ❖ ❖

Harold and Ceci decided that the first step would be to try to land on the island as close as possible to where the remains of Cornucopia lay. To maximise their chances, he suggested that Ceci fly without Krishnan on this initial reconnaissance trip, as his weight may affect her options on landing sites when she reached the island. Apart from reducing the landing and take-off run, it would also help to economise on the fuel used and help her rate of climb after take-off; particularly important, she emphasised to him, if the landing strip was short with tall trees at either end. The other option that lay open, she pointed out, was that the empty front seat might prove of value in carrying out a survivor or some bullion. Having discussed matters for some time, Ceci was keen to be off and the aircraft was manoeuvred into place ready for take-off. Harold, now something of an expert, swung the propeller. The engine burst into life, its signature sound reverberating off the surrounding jungle. Birds flew and screeched above the tree canopy as Ceci taxied carefully down to the water's edge, where the receding tide had once again left firmer, wet sand.

With the final brief checks completed, she turned toward Harold, standing with Krishnan and his boat crew in the shade, waved, and then slowly opened the throttle. As the aircraft responded to forward speed she pushed the stick forwards after a few seconds, lifting the tail, and concentrated on keeping the small machine straight on the uneven surface. Within seconds she was airborne, clearing the delicately waving tops of trees at the end of their beach by a good fifty feet. Banking, she turned slowly through a hundred and eighty degrees and, still climbing, glanced downwards, seeing her man, standing alone, staring up at her from beneath the shade of his hands over his eyes. She smiled behind her goggles, and gently rocked the machine's wings.

The flight was uneventful. She approached the crash site on the west side of the island as slowly as she dared. There it was, only the large section of broken fuselage of the once huge flying boat gave any indication that it had been a powerful, four-engine aeroplane, capable of flying passengers across the world in comfort and luxury. There appeared to be little activity on the beach as she flew over, just above the surrounding trees with the engine throttled back, idling. One figure, a man, she could see, suddenly looked up from what he was doing over the remains of a fire and waved vigorously. Two or three others emerged from the shadowy tree line, including a child, belatedly responding, and she gently waggled the Gypsy Moth's wings in acknowledgement. Opening up to cruise revolutions, Ceci gently flew out to sea. It was clear that there was no possibility of landing on the beach where the broken machine and its survivors lay. It was too short, with tall trees at either end and debris scattered along the foreshore, which precluded it as a safe option.

Turning, she flew along the coastline only a few feet above the gently rolling, crystal-clear ocean, all the time looking for an alternative landing place on one of the island's other nearby beaches. There were none to the north, along the increasingly rocky coast. The only beaches that might otherwise have been suitable had obstructions ranging from rocky outcrops thrusting up through their narrow strip of sand to the wreck of a formerly substantial steel ship. Other sites had tall trees at either end of a possible runway, preventing a good landing approach. She turned and, climbing back to a thousand feet, and passing the survivors on the way, set off to look for a suitable site to the south of their location. The story was much the same as in the north; there seemed to be no viable options within reasonable walking distance.

Cruising back towards the survivors' beach, she considered the situation. It seemed blindingly obvious to her now that any rescue would have to be undertaken by boat. Krishnan's brothers would have to be instrumental in this. Circling the survivors' beach, she waved encouragement, dropped her prepared message and then turned to fly across the interior of the island.

Pulling gently back on the stick and increasing engine revolutions, she began a steep climb, aiming to cross the plateau in the centre of the island at almost two and a half thousand feet. As she approached the rising ground, heat and humidity was making the air unstable and very bumpy; the aircraft lurched in the active thermals as it slowly gained height in the hot air. Now she could just see the ocean in the distance, on the far side of the island: it was deep-blue and looked cool and inviting. Ceci thought for a moment about a swim when she got back to Harold and the others. Beyond, in the distance, lay Camorta, with Krishnan's village perched on its south-eastern end. The turbulence was increasing and she began to feel distinctly uncomfortable. She was unused to conditions like these, now and again having difficulty in controlling the flight path of her small aircraft. Her brow furrowed with anxiety, she began to perspire with the effort, and began to worry about what would happen if she found that she could not cope.

Glancing down from time to time, Ceci tried to estimate how far it was before she would be over the ocean again on the eastern side of the island, where she knew the air would be less boisterous. Suddenly, something flashed in an instant, catching her eye; it seemed to originate on the ground, in among the green at the far, northern end, of the plateau. Briefly it took her mind off her predicament lurching unpredictably and violently through the air. A few moments later she looked quickly again towards where she thought she had seen the brilliant flash. Nothing. 'Must have been imagining it,' she rationalised as she tried to deal calmly with the continuing turbulence. To her left she noticed that the ground had started to fall away more rapidly than the terrain ahead on her present heading. That might mean less turbulence, she reasoned. Keen for any respite from the surging, bubbling air, she turned the machine slightly more northerly to take any advantage it might offer.

Levelling from the turn, she caught sight of an aircraft shining brightly, the late-morning sun reflecting off its polished-aluminium wings and fuselage top. She could see that it was stopped at the end of a strip of torn and churned scrubland, standing all alone, just beyond the line of trees that ringed the plateau. Goodness, she wondered, how did that get there? Had it crashed? No, it was standing on its undercarriage. As she circled closer she could see that the aircraft door was shut and there appeared to be no sign of life. Perhaps it was a rescue aircraft and they were on their way to the beach; she hoped it was a possibility, between controlling her bouncing Moth and trying to see more. Banking away, she considered a landing along the strip carved along the plateau by what she now recognised to be the infamous Dutch-registered DC-2. It had tried to destroy them just the day before. The DC-2, being heavier and more robustly constructed, had managed to get down in one piece and apparently without damage, pushing aside or rolling over any obstructions that hindered its progress. She decided her lightly built aircraft would never survive a landing on such a rough and torn surface.

Finally, out over the sea again, she set course for Camorta, dropping her second prepared message for Krishnan's brothers into the beachside village. It was almost deserted; no boats lay on the beach, nor anchored offshore. Near the huts she could see some women and two small children. They ran into one of the huts as she passed over. Dropping the message and half-satisfied that she had done what she could, she set course for their island base, her mind brimming with ideas.

Harold heard the telltale noise of the de Havilland Gypsy engine and, with the boat's crew, watched Ceci position the small machine for a landing. It was approaching spring tides, the water was now fully up and the strip of sand along their beach was both narrow and dry, with the onshore breeze gusting heavily at times. Ceci made three attempts to land on the narrow, difficult sand strip, each time opening the throttle as the aircraft danced just above stalling as she progressed along the beach. She was feeling very tired after the stress of the earlier turbulence. Now, trying to land successfully in conditions that a highly experienced pilot would find challenging was sapping her last reserves of energy and skill.

She knew that her rate of descent was too high and as she opened the throttle too much, it pitched the nose of the aircraft up. Closing the throttle again, too quickly, the nose fell away as she tried to regain some speed and control. Her erratic flight path brought Harold's hand to his face; he mouthed her name as he watched the Gypsy Moth. To his inexpert eye it seemed like a disaster in the making. Her starboard lower wing brushed the tops of the trees on approach, and the lower positioning of the undercarriage tore away a few slim fronds. It was too late; she was committed to a landing when the prudent thing to do would have been to go around for yet another attempt, much earlier in her erratic approach. But her tiredness was telling, she had cast all her training and caution to the winds, preferring to rely on fate and good luck for a landing of sorts.

The main wheels hit the beach with an audible thump, throwing a mist of dry sand into the quivering air. Harold saw the rudder working rapidly side to side as Ceci tried to control the direction of the machine. It swerved from side to side; the tail-skid, now in contact with the ground, was tearing huge swirling rents in the soft surface. Suddenly the tail began to rise. The nose pitched towards the ground. Harold saw in an instant what was about to happen. A slow-motion picture unfolded in his mind. If the propeller contacted the ground it would splinter. The shock would cause severe damage to the inside of the engine.

There was another dull thud as the tail hit the sand again and the Gypsy Moth spun to the left and then drained the last of its energy in the ocean as it ploughed finally into the small waves butting the shore.

Wading knee-deep to the cockpit, he lowered the small side door, remotely conscious that his feet were in the waves. She was sobbing, great, sparkling tears running down her pale cheeks; shaking as he pulled the pin from her safety harness and tried to pull her upright and get her to step out of the aircraft.

He carried her across the short stretch of water, up the beach and into the shade of the trees. Ceci held onto him tight, her arms around his neck, still sobbing. Lowering her onto the sand, he sat beside her trying to comfort her and understand what she was saying, amid her gasping breaths. Krishnan and his crew pulled the Gypsy Moth from the water, expertly supervised by the Dutchman.

Finally, Ceci calmed and her story came out. Instinctively they knew that the Japanese were aboard the DC-2 and were determined to take any bullion the wrecked Cornucopia contained. For Harold, the situation assumed a new dimension, a new burst of patriotism and anger suddenly flooding his thoughts. A foreign power, possibly one threatening the Empire, was trying to steal gold that was intended to help England prepare to defend herself against a tyrant in Europe. They had to warn Cornucopia's survivors, if it was not already too late.

Much later, after their communal evening meal, Ceci decided it was time to confront Henrik van der Valk. She and Harold had discussed his presence the previous evening. Why was he really here, and what did he know? Still slightly shaken by his shipwreck experience, van der Valk was mentally unprepared to be questioned. Caught off-guard, he explained what had happened when they had chartered the DC-2 to three Japanese businessmen and their Singaporean partner, who claimed to be looking for the lost Cornucopia; and how he had witnessed at first hand the murder of his co-pilot and the Singaporean. He described his dramatic escape from the Japanese crew prior to their take-off from Port Blair's grass airstrip – his pain and fever after these events – and then being lost in the darkness and wandering about the island before being looked after by Krishnan's sister-in-law; this, he explained, was why he had taken no action in reporting the grisly events.

Harold made it clear that they had known all along that he was lying about his presence among Krishnan's family, and his glib clap-trap about being a pharmaceutical researcher when they had first met. Now he had been prompted, Henrik recalled the discussions in the flight office at Penang with the RAF crew about the possible location of the downed aircraft but still did not recall Harold from that time; Ceci had made herself scarce to avoid meeting her fiancé then.

With the weight of the deception off his mind Henrik van der Valk slowly became more expansive. He suspected that the Japanese were interested in something more than searching for the dead Singaporean's lost relative, although he did not know what. He now knew that two of the Japanese trade officials were exceptional pilots and were illegally using his machine for some purpose relating to the lost flying boat. Ceci and Harold recognised that they were now dealing with a situation that was deadly, which perhaps explained the dangerous antics of the DC-2 over the wreck site, when its pilots appeared determined to push them out of control, into the sea.

"What exactly is your interest in this crashed machine, and how does Krishnan fit into things?" van der Valk asked, quietly. His question implied that Krishnan had not mentioned that Cornucopia was thought to be carrying bullion on her final flight. He watched their eyes as they considered their answer; holding his broken arm gingerly – although it had not actually suffered any as a result of his plunge through the surf.

Harold spoke first. It was an opportunity for him to clarify his own thoughts about the situation, while at the same time making clear to Ceci his stance over the possible recovery of the bullion.

"It is possible that Cornucopia was carrying a high-value cargo, possibly bullion, belonging to His Majesty's Government. Our interest in this cargo, assuming that it still exists, is to ensure that it is safely returned to its rightful owners." Short and sweet, although he knew he sounded like a pompous civil servant.

"So the aircraft was carrying gold in some form. You haven't mentioned any passengers – like the Singaporean's relative?" There was a short pause before van der Valk continued, "It must explain why the Japanese are so very interested."

Harold had decided that, as van der Valk was with them, he would be bound to find out sooner or later what they were up to, either from Krishnan, or from them if he were involved in the eventual rescue of Cornucopia's survivors. He decided that, in view of the circumstances, and the obvious cold-heartedness of the Japanese crew, to have van der Valk on their side was preferable; he might be able to provide detailed information about Japanese and the twin-engine aircraft.

"Yes, Henrik, we are pretty sure that Cornucopia was carrying gold bullion as cargo destined for England. Whether it's still on board we have no idea. We've seen the state of the wreck from the air. It's a sorry mess, not much of it still together."

FIFTEEN

Colonel Hyami's navigation through the island's jungle undergrowth was less than reliable. After almost four hours he staggered onto a narrow strip of sand overlooking the ocean. He sat, back against a tree, thankful for the onshore breeze. Perspiration poured from his brow, and his shirt was wet with the effort in the rising humidity. He was, however, not sure now where he was in relation to the wrecked Cornucopia. The ocean glittered in front of him but he knew that his immediate priority was fresh water, to replace the huge amounts he had lost while fighting his way through the unordered green mass, solid from the peak to the beaches of the island. He recognised too easily that he had been foolish in not completely filling his water bottle from the remainder of their supply in the aircraft.

Cooler after half an hour resting, he struggled to his feet and moved cautiously out from the tangled tree line and thick undergrowth onto the sand and into full sun, its glare reflecting painfully off the pale sand. His ears were alert to any human sound but all that he heard was the gentle noise of the sea lapping the shore and the background hum of insects and the occasional shriek of birds somewhere in the jungle. Which way should he go – north or south? He considered the idea for a few moments, trying to remember the fleeting views he had had as they flew low over the site of the wrecked aircraft's final resting place. Instinctively he felt he should go north – up the coast. He believed that he may have overcompensated in tending more towards the south in his trajectory while struggling from the DC-2 down the steep covered slopes to the shore. Setting off northwards, he trudged heavily through the loose sand, trying to stay close to the shade of the trees but the route was littered with their roots ready to trip the weary.

His ears suddenly picked up the faint sound of an engine; he had become aware of its dull drone growing louder. Looking out to sea expecting to see a boat, he soon realised that the noise was developing too fast for a seaborne vessel. Then, as the noise increased, he realised instantly it was an aircraft. There, just about half a mile from the shore, a small blue-and-silver biplane flew a hundred feet or so from the sea's surface. Hidden, he quickly recognised the biplane as a Gypsy Moth, and ducked back further under cover as it flew past his position. He could see the pilot scanning the shoreline; the sun occasionally reflecting off goggles. Hyami surmised that the pilot was looking for a place to land, to make contact with Cornucopia's survivors. As the engine sound faded he determined to find the wreck as quickly as possible, and strode out as well as the sand and his short legs would allow along the shoreline northwards, towards what he hoped was his goal. An hour passed and he was feeling distinctly weak. Lack of water and any sort of decent meal over the past few days had depleted his physical reserves, but his mind gave no respite.

Climbing and clinging halfway up a tree he could see that the coastline trended out slightly towards the west, finally forming the southerly arm of a small, almost symmetrical round bay. To reduce the distance, he decided to cut across the top of the thin peninsula, through the trees and undergrowth, rather than follow the lengthier sandy coastline route. He moved slowly through the undergrowth, stopping every so often to catch his breath and to cool off a little. On his third stop he heard the faint tinkle of splashing water; it sounded not too far from his resting place. Carefully listening, he tried to determine from which direction the noise was coming. Stealthily, he moved towards its apparent source until, after a few minutes, he parted the greenery and was confronted with a small run-off of cool, clear water rippling down a rock face, before falling a few feet into a small, natural rocky basin below.

Splashing unhesitatingly through overflowing crystal-clear pools, he moved quickly, now almost manically to the falling water, scooping it off the face of the smooth rock above him, drinking it in with relief. It was nectar to his parched throat: cool, fresh and reviving. Suddenly, above his own noise he heard human sounds. Voices and laughter reached him. Taking a last handful of the clear liquid, he moved back quickly and silently into the surrounding undergrowth. Peering back he noticed one or two boot-prints in the surrounding damp area. With seconds to spare he obliterated any suggestion of his presence with a frond of broad leaves brushed hastily across the surface.

A little European girl burst into the watery clearing and ran splashing into the same shallow pools, laughing and giggling, picking up handfuls of water and throwing them back at an accompanying blonde woman. The woman pretended to chase the child, and there were squeals of laughter.

Colonel Hyami was not a family man, but his twin sister in faraway Kobe had two small children and he loved to play with them on the very few occasions he was able to visit them on army leave. Carefully hidden, he watched, entranced, as the little girl played in the running water while the blonde woman attempted to wash the wriggling, splashing child. There was constant laughter and shouting as each tried to soak the other. Finally, the little girl was deemed clean enough by the woman and was roughly dried and dressed before being sent back alone, along the path by which they had arrived. The woman remained, removing her torn blouse and shortened skirt. She hung her underwear onto a nearby branch, stepped into the pool and tried to get some sort of shower from the dwindling waterfall.

Hyami watched. He had never seen a naked white woman and was riveted by the scene through the leaves. Aroused, he recalled the exciting times with the two Singaporean girls in his rooms and thought what a satisfying conquest this tall, blonde European would be in suitable circumstances. She finished quickly, dried herself and dressed, leaving the pools and waterfall empty except for Hyami.

Leaving time for others to follow, Hyami remained concealed for a further half-hour before stepping out of his observation point. Carefully, he took a few more scoops of water to his mouth, filled his empty water bottle and turned onto the narrow path that obviously led to the survivors' camp and, he hoped, the bullion. Deciding not to risk using their pathway he moved slowly and infinitely carefully through the dense foliage on a line roughly parallel to the path. The view ahead lightened as he approached the beach. Stopping some yards short, he found a place where he could observe the area of the small bay where the wreck of the aircraft lay. He could plainly see the torn fuselage on its side with holes through which an occasional wave emerged. In the surf some way out he made out what appeared to be one of the flying boat's engines and distorted propeller regularly covered by water as the ranks of sparkling waves marched shorewards.

The blonde woman was standing over a man who sat with his back against a tree; they were obviously discussing something important, there was a great deal of gesticulation and pointing. Hyami could also see the child playing intently with something in the sand a few feet away from the talking adults. She wore a crude sunhat made from broad leaves, as did the seated man. Then, Hyami became aware of another man coming into the picture from his left. He was walking slowly, from the direction of the larger part of the aircraft wreck, dragging a large box through the sand; there was an occasional glint of water running from it. He plainly heard the man shout something, the seated man and the woman stopped talking and looked up towards him. The woman ran to the man with the box and held onto a handle at one end. She and the man carried the box to the seated man and dropped it carelessly beside him. Clearly it was very heavy.

The seated man moved towards it awkwardly – there was something odd about the way he moved, thought Hyami – and then the woman bent and helped him to stand. He could see that the man had no right leg below the knee; the stub appeared heavily bandaged and he was balancing on a forked stick tucked up under his arm. He also seemed to be wearing a sort of military-style khaki jacket. They were gathered around the box on the sand looking at it for a few minutes, and then the fit man walked towards a pile of Cornucopia's wreckage and extracted a long length of metal. Returning, Hyami saw him use it to prise open part of the box, which he could hear squeaking and splintering from where he was. The box was turned over and kicked a couple of times, then lifted; it appeared to be much lighter, its contents gone. The woman bent down and picked something up with both hands, cradling the object and laughing. The facts did not need to be written down for Hyami; he could see well enough even from his concealed location that the woman was caressing an ingot of pure gold. Every so often its cast facets caught the sun.

Watching every move, Hyami saw the fit man show the one-legged man another ingot. They were obviously discussing something. Then the fit man walked towards some trees on the fringe of their campsite and started to dig with a crude implement fashioned from part of the broken box. 'So there might be more,' thought Hyami, watching the man finally deposit the broken box with the ingots back inside into the hole and cover it again. He made a mental note of the location, and that there appeared to be only four survivors – the blonde woman and child he had seen showering, a thin, fit man and a crippled male in the remains of a sort of uniform jacket. He was pleased, fortunately, not many had survived. He turned slowly and deliberately, making his way with noiseless care back into the deeper vegetation. He set out with renewed motivation, back to the DC-2 parked at the furthest end of the island's central plateau, high above him.

Hyami knew now that there was some bullion at the wreck site and this, despite his exhausted condition, gave him new energy to grapple with the tangled undergrowth that grew abundantly on the slopes beneath the tree canopy. Physically exhausted, wet with perspiration and a dry mouth, he finally reached the DC-2. Clambering up the metal boarding ladder, he collapsed onto the nearest seat, breathing heavily. His pilot was nowhere to be seen. When he had recovered, after some time, he raised himself again, annoyed, and stood in the aircraft's open doorway looking about. Then he heard a faint noise off to his right. Taking his pistol from its holster, he crept, cat-like, towards the source of the noise, in his right hand the black snub-nose of the heavy-calibre weapon sniffed ahead, its safety catch off. Through the shrubbery he could see someone; it was his pilot, labouring at something on the ground, out of his sight.

As he arrived, Hyami could see that the pilot had almost completed the burial of his deceased and already partly decomposed comrade. Hyami was pleased to see that the lost pistol was tucked securely into the pilot's belt, recovered as ordered, after the previous evening's panic.

When the work was finished, Hyami briefed the pilot on what he had seen at the wreck site and they began to discuss their options. They knew that there were at least two other parties interested in rescuing the survivors and any bullion from the wrecked flying boat. His pilot reported seeing the Gypsy Moth flying over the DC-2's semi-concealed position earlier in the day. Hyami responded with his sighting of the same aircraft along the beach. As far as he could see, there was only one fit male in the survivors' group, and he doubted that they were armed. Hyami and his pilot, however, he pointed out, were two fit males, armed and militarily trained. They considered that they could make a surprise attack on the survivors' camp, liquidate the two males and if necessary the woman and child, after getting them to confirm the whereabouts of the bullion in detail.

The one insurmountable problem was moving any gold to a safe place before any of the other parties could do so. The option of carrying it to the DC-2 at its position on the plateau was discounted. It would take too long, even using the fit male survivor to help. And there would be limitations on how much they could carry in the aircraft, assuming the gold could be delivered there. He still was not sure what over a million dollars' worth of gold looked like, or how much it weighed.

It had taken him nearly four hours to travel unladen from the DC-2 down to the beach in partial darkness: going the other way, fully laden, would be time-consuming and a serious physical challenge. In addition, the usable length of their makeshift, vegetation-strewn and rough airstrip was very short, bordered at each end with some very tall trees. In the heat and humidity, even with their low fuel state and with only two people on board, take-off would be dangerous, as they both well remembered from their previous emergency visit. Adding the bullion's weight into the take-off equation was perhaps not an option – although at present they were not aware of how much gold there was.

Both Japanese knew that to land at any airfield within Malaya, India, at Port Blair or even Singapore could lead to their being arrested on suspicion of murder, although Hyami was confident he could satisfactorily cast blame onto the Dutch charter captain for these events. There was one other thing that still concerned them: they were still not sure what had happened to the Dutch charter pilot after his unfortunate escape, alive they assumed, from the aircraft at Port Blair.

They spent almost the whole night looking at possibilities and decided on a risky strategy but probably the only one open to them.

❖ ❖ ❖

By mid-afternoon the other three Cornucopia survivors returned to the camp, having seen the small biplane again as they fished or gathered edible fruits. Colonel Deverall had not proved so successful a fisherman as David Rawlinson. He brought only one medium-sized fish back after three hours of effort – he admitted to having fallen asleep at one point in the warm sun. Snell and Rawlinson, however, had managed to collect a wide variety of fruits and later Snell started to prepare, with Sarah Gregson's help, the evening meal. While they cooked and ate supper, the atmosphere was quite light-hearted; the new note dropped that day from the Gypsy Moth told them that rescue efforts were still under way. The alien boot-marks in the sand that surrounded their communal shower facilities had gone unseen and all seemed to be well.

❖ ❖ ❖

In Ceci's camp there was an air of depression after the catastrophic events of the last twenty-four hours. They knew that they had to warn the survivors of the possible dangers to them from the Japanese-crewed DC-2 she had seen on their island's central plateau. They had just about four gallons of fuel left in the drum originally left by Krishnan, plus about twelve gallons remaining, as far as they could determine, in the Gypsy Moth's two tanks. It was enough for about two hours' careful flying, possibly more if she was not carrying a passenger in the front seat. In still air Ceci reckoned she would have about 140 miles range, but she was too aware that much would depend on wind direction: a headwind, depending on its strength, could seriously reduce this range. Alternatively, a tailwind could extend the distance that she could fly before finally having to land to avoid running out of fuel.

One thing was unalterable: the distance from their base to Port Blair. There they could alert the authorities; it was estimated by Ceci to be about two hundred and forty miles in a straight line. Together, they sat dispersed around the campfire pondering the matter as evening quickly gave way to tropical night. Krishnan was unsure when his brothers would return to Camorta with their larger boat so it was decided that for the moment they would have to discount help from that quarter. What of the Royal Air Force and Ceci's fiancé? The Walrus aircraft had not been seen since Ceci and Harold had escaped naked from the water, and its pilot's prying eyes, during their evening swim some days before.

They also discussed the possibility of her flying alone south-east to Banda Aceh in Sumatra, but this was discouraged for two reasons. Henrik van der Valk had had experience of the country. Firstly, he said that it would be unwise to alert the authorities there to the possibility of a large cache of bullion, and secondly, she would have to fly over a hundred and seventy miles of ocean, without any 'safety' islands en route. In any event, without a good tailwind to assist she would not be able to make it. The implications were clear: if Ceci had any engine problems while flying north she would at least have a chance to force-land onto or near one of the many islands, whereas if there were engine problems while she was flying south-east to Banda Aceh it would probably end in disaster. There were no islands; only the sea for 170 miles. Harold readily concurred with the Dutchman, reaching out and holding Ceci close to him at the thought.

It was finally agreed that Ceci would fly alone to the island of Car Nicobar, about ninety miles north of their island base, and try to land there. Depending on the winds at the time it was unlikely she would be able to return by air unless she could find a source of suitable aviation fuel, and engine oil – it was also becoming critical. Unlikely, they all agreed, at such a remote location. Car Nicobar lay at the southern limit of the Ten Degree Channel, the geographic divide between the Nicobar and Andaman Island groups.

Krishnan knew of a number of settlements on the island and thought that it should be possible to arrange for a boat of some sort to carry Ceci across the Ten Degree Channel northwards to Port Blair, where she could contact and raise the alarm with the appropriate district authorities. On her way flying north, she would divert slightly from her direct track to drop another note to Cornucopia's survivors, warning them about the Japanese, the possible threat they posed and advising of her planned course of action.

They all spent a restless and cold night waiting for dawn to announce its arrival, hoping for clear skies. As the eastern horizon began to lighten, Harold, Krishnan and van der Valk manoeuvred the Gypsy Moth to the end of the beach, its nose facing into a gently growing morning breeze. The remaining fuel was collected and pumped carefully from the drum into the aircraft's tanks by Harold. He then spent some time inspecting the aircraft looking for anything that might create a problem for his Ceci, who was still sleeping.

With the aircraft prepared, Harold gently woke Ceci with a now-customary tin mug of hot tea. She looked at him and smiled, brushing her tousled hair from her face but he could sense her apprehension. She looked exhausted. She knew that a lot depended on her reaching some form of authority that could help them rescue Cornucopia's crew and passengers and salvage any bullion on board. Dressing quietly, she contemplated the responsibility that lay with her. Then, refusing any breakfast, she made her way to the aircraft, with her flying jacket and cream linen helmet over her arm.

Harold walked with his arm gently around her shoulder, encouraging. At the aircraft she became a professional airwoman again, checking engine oil, fuel, rigging and controls. Harold followed her around at a distance, not mentioning that he had undertaken all of these essential tasks while she slept. Satisfied, Ceci climbed into the small rear cockpit and conducted a series of brief checks there until finally she shouted, "Switches off, fuel on, throttle set." Harold tickled the small button on top of the engine's carburettor until he heard petrol running from its overflow pipe onto the sand below. He closed and secured the starboard engine cowl, then pulled the propeller through six turns, sucking the potent petrol-and-air mixture into the engine's four large cylinders. Checking that the two large stones that served as chocks under the aircraft's wheels were secure, he stood poised, ready to start the engine.

"Switches on!" he shouted.

He looked at Ceci. She responded with a quick movement, flicking both magneto switches to 'on', and showed him a thumbs-up. Harold pulled the propeller swiftly down, as he had been taught. The engine fired immediately, crackling away, warming up. Henrik and Harold stood on either side of the aircraft as it warmed, awaiting a hand signal from Ceci to remove the makeshift stone chocks. After a few minutes she was ready. Checking that the message for the survivors was easily accessible, she looked up and waved the chocks away. Once they had been tugged clear, the engine was throttled up and the aircraft immediately started its take-off roll. She turned for a second, smiling at Harold, then, tail up, she was gone, turning out to sea as she climbed the small biplane into the clear blue morning.

In the cockpit she noted her time of take-off and set the compass to steer 355 degrees, almost due north. As she was climbing, the islands below her provided a series of huge visual stepping-stones leading towards the Ten Degree Channel and her destination, Car Nicobar Island.

As she approached the survivors' island and their beach, she grasped her message tightly, tied up in a piece of white cotton with a large stone attached. Overhead the wreck site she could see no one on the beach. Circling out to sea she flew back again, hoping the Gypsy engine's noise would prompt some reaction. Nothing. Although she had enough fuel to get her to Car Nicobar, she was worried about spending too much time cruising over the apparently vacant beach. It was odd, she thought, no one about, as, throttling back, she gently descended towards the broken Cornucopia.

In the absence of anyone below, she wanted to drop the message somewhere that it would easily be seen and read. Now gliding, with the engine quietly ticking over, she readied herself, intending to drop the message in an area that was obviously well used, judging by the disturbed sand and the remains of a campfire. As she settled closer to the trees the air became unstable, the aircraft pitching and jiggling in the warming morning sun.

She raised her arm to throw the message. As she did so the aircraft was picked up briefly by a thermal and pushed rapidly upwards. The sudden movement startled her and impaired her aim as she let go of the message. She tried to watch its fall as she climbed the aircraft away from the beach and its backing trees with the throttle wide open. She looked back for an instant, and a small spurt of sand caught her eye as she turned; it was well outside the area she had been aiming for. 'Bugger, bugger, bugger,' she scowled. Turning back over the beach again, she saw a woman and a small child emerge from the trees, waving excitedly, why had they not come out earlier when he engine must have alerted them to her presence above? Ceci watched for a moment. The pair walked towards her original target area by the campfire, not looking at where the message had finally landed.

Rocking her wings slowly she turned back onto her chosen northerly heading and climbed away, hoping that by chance one of the survivors would see the vital note fallen between the beach's fringing trees.

❖ ❖ ❖

What they needed was a boat. The problem was how to summon one. Colonel Hyami and his pilot decided to try using their aircraft's high-frequency radio. Although they were not experts, they knew that under normal atmospheric conditions the radio they carried would not transmit more than sixty, possibly eighty miles or so, and often much less in poor atmospheric conditions.

To call for help they needed to get a message to their trading agent in either Penang or Kuala Lumpur. The only way they could accomplish this, they had earlier discussed, was to fly to a point where the aircraft's radio signals, on a discrete frequency, could be picked up easily. That meant getting airborne again and flying eastwards, towards Malaya.

They also knew that their problem was compounded by the fact that their fuel reserves would only let them fly to within about eighty or so miles of the Malay coast, if they were to have enough fuel remaining – giving them a chance to return safely to the rough plateau runway high above Cornucopia's final resting place. Hyami's pilot spent a long time in the cockpit undertaking calculations, looking at fuel usage under various operating conditions, taking account of temperature and altitude. He spent time dipping the fuel tanks with a long measuring rod to determine exactly how much fuel they actually had, and not relying on what the tank gauges in the cockpit said they had. From long experience he was aware that all fuel gauges were notoriously unreliable.

The pilot's verdict suggested that they had sufficient fuel to reach within theoretical radio range of Penang, some eighty miles offshore. They would circle slowly there for about ten minutes while transmitting, and then would have just enough petrol remaining to land back on the plateau airstrip. After that they would have insufficient fuel to take off again. Clear contact with the agent was therefore imperative, stressed Hyami. The final problem in this scenario, the pilot explained, was the incalculable wind direction and speed over the flight distance. Without access to any form of meteorological service they would have to guess – it just increased the risk, he shrugged.

In view of their crucial need for future fuel supplies, the pilot explained to Colonel Hyami that the chances of their radio transmissions being received, and any responses to them being heard, were likely to be much better at night. The cool, night-time atmosphere usually gave better radio reception. Also, he explained, for greater fuel efficiency it would be better to fly when the air was cooler and denser – the engines would be more efficient. The conclusion was clear to both the professional pilot and his diminutive army master. They would have to take off at dusk to take advantage of the cooler temperatures to accomplish their aim. It would mean navigating back to the island in the dark and making a risky night landing while very low on fuel. Hyami sat back and considered the facts.

He had to do it. His face and reputation in Tokyo demanded it. There were few other realistic options. The two men then spent the day clearing dead and broken vegetation and detritus from within the DC-2's undercarriage bays and removing as much loose equipment as they could from inside the machine, including all its passenger seats – they needed to substantially lighten the aircraft.

With a combination of brute strength and large pieces of broken timber they managed to push and lever the aircraft around so that it was facing directly down the rough airstrip, where, fortunately, for the moment, the wind was coming from the right direction. The pilot stressed to Hyami that facing into wind for take-off was important, as it would help them to get airborne in the shortest possible distance, allowing them to climb well clear before reaching the huge wall of trees that dominated the end of the plateau.

The heat, and the roughness of the ground, made moving the aircraft arduous work that left them both wet with perspiration and physically worn out. At one point, while resting from their exertions, they considered turning the aircraft under its own engine power. The pilot thought that the noise would alert Cornucopia's survivors to their presence on the island. Neither of them wanted that at this stage. The clinching argument for Hyami was that not manoeuvring with the help of the engines on the ground would save them valuable, and possibly vital, fuel.

For the rest of the late afternoon they scavenged the local area looking for fruit or anything else that would assuage the increasing hunger pangs in their stomachs. Just off the plateau, as the slope plunged into denser undergrowth, Hyami found a small pool of rainwater that was teeming with small swimming creatures. Taking an empty water container from the aircraft's galley, he carefully submerged the pan and allowed the surface water to pour into it. From his backpack he produced a first-aid kit, in which was a small glass bottle containing white tablets. He dropped two of them into the pan of water, and they fizzed energetically. The pilot looked quizzically at Hyami.

"They are water purification tablets, new for the army. We can drink this in a few minutes," said Hyami, with satisfaction. "I used them in Manchuria." Then they rested for a while and the pilot mentally prepared for the night's critical work.

❖ ❖ ❖

Ceci made good progress after overflying the crash site. Up at seven thousand feet the air was cooler and less turbulent, and she had a good view of the passing islands below. Her chosen height gave her a margin of safety should the engine decide to stop for whatever reason. After an hour she began scanning the hazy horizon ahead of her hoping to see Car Nicobar. From her dead-reckoning navigation she believed that it lay about fifteen to twenty miles away but could see that the visibility ahead was far from good. Her main worry, however, was her estimations of wind speed and direction. If they were substantially different from conditions at their base that morning, she could be pushed off-track and miss the island altogether – without seeing it – and run out of fuel somewhere over the deep Ten Degree Channel. She had made some allowances for variations in her assumptions about wind strength and direction, but in the tropics she knew that weather conditions could be very localised and fickle.

Ceci cruised on, now at nine thousand feet. Nothing appeared below her except a few local shower squalls briefly puckering the surface of a slumbering, dark sea. The sun beat down relentlessly on the aircraft. Including her diversion over the Cornucopia site, she calculated they had been airborne for an hour and twenty minutes. With sixteen gallons on board prior to take-off she reckoned that they had used between nine and ten gallons so far. The remaining six gallons would give her, if she was careful, another forty-five to fifty minutes' flying time. Ceci began to feel a little uncomfortable. She should have sighted Car Nicobar by now – it was a sizeable island. The squally showers had begun to sweep more frequently across the seascape below her, making it more likely that she might miss the island.

Worried, she pushed the control stick to the left and banked the machine around, back towards the south and the scattered islands she had left behind over just twenty minutes earlier. It struck her that it might be prudent to retrace her steps, to get a fix on one of the islands and then head north again, making some new allowances for wind direction, strength and time, increasingly evidenced by the growing number of rain-squalls passing just below her.

Overhead the last small island south of Car Nicobar, she knew from her chart that she was now about thirty miles south of her destination. Working in the tiny open cockpit with an unsuitable chart that seemed determined to be sucked out of her hands by the air-stream was a difficult and demanding situation, made worse by her increasingly worried state of mind.

Turning again, she headed north with new mental calculations allowing for new guessimated strength and direction of wind. From her observations of the run of squalls she set a heading that should bring her over Car Nicobar within seventeen minutes. The wind was clearly stronger now and seemed to have a greater south-easterly element to it, pushing her to the north-west. After ten minutes she closed the throttle slightly and the aircraft began to descend, bouncing in the unstable air, Ceci trimming the machine while peering constantly ahead looking for land. Her descent brought her within the scope of the now-regular run of boisterous rain-squalls that rushed over the ocean. 'It must be here,' she told herself, but no island emerged from behind any of the squalls. Running rapidly through her mental calculations again, she reasoned that she had less than ten minutes' fuel left.

"Where is this damn island?" she shouted to the rushing wind.

Sarah and Beth watched the small biplane fly away to the north, the little girl continuing to wave frantically until the machine and its noise were gone. Michael Kelly had had a bad night: intense pain had returned to his phantom right leg. Sarah had spent the late evening and part of the night changing dressings, cleaning the wound and watching over him. During that time she thought for one moment that she had heard aircraft engines, but could not be sure, above the sound of the surf pounding onto the shore and the wind shaking the palm trees that sheltered their small community. And anyway it was dark, she reasoned. They had carried Kelly into the tree line fringing the beach to better protect him from the rain showers and wind that had been a feature of the evening. Tired and worried, she had taken an opportunity to administer two of Mr Snell's special Chinese migraine potions. Michael had eventually slept soundly from two in the morning. Only she and Beth had seen the biplane overfly their campsite. Michael Kelly had been asleep and the other three men had gone fishing and scavenging at daybreak.

Sarah and Beth both looked around for a dropped communication like the one they had received before, but could see nothing. Disappointed, they returned to the awakening and revitalised Michael and prepared him for a shower. He sat on the same rock he had clung onto when Sarah had unexpectedly expressed her love for him. Despite the discomfort from his leg, he laughed at the antics of the little girl and her beautiful mother, nearly sliding off his perch into the pool below him. When she had been deemed clean, Beth was dried and sent back to the campsite on the beach with the promise of a new story if she was good.

Sarah undressed herself and then helped Michael to disrobe. Aided by crutch on one side and Sarah on the other, he made slow progress towards the natural shower, now in full flow after the previous evening's rain. The cool water washed over them and they held each other under its unusually powerful, heavy fall. Beth spent time walking among the trees that lined the beach, picking up special leaves and pieces of wood to adorn her various sandcastles and palaces. She picked up a small envelope of white linen pinned loosely together. It would make a beautiful flag for a sandcastle. The piece of paper inside would make a smaller flag for another turret.

❖ ❖ ❖

The Japanese pilot had completed his pre-flight inspection well before the sun's last rays were slowly extinguished below the ocean's western horizon. Hyami took his place in the cockpit's right-hand seat and waited patiently, apprehensive. He had set a discrete frequency on the radio, that of his Penang agent, and had taken time to write out a concise but coded Morse message ready for transmission once they were within radio range. A faint orange glow shone from the radio's frequency dial, indicating that at least the set was taking power. He was unable to check if it worked properly as they were too far from any receiving or transmitting station. In any event, they did not want to literally broadcast their presence.

Satisfied, the pilot boarded the aircraft, pushing the metal ladder away from the door and into the undergrowth; it was additional weight. Closing the door, he firmly secured it. Pushing past Hyami as he moved into the cockpit, he sat down heavily into the captain's seat. The next five minutes were spent carrying out pre-flight checks, the instruments glowing softly from the panel ahead of them. Priming both engines with fuel, he switched on both sets of magneto switches. Looking momentarily at Hyami, he nodded, then pressed the port-engine starter button. The propeller turned slowly and one cylinder caught: others followed, with noisy explosions and gusts of smoke. The noise was shattering in the twilight. Bats, birds and moths took flight, trees and bushes behind the aircraft lay flattened in the vicious vortex of wind. The starboard engine was fired up quickly in the same way.

Tightening his seat belt, and without waiting for the engines to fully warm up, the pilot pushed both throttles forwards, the noise overwhelming his senses. The DC-2 gathered way and was soon racing through the scrub and bushes, leaving a plume of dust, the pilot catching and deftly correcting any alterations to a straight line as it charged tail-up across the uneven airstrip. The trees at the far end stood black against the soft indigo-blue of the twilight sky. The DC-2 was approaching them very quickly, yet the main wheels were still thundering along on the ground. Every so often the aircraft would check momentarily as it smashed through some heavier patches of thick undergrowth. Glancing to his right, the pilot noticed Hyami's worried and perspiring white face in the faint glow of the cockpit lamps. Smiling a little, he pulled back on the control wheel just a little. The machine lifted off the juddering surface, flying smoothly, straight at the trees ahead.

With the undercarriage retracting, their speed built, but they were still only marginally above the aircraft's critical stall speed. The pilot continued resolutely, looking ahead, neither climbing nor descending. The two engines were roaring, building crucial lifesaving speed. Hyami gripped the seat armrests, fearful of the rapidly approaching mass of branches and solid black trunks. Without warning, the pilot turned the control wheel to the right; the aircraft banked to almost seventy degrees, its engines continuing to snarl at maximum power. Hyami, disorientated and frightened, looked out and down to his right. Amazed, he watched the wing slice cleanly and unimpeded through a gap in the black, solid mass. Straightening up, the pilot reduced engine power slightly. They climbed slowly away to the south-east and Malaya. He was smiling.

At four thousand feet the engines were throttled back further and the aircraft trimmed for a quiet cruise towards the island of Penang, just off the Malay coast, four hundred and sixty miles distant over a dark sea. Every so often they caught sight of isolated lights on the ocean's surface – a ship ploughing an unseen, watery furrow towards some distant port, or fishermen working the night hours dragging a meagre income from the deep. Working quietly, the pilot estimated that the flight to within eighty miles of Penang would take two hours and forty minutes. They should be there at around eleven thirty, a half-hour after moonrise. Every now and then Hyami would try the radio, but without any success.

❖ ❖ ❖

Fifteen minutes had passed, and according to Ceci's calculations she should be out of fuel, but the Gypsy engine continued to turn unhesitatingly. Increasingly worried, she continually craned and turned to scan the ocean ahead from both sides the wind-blown cockpit. She watched intently as yet another squall passed ahead, the localised wind causing brief white disturbances on the sea's surface.

Then she saw it. The white flecks, reacting for a few minutes to the wind's bluster, stopped in a regular line about a mile ahead. It was the only clue she needed. Beyond the enforced line, she could see trees bordering a beach, which became more visible as the scudding clouds were driven on. Off to her right, a couple of miles or so, she could make out three or four roofs clustered around a small inlet in the coastline, and there some fishing boats drawn up on a beach backed by coconut palms.

The engine coughed once and carried on turning. The hint was not lost on the Gypsy Moth's pilot. She pumped the Vickers pump handle frantically, hoping to gain just a few more drops of unspent fuel, sending it from the small tank in the front cockpit, up to the main tank above and between the two upper wings. Now though, the pump was sucking air, she could feel it alternating from easy to hard as she pushed the handle to and fro; it was a difficult manoeuvre in the cramped cockpit.

Turning to the right, she side-slipped the machine to lose height quickly as she prepared for landing on the exposed beach. The idle boats were positioned on the beach in such a way that it left little room for manoeuvre. Ceci was conscious that this landing would have to be good, one of her best, worrying that the gallant Gypsy engine would cut at any second and there would be no opportunity for a second attempt.

Lined up with the beach, she realised that the daily onshore breeze was gusting to full effect, blowing her sideways towards the tree line. Countering this by banking and side-slipping into wind, she managed to keep the Gypsy Moth roughly in line with the sandy runway, the machine bobbing and swaying in the excited breeze. Two feet above its undulating surface she gently pulled back on the stick, the aircraft flared, nose raised, for a classic three-point landing. As she did so, the engine stopped dead, starved of fuel. The landing was near perfect. The dry sand slowed the machine quickly, but Ceci feared that, at any second, too much deceleration would cause her to nose-over into its dragging surface. When the machine had stopped, she switched off the magnetos to the dead engine, undid her straps and climbed stiffly out, smiling at a small group of islanders who ran out, quickly gathering about her in awe.

❖ ❖ ❖

Between attempts at working the high-frequency radio, Hyami sat watching the ocean and its occasional lights, yawning. His prepared Morse message ordered his agent in Penang to arrange for a sizeable, fast vessel to be chartered under the agent's overall command with a loyal raiding crew. It was to make best speed to the position coordinates given and he was to bring weapons, food and water, and importantly, drums of petrol with him. Hyami would be watching from a position on their island's plateau, on the east-facing side in three nights' time, where they would rendezvous on the beaches below, before developing a plan to invade the crash site on the island's west coast.

To the east, ahead of them, they saw the moon begin its long ascent into a near-cloudless night sky. Under any other conditions it would have been quite romantic, thought the Japanese pilot. After nearly two hours and thirty minutes he began a slow, wide circle to the right, climbing gently to help with the radio's range. Hyami sat at the small radio desk trying to raise his agent by voice radio. There was no success; despite the local conditions the night air was full of raging static, perhaps from an electric storm somewhere over Malaya's humid interior. Using the Morse key, he sent his identifying signal over the discrete frequency. He had been on the radio, keying continuously for ten minutes but there had been no discernible response. Still they circled steadily. Finally, the pilot stopped the turning and pointed the aircraft to the south-east again. Perhaps they needed to be nearer, he reasoned. But they were both mindful of the need to conserve fuel if they were to return to the plateau safely.

Another six minutes' flying brought them fifteen or so miles nearer Penang with an additional two thousand feet in altitude. Now circling, Hyami tried again. Success. The Morse message was rapidly keyed out and after a few seconds he received a brief burst of dots and dashes in acknowledgement through his headphones. Shutting down the radio, they turned north-westwards chasing a waxing moon, which was gliding effortlessly and silently through the night.

❖ ❖ ❖

Ceci quickly realised that she did not understand the excited group of almost naked villagers surrounding her; they spoke a language she knew nothing of – and no one appeared to speak any English. How on earth was she going to make clear her need for fuel or her urgent need to get to Port Blair, she wondered? In this northerly part of the Nicobars, the population appeared to speak only some form of aboriginal dialect.

After a few frustrating minutes spent trying to communicate by exchanging smiles and gesticulations, Ceci was relieved to see a small entourage approaching the aircraft. The apparent leader, a small nut-brown man, bald, with rheumy eyes, held out a hand, which Ceci grasped with care – it was small and delicate. The man too was naked, except for a small strategic covering.

Regrettably, the man, who was no doubt someone of import in the neighbourhood, neither spoke nor understood English, nor the single dialect of Malay that Ceci had mastered in part. Indications were made for her to join them at a crude, low table that had been set up just by the boats resting on the hot sand, just within the welcome shade of the fringing palm trees. On it were placed a few wooden bowls of fruit and other vegetables, together with gourds containing some lukewarm liquid.

The simple alfresco meal was undertaken with good humour, neither party really understanding the other until Ceci, using sign language that she thought may convey her needs, drew a simple map in the sand with a stick. First she drew a crude picture of her aeroplane plus a large drum – signifying petrol – while making the sound of an engine.

Initially, it drew blank stares until one of the audience understood and explained his realisation to the others. They looked at each other and shook their heads. There was no petrol on the island now. Trying a new tack, Ceci drew a simple map in the sand indicating where they were now on Car Nicobar, which received some agreement from members of the small throng. She then sketched a boat sailing from Car Nicobar to Port Blair across the Ten Degree and Duncan channels, and the other, shorter stretches of water. On the boat she drew a caricature of herself with a few sailors on board. The group of onlookers muttered and gasped as she played out her artistic charade, accompanied by much rubbing of chins and heads. She stood back and waited.

They talked among themselves for a while, pointing and shaking their heads. Finally the head man took Ceci's stick in his small hand. Making a mark on the north coast of their island, he drew another small boat, nodding and muttering all the while. He then scored a track in the sand from the point he had made, across the sea to Port Blair. It occurred to Ceci that the message was that there was no one willing to go to Port Blair from this village, but there was possibly a boat and crew to be found on the other side of the island who would be willing to take her the hundred-and-forty miles or so to Port Blair on South Andaman Island. She had not reckoned on this. Having to get to the other side of the island and negotiate a boat ride was going to take valuable time: time was not a commodity they had.

❖ ❖ ❖

The Japanese pilot watched the aircraft's fuel gauges carefully and studied his watch. He knew it was going to be touch-and-go to get back to the makeshift airstrip. Having to fly further towards the Malay mainland, and spending longer than they had allowed for climbing and circling while sending the vital message, had used more fuel than they had allowed for. Even though the gauges were not totally accurate, he tapped them from time to time, looking for an improvement in their readings. Hyami watched, worried.

An hour passed, and they both relaxed slightly as the DC-2 cruised towards their hoped-for landing place. Then the pilot sat up quickly from his semi-slumped position watching the instruments and the darkness passing by outside. Now alert and looking intently in front of him, he reached out and tapped a gauge again. Hyami rose from his reverie, sat up straight and took notice.

"What is it? Is there a problem?" He looked across the darkened cockpit. The pilot continued to stare at his instruments, the furrow on his brow lit by instrument lights.

"Oil pressure is low on the starboard engine and it's continuing to fall," he said in a slow, calm way. Throttling back the offending engine a little, he trimmed the aircraft to compensate. Groping in a flight bag just behind his seat, he pulled out a large chrome-plated torch.

"Colonel, please shine the torch onto the right engine and tell me if you see anything unusual."

Taking the torch, the colonel focused the pencil beam of light onto the engine to his right side. There appeared to be nothing wrong: the cowlings were still bright and shiny in the torch light. Then he saw something else, a narrow dark line extending from where the cowlings met halfway around the engine, then cutting back towards the leading edge of the wing. Steadying the torch and looking more carefully he saw, as he watched, the line slowly extending, moving back and then around the leading edge of the wing until it disappeared up and over its aerofoil curve.

"There is something leaking out of the engine," he said in a voice half an octave higher than his usual bark, glancing across at the pilot. The pilot released his seat belt and, standing, leant over Hyami, looking intently at the starboard engine nacelle. He studied the flow of what he knew must be engine oil as it spread backwards, now covering the cowl and leading edge of the wing. He sat again, tightening his seat belt.

"We have a serious oil leak from somewhere within the engine cowlings. There's nothing we can do about it from here but if the oil pressure falls much more I will have to stop the engine."

Hyami looked at the pilot; he was very worried now but concealed his concern in the darkness.

"Will we make it back?"

The pilot shrugged his shoulders, looking into the darkness beyond the windscreens. Hyami bit anxiously at his torn and dirty fingernails.

Four minutes later the sickening engine was throttled back to allow it to run slowly for a few minutes. Still dissatisfied, the pilot cut its magneto switches. In its dying moments the propeller blades were turned to feather, edge-on to the airflow to reduce the drag of their huge blades. The aircraft continued on one engine, its revolutions increased to compensate for the loss of thrust. The pilot remained very alert now, watching the instruments for signs of more problems; a second engine failure would prove rather final over the sea in the dark. Their destination lay thirty miles away, north-westwards, if his dead-reckoning calculations were accurate. It would be another fifteen minutes or so before they could relax fully, on the ground.

❖ ❖ ❖

Ceci's mother was gently sobbing when her soldier husband returned late in the evening from yet another round of discussions concerning a forthcoming military exercise with recently arrived Australian troops. She pushed a copy of the local newspaper reporting information from a Rangoon daily at him. He sat down next to her and quietly read a short article on an inside page describing in little detail the finding of an aircraft wheel floating in the sea near Aye Island, a hundred and fifty miles south-east of Rangoon. The brief report said that the wheel and its still-inflated tyre was picked up by two fisherman, that it apparently still had parts of the aircraft's undercarriage attached and was covered in molluscs and seaweed. The article also mentioned that the recovered wheel was now in the possession of the district administration officer at the Port of Ye.

He knew enough of aeroplanes to realise that the wheel could not have come from the reported lost flying boat – it did not have wheels. He placed the folded newspaper on the heavy teak coffee table in front of them and sank back into the chintz-covered cushions of the large wicker sofa, putting his arm around his sniffling and trembling wife.

"Listen, old girl," he said gently, "I don't see how it can be a wheel from Ceci's aircraft. It was found near the Siam border. That's much too far for her little aeroplane to fly. Anyway, dear, she would have real problems finding fuel for it in such a remote region. Let me get in touch with the district officer at Ye in the morning and see what he can tell us about it."

His wife watched him. A moment of belief came to her and she clung to it. Perhaps it had nothing to do with Ceci, she earnestly hoped. They sat together, her pale hand in his strong, tanned one, looking out through the veranda doors at the quietly closing day. The dinner gong sounded from the hall. They both sighed and she rose to go upstairs quickly to repair the damage to her face done by her earlier sobbing. Not bothering to change, he made his way into the dining room, a large glass of neat Scotch in his hand, and making a mental note to talk to Don Chivers, the RAF wing commander, about any further search plans in the morning.

Early the following day found the brigadier in the wing commander's office. His balding head was down, looking at charts of the area around the seas and islands just off the Tenasserim coast of Siam. He asked if the wing commander would sanction one final search in this area. Despite their different services, the wing commander was a good friend of the soldier.

"It may be difficult to get authorisation but if I say that we are continuing the search for passengers from the Empress machine then I may be able to swing it."

"Anything you can do would be splendid, Don."

"Don't worry Charles; I think we can do something. In the meantime I will telegraph the district officer at Ye to see what more he can tell us of the description of the recovered wheel. You and Miranda may be worrying for nothing over this one."

They shook hands and the brigadier left for his headquarters. It was just gone six-thirty on a bright Singapore morning, still fresh from a night of cooling rain. He did not feel bright, though, despite the wing commander's positive remarks. He loved his wayward daughter.

❖ ❖ ❖

The discussion, such as it was, lasted most of the afternoon. The head man and his villagers, together with what appeared to Ceci to be an increasing number of hangers-on, discussed and chattered about her map and the obviously understood need for her to get to Port Blair. There did not appear, however, to be an equivalent to the word 'urgent' in their language, she soon came to realise. As afternoon became early evening and everyone had been given an opportunity to draw or modify her original sand map, it finally became clear that someone would accompany her to a village settlement on Car Nicobar's north coast to negotiate a suitable vessel to take her to South Andaman Island, where Port Blair lay at its south-eastern end.

Accompanied by two village women, Ceci was taken to a larger hut in the centre of the small community and shown a small curtained-off room with a simple low wooden bed, a hardwood side table with a spluttering candle and a washstand. The washstand was beautifully carved; mahogany, she thought, and held a real porcelain bowl with a matching water jug decorated with roses. How this very obviously English item of furniture had arrived at this outlandish and remote location she had no idea, but she was pleased to be able to rinse her face and hands in the cold, clear water brought by one of the gently smiling woman. There was little air in the room. The small window was shuttered with a grass screen, and while the temperature was falling outside as the evening wore on, her room remained stifling. Brought up to be fastidious, she noted there was no WC. 'My God, where is the loo?' she wondered, worry lines creasing her brow

As darkness fell, the small community became quiet. Unable to sleep, she got up from the small, rather uncomfortable bed and pushed the rough screen covering the door to one side. There was no one about but she could hear muffled talking from adjacent huts. The coolness was delicious as it flowed around her and she breathed in its gentle perfume. Stepping outside, she looked about. There was no one she could see in the deepening twilight. Behind her the sea lapped the gently shelving shoreline. It was too tempting. Walking with care, Ceci edged her way around the outside of the hut and moved warily towards the beckoning, lapping waves. Here would be too exposed, and she continued for a few hundred yards further up the beach to a point where the dark trees almost reached the ocean, near to where her Gypsy Moth was parked. Entering the fringe of the jungle a few feet from the water, she undressed, all the time checking that no one had followed her. Satisfied, she ran over the short stretch of still-warm sand into the sea, taking care not to splash too much. It was delightful, cooling and refreshing after the sultry atmosphere in her village lodgings. Treading water, with only her head above the surface, she surveyed the beach and her aeroplane, just visible in the deep shadows beneath the palms.

There was someone there. In her aeroplane! How could she have missed them? She must have walked right past. Somebody was sitting in the cockpit; there was the vague outline of a person. The elevators and ailerons were also moving; it definitely was not her imagination. Suddenly, a small, shadowy figure stood up in the rear cockpit and appeared to stare about them. Then the figure got out and onto the wing. There was a short ripping sound, followed immediately by a muffled cry as the person half fell to the sand. The figure got up quickly and ran into the shadows. Ceci, still treading water and totally naked, watched.

"What the hell is going on?" she muttered.

Waiting a few minutes, she swam to the shore and lay quietly in the shallow, softly breaking waves while she watched the beach. It was difficult to see anything in the blackness; she could only sense the backdrop of trees, her aeroplane and the moving water. Kneeling, then standing slowly, she crossed the narrow beach carefully and moved back into the tree line looking for her pile of clothes. In the darkness, and like black cats, all trees looked pretty much the same, she realised.

"Where are they?" she mumbled and spent twenty minutes groping carefully around the area where she thought she had undressed, all the while bumping into bushes and shrubs, but without success. Her clothes eluded discovery, at least for the moment. This left her with a pretty problem: she was stark naked and about three hundred yards from her room in a hut near the centre of a strange village, inhabited by people with whom she could not converse. There must be a funny side to this – Harold would be highly amused at her concerns over nakedness in a village where almost everyone walked about with nothing, or almost nothing, on.

Just visible, Ceci could just see the soft glow of a dying fire coming from somewhere in the village; it gave her something to aim for. Walking within the tree line wherever possible, she crept towards the village, eyes and ears alert. Within the shadow of one of the upturned fishing boats she stopped, just about opposite the nearest village hut. There appeared to be no one about. It was now or never. Crouching a little, she sprinted towards the village, arriving at the back of one hut located on its very edge. From inside came gentle but regular snoring. Moving slowly around it, she just recognised her own, larger hut. Throwing caution to the wind, Ceci ran swiftly towards her shelter, bumping gently into an elderly man relieving himself quietly into the sand. He let out a grunt as he fell onto his back, still peeing, fountain-like. She rushed into her room and sat glowing on her bed, relieved and trying to suppress a fit of giggles.

So far, so good, but what about tomorrow? Tired and cooler, she lay down, pulling the simple cotton cover over her nakedness. She was soon asleep, an amused smile still on her lips.

❖ ❖ ❖

The DC-2 was proving a handful with only one engine turning. Even with full rudder trim applied to compensate for thrust on one side only, the Japanese pilot had to hold on left rudder, maintaining their direct course towards their island plateau airstrip. His left leg was beginning to ache with the strain. He was now very concerned, despite his experience and skill. Landing at night on an unmarked airstrip, assuming they could locate it again, was a challenge: to have to make an approach and land with only one engine increased the challenge considerably. He instructed Hyami to hold the rudder for a few minutes while he massaged his trembling leg, which had gone into painful spasms.

Keeping a careful watch on the oil pressure and temperature gauge for the remaining engine, he took the opportunity to recalculate their anticipated arrival over the island. Looking finally at the fuel gauges, he noted their needles almost touching the red 'empty' stops. Relieving Hyami of the need to hold the rudder, he indicated that they possibly had about six minutes' flying time to the island, according to his dead-reckoning calculations. When he slowly pulled back the remaining engine's throttle lever, its noise was slightly subdued, giving off a gentle rumble as they commenced a slow descent, both cockpit occupants watching the darkness ahead for signs of land.

Seven highly charged minutes went by; two pairs of straining eyes willed the island to be there. Eight minutes passed, and then nine. Suddenly the pilot said one word, softly.

"There." He pointed off to his left. There lay their destination, surrounded by pale phosphorescence as small waves broke around its coast in the darkness. The island's unique outline was now unmistakable as he turned the machine back towards the east, still descending. As during their previous landing, they did not want to alert Cornucopia's survivors to their presence.

Judging the turn accurately in the dark, the pilot gently side-slipped the disabled machine towards the lighter-shaded mass of the plateau lying within its opaque rim of surrounding trees. The manoeuvre ensured that he would easily make it to the landing site even if the remaining engine stopped through lack of fuel. High, and lined up with the makeshift runway, he reached up to the centre console above their heads and pulled off the remaining two magneto switches. The port engine died immediately. They were at once an almost silent, heavy glider, rushing to an earth they could barely see in the darkness. Hyami held tightly onto the armrests of the co-pilot's seat, his face for once reflecting his inner fears. Wide-eyed, he strained to discern the ground rushing up towards them, noticing for a fraction of a second a treetop flicking past the wing, just as their powerful landing lights came on. Ahead in their yellow beams lay the undulating strip punctuated with broken shrubs and debris from their previous two hazardous landings and take-offs.

Still side-slipping the machine as he sank below the very tall trees across the aircraft's approach path, the pilot held the aircraft just a few feet from the uneven ground, still travelling very quickly. As its speed slowed he levelled the wings and pulled the nose upwards. With flaps fully down, the machine sank heavily towards the ground, its undercarriage stretched out like talons to make contact.

The three-point landing that followed went to plan for the first few seconds, but as the full weight of the rushing aircraft collapsed onto its sturdy legs, the port wheel ran into a large and well-established shrub. The wheel's impact and momentary deceleration caused the aircraft to swerve to the left towards the tall stand of trees and undergrowth that bordered the landing strip. Instantly kicking on right rudder and pressing the brake on the same side, the pilot fought to stop the swerve.

In a fraction of a second the left wheel overcame the obstruction. The aircraft now began careering off to the right, obeying the pilot's last instinctive command. Slowing rapidly, the DC-2 still had energy enough to continue swerving right. The aircraft was now in an uncontrollable ground-loop. There appeared nothing that the pilot could do to restrain its gyrations. Suddenly, there was a loud crack. The aircraft stopped. It was facing the way it had come. In its lights, huge clouds of dust billowed around them. Some light was reflected back into the cockpit. The pilot could see Hyami holding his head in his hands. Blood was seeping out from between his fingers and he was moaning and cursing loudly.

Switching off all lights and controls, the pilot undid his seat belt and leant across the narrow space and pulled Hyami's hands from his face. By torchlight he could see that the colonel had a deep cut across his forehead and right cheek. It transpired later that as the aircraft had spun around, his head had been flung against the windscreen frames beside him, causing the injury and, no doubt, some concussion, thought the pilot. He pulled Hyami from the co-pilot's seat and led him back into the seatless cabin. He helped him to sit on the cabin floor with his back propped against the fuselage side and went in search of the aircraft's first-aid kit.

The kit was far from comprehensively equipped, but there was a bandage of sorts, which the pilot wound around Hyami's bloodied head. Unsurprisingly, he complained of a headache, but there was little in the kit to alleviate that apart from some simple aspirin. Having attended to Hyami's wounds, the pilot gave some attention to their situation. What was the cause of the loud crack they'd heard and felt, just before the aircraft had stopped? And what was wrong with the starboard engine? He would have to investigate when light came, around five o'clock. In the meantime, he tried to sleep in his cockpit seat.

SIXTEEN

The morning broke grey and overcast. A stiff breeze blew across the beach, causing the grass window curtain to flap against the rough walls of Ceci's hut. It woke her and she sat gathering her thoughts on the edge of the wooden bed, with its thin cotton cover wrapped around her. The door curtain parted for a second and a face peered in. A minute later, two women came in, smiling a little sheepishly. One held Ceci's 'lost' clothes, neatly folded; they appeared to have been laundered. The other carried a jug of water for the 'English' washstand. Ceci looked askance as the clothes were settled onto the bed. The woman said something softly, and then gestured that Ceci should wash, and dress in the clean clothes.

That accomplished, Ceci ventured out of the hut and was surprised to see that, despite the grey weather and roughish seas, all of the small boats had gone from the shore. As she sat under the trees eating some fruit brought by one of the ever-present women, the small, rheumy-eyed village elder came bustling towards her, his face serious. A few steps behind, a downcast young woman wrapped entirely in a deep-blue sari walked reluctantly, hands held together, as in a sign of contrition.

Reaching Ceci, the village elder turned towards the young woman and began berating her in obviously strong terms. Near to tears, she knelt in the sand looking down at her hands, which were folded into her lap. Ceci recognised her as one of the villagers who had greeted her landing with such enthusiasm the previous day. The elder then began a long high-pitched tirade, pointing and gesticulating at the young woman, who shortly began to cry quietly under his verbal onslaught. This lasted about fifteen minutes, at the end of which, Ceci thought she understood what had been going on.

The young woman had been the figure she had seen in the Gypsy's cockpit the previous evening; she wanted to fly in the aeroplane and had sat in the cockpit to see if it would fly her. She knew a woman could fly because she had seen Ceci fly. Something had disturbed her play in the cockpit, and, frightened, she had jumped out, ready to run back to the village. Stepping carelessly out onto the taut fabric-covered wing, she had put her foot had through the doped-linen-covered structure and had overbalanced and fallen onto the sand. While making her way back to the village the young girl had accidently stumbled across Ceci's pile of clothes and had opportunistically picked them up. Returning to her hut and realising what and whose they were, she decided to wash the clothes as atonement for the trespass and damage she had caused.

Ceci frowned; damage to the Gypsy Moth worried her. Jumping up, she walked quickly down the beach to where the aeroplane stood, gently rocking in the breeze. On the lower port wing, just outboard of the specially strengthened crew walkway was a large, 'L'-shaped tear in the fabric covering. By this time the old man and the young woman had also arrived on the scene, along with a dozen or so other villagers, mainly women and children. The nut-brown little man, eyes blazing further, again remonstrated with the young woman, who was now in full flow, tears coursing down her cheeks. The crowd formed a circle around her, mumbling. The man lifted his stick and started to strike at the young woman, who fell to the ground.

Ceci stepped purposefully between them, raising her arms so that the elder could not strike the prostrate woman. "No, No! Stop now!" shouted Ceci. The man stopped mid-swing, the small crowd amazed and fascinated by the scene.

"She ... it, mine," the man said, with both shame and anger, pointing at the wretch at his feet. Ceci understood now. It was his daughter who had caused the damage. His anger came from the shame that one of his own family, let alone a villager, had trespassed on a stranger's property and damaged it.

Smiling and gesturing for him to calm down, she stood firm between the young woman and her angry father. Bending down, Ceci pulled the young woman to her feet and helped wipe her tears. Then led her to the aeroplane and beckoned her to climb on the wing, onto the walkway. The woman looked worried, unsure of what was to follow, and backed away from the Gypsy Moth. Ceci climbed onto the wing, holding her hand out, offering encouragement. The man stood glowering, muttering all the time. Onto the wing the young woman climbed, and stood trembling beside Ceci, looking down at the gathering. Then, Ceci hinged down the small cockpit door and invited her to sit inside. Uncertainly, she did so, and the crowd laughed and cheered, her father looking astonished. After a few moments of trying the controls the young woman looked at Ceci with her huge brown eyes full of respect as she gestured clumsily her thanks and apologies. Ceci spent the next hour giving all of the villagers an opportunity to sit in the cockpit; by the time he became the last would-be pilot the village elder was now smiling.

The damage to the wing was not too serious. The woman was short and slight, and her small foot had torn only the aircraft's skin top surface. Ceci was confident that it should be easy to repair with needle and thread, at least temporarily. She set off to cross Car Nicobar to one of a number of similar villages on its north coast. The journey took her the rest of a tiring, hot day and early evening.

Again, lengthy discussions went on into the late evening, with the outcome that a father and his son would take Ceci to Port Blair. They would set off early the following morning, in a small sailing vessel, which Ceci, on inspection, could not fail to notice was equipped with a very small and ancient-looking auxiliary engine – covered with rust.

With dawn barely established, the boat was provisioned with water and some basic foodstuffs – mainly fruit, and some congealed cooked rice. Setting the sail while the islanders cheered and clapped, they slowly drifted into the waves. The wind had now chosen to blow from the north and the simple vessel with its small, tattered and inefficient sail was hard pressed, beating out into the choppy sea. Slowness of progress seemed to Ceci to have become a theme as they tacked yet again across the Ten Degree Channel for something like the twelfth time that evening. She could still see the unusual hills behind the village that they had left that morning. She doubted they had covered more than thirty miles in a straight line. As the night fell, the father took the helm indicating that Ceci should sleep, lying in the bottom of the vessel, sheltered from the strengthening wind and occasional dollops of seawater thrown back by the bow as they punched into short, steep seas.

She was vaguely conscious of a change in the vessel's motion as the uncomfortable night slowly passed. She was awoken on a number of occasions as the small boat tacked to take advantage of local wind-shifts, and by five o'clock on a cool morning she had had enough of trying to sleep in the hard conditions. Rising stiffly, sitting with her back to the weather coaming, longing for a hot, strong cup of tea or coffee, it seemed to Ceci an age since the one that Harold had brought her in a tin mug before she had set off. Pleased, she noticed their speed had increased slightly, the wind had shifted a few points to the east overnight, allowing the crew to ease the mainsail sheets a little, adding a knot or so to their progress.

With the dawn, the son took over sailing the boat and steered, while his father lay awkwardly across its broad beam, his head nodding as they lifted over each successive wave. Everything was damp and sticky with salt; the weather did everything possible to delay their progress. Blowing from dead-ahead again, they continued tacking again and again, very slowly gaining precious ground in the right direction. Eventually, after passing Little Andaman Island, the wind veered quickly to the west and they were finally able to lay a direct course for Port Blair. They arrived exhausted and hungry after battling for over forty-four hours from Car Nicobar.

Ceci went immediately to see the administration officer in the small port and recounted her barely believable tale. The officer meticulously wrote down every word and finally said he would forward details to Penang and Singapore, as well as to Delhi. Then she sent a telegram to her parents advising them of her safety at Port Blair. A further telegram went to her fiancé, Squadron Leader Harvey Wills, briefly describing the situation and letting him know where she was – and asking was there any way he could come to her with the Walrus aircraft?

❖ ❖ ❖

Harvey Wills was at that moment piloting the borrowed Fleet Air Arm Walrus northwards towards the Port of Ye in Burma on a twofold mission. The first objective was to discover anything about the aircraft wheel reportedly recovered from the sea at Aye Island; the second to undertake a search for Cornucopia and the Gypsy Moth in the group of mainly uninhabited islands off Burma's Tenasserim coast.

At Port Ye, Wills discussed the wheel find with an official and was given a chance to inspect the weed- and mollusc-encrusted artefact. He saw immediately that it was a large, heavy wheel; quite different from the much smaller wheels fitted to a de Havilland Gypsy Moth. He could also see that the wheel had been immersed in the water for some time, probably months; Ceci had not been gone that long. As he was returning to his aircraft, relieved to some extent, something occurred to him that might possibly provide an answer as to where the wheel had come from.

Sir Charles Kingsford Smith, the great pioneering Australian aviator, had disappeared somewhere between Rangoon and Singapore during his last race from Croydon Airport, near London, to Australia, in November 1935. Wills remembered the excitement at the time; RAF aircraft being sent from Singapore to search the route for the American single-engine Lockheed Altair aircraft, famously called The Lady Southern Cross. No sign of the aircraft had ever been found, although many theories abounded as to where its wreck may lie. However, and importantly, Harvey Wills was sure that the wheel was not from Ceci's Gypsy Moth and sent a cable to Wing Commander Chivers to that effect. The wing commander immediately passed the same information to Brigadier Charles Grosvenor-Ffoulkes, who, very relieved, called his wife. The fact that the wheel was definitely not from their daughter's aircraft relieved some of their worries, but they were still concerned as to her whereabouts and her safety.

❖ ❖ ❖

Squadron Leader Wills, with his young naval co-pilot, Sub-Lieutenant David Kildonan, made their take-off from the Bay of Bengal just off Port Ye, then turned south, intending to search the islands and ocean between Ye and Penang for signs of the lost Empress machine – it was the second justification for their flight. They made slow progress, a result of spending time looking at likely crash sites on the islands, many of which were uninhabited. They also had to contend with a strong headwind from the south-east.

Wills spent time wondering where his fiancée could be. Although relieved that the wheel secure in the administrator's office at Port Ye was not been from a Gypsy Moth, worry over Ceci's safety continued to dominate most of his waking moments. He let Kildonan have control for most of their arduous flight southwards to Penang. The young officer revelled in being given free rein, being allowed to swoop down and around the various islands encountered as they progressed southwards.

Their landing along the calm waters between Penang Island and the Malay mainland was accomplished with little fuss, and both crewmen clambered, tired and stiff, into the small tender that had come to assist their mooring and take them ashore to Penang's principal community, George Town. Once ashore, Harvey Wills sent a signal to Wing Commander Chivers advising him that they would be back in Singapore late the next morning. They stayed at the Peninsula Hotel and dined well, retiring early under swirling, cooling ceiling fans.

Breakfast the next morning was interrupted by a telephone call from Butterworth airfield on the mainland. They advised Wills that a signal had been received from Singapore overnight and asked if he would care to collect it or if they should send it over. He requested the latter. Both pilots sat about after breakfast awaiting the sealed signal, which eventually arrived just after eleven o'clock. Tearing open the buff envelope, Wills read that Ceci had been in contact by telegram with her parents and was safe in Port Blair in the Andaman Islands. A huge load lifted from his mind. The second part of the signal ordered him to Port Blair immediately and to await further orders by cable once there. What had Ceci been up to now, he wondered, and were his new orders connected to something she had done?

The distance from Penang to Port Blair was just over four hundred nautical miles. They had done the trip some days earlier and did not relish the idea of another three to four hours in the greenhouse-like cockpit under blistering tropical sun, with the Walrus's huge Pegasus engine and noisy two-bladed wooden propeller thrashing away above and behind them. They left shortly after lunch, having spent the remainder of the morning flying the machine off the water and landing-on at Butterworth airfield. The aircraft was fully refuelled and thoroughly checked over under the watchful eye of co-pilot Kildonan.

The Walrus had been designed to carry four crew; but in its search-and-rescue role, only the two pilots were aboard the sturdy 'Shagbat', as the ungainly Walrus was irreverently but affectionately known in naval flying circles. Their flight across four hundred miles of moodless water was uneventful to the point of boredom. Harvey Wills took some time to think about his relationship with Ceci as well as catching up with some missed shut-eye while his young co-pilot flew the machine at a steady ninety-five knots, three thousand feet above the sea.

After three hours or so, the dim shadow of the Andaman Island chain grew slowly out of the seemingly endless expanse of the Bay of Bengal, the heat haze and late afternoon sun making it difficult to pick out any detail until they were quite close. They landed on the airfield on this occasion, giving orders for the aircraft to be prepared for flight at short notice, anticipating their orders from Singapore. Again, Kildonan took charge of ground handling, ensuring that the aircraft was properly cared for and that their small amount of baggage was made ready to transport to the only guest-house within the port's small community. Wills, meanwhile, made his way to the district administrator's residence, hoping to read the signal he anticipated would be waiting for him. There was none.

"Perhaps it will come overnight and be waiting for you in the morning," the grey-haired civil servant had said. Leaving Kildonan to his own devices, Wills decided that his next priority was to find his sorely missed fiancée. Her cable had said she was safe here, somewhere in Port Blair. The place was small; there was only one guest-house. The administration officer said that he had not seen her since her arrival from Car Nicobar to report the finding of Cornucopia, its survivors and the Dutch-registered DC-2 with its seemingly dangerous Japanese crew. He spent the remainder of the evening walking around the small community hoping to find her but she seemed to have just evaporated.

❖ ❖ ❖

Hyami stood gazing eastwards into the thickening gloom, his head wound beginning to heal owing to his pilot's careful medical attention over the last two days. The horizon was indistinct in the deepening twilight. He wondered if his Penang agent would appear tonight, as ordered. The sun was setting behind him, its final gesture of scattered, rosy light quickly fading to leave only inky darkness. He reasoned it would be easier to see any signal light from a vessel in total darkness.

His pilot stood a few paces away scanning an arc of ocean from north-west to south-east with a set of powerful military binoculars. Disappointingly, no lights or boats interrupted his scan. They stood for a while watching, both silent. Suddenly the colonel turned and, tutting impatiently, walked slowly back up the short incline towards the top of the plateau and the DC-2. He turned briefly at the top, ordering the pilot to stay on watch for a few hours but to let him know immediately should anything occur. He would relieve the pilot in four hours, just before midnight.

The pilot found a spot to sit with a good view of the dark ocean and, making himself comfortable, leaned back against a convenient fallen tree. Occasionally he could hear creatures scurrying about in the undergrowth around him as he lit a cigarette, his large chrome-plated torch and pistol to hand on the ground beside him. Gazing seaward, he thought of his home near Nara, Japan's ancient and beautiful capital, and his young wife and baby son.

He had been in the military from a very young age, both his parents having died of typhoid when he was just eight years old. He had been very lucky to survive the epidemic. A distant uncle had reluctantly taken responsibility for him at the earliest opportunity and sent him to a military academy for his education. The regime had been tough, brutal at times, and at such a tender age he had often cried himself silently to sleep under the thin bedcovers in the crowded dormitories.

By the age of eighteen he volunteered and was accepted for military pilot training, after volunteering for almost anything that would release him from the mind-numbing prospect of joining the infantry. He was quiet and respectful, and proved to be an outstanding naturally gifted pilot, flying eventually with the Imperial Japanese Navy from some of the new aircraft carriers being built in the shipyards around Yokohama.

He loved those days, flying single-seat fighters on exercises high above the blue expanse of the Pacific Ocean. His skill was soon commented on, recognised by those in authority who were able to influence his future. Later, he was given an opportunity to undertake test flying of new military aircraft and managed to hone his flying skills to a very high degree in a variety of aeroplanes.

Then, one bright spring day, while he was testing a twin-engine torpedo bomber over the ocean outside Tokyo Bay, the aircraft started to break up in the air after performing high-speed manoeuvres. He was very lucky to survive the accident, and was pulled from the water by vigilant fishermen. His accompanying test engineer, fatally trapped, went down with the broken machine.

Four months in a military hospital just outside Tokyo eventually severed his connections with all those who had guided his career to that point. It was where he met his future wife. Just before he was discharged from medical care, he had been approached and interviewed by two black-suited government officials asking him if he would be interested in working on some special assignments in the south-west Asia region.

Three days before the government officials had arrived, his squadron commander had taken time to visit him. There had always been much mutual respect between them. He knew, even as the greying commander sat opposite him in the stark white visitors' room, that the news he was about to hear would not be welcome. The injuries he had sustained during the accident had left him with restricted movement in his right leg and left arm. It meant that he was now classified as medically unfit to continue with his first love, flight-testing, or to return to a navy carrier squadron.

The commander faced the pilot for a few moments, empathising with the awful disappointment that must be flooding the young man's mind behind the calm, expressionless eyes. But he had learnt to suppress any outward expression of emotion from a very early age, initially as an adolescent defence mechanism against a careless world, and later as a mechanism to cope with a military way of life – unquestioningly accepting good or bad orders and strictures.

There was a single option left that would allow him to continue with a military flying career: to join the Imperial Army and perhaps fly communications aircraft – in essence, become a military taxi driver – transporting elderly generals and arrogant staff officers about. He was not enamoured of the idea. The commander stood erect and formal. They shook hands, each looking for a way into the mind of the other. As the door closed behind him, the pilot sat, internalising the shock, no emotion escaping.

No quick decision was forced from him and he spent some weeks at a rehabilitation centre near the sea regaining his physical and mental strength. During this time opportunities to meet again the petite nurse occurred regularly. It was she who had woken him gently during painful nights to administer drugs in the initial months of his extended stay in hospital. Later they married settling in the old city of Nara, bringing a baby boy into the world, the image of his father. His wife's family had been brought up in Honolulu, she and her mother returning to Japan in 1935 when her father died as a result of a traffic accident in the dockyards there. The couple had spent holidays to the islands, visiting her Japanese and American friends and he had enjoyed it, particularly the relaxing way of life there among the Americans.

Feeling frustrated and needing to be active again, he finally contacted the government officials who had interviewed him in hospital, all those months ago. He was eventually offered a position that would give him a chance to travel outside Japan with a trade mission, ostensibly looking for opportunities to trade in essential raw materials and manufactured products. It would also provide him with opportunities to fly occasionally. Having a new wife and likely further responsibilities in the shape of children, he accepted the position, which paid well and, it turned out, was ultimately controlled by a special branch of Japanese military intelligence in Tokyo. His first step in his new career was to spend time at a special school, where he learned the new 'Purple' encryption code that was to be used by the military and diplomatic services in future.

His thoughts then turned to his friend, who lay in a new shallow grave, in the warm soil just a few hundred yards from where he was sitting. They had been through much together. His death was unnecessary; its cause was Hyami. The pilot truly missed his friend.

There was no sign of life on the expanse of ocean under his gaze. After four hours he heard something moving through the shrubbery in the darkness above him. Hyami signalled his approach noisily and the tip of his cigarette glowed red like a beacon.

"Any sign?" he enquired.

"None at all, Colonel," he shook his head and left the look-out spot, returning thankfully to the aircraft. He loaded one pair of seats back in the empty fuselage, locking them into position. Tired, he sprawled as best he could, and restless sleep soon overtook him.

❖ ❖ ❖

Harvey Wills was frustrated at not being able to find his fiancée, returning again to the administrator's office early the next morning. There was still no signal from Singapore and he began to wonder what all the urgency and fuss was about. While sitting chatting and drinking tea with the administrator he heard Ceci's voice in the hallway. At last! He jumped up from his chair to greet her, knocking over his tea in his haste. Ceci had expected to see him at some stage, but was a little taken aback as he strode smiling from the administrator's office into the hallway.

"Ceci, darling, where have you been?" he whispered hoarsely, putting his arms around her. "Your parents – we – have been sick with worry. Why didn't you stay in touch if you really needed to get stuck into some hair-brained scheme?" He tried to kiss her but she turned her face quickly, in faux coyness.

She put her arms around the familiar uniformed shoulders, more in response than affection. She knew then, in an instant, that any feelings of love for this honest and decent, and rather distant, man had somehow evaporated. The engagement announced some months ago had perhaps been a little premature. Now, in this moment, she was sure – this was not the man for her. It was so unfair on him, she thought.

"Harvey, thank goodness you're here. We need your help." He looked down at her; her greeting was warm but failed to match the affectionate, even passionate, embrace he imagined he would receive from his future wife. The administrator put his head round the door into the hallway, coughing discreetly.

"I have just received a signal from the telegraph office addressed to you, Squadron Leader." He handed a sealed brown envelope to Wills, who took it absent-mindedly, almost afraid to let go of Ceci, and after a minute uttered his thanks to the administrator's retreating back. Wills tore open the envelope and studied the flimsy white signal sheet inside.

It ordered him and his crew, in typical military language, to investigate and to assist the local authorities with the rescue and recovery of passengers and crew believed to be from the Empress Airways Short S.23 'C' Class flying boat Cornucopia – reported lost en route from Penang to Rangoon. The aircraft had been reported to be located on the west side of an island in the Nicobar chain – it then gave the latitude and longitude position coordinates. Wills and his crew, it went on, were to recover any cargo that may remain with the aircraft and to ensure its safety until arrangements could be made for its safe and secure transport to a suitable British-administered facility. He was also requested to provide any information concerning a young woman: Cecilia Grosvenor-Ffoulkes, who was believed to be in the region and who had provided the original information concerning the lost Empress machine. He was also ordered to confirm receipt of the signal, and to advise of any courses of action he deemed appropriate. The signal was signed by the British army garrison commander in Singapore and his own CO, Wing Commander D. Chivers.

Wills and Ceci went outside and walked together along the unmade path that led back to the small port area and the telegraph office. He held her hand, but it was as though he was holding the hand of a reluctant child. He sensed she wanted to be free from further commitment or imposition. They walked, talking little, she looking down at the path, but now and again looking up at his uncertain expression. He knows, she thought, feeling embarrassed and guilty.

❖ ❖ ❖

Hyami sat in the same spot as his pilot had occupied, studying the sea in front of him. For two hours there was nothing to see; he was both bored and anxious at the same time. Just after two-fifteen, he thought he saw something, a tiny source of light moving slowly and a little erratically in the darkness towards the island from the south-east. Watching it for half an hour, he saw that despite meandering from time to time it was definitely moving in the general direction of the island. Picking up the torch, he aimed it carefully at the moving light. He twice flashed a Morse signal – a group of three letters known only to him and his agent.

Seconds later, there was an instant reply from a powerful lamp, its short burst of letters confirming the agent's identity. He was relieved and went back to the aircraft to wake his pilot; they had to make their way down to a beach on the east side of the island by daybreak.

The jungle was, if anything, more dense and difficult to penetrate than that on the island's western side. The journey was made more hazardous by the increased steepness of the terrain, broken occasionally by deep gulleys, often concealed by dense vegetation. Struggling and stumbling downwards, Hyami thought of the difficulties in transporting drums of fuel up the slope to the empty but essential DC-2; it concerned him. Both he and the pilot fell at least once into overgrown gulleys as they made their way down the island's rugged slopes. Finally, bruised, exhausted and desperately hungry, they emerged onto a narrow strip of rocky beach that was weakly lit by the sun's first rays. It was just after 6 am.

The vessel was still some way offshore and the two unwilling explorers sat watching its progress for almost an hour. As the vessel grew closer they could see that it was indeed a large, black wooden ship about a hundred feet long, paint peeling from its battered hull and off-white superstructure. It was complete with top cabin, a small open bridge of sorts, a foremast and a short, thin smokestack from which a seemingly continuous stream of heavy black smoke drifted aimlessly in the calm morning air.

He recognised his agent as the vessel dropped anchor a hundred yards off the beach. The Malay waved slowly from an open window on the ship's excuse for a bridge. The colonel briefly waved back in response, walking down towards the shoreline, anticipating a boat to take him aboard. When it arrived, he insisted that one of its two-man crew carry him over the few feet of water so that he did not get his now-battered boots wet. The pilot was ordered to remain on the shore until he returned.

On board, Hyami greeted his agent in a perfunctory manner and was introduced to the vessel's captain, and leader of its odd and threatening-looking crew. Famished, Colonel Hyami demanded breakfast, not forgetting to have some sent ashore to his pilot. After breakfast, and having taken advantage of what passed on the ship as a bathroom, they sat on the afterdeck under a hastily rigged awning, around a green baize card-table ready to plan their action. This was a gamble for all of them.

❖ ❖ ❖

Ceci explained what had happened to her since leaving Singapore. Inevitably she was obliged to introduce Harold Penrose into her story, but tried to suppress anything that did not relate directly to their search, and the finding of Cornucopia. Harvey Wills watched as she spoke, his heart slowly sinking. Deciding to put his emotions to one side for the moment, he questioned her about the location of the wrecked Cornucopia, the DC-2, her Gypsy Moth, Krishnan and his brothers – and myriad other pieces of information that would allow him to reach a rescue and recovery plan of some sort.

Their initial steps, it was decided, would be to recover the Gypsy Moth from Car Nicobar Island. They would fly the Walrus with Ceci, and thirty gallons of petrol in five-gallon cans, to the beach village on the south side of the island, where she had landed. Having refuelled the machine, she would then fly north to Port Blair and wait, out of harm's way.

Harvey Wills and David Kildonan would then continue in the Walrus to the wreck site with food and water for the survivors, to assess the situation before returning with some survivors to Port Blair. While there, they would look for the DC-2, reported to have landed on the plateau on the island's high plateau. Kildonan expressed some concern over the timing and distances involved. They discussed at length the implications of their course of action: the range of the Walrus was about six hundred miles, the distance from Port Blair to the wreck site two hundred and thirty miles. Allowing for the diversion to Car Nicobar, and the fact that the weather could hardly be relied upon, they would have to be careful about their fuel consumption if they were to have enough to undertake a return flight to Port Blair. Wills felt that the priority was to reach the survivors quickly and provide whatever help they needed without further delay, as the crew and passengers had been on their own now for well over two weeks. Sending a brief a signal to Singapore, he outlined his plan and initial course of action.

Stocks of petrol at Port Blair were limited. Irregular deliveries were made by visiting ships from time to time, but the recent increase in air activity had depleted the island airfield's reserves considerably. They managed to find, fill and filter only three five-gallon cans with petrol for Ceci's machine. With fifteen gallons she could remain airborne for about two hours – ample duration, they all agreed, for her to cover the distance between Car Nicobar and Port Blair.

There was, however, reluctance by the district administrator to authorise complete refuelling of the military Walrus. Kildonan's calculations suggested that, provided they were economical in their use of the aircraft's throttle, and did not overload the machine, they could manage a return flight to and from Cornucopia without too much difficulty.

They took off and set a course south for Car Nicobar, getting airborne by three o'clock on a hot and humid afternoon. Food, water, petrol, the two pilots and Ceci were crammed into the cockpits of the Shagbat. Keeping engine revolutions low, they crawled slowly across a hard, pale-blue sky. Over the Ten Degree Channel they observed a lively sea below, with white flashes appearing, then rolling across its surface as waves began to build and break. The wind was rising and slowing their progress. Looking down, they could see its effect on a few small vessels that were making painful progress across the channel, plumes of fine spray bursting from their bows as they cut a watery furrow, which was soon obliterated by the wave's surge. Ceci sat quietly behind Harvey Wills watching him, at a loss to understand the state of her emotions.

❖ ❖ ❖

The ship's captain and Hyami eventually agreed a plan to capture any gold lying at the survivors' wreck site on the other side of the island. The first step was to manhandle the fuel drums up to the

DC-2's location, however difficult, and to refuel the aircraft ready for a quick get-away – once most of the gold had been loaded onto the decrepit black vessel, and having dealt appropriately with Cornucopia's crew and passengers. Hyami had still not decided what to do with the four Europeans he had seen at the aircraft wreck site.

After breakfast, Hyami ordered his pilot to take one of the ship's crew and return to the aircraft, each carrying a drum of petrol. Once there, they were to manoeuvre the machine by pulling and pushing, as the pilot and Hyami had done before, so that it was positioned in such a way as to be able to take off quickly should the need arise.

They were also ordered to carefully camouflage the machine with branches and similar material against aerial observation. Hyami was now back on form, barking out his orders, strutting about in the sand, his bandaged head wagging about imperiously. The pilot picked the biggest and beefiest of the motley ship's company and led the way back up the steep eastern slopes; each carried a five-gallon canister of petrol on their backs, plus a little water and food – it was going to be heavy, thirsty work, the pilot suspected.

Meanwhile, other members of the ship's disparate crew set about unloading the rest of the fuel. Hyami also insisted on inspecting the weapons they had brought with them; it was an odd collection of rifles and pistols, some rather ancient, together with a box of four grenades of indeterminate age. Later that morning, each of the ship's nine crewmen was given a weapon to clean and check, together with two five-gallon cans of petrol to carry up to the DC-2. With over seventy pounds strapped to their backs it took a gruelling six and a half hours for them to deliver the first load of fuel and to return eventually to the beach and ship. They sat, battered and quiet, around the deck of the rolling vessel, some wondering what they had got themselves into.

On the plateau the DC-2 had once again been pushed, pulled and levered into a position that would allow it a straight run down the torn runway. With help from the later-arriving ship's 'porters', the pilot poured just fifty-five gallons of vital petrol into the machine's tanks. It was not much but it would get them off the island. They then cut and placed large branches with green fronds across the polished skin of the aeroplane, ensuring that not a glint from its silver reflective sheen could escape. Once most of the ship's crew had finally left, staggering down the slope to the beaches below, the pilot started to investigate possible problems with the oily starboard engine, and made a full inspection of the aircraft for signs of damage after the loud cracking noise they had heard as they landed three nights earlier.

The oil problem proved to be easy both to find and to fix with the few tools they carried; it was a simple matter of reconnecting and tightening a rubber oil hose that had become partially disconnected from the starboard engine's oil tank. In the medium term, the pilot recognised that it could prove to be a problem. The leaking oil pipe had allowed a significant loss of precious engine oil that their small on-board reserves were unable to replace completely.

In the failing light of early evening, and not made easier by the layer of leafy camouflage hanging from the aircraft's structure, the pilot spent time looking carefully around the aircraft for anything that might reflect damage, or something that would explain the resounding crack.

In particular he spent time groping around in the undercarriage bays and tailwheel, cleaning out bits of branches, leaves and detritus and looking carefully for any tell-tale signs of structural failure or damage. There was nothing he could see that suggested a problem, yet his past experience as a test pilot told him that the loud noise they had heard signified that something, somewhere in the aircraft had experienced serious mechanical damage.

Hyami, still energetic, spent the late hours finalising his plans for recovering the gold with his agent and the ship's captain. They agreed that they would do it tomorrow, at twilight, so that after a successful raid on Cornucopia, the small, tattered ship, loaded with booty, and the aircraft, with Hyami on board, could, hoped, escape under cover of darkness. He had planned that the black ship would make a prearranged rendezvous, unobserved, with a Japanese merchant ship in the Indian Ocean. The ship would return to Japan with most of the captured gold on board while a triumphant Hyami would fly home, using the DC-2, carrying a small amount of the looted gold.

Before the plan could be put into effect, there still remained the need to fully fuel the DC-2 if they were to make their way to Japan without stopping in any British controlled areas. The aircraft had a range of nine hundred miles, so, after discussion with his pilot, Hyami decided to fly direct to Medan in northern Sumatra to refuel. They would then continue further south-east over Sumatra to Palembang for more fuel, then continuing, curve north-eastwards through Kuching, and Manila, in the Philippines, until finally, island-hopping across the Pacific via Formosa to arrive in Japan; no doubt to be met by approving looks and comments from his masters. It was a long and dangerous flight over remote seas, swamps and jungle; there were no guarantees of precious fuel being available at some of the airfields that they intended to visit en route.

At daybreak the small ship's crew were fed, then cajoled with further promises of riches into carrying further supplies of petrol up what had now become an established path, avoiding most of the hazardous pitfalls that lay in wait behind tangled undergrowth. The pilot took each precious can and poured its crucial, combustible content carefully into the DC-2's cavernous tanks until, finally, they were brimming. Thankful, the exhausted crewmen staggered back down onto the beach, hot and thirsty, after their final gruelling struggle with the awkward, heavy petrol cans. They collapsed, sprawling over the rocks in afternoon shade.

Aware of his need for their total co-operation and commitment, Hyami insisted that they should rest undisturbed for the remaining few hours before their intended action. Surprisingly, he had arranged for a full and proper meal to be prepared ready for their return from the plateau. But they were too hot and tired to appreciate any food.

The ship's diesel engine was run for a few minutes to confirm its fitness for the task ahead, Hyami screaming for its shut-down as plumes of filthy, greasy-black smoke erupted from the vessel's stack, rising into the warm air and providing a useful marker for anyone intent on finding them. As the late-afternoon shadows lengthened, the crew were summoned back on board from their prone, random scattering along the shady beach. All trace of their occupation of the remote and pristine beach and its surrounding jungle were carefully erased before the final man came aboard, and the anchor was raised. Once all were aboard, the ship turned to face the sea for its short voyage around the south coast of the island. Hyami began briefing the crew. There were to be no prisoners, none who could bear witness to their actions.

❖ ❖ ❖

Turning around Car Nicobar after a slow but uneventful flight, the Walrus landed safely off the beach where Ceci's Gypsy Moth lay undisturbed against the trees. The aircraft taxied up to the shelving shoreline, and the engine stopped. Kildonan managed to heave a line to a young villager, who secured it to a stout tree. Again, everyone from the village, apart from its young men, was out in force, led by the village elder. They helped to carry the fuel heavy cans from the Walrus up the beach, where Ceci carefully poured their clear, shimmering and vaporous contents into the Gypsy's top tank. The empty petrol cans were made a gift to the village elder.

Preparing to leave again, Harvey Wills walked with Ceci, well away from the crowd. Stopping, he held her hands gently in his, looking carefully into her face; her eyes were downcast. He thought that now – this moment – he needed to ask the question; although he already knew what the answer would be.

"Darling, Ceci. What's happened, have you stopped loving me?" he searched her face for some clue as to her true feelings.

She fell helplessly against his shoulder, and he could feel her silent, stifled sobs. This was answer enough, if not explanation. He held her for a while, savouring the feel of her, until, resigned; he gently kissed her salty cheek and pulled away. She turned away as he left, not wanting the gathering to see her distress. Wills returned grim-faced to the Walrus, casting off the temporary mooring rope, he splashed through the shallow water and heaved himself on board, water pouring from his boots and uniform trousers. With barely a word, he prepared for flight, taxiing the ungainly-looking amphibian out into the sea beyond the growing breakers and took off. Ceci watched, crestfallen. Why had she not explained? It was the very least she could do under the circumstances. Ceci was genuinely concerned for him; it must be such a let-down – a real blow – and what would he do now?

The village elder's daughter walked slowly to where Ceci sat, half-concealed in among the trees backing the beach. She sat quietly next to the sobbing young woman, placing a comforting arm around her shoulder.

Despite a favourable tailwind back to Port Blair, Ceci decided to stay on Car Nicobar for the night, she did not feel up to flying on her own in her present emotional state. The young woman walked with her back to the village, welcoming her into her own small home.

Unrefreshed by eight hours' unbroken sleep, Ceci arose and wearily looked out of the small window that faced the sea. There was a great deal of activity on the shore; young men and women were lifting baskets and boxes full of goods from a small rowing boat pulled up beyond the surf, and carrying them up into the village. Beyond lay a long, high-bowed vessel, anchored a half a mile out, its crew passing more boxes and baskets to men in other small craft secured along its side. Ceci quickly dressed and joined the throng hard at work. It was clear that the vessel was a trading craft, carrying anything and everything for the islanders.

Then it occurred to her that they might be carrying petrol. Rushing back to the head-man's house she saw the three empty petrol cans still lying outside. Taking one, she ran back just in time to ask a boatman preparing to row out to the trading schooner whether they were carrying petrol. He looked at the animated young white woman, mouth agape, trying to understand but it was clear to him what she wanted. Ceci opened the can and put her nose into the hole, making a sniffing gesture. He watched, somewhat bemused for a moment and then, taking the proffered can, he too sniffed its volatile vapour. The penny dropped. He nodded vigorously. Ceci held up her fingers, trying to indicate how much. Again, his comprehension was being stretched. Getting into the boat, she pointed out towards the schooner enquiringly. This he clearly understood, and rowed.

On board the ship she managed a fractured conversation with a tall, bony man wearing a torn and weathered orange shirt with very off-white trousers, cut off at the knee above a pair of very large, strong feet. He seemed to be in charge of things. Whether he was the captain or not Ceci was unsure. After supervising the loading of another heavy rowing boat with goods and sending it on its way, he led her down into the dim, pungent-smelling hold, full of everything from spices and brushes to rolls of sticky tar paper. Towards the stern, he dragged away some heavy wooden boxes, revealing a neatly stacked pile of shiny tin cans, all roped together under a net. They were about the same size as the ones collected by Harvey at Port Blair. Carefully pulling the net aside, she prised three of the cans out onto the uneven deck. The man looked at her as she pulled some dirty notes from her pocket and held them out He inspected the currency without taking it from her hand then, nodding, said, "Not good."

She looked at the money. It was certainly a little creased and torn but it was still money. He bent and picked up the three petrol cans with little effort and walked back to the short wooden ladder that led up to the vessel's main deck and the sunshine. Ceci followed, not quite sure how to resolve the situation. Was he going to let her buy the fuel?

As she straightened up from the ladder, shielding her eyes from the bright sun, she became aware of a smiling face watching her. It was a face she knew but could not place for a moment. Then, at the instant of recognition, the young girl began to laugh delicately behind her raised hand. It was the intruder from the Gypsy Moth, the would-be nocturnal pilot, the girl who tried to comfort her yesterday.

Laughing, the tall, bony man turned, "She sister, you stop hitting."

The young girl was also the same who had submitted to violence from her father before Ceci's intervention. They all smiled at each other, and language seemed unimportant at that moment, although they could have spent hours in each other's company, just chatting.

The girl's tall brother carried the cans to the ship's side and hailed the waiting oarsman below. The cans were casually cast down and expertly caught. Ceci kissed the girl on the forehead and shook the enormous brown hand of her brother. Swinging her legs over the gunwale and timing her drop into the small boat with the surging swell, she was rowed ashore, waving and smiling.

Another fifteen gallons of fuel would give her a full pair of tanks when added to the fuel brought from Port Blair with Harvey in the Walrus. The brief reminder of Harvey dampened her spirits again as she filled the Gypsy Moth with petrol. The guilt would stay with her for some time to come, she knew.

She had decided. She would not go back to Port Blair to await the outcome but would fly south, to their small camp, and Harold. Filling the tanks in the heat of the forenoon was uncomfortable work; the petrol sloshed about, liberating volatile fumes that drifted around, making her feel light-headed. After a short break in the shade, she started to inspect the Gypsy Moth, readying it for flight. As she worked her way around, testing struts and rigging, flying controls and engine bay, she came to the wing where the hole had been made by the girl. She had actually forgotten about the problem, but it had been repaired, neatly sewn with dozens of tiny stitches so that no gap appeared in the rent; it was perfection. She looked up, amazed at such handiwork, and was grateful.

Lifting the tail, Ceci managed with difficulty to swing the aircraft around to face down the beach. Walking back the short distance to the huts, she thanked the village elder for their hospitality to her, and collected her few belongings, taking a final rinse from the porcelain bowl in the English mahogany wash stand.

She would have to start the machine herself, and placed two halves of coconut shells under the wheels as makeshift chocks. When everything was ready, she switched on the two sets of magneto switches and pulled. The engine caught immediately, its signature bark resounding off the fringing trees. Throttling back to idle, she bent down, clear of the whirring propeller, carefully removing the two shells under each wheel, then climbed aboard. A few minutes later she was looking down on the industrious scene on the beach. They all stopped to watch, waving as she made a shallow dive along the beach, gently waggling her wings before climbing to the south under maximum power.

❖ ❖ ❖

The crew of the Walrus found Cornucopia with little trouble, overflying the island first to check on the location of the DC-2 that Ceci had reported. They could certainly see where something had torn up the ground on the plateau that topped the island, but no sign of any aircraft. Descending, they reconnoitred the beaches and seascape prior to landing on the bay's calm waters, just off the wreck site. As the Walrus taxied in towards the beach, the small group of survivors stood waving and laughing. Cutting the engine, Wills allowed the aircraft to drift in towards them until its keel gently rode a foot or two onto the shelving sand. Greeting the two pilots with great enthusiasm, they unloaded boxes of food from the laden Walrus. Their diet had become increasingly monotonous as the days had passed, and the tins and baskets of fresh food looked tempting. Purser Snell started preparing a celebratory dinner for the two pilots and the survivors; there was even a welcome bottle of single malt in the stores.

Squadron Leader Harvey Wills was introduced to Captain Michael Kelly, who had managed to hobble with Sarah's help to the edge of the surf. After shaking hands and exchanging greetings, they retired to the shade of the trees to discuss a proposed rescue plan, and to brief Wills as to what had happened to them since leaving Penang. Kelly quickly ran through the salient events, including the finding of the magnet attached to his aircraft compass. Sarah showed Wills where the recovered bullion was buried, and later told him about Michael Kelly's injuries and what she had been able to do to help him.

The Squadron Leader returned to his beached aircraft to collect its first-aid kit, which he passed to Sarah Gregson. She was grateful to have it, having been finding it increasingly difficult to make do with the bandages from her torn clothes. The small pouches of sulphonamide powder would be useful in keeping any further infections at bay.

Over an early alfresco dinner the two military pilots and survivors got to know each other better, aided to some extent by liberal toasts of whisky: the bottle did not last long. They discussed the reported sighting of a Dutch-registered DC-2 on their island by the pilot of the Gypsy Moth. Harvey Wills went on to say that there had been no sighting of the DC-2 as they had flown over its landing site atop the island. Colonel Deverall reported their expedition up into the island's interior, soon after they had been wrecked all those days ago, and their spying on what was probably the same machine just before it had taken off. Then Michael Kelly recounted the extraordinary events over their beach when the DC-2 and Gypsy Moth had performed their dangerous aerial jousting.

Harvey Wills swallowed hard when he heard this. As a professional, Michael Kelly was well placed to give a detailed commentary on the near-suicidal flying by the pilots of both machines. He reported that the Gypsy Moth had flown over their camp a few days earlier, but without dropping any form of communication, as it had done on previous occasions.

Twilight enveloped them, and they relaxed in the knowledge that some of them would be flown off the island in the morning; it had been decided that Sarah, Beth and Purser Snell would go, together with a few boxes of gold. David Kildonan would stay with the survivors, allowing more passengers to fly back to Penang.

❖ ❖ ❖

The black ship, near invisible in the growing darkness, made deliberately slow progress around the island, skirting its southernmost point until, moving at a few knots northwards, it approached the southerly end of the small bay in which Cornucopia's smashed hull lay. Hyami was a consummate professional as a military commander; as they sidled up the coastline, he ordered the ship to stop and anchor briefly, just before entering the bay. Ordering away a small boat, into which he clambered with one crewman, they rowed stealthily up the coastline until, finally, he was just able to see the white carcass of the Empress flying boat.

He was surprised and annoyed to also see a military flying boat resting on the shore just beyond it. Through his binoculars he was just able to pick out some figures seated around a fire between the shore and the dark backdrop of the surrounding jungle. He noticed they appeared to be quite animated. However, discovery of the military machine was a blow to his hopes of an easy recovery of any gold. It suggested strongly that they would have to fight.

They rowed back to the ship. Once on board, Hyami reported the new situation to the captain and crew. It was decided that they would leave their approach to the wreck site until the early hours of the morning when, they hoped, the four survivors and, hopefully, the pilots of the military amphibian aircraft would be sleeping deeply. They had four hours to kill, and most of them took the opportunity to catch up on some sleep. The black vessel, at anchor, rolled gently in the oily swell while Hyami, his agent and the ship's captain sat watching the dark coast.

❖ ❖ ❖

The Gypsy Moth behaved perfectly as Ceci flew south towards Harold, Krishnan and the rest of his ship-wrecked crew. She circled Krishnan's village on Camorta, seeing a large fishing boat bobbing offshore. Men were working on the shoreline as she continued to circle, trying to attract their attention.

"Damn," she muttered, "nothing to write with, nothing to write on. Bugger!" Her last resort was to zoom down over the beach and back up, and fly off in the direction of her island base waggling her wings, hoping that they would get the message. This she did no less than three times. The men continued to wave, at least on two occasions, but seemed to take little notice of her third attempt.

Giving up in exasperation, she flew on, surprising the small community at her temporary base as she turned smartly, lined-up and landed on a wide damp-firm beach, before they could gather their thoughts. She was out of the aircraft quickly, running back along the beach towards Harold Penrose. He grabbed her as she jumped into his arms, and held her. This was it, she knew.

"My God, I've missed you, Ceci." The words were out before he could think – and seemed inadequate. Ceci said nothing, just happy to be in Harold's arms again. Later, after they had eaten, Ceci had told him what had happened at Port Blair as they went for a long walk hand-in-hand along the sand, followed by a cooling swim in the still waters. They made love on the wide, empty beach, the moon hiding its face behind wispy clouds as they coupled passionately.

❖ ❖ ❖

The crew were awakened and made ready. Weapons were loaded and checked again, shovels put into the two heavy wooden rowing boats that would take Hyami and his raiders silently onto the sleeping beach. The black ship was anchored just inside the southern arm of the small bay. They carefully disembarked, four to each boat, and began rowing deep into the bay, towards the shore where Cornucopia lay. There appeared to be no signs of life on the beach, just the dying glow from a fire.

Hyami ordered that the two boats should approach the beach on either side of the wrecked flying boat. It would give them a better chance of surprise should one group be detected in the darkness. They placed the oars carefully into the water on each stroke, trying not to splash in the almost motionless sea. The two crews sat watching ahead, alert and ready.

As his boat ran softly up onto the sand, Hyami jumped ashore. Holding himself low, he placed a finger over his lips, encouraging silence from his rag-tag accomplices as they disembarked.

Immediately to his left he could see the white, broken mass of Cornucopia. Beyond it, the other crew would be making their approach under the command of the ship's captain. He noticed the shadow of the military flying boat off to his left. It was now high and dry on the beach where the tide had left it. Creeping almost silently in the fine sand, taking advantage of the shadows, he led his group around the beach and into the deeper darkness of the tree line.

Sarah Gregson awoke. Beth was crying in her sleep and she rose to comfort the agitated little girl. Picking her up, and talking softly to her, she glanced out from their crude shelter towards the beach and its fringing jungle. Something glinted for a second in the near-darkness; she looked harder, thinking it unusual. Then she heard a noise. Perhaps someone had gone for a pee and had knocked into something? Bending and stroking the little girl's hair, she prepared to put her back into the small bed made by Purser Snell. She glanced up once more. There was someone there, just inside the tree line. In fact, it looked as if it could be more than one person, but it was so difficult to see.

By the time she had set the sleeping Beth down and pulled a cover over her, Sarah was now fully alert. Leaving the shelter, she walked towards the remnants of the campfire, expecting to meet one of the group, as she sometimes had for a nocturnal chat until tiredness caught up with her again. As she stood waiting, wrapped only in the remains of a thin cotton bunk cover from Cornucopia, she was glad of the warmth from the glowing embers.

In a second, something wrapped itself around her throat. She quickly realised it was a rough, muscular and hairy arm, and it was accompanied by a strong, unwashed odour. He pulled her down onto the sand and grappled for her mouth unsuccessfully.

She let off a short, shrill scream. The fist hit her in the mouth. She tasted blood, warm and salty, before he turned her brutally onto her face, holding it into the sand. Kicking and struggling resulted in two heavy blows to her head. She remained still.

Michael Kelly heard the scream. Waking, he waited for a few seconds. Was it a dream scream? Was it real? Looking across, he could see that Sarah was not there, next to him. Mildly alarmed, he sat up, grabbing for his wooden crutch. Kneeling, he pulled himself upright using the tree that supported part of the shelter. Crutch under his right arm, he staggered out from cover, looking about in the darkness.

There were shadows moving about to the right of Cornucopia; he could just make out the dark shape of a boat being pulled up the shoreline and phosphorescent splashes as men raced through the water. It struck him in an instant: if this was a rescue, why so quiet and secretive? He shouted out to the moving figures.

"Hey! Who are you?" His shout awoke the campsite, as did the subsequent volley of shots that arched over their shelter. Lying down, he called out again.

"Sarah, where are you?" No reply. But Beth was crying again and there was the sound of men breathing hard and grunting with the effort of running up the sandy beach towards him.

Hyami co-ordinated the raid, rushing the sleeping area around the shelter and campfire; his crew pointed weapons at the assembled survivors and shone torches into their faces. Sarah was dragged from where she had been brutally pulled down, and left gasping at their feet. It was difficult for her to breathe; she rolled over, revealing a bloody face caked in sand. Kelly crawled quickly towards her, half falling at her side.

"You bastards! What do you want – why do this to a woman?"

he shouted angrily, pointing at the Sarah lying painfully beside him. One of the crew stepped towards him, lashing out with his rifle, striking the crippled captain painfully across the shoulders. He fell across Sarah, writhing, trying to raise himself.

Hyami ordered that the survivors be tied up. Sarah and Beth were roped together back-to-back sitting on the sand, Sarah trying to comfort the sobbing and petrified little girl as best she could. Kelly's crutch was thrown onto the fire, burning brightly for an instant as he was tied up, face down. David Rawlinson and the pilot Kildonan were roped together, Rawlinson swearing and cursing until, like Kelly, he was struck a vicious blow with the side of a rifle that took his breath. It left a bruise from his left shoulder almost to his waist, the skin broken and bleeding, the blood seeping through his shirt.

From the trees there was the sound of struggling and shouting. A shot was fired. More shouting followed. Then, the crump of heavy blows being struck. George Hudson was pushed, staggering, into the arc of light from the fire, his arms held taut behind. His face was covered in blood, which was dripping from his chin down his front. Two of Hyami's crew had seen and caught him running up the slope away from the camp. Their gunshot served as a stark warning to George that his intended action might prove fatal. He stopped, hands held up. The two men had beaten him for pleasure with their weapons. Hyami walked to where Hudson lay, panting and bleeding.

"Escaping, were we, English? We need to do something for those nasty wounds, don't we Mister?" his lip curled in menace. Burying the toe of his boot in the beach, he kicked a cloud of sand into Hudson's unprotected face. The movement was quick, with no forewarning, and the prostrate Hudson had no time to avert or close his eyes. The pain was shocking.

The moon, now risen and nearly full, cast cold, silvery light on the scene. The black ship's captain looked around at the prisoners. There were four men, a woman and a sobbing child. Hyami had told him that he had counted four survivors when he had reconnoitred the site earlier. Now they had six, the additional two no doubt accounted for by the pilots of the military flying boat stranded on the sand; he had noticed that one of their captives seemed to be wearing a uniform.

Four of the raiders retrieved shovels from the rowing boats and began digging frantically at the place where Hyami had remembered seeing the bullion box buried during his reconnaissance visit. Soon, there was a triumphant cry from one of the men. He bent, and with help, lifted something large and obviously heavy from the sand and enmeshed roots under the trees. They smashed the box with their shovels, the wood splintering noisily, allowing them to pull four gold ingots out. Hyami strode to the diggers and snatched one of the ingots from their hands. Looking closely at it in the torchlight, he could see the regular shape of a solid lump of metal with its markings. It was heavy, it was gold: of that he had absolutely no doubt.

With all hands working fast, the bullion was recovered from its shallow grave and stacked on the shoreline ready for transporting out to the black ship. Hyami was elated; it had taken a remarkably short time to restrain the survivors and capture the precious metal. The black ship was summoned from its anchored position by Hyami firing three gunshots in quick succession from his heavy pistol. As its shadowy form hove close into view, men were already rowing out towards it with four boxes laid carefully on the bottom boards of the two heavy rowing boats. Two raiders were sent with four of the heavy ingots, in their wooden boxes, secured by broad webbing straps to their backs, to the DC-2, high up on the island's central plateau; Hyami sent a message with them for the pilot to say he would be with him within one or two hours and that he must prepare the aircraft to leave.

Colonel Deverall, Squadron Leader Wills and Purser Snell watched carefully from their cover about two hundred yards away, concealed in a shallow dip in the sand just where the beach met the fringing trees. They had been playing cards in candlelight when the rest of the party had retired, and had moved away to a convenient spot where they would not disturb the sleepers. They had played a few rounds of poker, talking and laughing, cheered by the remains of the malt whisky. Finally, they had succumbed to tiredness and lay for a while, chatting under the trees and watching the abundant stars overhead until finally falling asleep. The noise of shooting and shouting awoke them quickly, but they were prevented from running immediately to the rescue by Colonel Deverall.

Watching as best they could, listening to the shouts and shots, they felt horror and anger at the events they could hear unfolding further down the beach. The rumpus stopped as quickly as it had started. Now and then they could see the outline of two men walking quickly towards the jungle; they would pass only a few yards from their position. The two men, talking to each other and obviously quite pleased with themselves, entered the tree line and disappeared. Snell darted quietly after them before Wills or Deverall could stop him. The two raiders, convinced that no one else was about, crashed noisily through the jungle, their torchlight easily followed by the pursuing Snell.

He thought that they were obviously fit and no doubt well

motivated as they moved quickly up the steepening incline through the heavy undergrowth. Snell was having trouble at times keeping pace with them. He was also worried because his spontaneous pursuit had not really been fully considered. He was not exactly sure what he was going to do. He had no weapon but he knew where they were probably going. He had been this way before with Colonel Deverall; on that occasion they had seen the shiny Dutch aeroplane at the top of the island, and had almost been seen themselves.

Trying to contain his heavy breathing as he followed at a discreet distance in the darkness, he considered what he might do to stop the two men, possibly even capture them. Then an idea occurred to him that just might thwart their likely plans, if he could find the raw materials.

❖ ❖ ❖

Deverall and Wills crawled from their hiding place, moving silently towards the trees, intending to circle around the campsite to where the Walrus lay. It was stranded well up the beach; Wills and Kildonan had somehow forgotten to allow for the tide when they had beached the machine in the shelving waters the previous afternoon. Wills knew that in the cockpit there was a Very pistol, used for firing magnesium signal lights into the air. Unfortunately, the two machine guns usually fitted to the Walrus had been removed prior to the search mission to reduce weight, allowing them to lift any survivors found back to civilisation. He might, however, be able to create some confusion and possibly sabotage the raiders' plans if he could retrieve the Very pistol and perhaps fire a few of the highly incendiary cartridges into the ship they could now see brightly lit just offshore. And then he remembered being told of Deverall's service revolver, which had been recovered from Cornucopia, cleaned and kept wrapped in cloth under Michael Kelly's bed in the shelter.

Under Hyami's direction, the raiders' attention was directed at moving the bullion by boat out to the waiting ship.

"Damn the bloody moon," Wills muttered quietly to Deverall as they crawled along around the outer edge of the beach. The raiders were probably too busy loading and rowing to notice them, he hoped, but they could clearly see one armed man standing guard near the fire, watching over the captives. The guard was under instructions to shoot dead anyone who attempted escape or made a nuisance of themselves. Hyami's recent and proven Manchurian suppression techniques were being given free rein again on this night. The prisoners lay or sat, watching or listening to proceedings, wondering what their fate would be once the bullion loading was completed.

Deverall and Wills hatched a very simple plan together, whispering desperately, concealed in the jungle.

"As their main concern is to capture the bullion, we should wait until they're ready to row out with the last load. I think it's then that they might take action against our friends." Deverall hypothesised. Wills nodded agreement in the darkness.

"Okay, if we can reach your revolver in Michael's tent, and the Walrus's Very gun independently, we might be able to confuse them to a point where they abandon any ideas of harming their prisoners and make for the ship with the gold," said Wills, carefully scanning the campsite.

"Yes, but how will we co-ordinate our efforts in the darkness? We need to be able to disable that guard by the fire quickly so that he can't hurt anyone," interrupted Deverall.

"If we synchronise our watches now and leave, say ... ten

minutes, then I'll fire a Very light in the direction of the ship or the nearest rowing boat. That will be your signal to fire at the guard first, and then shoot at anyone else who presents a target, with the revolver."

"Agreed," whispered Deverall. Synchronising their watches, they separated in the darkness, Wills making for the stranded Walrus aircraft, Deverall hoping to penetrate the campsite unseen and get into Kelly's sleeping quarters to collect his service revolver.

Wills had the most difficult job; it proved necessary to move quickly and quietly through the trees until at a point where the size and shape of the Walrus would mask his approach to the aircraft from the jungle's edge. Leaving the dark shelter of the trees, he would have to crawl about two hundred yards diagonally across open, undulating beach in the moonlight. He knew that he could not be seen by the raiders on the beach or from the campsite, but anyone using binoculars on the ship, or even glancing back from a rowing boat, might just be able to pick out his moving shape against the pale moonlit sand.

Belly down, Wills crawled as quickly as he dared across the exposed beach, all the time watching the dark mass of the ship, anchored just offshore, and the comings and goings of the boats. Deverall, meanwhile, managed to creep soundlessly through the jungle, past the waterfall and around to the back of the campsite, eventually entering Kelly's sleeping quarters, sliding deftly under the leafy sidewall. He groped about under the simple bed, feeling for the pistol. It was not there. Time was running out. He had actually seen Kelly put the weapon under the bed days ago; it must be here. Fearful of making too much noise and attracting unwanted attention, he very slowly pulled the roughly constructed bed up, leaning it against the tree. It was nearly eight minutes since they had separated – Wills would be ready to fire the signal light shortly. Down on his knees, he calmly swept the sandy area with his fingers where the bed had sat, perspiration dripping from his brow.

His fingers finally touched something near to where the head of the bed would have been. His hand closed over the weapon, still wrapped in cloth. His only concern now was whether the ammunition was still okay after its days submerged in Cornucopia's waterlogged hull.

Moving silently from the cover of the sleeping quarters, he unwrapped the heavy revolver. He could just see the guard standing facing him, thirty yards away. He was distracted, watching and kicking something on the ground in front of him, the glow from the fire's embers lighting his face.

Wills had finally slunk snake-like into the cockpit of the Walrus, pulling the Very pistol from its canvas stowage just behind the pilots' seats. As he grabbed a handful of cartridges from an adjacent canvas holder his heart jumped into his mouth when one of the heavy, brass-bound shells fell, rattling noisily onto the metal cockpit floor. The raiders were too busy plundering to hear a sound from inside the Shagbat.

Pushing half a dozen of the large cartridges into his pockets, he climbed stealthily out of the aircraft crawling on the raiders' blind side towards the aircraft's nose. Glancing at his watch, he saw that he had just twenty seconds before he was supposed to fire the first signal flare. Opening the muzzle of the Very pistol, he pushed the large cartridge into its barrel and snapped the breech closed, hearing the catch click home.

'Let's hope you're ready, Deverall. Here goes,' he muttered as, holding the weapon as far away from him as possible, he took rough aim at a rowing boat just leaving the beach, heavy and low in the water. He fired. He had never actually fired one in anger before and the recoil and noise of the weapon's explosion, followed by the arcing signal light, shocked him for an instant. From across the beach he heard the single sharp report of a heavy revolver. Glancing in that direction he saw the fireside guard crumple in the flaring red signal light.

He turned his attention to where the red signal flare was falling; it was going to miss the rowing boat he had aimed at, and finally fell wide, hissing into the water. Pushing another cartridge into the hot breach, he fired again. This time the flare was glaring white against the dark sky, creating stark shadows around the campsite. Not waiting for it to expire, he loaded another and fired again, aiming at the ship, which was now lying barely a hundred yards offshore.

Deverall took advantage of the noise and light provided by Wills's action and knelt, taking careful aim at one of the raiders, who was loading some of the last of the bullion cases into a waiting boat. He knew that it was a long shot for a pistol, however expert the marksman. Deverall could only hope to confuse and worry the raiders with his efforts. He struck lucky. The man, holding onto one end of a box, suddenly screamed and fell sideways into the water, the box falling into the water beside him with a huge phosphorescent splash. He guessed he had managed to hit him in the leg and grinned grimly to himself. Another of the raiders ran to the boat and was trying to lift the wounded man from the water and drag him into the boat. Deverall sighted again and pulled the revolver's trigger. Nothing – the round was a dud.

Someone started firing from the ship but it did not appear to either Wills or Deverall as though the gunman had any real target in sight. Running in the darkness, the colonel made it to the campfire. The gunman on the ship had now chosen this as his general target area, firing indiscriminately. Every so often a round caused a spurt of sand to jump as it struck home among the cowering survivors.

Picking up the rifle dropped by the now-dead guard, Deverall cocked the weapon and took aim at the departing rowing boat. There was a flash from the muzzle; he saw the oarsman lurch sideways, leaning over the side of the small vessel. In the light of another of Wills's flares, red this time, he saw the other man in the boat stand up, trying to pull the injured rower off the thwart so that he could manoeuvre the heavy boat. Deverall fired again. It was clear that he had hit the second man square in the chest, his arms shooting up at the moment of impact. The victim fell back into the boat. The injured oarsman, motivated by fear, sat up fully and contrived to carry on rowing back to the ship.

Deverall saw that there were still a few boxes of bullion left on the shore; however, there did not seem to be any other boat coming back to collect them. He continued firing towards the rowing boat until it disappeared into the darkness around the side of the ship, and the rifle had run out of ammunition. Still gripping the revolver, he crossed the beach, keeping low, there were still occasional rounds being loosed off from the black ship towards them. He needed more light if he was to use his remaining and precious ammunition to useful effect.

As Deverall arrived at the Walrus, Wills was trying to clear a jammed cartridge from within the Very pistol's breach. Somehow the brass band around its base it had become distorted and stayed stuck, refusing to be ejected. They banged the gun onto the side of the Walrus to try and free it until, finally, after precious minutes, the burnt cartridge dropped onto the sand. Loading another round, Wills stood, defying the incoming bullets and taking aim at the mass of the ship, which was swinging around as its anchor was hauled in. As it swung broadside, presenting a larger target, he fired. The signal flare, burning bright-green, arced low over the beach casting an unnatural, vivid light across its expanse before crossing the lapping waves and out into the bay. From its apogee it began to fall slowly towards the ship. It landed on the roof of the vessel's bridge, burning brightly there for a few seconds, appearing to splutter out.

Deverall cast about as another flare ascended, looking for any other raiders who may be still on the beach. Wills let off his last flare towards the stationary ship. As it reached its zenith, lighting up a huge area, Deverall sighted a single individual, a grey shadow, two or three hundred yards behind them, running quickly for the cover of the jungle. The target was very small and carrying what appeared to be a rifle. Holding the pistol with two hands out in front of him, he carefully lined up with the swiftly moving target and pulled the trigger. The figure moved into the shadows, still running. Deverall had no more ammunition left.

Watching together from their vantage point behind the Walrus, they could see that the bow of the ship was pointing seaward and that the vessel was gathering way, a phosphorescent froth emerging from under her stern. Still somebody was shooting from the ship but the shots were wayward and presented only a small risk to those sheltering ashore. The two military men ran back towards the campfire, fearful of what they would find.

David Kildonan and Rawlinson were rolling about on the sand together, almost free of the bonds that had held them back-to-back. Deverall pulled Sarah's erstwhile surgeon's knife from the kitchen bench they had built beside the fire, and slit the rope freeing them. Rawlinson jumped up and ran towards his captain, who was still lying awkwardly across Sarah Gregson. Gently, he turned the pilot over and laid him carefully on his back.

"Take more than a bloody Jap to stop Michael Kelly!" He winced as he gasped out the defiant statement, then, "Check Sarah, quick." Relieved of his weight and the ropes securing her to little Beth, Sarah sat up on one elbow, looking about and rubbing her battered face. Her daughter, sobbing uncontrollably, held her round the neck, repeating, "Mummy, Mummy, Mummy!" David Kildonan helped her to her feet, leading her to a makeshift seat in front of the fire. In its flickering light he could see how brutal the attack had been. She had been lucky, no teeth had been dislodged. But her face was swollen and her lips cut and split.

"You're going to have a great black eye in the morning, Ma'am," he remarked. Rawlinson then turned his attention to George Hudson, gently brushing the loose sand from his face where he could. Then he made his way in the darkness to the waterfall with a large pan from Cornucopia's galley. Deverall went with him, taking the empty pistol and torch in case they met someone untoward. The colonel felt that as a last resort he could throw the gun at any assailant.

The next hour, under the moon's fading, cold gaze and a revitalised campfire, was spent cleaning and attending the survivors' wounds as best they could. Deverall and Wills were concerned for the safety of the unusually impetuous Purser Snell. Kildonan, with the help of the colonel, collected the eight boxes of bullion left at the water's edge and carried them breathlessly into the jungle, far from their original hiding place. Wills later went to inspect the Walrus aircraft. The tide was on the make and soon the stranded aircraft would be afloat again. He wondered what to do in the light of the raid. Should he try to find the black ship and somehow stop it? He was mindful that they had just enough fuel aboard to reach Port Blair again. Or should he return to Port Blair at first light with some of the survivors, as originally planned? He discussed the issue with Michael Kelly, Colonel Deverall and David Kildonan. It was finally agreed that he should fly direct back to Port Blair with survivors and see if he could summon naval help to look for and intercept the black ship at sea.

❖ ❖ ❖

Harry Snell followed the two raiders up the side of the island. Their pace had slowed somewhat as the weight on their backs and the challenge of the dense jungle and difficult, steep terrain took its toll. They both seemed completely oblivious to the noise and lights they were showing, obviously believing that they were quite safe, having subdued the crew and survivors of Cornucopia. After almost two hours he lost sight of them; above him, a few pale beams of moonlight were penetrating the canopy. They had reached the plateau about ten minutes ahead of him. He approached the edge of the tree line with absolute caution. Both men were armed, and if their behaviour on the beach was any guide, they would think nothing of liquidating him without compunction. Moving quietly towards the last few trees, he stood silently for a few minutes, listening and looking. There was some noise off to his left. As he moved a few yards further out from the trees he could see occasional flickers of light from a torch moving away from him, quickly now, down towards the end of the plateau and its tall trees, half a mile or so away.

As he watched, he was just able to discern some odd shadowy

movements right at the very edge of the trees. It appeared to him that the forest was being blown down, yet there was no wind, it was moving very unnaturally. Then the picture resolved itself as the shiny aircraft, reflecting moonlight, was partially exposed, its nose pointing down the makeshift runway almost towards him. He could not see how many men there were, but he considered that there were probably more than he could handle on his own. Pulling back into the shadows again, sitting, he wondered how he alone could prevent their escape. He knew now that his original idea had no hope in the circumstances.

Suddenly, just a few yards from his concealed position he saw a small, armed man stumble noisily through the loose vegetation in the direction taken by the two raiders some minutes before. Should he attack the man? He briefly considered the idea but discounted it – the man would almost certainly hear his approach and perhaps have time to let off a shot before he could overwhelm him. Snell watched the man moving down towards the increasingly exposed aircraft. On its wings, he could just about see figures throwing branches onto the ground. 'No wonder the Squadron Leader did not see the aircraft when he flew over; they had it well and truly camouflaged. I have to find a way to stop them somehow,' he resolved. As he sat on a large, half-rotten tree trunk with his mind racing frantically, the idea came to him.

He stood and tried lifting the trunk; he could barely move the huge, rotting timber as pieces broke off in his hands. Looking around him, he found what might serve his plan. Just outside the tree line lay a pile of fallen trunks more modest in girth than the one he had been resting on. Stepping carefully towards them he could see that they were all meshed together with broken branches. Taking firm hold of one that lay towards the outside of the pile, he moved a little, then heaved solidly at it. As it shifted, entangled branches cracked and the pile shuddered. Finally, pulling it clear, he looked towards where the aircraft now stood, completely exposed in the moonlight. In particular, he noticed the direction it was facing. He judged that if it were to take off along its present line it would pass not too far from his side of the makeshift take-off strip. Stooping, he began to drag the awkward and heavy trunk slowly along the ground, trying to minimise the noise it made, and all the time checking his position in relation to the aircraft.

Looking back towards the aircraft yet again, he let the end of the timber fall across the track of the runway. Gathering his breath, he moved silently back towards the timber pile. A burst of noise from the aircraft surprised him; one of the engines had started. Minutes later it was followed by the second. Noise was not an issue any longer – he grabbed another thick trunk and, from somewhere, managed to generate super-human effort, pulling it straight from the pile, making branches and twigs snap and drag. Lifting the free end up onto his shoulder and leaving the remainder dragging behind him, he staggered across the moonlit ground. He sensed rather than saw the aircraft begin to move, its engines hurling sound across the plateau as its propellers tore at the air. He tried running. The trunk was slipping off his shoulder. He made his strides longer, more deliberate.

Out of the corner of his eye he could see the machine was now moving towards him. Two powerful landing lights, shining ahead, had not yet reached him. The air and ground seemed to hum with the vibration and power generated by the two radial engines and their whirling propellers. Totally exhausted, he dropped the timber end-to-end with the previous trunk. Both he and they now lay directly in the path of the DC-2, which was accelerating hard towards him.

The racing machine had its tail up and the yellow beams from its landing lamps spread fingers of light ahead and over the rough undulating ground. The Japanese pilot saw him first in their glare. A man was staggering off to the right, towards the trees. He shouted at Hyami, not able to point with his hands firmly on the controls. As they hurtled onwards, it was clear that the man would not make it out of the way of the rushing machine. Pushing slightly on the rudder bar at the last second, he aimed to strike the man just as they left the ground. With the two main wheels still hammering on the ground, the machine bucked and heaved with increasing ferocity as speed built. They were on him in barely seconds; Hyami just had time to see the figure fall as one of the huge propellers crossed his path.

The crash was resounding. The aircraft slowed for an instant. Then it leapt high into the air, uncontrolled. Something solid, heavy, struck its belly and it jumped unnaturally upwards. The pilot fought for control, baffled. What had happened? The throttles were fully open; they had no more to give. Instinctively, lowering the nose, he tried to coax the machine into flying. It teetered just above the stall. The trees at the end of the plateau were coming at them, fast. The aircraft was much heavier on this occasion. Hyami tensed, half-covering his face – waiting for the inevitable – a tearing, rending crash. They had managed to gain some fifty feet. The black trees ahead were at least three times that. The engines screamed. Selecting undercarriage 'up' and gently pushing the control wheel forwards slightly, the pilot let the aircraft descend; he was intent on expending valuable height in exchange for desperately needed speed. It was dangerous and expert flying. He revelled in it.

But there was something wrong. The machine was pulling to the right. Countering with left rudder was causing excess drag, slowing them when speed was crucial. Test-flying had been easy compared to this. Leaving it as long as he dared, the pilot firmly pulled firmly back on the column; the aircraft reacted and nosed rapidly upwards, carried by their forward momentum. They smashed through the upper few feet of the taller trees. He relaxed slightly. They sank down the slope of the island, quickly gaining flying speed until, levelling off, they altered course for Medan in Sumatra.

Purser Snell heaved himself up from the ground into a kneeling position, standing shakily, amazed to be in one piece, not quite knowing what had happened amid the shattering noise, dust and blast. One thing he was sure of, however, was that his efforts to stop them leaving had been foiled. He could hear the drone of the DC-2 gradually declining in the distance. Taking time to look around, he could see that something had hurled one of his carefully placed tree trunks fifteen yards or so from where he had deposited it seconds before being nearly diced by thrashing propeller blades. Off to his left, something large lay hissing softly in a dark fold in the ground.

Valour being the better part of discretion in this instance, he moved carefully towards the unusual sound. The hissing had declined to a modest whistle by the time he reached the aircraft's starboard main wheel. Feeling it in the semi-darkness – the moon had sunk – he detected a sizeable tear in the wheel's rubber tyre; any remaining air was finally expiring. Looking and feeling further, he could make out large sections of metal attached to the wheel, part of the undercarriage, he surmised. With any luck, he had now given them a real problem when it came to landing, despite being unable to stop them from leaving.

On the flight deck of the DC-2 there was anxious discussion. The pilot reported that the machine was handling oddly and the starboard undercarriage indicator showed that that wheel was not retracted properly. The ex-military test pilot instinctively knew that the two factors indicated the same problem. He decided to take a risk and select undercarriage 'down' again to see if it would make any difference to the handling. The port wheel came down and was clearly indicated on the instrument panel display as 'locked'. The starboard indicator showed nothing. Passing the torch from his bag to Hyami, he requested that the colonel go to the rear of the passenger cabin and look out of the aftmost window to see if he could see forward and under the wings on both sides. He needed to know the state of things back there, and it was impossible to observe the wheels from the cockpit side windows.

Hyami returned a few seconds later with a worried expression. Trying vainly to sound cool and calm, he looked at the pilot in the dim cockpit lights.

"There does not appear to be a wheel under the right wing similar to the one under the left wing!"

The pilot selected undercarriage 'up' and watched the cockpit indicator. The left side, according to the instrument, showed the wheel retracted; the right side indicator showed no change – a bright red lamp glowed.

"Whatever we hit during the take-off must have caused damage and the loss of the starboard wheel." He paused. "It might also have had something to do with the loud cracking noise we heard after our last landing back there. I inspected as far as I could but found nothing obviously wrong; perhaps we did damage some structural part of the undercarriage mechanism. Hitting something, I don't know what, something very solid on the ground may have caused it to finally fail during take-off." He turned to Hyami and the two frightened raiders standing behind him.

"I suspect that the second bang as we jumped off the ground was the wheel bouncing up and striking the underside of the aircraft."

"So how will we land at Medan?" Hyami shouted above the engine noise.

"With difficulty, Colonel ... with considerable difficulty."

❖ ❖ ❖

Ceci woke early, keen to see how things had worked out with Cornucopia's survivors and Harvey and the Walrus. Krishnan's brothers had not put in an appearance. He was still very depressed at the loss of his boat and the lack of any action. Even some fresh supplies brought from Car Nicobar in the front cockpit of the Gypsy Moth failed to raise spirits. Henrik van der Valk suggested that he try to fly the Gypsy Moth to Camorta to look for a landing site. Ceci made it clear that she had done that already, with and without Harold: there was nowhere suitable to land, she was adamant. In any event, she asked, how was he to do it with a broken arm?

Over a rushed breakfast, taken standing about, they discussed what to do next; finally deciding that, with the precious little fuel remaining in the biplane and only about two gallons scraped together from the other empty fuel cans, she should fly to Cornucopia. She would be able to see what had happened, and drop a further message.

With help from van der Valk and Harold, the machine was prepared, squeezing every last drop of petrol from the near-empty cans. They turned the aircraft and pulled it onto the firmer sand at the water's edge yet again. Harold swung the propeller and the engine came alive after the third try. Airborne with no dramas, Ceci turned immediately on course for the wreck site, cruising at two thousand feet. The air was warm but there was little thermal activity this early morning, for which she was grateful. Glancing out to the south-west at the vast, empty expanse of the blue-grey Bay of Bengal, she was surprised to see a pall of black smoke rising almost straight up some miles distant. She could not quite see what was at the source of the smoke, but whatever it was, it looked pretty dramatic.

"Now I have a problem," she muttered to herself. She had to decide whether to go to investigate the smoke, with her limited fuel, or just ignore it. She decided the second course was irresponsible: people's lives may well be at risk.

Turning towards the plume of smoke, she flew lower over the sea. As she approached, she could see quite clearly bright flames flickering at the centre of the smoke. From overhead, the black ship appeared wreathed in smoke; men were rushing about with buckets, throwing sea water onto the blaze, which seemed to have burnt away large sections of the vessel, in one place almost down to the waterline. Any superstructure that might have existed had almost disappeared, leaving only the walls of one corner of the bridge still standing.

Amazingly, the ship was still slowly under way, and heading in a generally easterly direction. Off her stern one rowing boat was being towed; there appeared to be someone lying in it. She knew that she could not loiter too long over the stricken vessel with her limited fuel, but as she circled, she could see that the crew were slowly succeeding in controlling the blaze. After ten minutes they seemed to have subdued any naked flames but black smoke and steam continued to pour upwards from decks and hull. Nobody on board looked up to acknowledge the aircraft's presence. They were working desperately to douse the flames. Ceci felt that the best she could do would be to add something to the note she intended to drop to the survivors at the wreck site. Perhaps when the Walrus returned from Port Blair they could investigate and give practical help, although she had no idea when that would be.

Heading back to the islands, she managed to scrawl a crudely written addendum to her note to the survivors and Harvey, giving the ship's rough position, heading and their situation.

❖ ❖ ❖

Sitting down feeling tired and hungry, Harry Snell was bracing himself for the long trek back down the island's slopes to Cornucopia and the survivors. The eastern sky was barely beginning to lighten and he wondered what had happened on the beach after he had left so impetuously. He had heard a lot of spasmodic shooting and seen the glow of bright coloured lights in the night sky as he had followed the raiders upwards. He made a mental note to be cautious when he returned – the raiders may still be there and he was not keen to become another captive.

Before moving down the slopes he thought it might be an idea to look around the place where the aircraft had been standing. It crossed his mind that there might be something worth seeing. Walking slowly down the torn runway, he was amazed to see how much damage had been done by the aircraft; even quite large shrubs and bushes had been torn and splintered by the machine's big main wheels as they had charged over the ground.

In the early-morning half-light he came across what appeared to be a grave. The soil was freshly turned and there appeared to be a small cairn of rocks placed at one end. He wondered if one of the raiders had been shot or hurt in some way, and succumbed. Then it struck him; it might be the body of the man Deverall had seen in some sort of trouble when they had both spied on the machine soon after reaching the island. There were no markings anywhere on or around the grave. He touched the small cairn of stones to see if there was any clue as to who lay beneath them. Carelessly poking about, he dislodged some of them and, trying to repair the damage done, started to rebuild the pile.

Then he found it. A small piece of thick, folded paper inside a small oval leather box similar to boxes he had seen for sale in Singapore for carrying pills. Opening the paper he saw an incomprehensible few lines of hieroglyphic script. It meant nothing to him but he had travelled enough to recognise that it was almost certainly Japanese. And, he concluded, it was almost certainly the body of the young Japanese man they had found abandoned after the aircraft had left from an earlier visit. He put the small box with folded paper into his shirt pocket, buttoning the flap over it.

On reaching the place where the aircraft had stood he found piles of broken branches and mish-mash of torn shrubbery that had been used to cover the machine. It seemed they had done a good job; the crew of the Walrus claimed not to have seen anything when overflying the plateau the previous day. Here and there lay a few empty cans; he picked one up and sniffed. "Petrol," he muttered. There was not much to see; nothing worth noting and he started to make his way towards the far tree line, intending to descend to the camp.

"What the ...!" He tripped and fell heavily, banging his shins on something sharp and hard. Sitting up, he swore and started to rub the front of his legs.

"More bloody cans! Why can't people be more bloody careful where they leave their rubbish?" Standing, he picked up one of the offending cans – this one was heavy, full of something. Checking further he discovered six other full cans of petrol lying among and under the camouflage branches together with an ancient rifle with an ornately decorated stock. Significantly, he remembered, over their dinner the previous evening, Harvey Wills had said that he wanted to take the first batch of survivors back to Penang but that he had only sufficient fuel to reach to Port Blair. From there they would have to be transported by ship back to the Malay mainland or to Singapore.

Snell wondered if just three full cans would make any difference to those plans; it was, after all, fifteen gallons. He tried to lift three of the cans together. They were heavy and awkward to carry but somebody must have brought them up here somehow. He guessed that their combined weight was something over a hundred pounds. There was little prospect that he could carry them down to the beach by himself; he would have to think again. Looking around, he tried to think of something that would help to alleviate some if not all of their dead weight. Picking over some of the camouflage branches an idea occurred to him. Along with the various cans scattered about were lots of short pieces of cord. Having once been a boy scout, he imagined the cord was probably used to lash the cans together for transporting up onto the plateau. Perhaps he could contrive some sort of carrying frame, he pondered, using the cord to bind it all together.

Tying each full can securely along the length of two stout and forked branches, he put one end of each branch up and onto his shoulders, leaving the other ends to trail on the ground behind him. With the weight so distributed he thought he would just manage to pull the suspended fuel cans behind him. After a trial run and a few adjustments, including the addition of a strop to hold the branches more firmly onto his shoulders, he set off with the ornate rifle slung over the protruding ends of the two branches in front of him. It had taken him over three hours to reach the top; he hoped to descend a little quicker, despite the load. He looked at his watch: it was just before five and the sun was on the move.

❖ ❖ ❖

Most of those on the beach had slept, despite their injuries and the violent interruptions of the previous night. Wills rose first and looked out to sea. There was no sign of the ship and they'd all heard the aircraft taking off during the early hours. He desperately needed to get back to Port Blair as soon as possible, to report the situation and to alert the authorities in Singapore and Penang. Perhaps they could search for the ship and the aircraft, although he knew it was a pretty forlorn hope in thousands of square miles of ocean. But one thing they were pretty positive about was that the raid would have been undertaken at the instigation of the Japanese crew of the DC-2. It might be reasonable to assume that the gold was eventually destined for Japan. Could it be intercepted, perhaps?

The Walrus was now fully afloat on the rising tide, swinging head to the gentle wind. He waded out to her intending to inspect the machine carefully to be sure that she had not suffered any serious damage as a result of the shooting last evening. As he walked down the short length of sand in his shorts he heard someone behind him. It was the colonel.

"Morning Wills. How are you feeling?"

"I'm okay, Colonel – you? But I'm a bit concerned that we

haven't heard anything from the purser. Rather foolish to have run off like that, I thought."

The colonel nodded in agreement.

"Yes, I'll give it a couple of hours, until, say, seven-thirty, then I'll go looking for him. Hope to God nothing's happened to him, he's a useful fella on the culinary front."

Wills waded out to the quietly rocking amphibian and began looking around its hull and engine. The colonel, meanwhile, breathed life back into the fire and put a pan of water over it to boil. Wills completed his inspection. The Walrus, it appeared, had miraculously not suffered any damage, despite the amount of lead that had been loosed off in the darkness. Wading back to the beach, he noticed a large, heavy rowing boat nudging the beach a few hundred yards north of the camp. On reaching it he was a little surprised to find a man's body lying in the bottom; he had been shot through the chest. Protruding from under the corpse was a rifle. Rummaging through the man's clothes, he found no form of identification.

'That's two to bury, more work!'

"Don't look in a mirror, Sarah; you won't recognise the person looking out!" She lay back touching her swollen face. Michael crawled to her.

"Its just as well I know you. I don't think I'd be too interested in a woman who looks the way you do right now." She tried to smile but it was too painful. Then she managed to utter,

"You can keep your remarks to yourself, Captain, thank you." With Kelly's help she sat up, leaning against him.

"What are we going to do now, Michael?"

"Well ... as we agreed, you, Beth and George Hudson, in the event that Mr Snell doesn't turn up, are going to Port Blair in the

Walrus. At least they'll be able to give you some proper attention there. Then arrangements will be made to take you to Singapore, where I will join you later."

"Why don't you come with us now? Why wait? You need proper attention to your leg. I do hope poor Mr Snell is okay. I'd hate anything to have happened to him."

"I may be a cripple, Sarah, but I'm still the captain of Cornucopia. In the best traditions of the sea, I shall be the last to leave the ship ... flying boat, rather."

Sarah looked round at him and managed a faint smile before it hurt.

"Bloody men!" she spluttered.

As the camp came to life breakfast was prepared. Purser Snell's absence meant that its organisation was less than effective but they managed to fill everyone's needs. Beth, after the night's trauma and broken sleep, seemed to be acting as any normal child would when faced with a huge, sandy beach. With everyone gathered, Wills explained that he would try to get to Port Blair and back in the same day. Depending on what time he returned, he would then try to make a further trip back to Port Blair before dusk. Sarah, Beth and George Hudson gathered their few bits and pieces together. Having buried the two dead raiders, Wills and David Kildonan used the rowing boat to carry four boxes of the remaining bullion out to the aircraft. They lashed two boxes into the empty rear gunner's position and two into the front gun position. The survivors were loaded into the rowing boat and they were preparing to shove off from the shore when two shots were heard, one immediately after the other, coming from somewhere in the jungle above them.

"It's a signal," said Colonel Deverall, looking up. They stood looking back at the jungle from the water. There were no clues as to who had fired, where or why.

"It might be Snell, he may be on his way down to us, or in trouble!" shouted Wills from the moored aircraft.

"Hang on, I'll come ashore." He waded ashore, running to where the rifle he had found in the rowing boat was leaned against a tree in the camp area. Cocking the poorly kept weapon carefully, he moved cautiously towards the trees, unsure where or if anything would emerge. They waited for fifteen minutes: still nothing. Then they saw agitated birds flying out of the trees as if disturbed by some predator. Somebody or something was moving slowly down the jungle-covered slopes towards them. There was a shout.

"It's Snell!" said Kelly excitedly, "Quick, see if he's okay."

Deverall and Kildonan plunged into the undergrowth and started up the slope, shouting Snell's name. A call came from somewhere high above them. After a few minutes they came across the limp and exhausted Snell, slumped on the ground with two heavy branches lashed over his shoulders, trailing three bright silver cans. They led him staggering out onto the beach and sat him down. He told his story in a few breathless minutes and then gestured towards the cans of petrol.

"Thought you could use these, Mr Wills, maybe help you on your way." Harvey Wills thanked him, as did the others, but the additional fifteen gallons, however well intentioned, was not enough to enable him to fly the distance to Penang. It was almost twice the distance to Port Blair. The exhausted Snell looked crestfallen.

"It's not wasted effort, Mr Snell. The amount of fuel we have is just about enough to get us back to Port Blair; any additional juice is a bonus. If we hit headwinds, we may well need it." Kildonan slapped the purser on the back.

"I think you've done a bloody good job, Mr Snell. Be interesting to see how they land that machine with only one main wheel, though." Wills and Michael Kelly nodded, smiling conspiratorially.

"What it does mean is that any gold they took on the aircraft will cause a great deal of interest wherever it comes down. They won't be able to keep that quiet for long, always assuming they survive the landing," said Kelly. Sarah, holding her daughter on her knee, broke into the discussion.

"Where do you think they are headed for? Harvey thinks that would probably be picked up by the authorities as soon as they landed if they went to Penang, Port Blair or even Singapore. He's sent a signal reporting the aircraft at Port Blair days ago, isn't that so, Harvey?"

He nodded, "The only route I can see them taking from here back to Japan, and we have to assume, I suppose, that that is where they eventually want to get to, is through Sumatra, along the Javanese archipelago and then north-east via the Philippines, hopping on to Formosa and Okinawa. It's a very long way. I can only assume that they have it all fully planned with fuel stops arranged and so on."

"Well, from what you've said, it seems unlikely that they'll get much further than the first refuelling stop," interrupted Colonel Deverall to nods all round.

They poured Snell's petrol carefully into the Walrus's tanks and prepared again to take the three passengers out to the aircraft. Their departure was interrupted for a second time that morning. Wills recognised the sound of the Gypsy's engine early in its approach to the wreck site.

Looking up, almost directly into the sun, they watched the small blue-and-silver biplane sideslip down the side of the island's central highland until it was over the beach. Wills recognised Ceci's machine immediately. Why was she here? She was supposed to be waiting for him and the rest of the survivors back at Port Blair. And where had she got hold of the fuel to get so far south? Banking steeply out to sea, Ceci headed back at low level towards the crowd of interested onlookers. Overhead, she threw her weighted message over the side, firmly attached to a streamer of coloured cloth. The streamer fell just a few yards from the group. Beth ran to fetch it, pleased with the present of coloured cloth.

The message advised that she had picked up fuel from a visiting trading vessel at Car Nicobar and returned to her base, where Krishnan's shipwrecked crew were waiting to be picked up by his brothers in their boat. They were normally based at their village on the south-eastern end of Camorta. They needed more fuel and food if possible. A crude map of the island had been drawn with a large X showing the site of the base. Ceci's handwriting was not usually the most decipherable, but the second part of the message, obviously scrawled at some later time, made mention of a ship on fire about twenty miles out, to the west, and mentioned the fact that it appeared to be making way slowly towards the Nicobars. Could they investigate?

Once again they prepared to leave. Sarah, her daughter and George Hudson made themselves comfortable in the Walrus. Sarah and Michael spent a few minutes together talking, looking hopefully into each other's eyes. Their relationship was tacitly acknowledged by the others, and no one took exception. Leaving a package of leg dressings for Purser Snell to apply, she kissed Michael Kelly and hugged him – Beth watched, not quite sure.

Harvey Wills started the engine eventually – it was reluctant to fire initially – and taxiing clear of the small bay, he began their take-off run. Cutting a white score through the blue, they were soon airborne, water streaming off the machine's glistening hull as it headed out across the huge expanse of ocean that finished somewhere to the west on India and Ceylon's east coasts. At three thousand feet they soon spotted a smudge of black smoke well offshore and headed out towards it. In the short time it took to fly to the stricken vessel the smoke appeared to virtually clear: whoever had been fighting the fire seemed to have got it under control.

Despite its charred condition and the wisps of smoke and steam still drifting off the ship, Wills thought he recognised the smoky black hull. Hudson took the aircraft's binoculars and focused on the ship, which was continuing to make way slowly eastwards. Studying the vessel for several minutes, he was fairly sure that it was the ship that had raided them, stealing the bullion. Why it had caught fire was unclear, but what was important was that they had found it. Now it was heading back towards the southern Nicobars. As they flew over the vessel, the crew looked up. Nobody waved, but instead cast sullen stares up at them. Two of the men had what looked liked rifles in their hands but nobody took aim to shoot.

Wills and Hudson discussed a course of action that included flying back to Cornucopia and dropping a note warning the remaining crew and survivors of the state of the ship and the fact that they estimated its distance offshore at about eighteen miles, probably travelling at one or two knots. After a few minutes Hudson had hastily written a message and they dropped it over Cornucopia's beach. They then turned north towards Port Blair, where they landed on the water safely two and a half hours later.

Keen to fly back to Cornucopia as soon as possible, Wills tried to rush the two native crewmen manning the fuelling barge that had come out from the harbour to replenish the aircraft's depleted tanks – the airfield had become too boggy after overnight rain. But the two elderly men continued at their own pace, much to Wills's frustration. He took the opportunity to go ashore with the three survivors. The administrator came to meet him, taking charge of the carefully loaded bullion, and to ensure that Sarah, Beth and George Hudson were properly looked after. He expressed his unhappiness at the further extensive drain on their now-greatly depleted petrol stocks.

No signals awaited Wills but he sent a short cable to his CO advising the latest situation, and reporting on the suspected state of the DC-2, together with his brief thoughts on its assumed destination. He also reported his concerns about the smoking ship and its crew, who had stolen some of the bullion, together with its present state and position. Finally, before returning to his aircraft, he arranged to borrow some rifles from the administrator's armoury and some boxes of .303 ammunition.

Now alone, he taxied out from the harbour area, and once airborne set off again for Cornucopia's remaining survivors. It had taken nearly two frustrating hours to refuel the machine and sort out the other matters that demanded his attention. Looking at his watch before pushing the throttle forwards, he noted that it was just before three in the afternoon: against a slight headwind he would not arrive back at Cornucopia much before six in the evening.

He thought it unlikely that they would make a further return trip to Port Blair today: he was dog-tired. The previous night's attack had ensured that any sleep came late, and this, combined with an early start, was now making him start to feel drowsy as the faithful Shagbat cruised on under the hot sun towards the south. Staring out at the ocean below him, occasionally checking the compass and engine instruments, he was lulled by the regular beat of the engine, and his eyelids began to feel heavy. Opening the side windows of the small cockpit introduced a draught of lukewarm air that helped initially to stave off sleep, and he began singing to himself.

It was the noise that woke him. Demented air tearing through the aircraft's rigging and structure alerted his semi-conscious mind. His eyes had closed a few seconds too long. His brain had sunk fleetingly into relaxing oblivion. The Walrus's normally stable flight had been disrupted by a stray thermal bubble. The port wing dropped, the machine started to slowly spiral down towards the sea. With no correcting control from the cockpit the spiral was exaggerated. When Wills awoke, the sea was twisting around in the windscreen's frame. Fighting against intensifying gravitational forces, he pushed the control column sharply to the right to counter the leftward turning of the Walrus. He closed the throttle, reducing the speed and stresses building on the airframe. It straightened but continued to dive, the wind screaming through her vibrating struts and rigging wires. A less experienced pilot would have pulled back strongly on the control column, unaware that it would have torn the wings off the machine.

Wills, very alert now, gently exerted rearward pressure on the column. The noise entering through the open cockpit windows reached a penetrating crescendo. The Walrus vibrated madly. The sea rushed up towards him, the altimeter needle, he noticed, unwinding worryingly fast. Any precipitate action would prove final. Continuing to apply gentle back-pressure, he slowly began to bring the nose of the plunging aircraft up towards the broad horizon. He could feel increasing gravitational forces pushing him down into his seat as he played the diving machine carefully. Less than fifty feet from the waiting ocean the Walrus ceased its descent. Wills breathed out, nursing the aircraft back to two thousand feet. He remained fully awake, watching the sea and clouds pass by, shocked by his transitory lapse. They would never have known what had happened.

Now two and a half hours out from Port Blair, he began to look for the black ship. There was no smoke now to guide him towards her, and he knew too well that finding even a sizeable ship could prove difficult if not impossible on the endless ocean.

Turning out to the west, he steered to roughly where he had last seen her, earlier that morning – seven and a half hours ago. Forcing his tired brain through some quick mental calculations, he reckoned that if she had maintained the same apparent speed over the intervening period, she would be closing the coastline of the Nicobars now. Swinging the ungainly Walrus back towards the east, he kept a watchful eye on the sea below. There was nothing to see. He climbed the machine, hoping altitude would give him a wider view. After half an hour of flying around the area there was still no sign of the ship. Perhaps she had finally sunk. She was in a pretty bad state when they had last seen her.

Announcing his arrival with a burst of sound over Cornucopia's wreck site, he touched down just outside the bay and taxied to the shore, mooring the Walrus so that she would not take the ground as the tide receded. David Kildonan rowed out to meet him, helping to bring the rifles and some more food ashore.

❖ ❖ ❖

The captain of the fired damaged black ship looked around at the terrible state of things. His decimated crew were exhausted after their successful raid on Cornucopia's bullion; he had lost three men in the action and two had gone by air with Hyami. The bullion lay below trapped in the hot, smoke-filled hold.

The engine room, with its veteran diesel engine, was also untenable, full of smoke and fumes. The engine turned, uncontrolled, providing about two and a half knots of effort towards the island chain in the distance ahead of them. The fire had somehow started during the night, somewhere on the bridge. Fanned quickly by the boat's forward speed into an inferno, it had threatened to destroy everything, leaving them swimming for their lives. Turning the vessel ensured that the wind blew the flames away from the vessel's main structure, preventing a total conflagration. The flames had burnt through the steering cables and engine controls, and they were now at the mercy of the elements, and their remaining fuel. What was certain was that they were going to end up running aground on one of the many islands that lay directly in their path ahead. The captain also knew that the military flying boat that had appeared that morning would almost certainly report them to the British or Indian authorities.

❖ ❖ ❖

The Japanese pilot considered their situation. An attempt to land with their only main wheel extended would probably lead to disaster. Even if he managed to land successfully on the airfield at Medan, on only the port main wheel and tailwheel, he knew that as their speed fell off, the right wing would be unable to support itself. If the wingtip dug into the ground during landing, the DC-2 could cartwheel spectacularly with fatal and almost certainly incendiary results. The answer to their landing problem, he knew, was to belly-land the machine, wheels up, onto something soft like marsh or estuary mud. But it was dark beyond the windscreens, the moon had set an hour or so ago and he had no real idea of their exact location. He was aware, however, that down the east side of Sumatra there were a number of large rivers emptying tropical rain into the Strait of Malacca, and that the surrounding coastal region was mainly swamp and marsh.

He discussed the issue with Hyami, who was torn between saving himself and saving the gold – and all that it would do for his reputation in Tokyo. While it remained dark, all they could do was to continue to fly south-eastwards towards Medan and possibly beyond.

They bypassed a darkened Medan during the night and as a grey dawn appeared they continued, heading for the small port of Dumai, lying on the mainland, behind an island set in the Malacca strait. He estimated they had just enough fuel to reach Dumai. He hoped that with luck they would find a suitable area of soft, yielding ground to put the machine down safely, undercarriage up, on its belly. The pilot's maps of the area showed signs of marsh and rice paddy, all fed by innumerable watercourses. After landing, if they made it, their intention was to take the bullion from the machine to the small port, and charter a ship, enabling them to continue – but those worries could wait until later, the pilot thought.

Despite their situation the two raiders and Hyami slept fitfully as the aircraft continued on its way, occasionally overflying small villages and townships in the darkness, their remote presence sometimes revealed by a few weak lights. Desperately tired, the pilot struggled to stay lucid and alert. At altitude the dawn grew lighter ahead of them: below, the surface was still dark with occasional patches of white ground-mist reflecting traces of the early light.

To his left and some eight thousand feet below lay the Strait of Malacca, an occasional white score signifying the location of a ship cutting through its solid grey ribbon, trailing a near-symmetrical wake. After Medan had passed below them some time ago, its one or two lights standing out against the inky blackness, the damaged machine was turned slightly left, following the long Sumatran coastline as it wove its way south-east around endless low-lying bays and saturated river mouths. Finally the sun burst dramatically above the horizon, flooding the cool flight deck with pale orange light. Against the sun's glare he could just make out the strait as it narrowed far ahead. Beyond, the island of Rupat was growing tangible from out of the ground-mist. There, he knew, in the curve of the waters that surrounded the westerly edge of the island, lay the small port of Dumai.

Pulling back the two throttle levers, he allowed the machine to slowly descend. Hyami awoke abruptly, startled by the change in engine note. There was no activity to be seen in or around the small port, the population still slumbering as the aircraft passed above. Just to the south, alongside the strait, was what appeared from their height to be an area of flat marshland – no trees or large shrubs to hinder an aircraft's uncontrolled belly-landing along the wet surface. Further inland were rice paddies with meandering cart tracks between flooded fields that reflected early clouds.

The pilot turned out across the strait, preparing the machine for its final landing. Propellers were set to fine pitch, flaps half-lowered and the crew securely strapped into their seats. The two over-wing hatches were removed as a precaution. He intended to make a long, flat approach just above the stall using the engines to control the machine's speed and attitude. Lining up with his chosen landing path, he gradually reduced engine power, trimming the aircraft carefully each time to compensate for the loss of thrust. Through the cockpit windscreens, images gradually resolved until they were able to see individual leaves and grasses as they flashed by a few feet above the sodden surface, glinting wetly in the new daylight.

Selecting full flap for the last time, he allowed them to extend before pulling back fully on the throttles. Then, as he cut the magnetos the motors stopped dead. Hyami did as instructed earlier and pulled the switches to the aircraft's batteries. The DC-2 was effectively dead, but not down – yet. The pilot was not sure quite what to expect, but to him the landing felt like touching down on a huge plate of sushi. The machine slithered and bounced across the slimy landscape, showing little sign of slowing. Finally gravity imposed its will and the machine began to sink gently into the gooey surface, sliding sideways for the final two hundred yards. It had been an anti-climax. There had been little noise except for sheets of hissing spray jetting out from under the wings and belly as they rushed pell-mell across the sodden, misty landscape.

Once stopped, the aircraft began to settle, wobbling worryingly as huge bubbles of primeval gas erupted around and she began sinking into the soft, sucking morass. For a brief moment they all thought the DC-2 was going to slide under the surface, but finally, she stabilised, muddy water a few inches below the main door cill. Nothing moved outside: it was eerily quiet. The faintly translucent mist swirled around them, evaporating in the growing sun as it did so. It was as though they were the only people on this part of the earth. The pilot noted the time: it was six-fifteen on a virgin morning, as yet unsullied by man and his greed.

Out of his seat quickly, Hyami moved back into the cabin, his fears now allayed. Stamping about on the metal cabin floor, he ordered the two raiders to untie the bullion bags and to place them near the aircraft's main door. Bending and grunting, he crawled through an open over-wing hatch and stood on the wing, gazing about him. A few moments later the pilot joined him.

"We are some way from the town. How do you suppose we can get the cargo to the port from this position?" Hyami's question had just a veneer of recovered sarcasm in its delivery.

'He no doubt assumed I could deliver him and the gold conveniently straight to the quayside,' thought the pilot.

"I think we shall have to wait, Colonel; wait until someone comes to the paddies, or along that track over there. It's still early," he said, pointing. Hyami clambered back inside the machine; it rocked slightly on the unstable, marshy surface. Barking again, he ordered one of the raiders to try to walk through the marsh to the track, a distance of about a hundred yards or so. The younger and lighter of the two men put one foot down on its spongy surface while sitting in the aircraft's doorway. It was soft and watery on the surface but seemed reasonably solid further down. Experimenting, he tried standing; his feet sank a foot or so into the mire but no more. Climbing through the wing hatch, he walked to the end of the wing, followed by his muddy footprints. He gingerly stepped off, intending to take just a few careful steps to test the surface again before setting off to what appeared to be solid land.

He was about eight or nine feet from the wingtip, half-smiling at his careful sticky progress, when he seemed to enter an area where the underlying mass was less supportive. It was as though the surface opened for a moment as he suddenly jerked downwards, his knees sinking suddenly below the surface. The sudden movement caught him out, unbalancing him; he fell forward, arms outstretched. Hyami watched interestedly as the man tried to push his chest away from the viscous mud, but each movement seemed to make matters worse. Now the man was frightened and shouting for help. The pilot rushed back along the wing and into the rear of the aircraft. Picking up a stout piece of lashing rope, he crawled quickly back through the wing hatch and ran back out to the wingtip. The aircraft wobbled disconcertingly. The lower half of the man's trunk was now completely submerged but now at least he had managed to assume a more upright stance.

The pilot threw the rope. The man, frightened, flailed about trying to grasp and hold onto it. Each rapid movement saw his body sucked further into the mud. Panic was setting in. The young man snatched the entire rope out of the pilot's hands, almost pulling him over. Hyami stood watching. The sinking man was now submerged up to his armpits. The muscles in his neck bulged as he tried to hold his face and head away from the ravenous, encroaching slime. The second raider could only watch, transfixed. Hands to his mouth, he saw his colleague being devoured by the remorseless surface. Now, lying down on the wingtip, the pilot asked Hyami to hold onto his legs. Supported, he slid out carefully onto the greasy surface. Spreading his weight, he reached out, but he was three feet too short.

Petrified and crying, the sinking man resorted to a kind of upward swimming motion in an attempt to release himself. His final, desperate thrashings merely quickened the inevitable. He gasped frantically in short bursts, his eyes wide with awful realisation, and his one visible hand was covered in mud and outstretched, imploring help. He craned his neck and turned his face upwards in a desperate effort to keep breathing air, but with a final lurch, his head was sucked down. Two thick bubbles remained, produced by his final breath. His hand clawed the air for a few seconds, until it too sank, fingers straight and tense, below the surface.

The pilot scrambled back onto the wing and stood up, his front dripping with the foul-smelling mud. Nothing remained; no sign that any human had been there just seconds before. It had shocked him; so unexpected and quick. They all went back inside the aircraft; they would have to wait for rescue.

An hour or so later there was a shrill call from a small man, old and bent, standing on the bank by the cart track. They waved from the door, requesting help. Neither spoke the other's language but it was obvious what was required. The sun was well up before a crude cart drawn by a single, emaciated ox arrived on the track opposite. In the cart was what appeared to be a small, flat-bottomed wooden boat. The old man, helped by a youth, pulled the craft out of the cart, lowering it down the bank onto the surface of the marsh. It did not float conventionally, but sat on the gluey surface as though it was frozen. The youth slid down after it, clambering into the small vessel, the man passing him two stout poles, slightly flattened at the ends. As the youth moved about, the hull sank a few inches into the soft slime. He stood carefully and slowly poled, and occasionally rowed, the wobbling boat out to the aircraft. It was slow work and heavy going in the humidity and increasing heat.

Alongside the aircraft's main door, the youth was pulled inside. Through a combination of shouting, exaggerated arm-waving and pointing they finally drove the message home. They wanted to be rescued, along with the two boxes lying by the door. Hyami ordered the remaining raider to help lift one of the bullion boxes into the boat and then clambered in himself. The youth stood carefully in the stern and begun again an action that was a cross between rowing and punting, the boat jerking at times across the slithery surface. At places it seemed to perform as a normal boat, displacing water and thin mud; at others it tended to skid, supported by a thin crust of heavier mud. The colonel sat rigid, worried, after earlier events.

With both wooden boxes safely loaded into the cart, Hyami joined the pilot sitting atop them, signing to the old man to take them to town. The remaining raider was still in the process of being rescued from the aircraft by the youth as they squeaked slowly away in the lurching cart. Hyami had no thought for him now that he was on his way with his booty. Finally, they arrived at the small port ordering the driver and his tired ox towards the waterside and the few boats caught up to the bank and quay.

Hyami's priority was clear to the pilot – to get to a place where proper and secure transport could be arranged for him and the bullion. His first step was to charter one of the moored trading vessels to take him and his prize onwards to Jakarta, where local anti-Dutch supporters would facilitate his and its progress to the Japanese homeland. Language difficulties proved an immediate stumbling block. Neither he nor the pilot spoke any of the local languages or dialects. Finally, and ironically, they came across an ancient Englishman asleep in the back of a near-collapsing, dim and doubtful tea house, where charter negotiations were held with some difficulty. Hyami thought the Englishman was either drunk, or in an advanced state of dementia, but after two hours of discussion, the polyglot Englishman providing translations of a sort, they settled on a deal with one of the schooners' agents.

The vessel was leaving that evening and Hyami wanted to get his bullion on board and secure as soon as possible. The ox-cart driver was instructed to load the boxes onto a teak-planked vessel with red-painted prow that lay last in a line of vessels moored to the river bank. Standing on the boxes, Hyami urged the driver and his animal quickly on, pushing through the increasing hustle and bustle as vessels were loaded and unloaded with great activity and noise. With Hyami impatient and on the edge of losing his temper, they finally arrived. Strong, surly, barefoot sailors stood watching from the vessel's decks as the old man wrestled to lift the large, heavy boxes off the cart. Hyami bellowed, and the vessel's young captain came to the ship's side. Remarkably, he spoke a little English.

"What is it for you?"

Hyami turned and looked scornfully at him, replying in fractured English:

"Get men, take boxes on. Tell them careful." The captain shrugged his shoulders, not quite understanding everything the little oriental had uttered. Although unused to such treatment, he gave a curt order. Two tough-looking crewmen came ashore and prepared to lift the first box off the cart. The boxes had suffered rough treatment since originally being loaded into Cornucopia; their integrity had been breached in a number of places. As the first box was grasped and pulled sideways, a piece of one side broke away in one of the sailors' hands, and splinters drove into his palm.

Cursing and shouting, he let go, and the box fell awkwardly onto the dusty earth. It did not break open but further splintered pieces detached themselves from the broken side, partially exposing one of the ingots. Hyami, looking elsewhere at that moment, failed to see the incident. The wounded sailor, clutching his hand, bent to see what damage had been caused.

The afternoon sunlight caught the sullen gleam of the captured gold through the box's fractured side. The sailor saw it and pointed it out in a shocked whisper to his colleague. Hyami, turning, was outraged at the clumsy handling of his goods and leapt down from the cart, berating the men and pushing the broken pieces of wood back onto the box. Neither man understood or cared what Hyami said. With both boxes aboard and placed carefully in the vessel's cavernous but rapidly filling hold, Hyami embarked – alone.

The pilot had had enough of being subservient; doing the bidding of a man he had unwillingly served without comment or criticism for over a year. Koya Yoshi wanted to go home, to Japan, that was true; to his wife and young son in Nara. But travelling with this self-centred, cold-hearted, lethal and indoctrinated military man had become too much. When the pilot announced his intention, Hyami, contrary to Yoshi's expectation, stared arrogantly at him for a few seconds, cleared his throat, spat and turned sharply on his heel. He did not look back as he walked along the wooden deck, led by a young man. With the pilot he had lost face. Tired but relieved, the pilot walked back along the line of moored vessels to the tea house looking for the Englishman.

❖ ❖ ❖

Albert Cox had been a district officer in Malaya for sixteen years. He was forty-eight, had never married and had enjoyed the trappings of local power that his position had bestowed, until the day he was tempted. As he would readily admit, he stupidly and willingly succumbed. He absconded with a large sum of money from the district imprest fund. The fund was government money entrusted to him and used to meet the expenses of his administrative area. The sum was not huge; that was his first mistake – it would not keep him in luxury for the rest of his days – and secondly, it was a spur-of-the-moment transgression with little real thought given to where he would go to live off the modest fruits of his crime.

Escaping by trading vessel to Sumatra before his offence was revealed through the usual quarterly audit, Cox settled into a life of ease and raw alcohol. He lived and slept usually where he fell, sometimes at the roadside, in the tea shop, a local go-down; it hardly mattered to him now. At first he tried to keep up appearances, but the heat, the slow pace of life and the effects of alcohol and a poor diet gradually ate into his resolve. He was now reduced to a tramp-like existence, returning occasionally to the secret spot where he had stashed his rapidly diminishing ill-gotten gains. Unshaven and dressed shabbily in torn and dirty blue shirt with no collar and a pair of now-too-small grey trousers, ripped at one knee, he lay in a corner slumped across one of the tables in the hot, smoke-filled and fetid room. Every so often the low hubbub of voices was interrupted by regular and loud intakes of breath from his open mouth, dribbling disgustingly onto the rough tabletop.

He was a wreck, but not beyond redemption, thought Yoshi, staring down at this example of human flotsam. Reaching out, he pushed at the Englishman, trying to wake him. The man rolled and groaned, briefly opening his blood-shot eyes.

"Whatjuwant, bugger off, you yellow basta..." He was asleep or unconscious before he could finish the insult. The pilot pushed him again. Cox moaned, without opening his eyes this time.

"Didntja hear wha Isssaid?" The words stumbled together from his mouth, more saliva wetting the tabletop. The pilot, aware now that all eyes in the room were on him, moved around and behind the prostrate man, then pulled him upright into the back of the rickety cane chair.

"Ere, whatju doin, bloody Nip?" He attempted to stand, his hand a fist but the alcohol had a long-established grip on Cox's metabolism and balance. He fell heavily back into the chair – it cracked. The pilot realised that this was going to be a long job requiring some tact and patience. Bending low in front of the sideways-sagging Englishman, he pulled him forwards until he was lying across his left shoulder. Standing slowly, with the man over his shoulder, he walked out of the oppressive room, ducking through the low doorway into bright sunlight and hot breeze coming in off the strait.

It took three full days for Cox to reach a state resembling compos mentis. The pilot swilled him down with water from borrowed thick leather buckets behind the tea shop, the proprietor watching and laughing as he did so. As Cox approached reality, the cool water hastened the desired result. On the third day, with a proper meal of rice and chicken inside him, and some hastily purchased clean clothes, the pilot began to quietly and carefully set out an idea to Albert Cox that might offer an opportunity to both of them. Yoshi's English was scant; what he knew was largely learned during his visits to Hawaii with his wife, but he managed to communicate his idea well enough to enliven Albert Cox.

Finally, they went to the site of the DC-2's last landing. The pilot was dismayed at the condition of the machine as it lay with its nose now submerged beneath the swampy surface with just the tops of the pilot's windscreens visible, and its tail jerked high up into the air. Watching, they could see that the aircraft was gradually submerging into the morass with barely a sound even as they watched.

A group of locals had gathered around the stricken machine in small flat-bottomed boats, attempting to salvage any bits and pieces worth having; there was much chattering and shouting but there was little that they could take. Suddenly there was a tension in the group, accompanied by shouting; the small boats pulled back quickly from the still-shiny hull. There followed a series of loud gurgling noises, and she began to slip slowly forwards and down, like an elegant ship sliding gently beneath calm waters. They saw a mixture of mud and water pour through the open wing hatches and then, as she settled, it flooded across the main door cill, rapidly filling the cabin, and hastening her demise. Within fifteen minutes she was gone, leaving some minor disturbances on the surface indicating where the beautiful, twin-engine, polished-aluminium aircraft had once sat.

❖ ❖ ❖

The black ship was just about half a mile off one of the southernmost Nicobar Islands, its still-pounding diesel engine delivering power and one to two knots as it cut through the tranquil waters. They had made a jury rudder from some of the burnt wooden panels that had formed the ship's superstructure. Their crudely formed rudder, however, gave them little control over the vessel's direction; they were unable to submerge it deep enough into the water to be effective. Finally the strain of trying to manoeuvre such a large ship with the make-do rudder proved too much and it finally disintegrated. In less than half an hour they would be aground somewhere on the approaching shoreline. The captain, Hyami's agent and the three remaining crew watched, powerless, as the inevitable took place.

Still driving forwards, her bluff bow ran up the beach about thirty feet, the slowly pounding engine continuing to turn. The event was surprisingly smooth and barely threw the crew off balance owing to the gently shelving nature of the shore that fate had selected for their landfall. She sat slightly over onto her port side in the deep groove cut by her keel through the sand. The propeller continued turning slowly, thrashing the shallow water at her stern.

Throwing a rope over the side, the captain and one of the raiders clambered down onto the beach to assess the situation. It was obvious that his vessel was unlikely to cut a wake through any seas again; there were signs of strains in her worn planking. As they walked around her, the labouring diesel engine seized, deprived of cooling water from its inlet pipe now well above sea level.

The captain stood back and looked at his desolate ship and their situation. This was not part of the plan. His contract was to help mount the raid, collect the bullion and deliver it to a Japanese freighter at secret coordinates some five hundred miles out into the Indian Ocean. He had managed the first two tasks but was now left with a wrecked ship, three men dead as far as he knew, and a number of boxes of bullion, with no way of getting them away. One thing was for sure, Hyami was going to have to pay for a new ship from the bullion; he had firmly made up his mind about that. For the moment they decided to remain on the vessel with the bullion, but somehow they had to arrange a rescue. They still had the heavy rowing boat gently bobbing about in the surf tied behind the ship, with the body still in it.

❖ ❖ ❖

They must have understood. Krishnan's brothers arrived off Ceci's beach base in their large trading vessel; her diving and manoeuvring over their village on Camorta had had the desired effect. It was they who had originally delivered Ceci, Harold and the Gypsy Moth to their island base from Penang; it was not difficult for them to deduce where she was heading, encouraging them to follow. They all spent next hour talking, occasionally laughing, and exchanging news, in particular about the loss of Krishnan's vessel and the eventual finding of the lost flying boat. They ate on board, rocking gently in the swell, Ceci and Harold glad to have something other than fish and rice for an evening meal. Under a gently swinging lantern they sat, replete with chicken and pleased to have help at hand. In the morning, it was agreed, they would cruise round to where Cornucopia lay and if possible uplift the gold with any remaining survivors, and return them to Penang direct. They would also refuel the Gypsy Moth and take some stores of fuel onto Ceci's beach. Henrik van der Valk sat quietly throughout the evening holding onto his arm; he complained of some pain despite another warm native poultice being applied to ease the ache.

SEVENTEEN

Hyami paced frustratedly around the wooden decks of the two-masted trading schooner, observed interestedly by its small crew and captain. She was heavily built from tropical hardwoods and measured about a hundred feet from her high, red-painted prow to the blunt overhang of her stern. She was not typical of the region's sailing vessels and no one seemed to know where she had come from. Some locals thought she had originated from Arabia.

Her heavy teak decks were pierced by two large openings that led down to her capacious holds, which were now almost full. The crew were preparing for sea; hatch covers being secured over the fore and aft openings. Between the two hatches, protruding above the deck were two raised wooden skylights with glass panes covered with protective metal bars. They provided daylight to two small cabins below. As evening quiet overcame the small port, the captain ordered all ties with the land severed. Hyami stood holding onto the ship's rail, absent-mindedly watching the gap between the vessel and shore open up, while the crew coiled and stowed the mooring warps. His mind was firmly on other matters. Slowly, the schooner nosed out into the unsheltered waters of the Malacca strait; night fell quickly covering the schooner's departure. The crew secured the huge, heavy, loose-footed cotton sails as they were hauled up two tall, tapered wooden masts, the wooden luff rings clattering noisily until quietened as the sails filled with warm wind, driving them on and out into the deep eastern twilight. In the strait the wind was brisk; white horses skipped in the darkness, their antics betrayed by regular dashes of brilliant foam across a heaving surface.

Tired after the events and fears of the day and previous evening, Hyami returned to the tiny cubby-hole that served as a sort of cabin below the solid decks. He lay on his narrow bunk looking up at the deck-head a few inches above, listening to the sea gurgling past on the other side of the planking and the creaks and groans of a wooden sailing vessel under way. Sleep was a long way off – his body was trying to disperse the adrenaline produced over recent hours. Two hours later, with the vessel beginning to pound through an increasingly boisterous sea, he finally gave up and rose, struggling to keep his balance in the pitching cabin. Standing on deck, he could see no one except the helmsman's silhouette in the pale glow of the ship's binnacle. The air was full of swirling dampness; the sails were full and taut, the leech of one sail vibrating heavily causing its mast and gaff to do the same.

He looked to weather; there was nothing to be seen except rows of white breakers approaching out of the darkness, disappearing below his sight to break under the plunging bow. The land was far-gone. He stood and watched the scene for a while longer, then turned to make his way aft, intending to talk to the helmsman. Making his way, he needed to grasp hold of anything he could to support his moves on the wet, pitching deck. He saw light glowing upwards from one of the raised deck hatches and carefully made his way towards it. Looking down through the salt-streaked panes, he could see the two crewmen who had helped to offload the bullion boxes from the dockside. They were in animated conversation with the ship's young captain. Pulling himself around the hatch, aiming to drag himself along its side as he progressed aft, he glanced down a second time into the spartan, poorly lit cabin. In one corner there lay one of his bullion boxes. It was smashed open, the lid with its inscription lying on a bunk. The captain, he could see from this angle, had one of the precious ingots cradled in his hand, elbows resting on the table, and they were all laughing. It was hardly necessary for Hyami to hear what was being said or joked about; he knew too well that they could not afford to let him reach any destination alive.

Hyami stopped, ducking down to avoid being seen from below. He sat for a few more minutes, considering what to do next. Thinking on his feet, under pressure, was something he had mastered; it more often than not led to violence of one sort or another. Back in his tiny cabin was the large, heavy pistol he had remembered to bring with him from the DC-2. If he could get to it without being seen he might be able to take control of the vessel and its five-man crew. He considered for a few moments. It would mean eliminating at least three crewmen: five would prove too many to keep track of in this situation. At the point of a gun the two remaining crewmen would probably be sufficient manpower to sail the ship under his command. He moved quickly and quietly to recover his pistol, mentally preparing to liquidate the three seamen in the captain's cabin. The crewman manning the helm would probably not hear the fatal shots above the noise of wind and sea. Where the other crewman was he presently did not have a clue – sleeping off watch, he guessed.

With the bulky weapon held firmly in his hand, he made his way again in the semi-darkness along the pitching deck towards a short ladder leading down to the galley area and the captain's lamp-lit cabin. More than once he was caught by seas breaking heavily over the vessel's bow and was soaked by the time he reached the narrow hatchway. Putting the pistol into his drenched trouser-waistband, he slid back the hatch, and turning, descended slowly and silently, holding onto the sides of the narrow ladder firmly; swaying with each lurch of the hard-pressed vessel until he reached the darkened space below. Hyami could now make out some sort of excited discussion taking place within the small cabin on his left. A crack of feeble light shone under the door. Removing the pistol deliberately from his waist, he cocked it as he edged in the near-darkness towards the cabin door. There was a movement within, and then someone was noisily turning the handle. It opened a fraction then, on somebody's second thoughts, banged closed again as a new round of talking began. Hyami stood back under the ladder waiting patiently for events to unfold.

The door opened again fully, spilling a path of weak yellow light out into the dark space. As the man emerged, Hyami fired, point-blank. Hands clasping his chest, the young captain fell mortally wounded, with blood pouring from an enormous exit wound in his back and rapidly spreading a dark and sticky stain across the deck. Immediately behind the unfortunate captain, one of the crewmen tried to turn and close the door. The benefit of surprise and Hyami's experience told. The large-calibre bullet struck the man in the side of the head just above the ear, the right side of the skull erupting as the bullet liquefied its contents. Bone and tissue splattered against the door and frame. The man fell out of the cabin at Hyami's feet, across the rapidly expiring captain.

The third crewman just managed to slam the door closed as his colleague fell, shouting something unintelligible as he pushed the heavy brass lock across to secure it. The sailor knew that it would only provide an additional few seconds of grace, but the cabin had a small access hatch into the adjacent packed hold. He scrambled frantically, pulling the table and bench away from the hatch cover. Bullets splintered through the teak cabin door as Hyami fired blindly, hoping for a lucky hit.

Once through the narrow access hatch, into the hold, the man staggered aft in total darkness, towards the steering position. Bumping, banging and staggering into items of cargo swinging about in the vessel's lively motion, he reached the hold's aftmost ladder. Pushing the stiff, wet covers aside with difficulty, he struggled up onto the streaming deck just behind the after mast. Hyami finished the bullets in the magazine through the door, then, while waiting for some reaction, quickly reloaded the murderous weapon, standing back beneath the ladder in the dark.

Nothing. He waited. Listening intently, he tried to make out whether anyone was still alive in the small cabin; no light came from under the door now. After five minutes he was convinced that he had been lucky and, holding onto the ladder's rail, he began to kick at the door, pistol ever ready. The hasp of the brass bolt was soon persuaded to relinquish its hold on the stout wooden frame, and the door swung open, smashing violently against the adjacent cabin wall. Only a suffused grey light came from the deck light above, barely illuminating the scene. It was difficult to see much. Hyami, holding the pistol firmly out ahead of him, stepped slowly into the cabin. Tense, he turned about, looking; there was nobody there – dead or alive. Nearly tripping, he saw the table and bench on their sides and then the rectangular blackness of the open hatchway in the cabin wall.

Bending carefully, he looked into the hole. There was, as far as he could see, nobody. But it was pitch-dark. Listening served no purpose – all sorts of noises were emanating from the space as the schooner plunged on through the night. He backed away from the opening, looking about him; there on the floor was a box of Lucifers lying near to his scattered bullion. Picking them up, he returned to the open hatch and peering in, struck one of the matches in front of him. The few seconds of its burning left him no wiser. There were dozens of places where anyone could secrete themselves among the rows of boxes and barrels roped and netted about in the pitch-black space.

Passing out of the captain's cabin, he moved slowly up the ladder towards the deck. The weather appeared to be worsening; even as a landsman he could feel that the ship was being hard pressed at times in the strengthening gale. She was heeling dangerously: her lee rail now constantly awash. Every now and then she would smash into a larger sea with a resounding bang that checked her plunging stride momentarily. Somewhere there were three men to deal with; he crawled slowly aft on the weather deck.

In the light from the binnacle he could just see two of them. One had a gun, a rifle, and was waving it about, pointing it at every one of the hundreds of noises that mingled with the wind's overriding whine. In these conditions Hyami knew that to kill with the pistol he had to get much, much closer. Completely soaked from being constantly washed by seas breaking over the weather rail, he slid on his belly along the saturated deck, keeping his head and body in contact with its teak planking.

About ten feet forward of the helmsman's position, fixed on the centre line of the deck, was a box structure with a large cast-iron eye fitted to its top. It was used to support the base of a tripod used, crane-like, for lifting heavy items from the vessel's holds. Hyami moved carefully towards it until, unseen, he managed to roll with a rush of water across the deck to hide behind it. Keeping the weapon clear of water, he knelt, gradually raising his head in preparation for aiming. There was a sudden, unusual noise from behind him. Glancing back, he saw a shadowy crewman, upright, clinging and moving slowly along the deck towards his position, shouting out something at the two men gathered around the helm. Hyami swore under his breath, muttering, "So there you are." The sailor, only a few feet away, had now seen him despite the darkness. He was pointing out his position excitedly.

He hit the deck awkwardly as the ship lurched, but it was of little consequence – he was within a few seconds of death. The limp body slumped, and then rolled down against the lee rail, the rushing water briefly turning dark. The man with the rifle, seeing the pistol's flash, fired blindly then staggered forwards, fully exposed to the wind, and the pistol's muzzle.

Even in the tumultuous conditions the Japanese colonel could not miss at such close range. The rifle dropped to the deck, sliding overboard. The sailor was jerked off his feet for an instant, and then followed the rifle, after being caught up for a few seconds in the leeward guardrail. It was now Hyami and the indispensable helmsman.

The gusts were merging into a continuous and stronger gale, the ship dangerously pressed to the point where her gear may fail. She was becoming unmanageable with increasing frequency. In normal circumstances, and with a full crew, they would lower or reef some of the sails, but now, at each gust she would heel hard over trying to round-up into the eye of the wind. The lone helmsman fought to counter these natural responses with the rudder. Hyami shuffled carefully towards the man, the weapon's black snout just visible.

Another series of heavy gusts hit them. She rolled violently, uncontrolled, green seas pouring over the decks. Her bows, disregarding the rudder, thrust hard up into the wind causing the heavy sails to shake violently and the whole vessel to vibrate as she sat helpless 'in irons'. Then, hit by a large cross-sea, she was knocked through the wind onto the opposite tack.

Despite the helmsman's best efforts he had been unable to prevent the schooner's involuntarily change of heading. The flapping sails jerked hard across the deck as she fell unbid onto the opposite tack. The heavy sisal sheets holding the clews of the loose-footed sails whipped instantly across the deck where Hyami stood holding onto a stanchion. As she fell further off the wind, the sails filled instantly with a bang, harnessing the full power of the tearing gusts. One of the mainsail sheets caught under his right leg. With such unrestrained natural power in play, it whipped upwards, catching him off balance, lifting him vertically into the air. Falling, the vessel rolled violently, lurching further to leeward, aided by a series of rogue seas striking heavily at the bow. Where the deck should have been when Hyami landed was now surging white water.

The remaining crewman had only his own safety in mind as the vessel now careered uncontrolled, downwind, sails pressed heavily against the stays, and the dangerous prospect of a gybe increasing. Aware that a gybe under such conditions would probably rip the masts out of her, he risked everything. Frightened at leaving his position at the helm, he made his way forward, knife in hand, slashing madly at sheets and halyards. Released from their constraining influence, the sails took some minutes to thrash themselves into rags before finally falling to the deck or into the sea. Somewhere, downwind, the coast of Sumatra lay low and indistinct in the wild darkness.

As each successive crest passed under him, Hyami could see the grey shadow of the vessel and the pin-point light of the binnacle moving rapidly away, plunging before the driving wind and spume.

He had just a few minutes to come to terms with the hopelessness of his situation before, struggling and choking at each submersion, his lungs filled with sea water. His final thoughts as his nervous system shut down vital functions were of rage at his failure – then nothing.

❖ ❖ ❖

Leaving early, Harold Penrose, Krishnan, his crew and brothers, together with van der Valk, sailed from Ceci's base, making for the site of the broken Cornucopia. It was barely light. The dawn was grey with little prospect of a shining entry from the sun, dark, lowering clouds spread menacingly across the eastern horizon.

Ceci and the Gypsy Moth, now with full tanks, were going to follow by air. She intended to make yet another search of the coastline north and south of the wreck's location, hoping against hope that this time she would find somewhere nearby that might prove suitable for a landing. She was not convinced, however; she had been very thorough on her earlier reconnaissance of the wreck island.

It took some time to reach Cornucopia. The weather and seas were turning boisterous again and they surprised Cornucopia's remaining survivors and the Walrus's crew by their unheralded arrival. The late afternoon and early evening were spent retrieving the eight boxes of bullion that had been left behind and collecting together their few personal effects and loading them on board Krishnan's schooner. Talk turned to the likely location of the black ship that both Ceci, and later Wills, had seen the morning after the raid, well out to the west of the island chain. They speculated where she might be now. Had she sunk, or had her charred hull made a landfall on some island to the south of them? Putting the pieces together, they believed, from Ceci's report to Harold

Penrose, and Wills's own observations, that she had probably made it to one of the nearby islands. If that was the case they thought she probably still had the greater part of Cornucopia's bullion cargo on board. It was the consensus that they were duty-bound to locate and recover it.

Harold patiently explained his idea for locating and recovering the bullion and arresting the ship's crew. He proposed that Wills and Kildonan undertake a search of the nearby western and southern islands of the Nicobars. Wills's observations of the smoking ship had shown him that the crew's ability to manoeuvre her under any degree of control was limited, and that they would probably end up on the first island that crossed their path. From his aerial charts he and Kildonan tried to estimate, within reason, which islands might be the ship's probable landfall, based on the direction she was heading in when Wills last plotted her position from the air. They made some guesses as to the ocean's tidal effects on her course. If they could find her, they would mount a raid of their own, using Krishnan's brother's schooner to transport all their able-bodied men and the weapons Wills had brought from Port Blair in the Walrus. After much discussion and calculating, led by Harold, the Walrus crew felt confident that they had narrowed the search area down to three or four particular islands, but would quickly inspect all others en route.

Sleep assumed priority. Deverall, Snell and Kelly remained on shore with Wills and Kildonan. Krishnan, his crew, Penrose and van der Valk slept on the schooner. It was a warm night despite the restless wind causing the vessel to snub at her two stout anchor chains waking most of those sleeping on board at least once. Kildonan rose once during the early hours to check on the state of the Walrus, which was swinging to her mooring, now that the tide had risen. Above him, clouds were racing across the heavens, making the crescent moon pitch and toss through their turbulent strands as it headed west.

The morning was brighter, the wind a gentle breeze with a few remnants of cloud, having exhausted most of its energy overnight. After two cups of strong coffee, Wills and Kildonan were airborne with Colonel Deverall and Penrose in the front and rear gunner's positions, operating as observers, Deverall using a large pair of military binoculars. Flying south, they concentrated hard on seeing the detail of the island coastlines that passed beneath them. Now and again they descended to within a few feet of the sea and its bordering beaches, turning around some piece of coast to inspect its beaches and jungle overhangs more closely.

The ship stuck out like a sore thumb when eventually they found her, sitting stark, almost upright in the middle of a broad stretch of yellowish sand that set off her blackness. She could not have been more obvious. Circling carefully at five hundred feet, they looked carefully down at the stricken ship. No one appeared to be on board or in her immediate vicinity; it was as if she had somehow arrived on her own and now sat forlornly awaiting her fate. Kildonan was keen that they land in the sea and taxi ashore to investigate further. Wills vetoed the plan; by some ridiculous oversight, they had only brought one weapon aboard the machine, and were not sure how many of the ship's crew were probably hiding within the fringing jungle. However many there were, Wills was sure they would all be armed, and any damage to the Walrus could give him a real problem. The aerial observers were conscious that they too were being observed as they turned over the beach, the aircraft's engine roaring noisily as they manoeuvred, looking. They could clearly see scuffed tracks in the sand, leading from a rope ladder suspended from the ship's rail, which led along then up the beach, disappearing finally into the shelter of the trees. There was no sign of the bullion boxes from their aerial position. The vessel's hatches appeared sealed, wisps of smoke occasionally drifting. The large, heavily built, rowing boat that Wills had seen being towed behind the ship was now missing, along with its dead cargo.

Two hours after leaving, the Walrus landed back in the small bay opposite Cornucopia and its crew were soon ashore, sharing details of their reconnaissance. Michael Kelly chaired a beach meeting with everyone sitting around him on the sand or on makeshift log seats as they refined some ideas to recover the bullion from the stranded black ship. It was decided to sail overnight to the island where the ship sat. Depending on winds and tide, they would aim to arrive off the beach around four-thirty, before the sun rose.

Kelly insisted that everyone would go – they would pack up the Cornucopia camp this evening and probably not return; altogether there would be thirteen of them including Krishnan, his two crew and his two brothers and their crew. Squadron Leader Wills and Sub-Lieutenant Kildonan would remain at the Cornucopia site until morning, and then, with the Walrus fully fuelled from the stores on the schooner, make for the island and the black ship, ready to co-ordinate their efforts in any way possible in the recapture of the bullion and the crew of raiders.

❖ ❖ ❖

Yoshi and Cox looked an unlikely pair as they sat again in the ramshackle tea house negotiating with the owner–captain of a small coastal trading steamship for passage direct to Batavia. The captain wanted to call at Singapore for cargo, but neither Cox nor his new-found Japanese friend would risk a visit to the British-controlled colony at the moment. Albert Cox still had a little money left from his ill-gotten gains, but paying the captain would leave them both penniless. They had few options, and eventually agreed to the captain's demands. They would sail as soon as the unusually inclement weather had cleared the Malacca strait, probably tomorrow. Their plan was to pursue Hyami, trying to intercept him as he made his way along the Javanese archipelago on his way to Japan with the stolen ingots. If successful, it would mean that they could return the gold to its rightful owners and Cox may be forgiven for his serious lapse in integrity by the British authorities – perhaps they would also get some sort of cash reward. Yoshi would ask the British authorities for assistance in returning to Japan and help in removing himself, wife and son to Hawaii. They both recognised that their plan was naive in some ways but felt they had few other choices open to them.

The two of them boarded the small coal-fired vessel and sat together in the shade of a dirty awning strung between a short, stubby after mast and the ship's once-white superstructure. The captain intended to sail south-east down Sumatra's low-lying coast, through the maze of islands that lay south of Singapore to the port of Bangka, lying on the east side of an island set in the Java Sea. The following morning, very early, they were under way; the ship left a black, smoky trail suspended in the bright, clear air. Towards evening, with the Sumatran coast barely visible off to starboard, they approached the narrowest part of the Malacca strait; far ahead in the dusk lay a mass of islands and shallows across their path. It was possible to see other vessels, some lit with navigation lights, others ploughing through the deepening twilight incognito. Cox and Yoshi joined the ship's captain on the bridge, supping scalding-hot tea and staring ahead.

It was just a greyish shadow at first.

"Another unlit native fishing boat?" queried Cox of the captain. But there was something a little unusual about the vessel's movements; she seemed almost to be drifting, shaping no proper course despite a useful breeze. As they progressed, the unlit vessel changed direction a number of times for no apparent reason. Closer, they could now see that she had two masts, one of which had a small sail partially and badly set. The pilot moved across the bridge and sighted the strange vessel across the steering compass. He mentally noted the heading. Cox and the captain looked on. In the final remnants of daylight they could see the wayward vessel still changing course from time to time – there seemed little logic to her movements. Again Yoshi moved from his position leaning against the bridge rail, and standing over the ship's compass he noted the vessel's bearing again. The compass bearing had remained the same over the last fifteen minutes: they would collide with the ship if she, or they, failed to alter course substantially, and soon. Their problem was that they could not guess in which direction she was going to turn next.

The captain followed Yoshi's actions approvingly; only too aware of what was being assessed. They were now less than a quarter of a mile from the depleted sailing ship. The captain kept watching as she seemed to drift towards them, showing no apparent sign of life, no lights showing anywhere on board. Taking the wheel from his crewman, the captain began tracking the darkened vessel while they all tried to determine whether it was under control, abandoned or in some other difficulty.

The captain finally recognised the ship despite the lack of natural light. As they closed, a lamp was played over the silent vessel by a member of the steamship's crew, reflecting the high, red prow gently forging through the swell. It was the same vessel in which Hyami had taken passage to Batavia: the one onto which Yoshi had watched the two boxes of bullion being loaded. Manoeuvring slowly and expertly, the captain managed to get alongside the sailing vessel. They could now see that the sails were torn to ribbons, just large shreds of cloth, and that no one manned the helm near the stern. She appeared to be abandoned. The vessels bumped heavily as they came together; two members of the ship's crew leapt across and secured two large warps to the drifting schooner, locking them together. Intrigued, Yoshi followed, climbing over the rail, wondering where his erstwhile commander and his gold were.

It did not take long. He and Cox, with the captain and two crew members, secured the vessel, cutting down the remnants of sail. Yoshi quickly searched the decks then lowered himself carefully down a narrow open hatchway. He slid then tripped on something soft in the black space at bottom of the ladder, noticing that there was a faint smell of cordite, no doubt from a weapon's discharge. Not bothering to bend down, he knew too well that on the floor was semi-congealed blood and at least one body, which was confirmed as the steamship's captain reached the top of the ladder with a lamp. Taking the lamp, Yoshi stepped over what appeared to be a second victim; he noticed the man had much of his head missing on one side. The steamship captain, joined by Cox at the bottom of the ladder, watched as the lamp beam flicked across the unfolding scene. They all gagged at the carnage lying in the doorway to the cabin.

Inside, the pilot looked and felt around in the cabin's semi-darkness, while the captain took his lamp to look elsewhere. The light-coloured wooden box, what remained of it, stood out against its grey surroundings. Bumping into Yoshi, Cox muttered an expletive as he bent down to pick up something off the floor that had been trapped under the edge of the overturned table. Standing, he grunted, holding up a large, regular-shaped object. The pilot looked at the chunk in his hands; the glow from a flickering match lit an oblong ingot, glistening softly. Cox looked at it open-mouthed.

"Is this what I think it is?" he whispered. The pilot looked him in the eyes and nodded. They heard the captain's feet stomping down the ladder from the deck.

"Has he seen it?" Cox looked sideways at Yoshi.

"I think no," said Yoshi, looking pointedly at Albert Cox. "There must be other gold, this not all loaded."

In the cabin's oppressive gloom they managed to pick up the table and lift the smashed wooden box onto it. Its weight confirmed that other ingots lay inside. A thought crossed Yoshi's mind: 'So where is Hyami?' Taking Cox's ingot, he placed it with the other seven in the base of one box, urging Cox to leave the cabin. Yoshi dragged the two dead men aside, allowing the bullet-holed door to shut slightly, held firmly in place by the two cadavers. Yoshi and Cox were both aware that somewhere on this vessel there should be another identical box with four more high-quality ingots.

Reaching the deck again, they could see that someone had now permanently rigged a large light on the steamship's bridge, which shone usefully over the schooner. Towards its stern there was activity, the captain bending, holding onto a person, trying to coax some response. As the young man stood up, with the captain's help, it was obvious that he had suffered some kind of breakdown and was exhausted. Shaking and shivering, holding onto his right wrist, his face was twisted in a painful grimace. The swollen wrist was inspected carefully by the pilot; it appeared to be broken or badly sprained. Cox sat the man down; tearing off a large piece of sail cloth, he made a sling around the sailor's neck, gently pushing the damaged arm into its enveloping support. As he did so, the captain tried to make sense of the gibberish that tumbled from the man's lips. He did not appear to be making much sense; no phrase was completed before he lost the thread and drifted onto some other, unrelated, detail of his ordeal.

Taking the captain's lamp, the pilot walked forwards, and with the help of one of the captain's crew pulled the canvas covers off the corner of one of the holds. He peered in, the lamp shining ahead of him. Some barrels netted against the hold's sides provided a useful route down inside the pitch-black space. Moving between the mixed cargo, he searched painstakingly for the second bullion box. Stumbling about for twenty minutes, he finally surfaced, beaten. It was not in the aft hold. He returned to where the captain and Cox were still trying to help the schooner's remaining young crewman. Some of the story had come out, in a fashion. The sailor told how a Japanese passenger who had come on board at Dumai had appeared on deck during the previous night with a gun and had shot two of his colleagues before being swept off the deck himself by the violence of the vessel's motion in the heaving seaway. He had tried to control the ship but the wind's growing strength had made it impossible for him to sail her alone. He told how he had cut everything to reduce her headlong dash downwind, unsure how far away the coastline lay in the darkness. Exhausted, he had finally fallen asleep at the wheel as they plunged to leeward, not knowing where he was, or where the out-of-control schooner was heading.

From piecing together fragments of his story it was apparent that he had probably been asleep for most of the following day. He asked where his captain and the schooner's mate were. They all looked at each other; he saw their faces in the flickering lamplight and knew. The steamship captain pointed towards his ship, which had been made fast alongside, and gestured to the young man to transfer aboard. The sailor looked at them all in turn and shook his head. It transpired later that night that the schooner's slaughtered captain was the traumatised sailor's older brother. Their mother still lived in Dumai and he wanted to take the damaged schooner back there somehow.

As this came out the captain scratched his head. He also discovered that he knew the young man's family, but there was no way he could take the schooner in tow, nor could he spare any of his own crew to sail her back to Dumai. Explaining the problem carefully, using all the English he could muster, he looked resignedly at the two foreigners. They all sat, rolling with the gentle swell that passed under the two closely moored ships, and nobody said anything for a few minutes. Then, standing, Cox said that he and Yoshi the pilot would take the vessel home somehow – with the help of the young sailor. The ship's captain looked both relieved and worried.

"How you make such big boat go, you not done before? Sail, they all broked," he said pointing at lengths of tattered cloth still hanging from the masts.

Albert Cox smiled briefly, remembering. In his youth he had sailed around the Western Approaches from Falmouth in heavy, gaff-rigged fishing boats, crewing for a pittance with his father and uncles, looking for the silver herring. He spent time explaining this to the huddled group; it was tortuous, with their limited understanding of English, but he managed, at times calling on his limited knowledge of Malay and Mandarin. The captain looked at Cox with new-found respect; the pilot too was impressed with his calm and diplomatic approach. This was not the man he had found in the smoky tea house.

Rafted together, the two ships spent the night drifting with the tide a few miles up and then down the strait. An opportunity was taken to tidy up the schooner and to 'deep-six' the two shattered and now-stiff bodies brought up from below. The cabin was washed out with buckets of sea water until all traces of blood and horror were removed from the scene. Early the following morning the two vessels parted, and as their coir umbilicals were pulled clear the steamship headed south-east to Bangka and Batavia, black smoke pouring from her stack. The schooner, now with small patches of sail hoisted, set course slowly to the north-west and Dumai.

❖ ❖ ❖

Ceci had not slept well at all. Being totally alone in their island base was a new experience, and she definitely did not like it. It had never occurred to her as she said goodbye to everyone that she was going to be all alone on an island. Each night-time noise from the surrounding jungle had her sitting up, watching and listening tensely. Finally, after sitting up for the umpteenth time and having a good look around, she sank into a dreamless coma, waking only because the sun, high in the sky, had penetrated the narrow gaps between the leafy walls and roof of their simple bivouac. Stirring, she reached out for Harold; he was missing. Lifting her head, she remembered: he had gone with the rest. Her duty today was to fly to Cornucopia and search again for a landing site near to their beach.

As she went for a quick dip in the ocean, she was pleased to see that the tide had left a broad, firm beach for her to operate from. The Gypsy Moth sat quietly, nose up, pointing seawards, seemingly sniffing the air. She patted its taut wings as she skipped past, glad that the day was here and she was leaving.

On her own, she would have to start the machine with no one in the cockpit. She'd done it a few times before, but she'd also seen the result of carelessness in this act at White Waltham aerodrome near London, one summer's day when learning to fly. The poor pilot had had too much throttle set as he had swung the propeller. The engine had burst fully into life, and he'd just had time to leap for his life as the machine, with its thrashing propeller, jumped its restraining chocks, careering across the aerodrome taking damaging side-swipes at various machines lined up neatly in front of the club house, before finally hitting the airfield boundary fence. Her flying instructor said it had been a good example of how not to do it, and that he had been lucky not to be cut into small pieces. With the event in her mind, she dried and dressed, determined not to make the same error – particularly now.

Without drama the Gypsy Moth lifted off, the engine's throaty roar echoing off the glistening jungle. She was late; the sun was reaching its zenith as she banked across the ocean towards Cornucopia's shattered remains. Arriving over the site, she looked for her survivors and Krishnan's brother's boat. Neither it nor the Walrus were anywhere to be seen. There was no evidence of anyone in residence. Flying around, just off the beach, she wondered at the situation for a few moments. It soon became clear to her that they had either all gone north to Port Blair or, more likely, in her opinion, gone south looking for the raiders' black ship. Opening the throttle, she allowed the Gypsy Moth to climb slowly towards the south, not quite sure where she was heading, but she had a few ideas to check out.

❖ ❖ ❖

They hadn't made good time. It was just after sunrise as they approached the beach where the black ship sat. Creeping along the coast of the small island they stopped short, anchoring a half-mile north of the ship's position. The shallow draught of their trading schooner allowed them to wade ashore, thigh deep, led by Colonel Deverall, followed by Snell, Penrose, Rawlinson and all but one of the vessel's crew and the partly incapacitated Michael Kelly. They were armed with rifles and sharp knives. Van der Valk joined them holding a pistol, his left arm seemingly having made a remarkable recovery, although still in a sling. Michael Kelly watched them leaving from his seat aboard the schooner with the remaining local crewman. Arriving later than they had actually intended, just after dawn, meant that all their actions could now be fully observed, and the element of surprise may well have been lost – Deverall was both concerned and annoyed.

He split his forces, one group, led by him, moving through the island's interior to approach the sad, stranded vessel from the south; the remainder, under David Rawlinson, creeping silently as near to the beach as possible without being seen, to wait until a warning shot was fired by Deverall when he was in place. All wondered where and how many there were of the black ship's crew; the ship itself appeared to be completely abandoned, but they must be somewhere, probably hiding within the tree line.

Rawlinson and van der Valk sat watching, the mixed crews a few feet further back in the trees, smoking, sitting quietly, alert. They had been there nearly forty-five minutes, without a signal from Deverall or a sight or sound from the black ship's crew. It occurred to Rawlinson that perhaps they were the party being watched and liable to attack; after all, he reasoned, the raiders would know that someone would come looking for them after the recent aerial activity over their vessel.

A further fifteen minutes ticked by; it had now been well over an hour since Deverall had moved off with his group. Rawlinson wondered what was going on. He sat back against a tree watching the beach for any signs of movement, concealed behind the lush, variegated greenery. Another ten minutes passed, and still there was no signal from Deverall. Should Rawlinson send one of the sailors around the beach, and through the tree line, to make contact? He turned and beckoned to Krishnan. The young man was in his element, loving the intrigue and possibility of a fight – and a reward. They discussed what to do. The group were becoming restless. Obviously there had been no contact between Deverall's group and the crew of the black ship; they should have heard something by now.

Picking one of his own crew, Krishnan was just instructing the slim young man on what to do when suddenly there was a burst of shooting from within the jungle. Birds rose squawking and crying as the shots echoed across the beach. But it was not possible to determine the location of the action precisely; the jungle was very dense, certainly more impenetrable than other locations they had visited. The shooting stopped; there were some muffled shouts, then nothing. Rawlinson and van der Valk stood up and crept gingerly with Krishnan towards the edge of their concealment. There was no action on the beach; no sign of any human activity, or any sounds now. After a few minutes they all moved back into the undergrowth and sat with the rest of the men to wait.

A hum turned slowly into a roar as the Walrus approached the site. Wills and Kildonan expected to see the black ship secured after an assault by Colonel Deverall's team. Over the beach, they were surprised to see no sign of activity or life. Banking out to sea again, they climbed and began circling about two miles offshore, discussing as best they could in the noisy cockpit what action to take. They had seen Krishnan's brother's schooner apparently anchored some way north from the beach where the abandoned black ship sat. Wills recognised Kelly sitting on one of the hatch covers as they passed overhead, and he gently rocked the wings of the machine in acknowledgement of a wave from the two men below. Kelly sat watching the Shagbat circling out to sea and wondered if he would ever have command of an aircraft again.

Splinters hit his arm as the bullet smashed into the ship's wooden rail a few feet in front of him. He turned just in time to see no less than five armed men running across the beach towards the water's edge, firing continually at the schooner. Kelly and the Malay crewman just had time to fall behind the stout wooden hatch-surround. Bullets continually zinged across the deck as the approaching raiders splashed through the shallow water and up to the schooner's side.

Kelly fired off a few reactionary shots but was unable to see a real target as the approaching men were now too close to the schooner, hidden from his view. Keeping his head down and looking back along the vessel's planked deck, he caught sight of someone clambering over the rail at its stern, rifle in hand. The figure was quickly followed by another man. Their rapid shooting towards Kelly's position made raising his head for a shot over the top of the protective hatch an act of certain suicide. The Malay crewman, armed only with a knife and wooden pole, slid cautiously down one side of the deck hatch wall. Kelly remained, constrained by his leg wound, and the fear of being hit by the blizzard of lead hurtling across the deck just above them. By now, he was certain that all the men he had seen running had probably managed to get aboard the schooner.

There was a brief cry and then the sounds of grunting followed by more short cries. He tried to turn, to see what had happened further aft, on the opposite side of the hatch. Three men were approaching with weapons carefully aimed. Behind, two other men were hauling the Malay crewman along the deck, blood running in a thin trickle from the top of the poor man's shoulder, more from the side of his mouth.

"We meeting for the second time I think, Mister," said one of the men, who was wearing a dirty white peaked hat. Kelly looked scornfully up at him from his position sitting back against the side of the hatch surround.

"No, you are not recognising me, it dark we met last." The Malay crewman was thrown roughly down beside Kelly. "Well, that is very convenient, Mister; you have brought us boat and provide us hostages. Well, well." The captain looked around, then gave his instructions. The Malay and Kelly were grabbed and spread-eagled, one on top of each of the two large hatch covers, and tied securely into place. The sun beat down on them mercilessly. Meanwhile, two of the raiders' crew raised the schooner's anchor; the vessel was then quickly made ready for sea, sailing slowly up the coast towards their beached black ship.

Both Rawlinson and Deverall heard the shooting coming from somewhere in the general area of where they had moored the schooner.

"What the bloody hell is going on?" shouted Deverall as he ran back towards where he had left the rest of his group, who were now sitting secreted in the mass of trees just off the beach. In his hand was the booby-trap gun that had been mounted in the fork of a tree with a tripwire cleverly running from the trigger across the floor of the jungle awaiting someone passing. Someone in his group had passed by, caught the tripwire and the weapon had discharged. No one had been hit by this ingenious contraption, but the shot had brought an outburst of ill-disciplined firing from his own men, one of whom had received a minor flesh wound. Deverall began to realise that they had been expected and outwitted by the crew of the black ship. He'd have lost points for this at Staff College.

Rawlinson, with his men following, moved as quickly as possible through the undergrowth back to the beach where their schooner was anchored. Perspiring and out of breath, they carefully broke cover from the trees. The vessel was not anchored, but moving slowly up the coast about half a mile offshore in deep water. Even as they watched, shots were fired indiscriminately towards them. Ducking down, they crawled quickly back into the tree line, a little shocked at how the initiative had been taken from them. A few minutes later an even-hotter Deverall and his men arrived. Rawlinson described what had taken place, and the colonel briefly described what had happened to them. They both felt a little foolish and very worried for Kelly and the crewman, who were now hostages – or dead.

Wills saw the schooner moving away from the beach and turned the aircraft towards it. The Walrus roared overhead, slightly banked to port; Wills looked down on the scene and was amazed to see two men, one of them clearly Kelly with his missing lower right leg, strapped across the ship's hatch covers. Straightening up, he reversed their course and flew back, this time allowing Kildonan to see the outcome of events over the past few minutes. The two pilots and the men on the ground were too aware that the initiative had been lost. The two hostages on the schooner made sure that the raiders had a clear run back to the beach and the black ship. It was now obvious that any counter-attack would result in serious repercussions for the crippled Michael Kelly and the bleeding Malay crewman.

Slowing, the schooner turned directly towards the shore and finally ran her bow a short distance onto the beach just behind the stranded ship. Three men leapt from the schooner's bow, running low towards the ship. The remaining two raiders crouched with weapons pointing at their hostages. Deverall watched through binoculars as the hatches were pulled open on the black ship; smoke poured from the openings. Turning every so often, the raiders fired a few shots in the general direction of Deverall's men, now hidden. Two of the raiders disappeared into the smoking hold, while one took up a position behind the remains of the vessel's burnt superstructure, holding a powerful rifle in his hands.

For ten minutes or so there was no activity, then both men scrambled hastily up out of the hold, diving over the hatch coamings and running towards the stern of the vessel, coughing. Seconds later there was a resounding explosion; the black ship lurched, then slumped over towards her starboard side. Deverall watched for a few more seconds and then turned in shock to Rawlinson.

"They've blown out the side of the hull on the other side, I think. It'll let them remove the bullion more easily, straight onto the beach." Smoke from the explosion was still rising from the open hatch as the third man relinquished his sniper position behind the superstructure and clambered quickly over the side of the ship, rifle slung over his back.

"Quick! We have to get round to the other side. We're blind

here, can't see what the buggers are up to." Rawlinson started to run along just inside the tree line, hoping to get around the beach so that he could observe what was happening on the black ship's blind starboard side. His running attracted shots from the two raiders on the schooner guarding Kelly and the Malay. Snell followed, not quite sure where this idea was going, but felt that standing watching with Deverall was achieving nothing.

They all stopped as one man cautiously appeared, waving a white flag, from around the bow of the black ship. In his hand was a large megaphone. He raised it to his face; the words were difficult to catch against the noise of the breeze and gently breaking waves.

"We take gold from ship now. Load onto schooner. If you make mistake interfering, we kill you friends. Stay back, not trouble. Okay?" He said it twice, slowly. Even with his basic English the message was obvious. It was a stand-off.

Wills landed the Walrus a mile offshore to wait for an opportunity that might allow them to regain the initiative. Around the stern of the black ship a man emerged, pulling a sort of cart with large wide wheels. Back on the ship's deck, two raiders sat half-hidden, with rifles ready. On the cart sat two or three wooden boxes. Even with its large wheels the cart required a lot of effort to move over the sand. At the bow of the schooner, the raider standing guard laid his rifle within reach, and with the help of ropes lifted the boxes up onto the gently bobbing schooner's bow one by one. His compatriot continued to hold his weapon at Kelly's temple. Deverall watched, frustrated, as the exercise was carried out five times until, finally, on the sixth trip, two of the boxes slipped sideways off the trolley. They lay dug into the sand and the man ignored them while he completed his trip and unloaded the remainder. The raider positioned on the schooner's bow began to pull the boxes aft, tipping them loosely over the rim of one of the part-open hatches until they fell into the hold. From their positions Deverall and Rawlinson could clearly hear them smashing as they struck the wooden deck and cargo below.

Once he had unloaded, the raider turned and wheeled his trolley back towards the two fallen boxes. His colleague on the schooner, now with a minute to spare, jumped down into the hold to sort out the fallen boxes below. Kelly watched him from his restrained position, his vision blurred by sweat, his guard alert.

Ceci saw the schooner first, its bow nudging the shoreline; someone was pulling something towards it. The black ship sat inert just beyond. It appeared to be a wreck, past hope, a huge jagged hole in its side, lying at an odd angle. 'So they managed it!' She prepared to beat up the beach in celebration. Everyone heard the approaching Gypsy Moth. The raider guarding Kelly and the injured Malay looked up and turned to look at the approaching small machine, now over the far end of the beach. Deverall, opportunistic, fired once; the shot felled the man. The colonel had had his rifle sighted on the guarding raider for some minutes, waiting patiently for such a break in concentration. The bullet tore through the man's side, severing his spine, the fragments of shattered bone ripping through the right ventricle of his heart. Tied up, Kelly could hear the man grunting and sighing for a final few seconds as he lay broken, head hanging down into the hatch, blood streaming down onto the deck below and gathering in a large, crimson pool. Deverall gave the order for everyone with a rifle to keep firing over the open hatch and take care to miss Cornucopia's restrained captain; it would keep the other raiders trapped below for the moment, and keep them from taking any vengeful action against the two hostages.

As Ceci pulled up steeply from the beach she sensed things were not as they should be. Offshore, she could see the Walrus, engine idling, the machine just making way through the water. 'Odd,' she thought, 'why aren't they ashore, helping in some way?' The situation on the ground became a little clearer as a neat round hole appeared unexpectedly in the lower starboard wing, just outboard of the walkway. 'They're shooting at me.' 'Who is?' was the next question rushing through her excited brain. Banking steeply around, she looked at the scene set out below her; there appeared to be a gunfight going on. They were shooting at her and into the jungle beyond the black ship. Off to one side of the beach, two men were running through the sand. It looked like Harold and another man, who had a rifle. Harold appeared to have a pistol, he was waving it. Two men lying along the deck of the black ship, hidden from Harold's view, were preparing to shoot at the two men as they ran along the top of the beach, gradually bringing them neatly into the sights of the two raiders.

The Gypsy engine roared away as Ceci thrust the throttle open, climbing up and around towards the far end of the beach. Turning again, engine still roaring, she sighted the two half-concealed raiders in the crossed struts that supported the aircraft's fuel tank. Diving at almost full throttle, she watched them carefully. They had seen her. One was pointing at her. They both turned, kneeling, calmly taking aim at the diving machine that was rapidly filling the sights on their rifles. It was coming straight at them, the noise of its power dive screaming. They could not miss. To all intents the Gypsy Moth was a static target as it flew directly at them; not wavering in its intent. As both gunmen fired simultaneously, the .303-calibre lead flew to meet the looming aircraft. One bullet flew down the port side of the machine harmlessly. The second hit the wooden propeller as it rotated at 2,100 revolutions per minute.

Sub-Lieutenant Kildonan had been watching Ceci's approach from a distance, sitting in the Walrus's cockpit, finally drawing Harvey Wills's attention to the blue-and-silver biplane. As it dived for the second time onto the beach they saw an eruption at the front of the aircraft, then large lumps of solid material flying off, arcing every way into the air. It was over in barely a second or two.

Captain Kelly felt the wind from her passing as the Gypsy Moth hurtled over the schooner on its way out to sea. He heard the engine racing unnaturally, trying to burst, he later remarked, laughing. Ceci couldn't for a brief moment understand what had happened; the throttle was wide open but she was losing speed as she tried to climb out from her dive. The aircraft vibrated madly. Her wonder was just for an instant. Then she realised: the propeller was gone. She must now focus only on landing safely. At her low altitude only one option was available. Ahead lay the sea: on it sat the Walrus. Closing the throttle had made life simpler; she didn't have to cope with the distraction of the noisy engine. She gave her full attention to her first-ever sea ditching.

"Christ," uttered Kildonan, irreverently, "She's not going to try and ditch the bloody thing, is she?" Wills watched; teeth clenched hard, willing something good to happen. He knew a Gypsy Moth was hardly ideal in a ditching situation. Its fixed undercarriage was the problem. He knew too well that as soon as it touched the sea's surface the machine would trip, and flip, onto its back. Ceci had no time for such matters. It would take all of her concentration to make the slowest approach possible to the swell's surface.

Anxiously looking out, assessing her height and the aircraft's attitude, she allowed the silent aeroplane to settle, pulling back gently on the stick as the water grew closer. Feeling the aircraft was about to stop flying, just on the point of stalling, she kicked the rudder bar hard to the right. The Gypsy Moth slewed sideways momentarily as she hit the water. They were enveloped in a huge cocoon of solid water and spray, the aircraft completely hidden from view.

The water settled; the breeze blew the spray downwind. She was afloat, upright, tail high in the air, nose deep under water.

"My God! Look! She's managed it! It's still in one piece, right side up!" Wills was already opening up the Walrus's engine, taxiing towards the waterlogged Gypsy Moth. Ceci, a little stunned, unstrapped and climbed rapidly out onto the wing, noticing again the neat round hole. She was shaking but unhurt.

As the Walrus drew near, Wills cut its motor, allowing it to glide through the water towards the stricken, fast-submerging Gypsy Moth. When they were alongside, Ceci clung to the coaming around the front gunner's position and clambered into its well, and only her feet were wet. She smiled, relieved, at the two pilots sitting behind the windscreens then looked back sadly at her beautiful Moth. Bubbles were erupting from around it before it slowly and gracefully disappeared beneath the surface. Watching her go, Ceci was numb, facing away from the men in the cockpit behind her. The silver-and-blue aeroplane sat on the sea-bed ten feet or so below, its image distorted, unreal through the gently moving, gin-clear ocean.

The Pegasus engine turned and caught with a puff of blue smoke, and the Walrus moved off slowly towards the beach. They could see from their position off the beach the remainder of the crew of the black ship now holed up inside its broken hull; every so often a fusillade of shots poured from its black interior. None of the Cornucopia party was hit, or in danger of being hit. The firing was unaimed and erratic. The remaining raider lodged in the hold of the schooner had been quiet during the sustained hail of shots over the hatchway.

A brief pause in the shooting from the black ship's crew prompted van der Valk to rush unannounced from his concealed position to the side of the broken vessel. Rawlinson, Deverall and the rest of the crew watched as he crept carefully around the bow of the vessel; he was shouting something to the raiders – it appeared to be Dutch. Suddenly he was gone, around the bow, hidden from view. Rawlinson and Deverall looked at each other, raised eyebrows, questioning

"He's either very brave or mad," said Deverall. During the lull while van der Valk was engaging the raiders, Snell and two of their boat's crew took the opportunity to rush the schooner. Kelly and the Malay man were still strapped helplessly to its hatch covers. Clambering up, Snell crept cautiously towards the open corner of the hatch down which the second raider had disappeared when his compatriot was killed. The two other crew men severed the ropes holding the two men, helping Kelly to hobble to the stern of the vessel – out of harm's way for the moment.

Looking down, Snell could see nothing. The hold was black; not a glimmer of light showed except that penetrating a few feet from the open corner. Shooting started again but this time the raiders were aiming at him. He fell clumsily, grasping the corner of the hatch cover and pulling it roughly over the opening. From his position lying on the deck, he was just out of sight of the gunmen. He tried knocking the wooden wedges back into place to secure the heavy hatch cover. Bullets were regularly smashing into the ship's rail and, now and then, into the corner of the hatch surround, splattering huge wooden splinters across the deck where he lay. Choosing his moment, he managed to get one wedge in place but could do no more without risking his life.

"We need to follow van der Valk. I'll take two men and see if we can creep around the stern and attack them from there, dividing their fire. You stay here, David, and take them if any should escape." Rawlinson nodded at Deverall's instruction. As the colonel and two young crew men began to run crouched towards the black ship, van der Valk suddenly appeared on its deck, a pistol in his left hand. Deverall stopped for a second. Had van der Valk killed or captured the remaining raiders single-handedly?

The Dutchman raised his right arm as if about to wave to them but the wave became a throw. Something small left his hand and flew towards the three running men, stopping them mid-stride.

"Down!" bellowed Deverall. He recognised the tiny silhouette of a grenade aimed unerringly towards them. The explosion threw damp sand and shrapnel across the beach. Fortunately the three men had fallen into a slight depression in the contours of the beach. The lethal blast had passed over them. Looking up through the mist of falling sand, Deverall could see van der Valk picking something from a box at his feet. Nobody from Rawlinson's group fired at the Dutchman – they were too stunned by events, as Rawlinson later explained to Deverall. The second grenade fell nearer to the three prone men, just into their sandy depression. It rolled a few feet on impact before coming to a halt between Deverall and one of the Malay crew. They lay, pressing their bodies firmly into the beach, tense and waiting for the explosion – and pain. Nothing. Ten seconds, still nothing. Deverall opened his eyes and looked nervously across at the murderous, rusty device lying only feet from him. Still there was nothing.

"It's a dud!" he shouted, and looked up towards the black ship, anticipating more. Van der Valk was gone; no one stood on the deck. He had picked up the remaining four rust-covered grenades in their box with difficulty, passing them down to one of the raiders, a pistol still clutched in his left hand.

Nothing happened for a few minutes, no shooting. There was silence on the beach, except for the rumble of the Walrus's engine as they cruised just offshore watching the action on the beach. Deverall with his two men ran back to where Rawlinson lay waiting, covered by the trees. A few words were exchanged as they watched.

"That bastard Dutchman has let us down rather badly, eh, Rawlinson?"

David Rawlinson glanced sideways at the colonel.

"I have to say, Colonel, that I was never truly trusting of him. There always seemed to be something not quite pukka about him. What do you think they're up to now?"

Deverall shook his head.

"I'm not too sure but they'll not give up the bullion they've loaded on the schooner without a good fight. They've taken a lot of risks and trouble getting this far. But they are becoming desperate."

Again matters were taken from their hands. Suddenly four men emerged from the blind side of the black ship, three with rifles that were aimed at the jungle surrounding Deverall and his partially concealed crew. Van der Valk was easily identifiable, his arm in a dirty sling, the pistol in his hand. In his right hand, they could just make out a grenade; on his belt hung others. The men were firing repeatedly as they ran, crouched low, towards the schooner, then van der Valk launched the grenade into a shallow trajectory so that it fell and exploded just outside the tree line, most of its blast and wicked shrapnel absorbed by the jungle's thick interior. No one was hurt.

Snell dared to raise his head just above the schooner's hatch surround, rifle at the ready. The four raiders were running, low down, towards him. One had stopped and was preparing to throw something. Kneeling, Snell took aim and slowly squeezed the trigger, the image of van der Valk secure in his sights about two hundred feet distant. The gun jumped from his hands, falling over the side of the vessel into the shallow water at her bow.

One of the raiders, glancing up briefly, saw Snell rise. Instinctively he had aimed and fired quickly. Either the raider was a superb marksman or, more likely, it was a lucky shot. The bullet struck Snell's weapon slightly to one side of the stock above the trigger guard. The shock of the impact tore the weapon away; Snell fell backwards onto the deck, concussed, with blood running from cuts to his face.

Now up to the schooner's bow, two raiders were still firing indiscriminately towards the jungle; the other two raiders were now on the schooner's blind side, clambering up the vessel amidships. Deverall and his men ran, still inside the tree line, tripping over roots and brush but moving away from the raider's general target area. Stopping for a moment, the colonel could see that three men were now aboard the schooner; one was bending down helping van der Valk climb onto the deck. Moving his men just out onto the beach, those with weapons started shooting at the escaping raiders on the schooner. One pitched into the sea face-down, not moving.

There was now some action right at the stern of the vessel: suddenly someone dived into the deeper water there and began swimming strongly away, curving gradually in towards the beach.

"Stop firing!" Deverall bellowed. Rawlinson had been watching events on the schooner with the binoculars and had seen the action on the stern. It seemed that the Malay crewman had somehow escaped just as a raider emerged from a hatch near the aft most hold. The raider held a long weapon, pointing it at Kelly. Then Rawlinson saw Michael Kelly being forcefully dragged along the deck, still a hostage for the raiders' escape.

"Stop you shooting, your man will be kilt." The broken English of one of the surviving raiders rang out across the sand. There wasn't much they could do if Kelly was to remain unharmed. Van der Valk moved down the deck towards the unfortunate Kelly, who had been sat on the forward hatch cover; the pistol was pushed firmly against his temple.

"I'm sorry for misleading you, Captain, but we intend leaving shortly. We have an appointment elsewhere, I'm sure you'll understand." There was mild mockery in van der Valk's breathless voice. The schooner's ancient diesel engine started, blowing puffs of thick black smoke shorewards. Expertly handled, the vessel slowly backed off the beach, swinging in reverse until parallel with the shore; the raiders alert on deck, weapons pointing at the beach and at their prisoner.

Wills watched the schooner moving away from the shoreline, turning out towards them. They were Kelly's only hope, but what should they do? Of course, they could always pursue the vessel from the air, at least until their fuel became critical or it got dark.

Then what? Wills thought. Ceci still sat in the exposed forward gunner's cockpit, fearful of the outcome. Wills decided to try diplomacy.

Taxiing very slowly through the water, he converged with the schooner. The three raiders stood watching him manoeuvring, ready to fire, and to kill Kelly. A hundred yards off, Wills shut down the engine completely, opening the cockpit door, leaving Kildonan to steer the machine. Standing, he cupped his hands.

"Let us take Captain Kelly off – we guarantee not to interfere with you or your vessel." Now holding onto Kelly firmly, van der Valk looked across at the aircraft off their starboard side.

"Captain Kelly is our safe passage; we will leave him somewhere safe tonight."

"Come on, van der Valk, the man is seriously wounded. I give you my word; we will leave you alone without pursuit if you let us take him off."

"I don't think so, Wills. I would feel so much safer with him than without. You will have to trust us, I think." Wills looked down into the cockpit, discussing the situation with Kildonan.

Ceci noticed first. The Walrus was drifting down onto the schooner in the onshore breeze. Looking up, David Kildonan immediately saw the situation and grabbed for the petrol cock. Flicking the magneto switches on, he pressed the starter. The propeller turned slowly behind them, the engine coughing and belching, unwilling to fire; it was hot. The wind had gained a little strength as the land had warmed. It was enough to increase the rate at which the cumbersome, now uncontrollable aircraft was bearing down on the schooner, which sat beam-on to their approach. Wills tried to persuade the engine to fire but it was not to be persuaded.

The Walrus's lower starboard wingtip hit the side of the schooner a glancing blow. The front gunner's cockpit, with Ceci ensconced, was next to hit the vessel. One of the raiders leaned out from the schooner's rigging and tried to fend off the flying machine with one hand, holding onto his rifle with the other. As he leaned out, pushing it away, he almost lost his balance, in danger of toppling into the sea. With a shout, he let his rifle fall. It fell neatly into the front gunner's cockpit, landing painfully on Ceci's legs and feet with a clatter. Managing to regain his balance, the raider backed away, now weapon-less, from the side of the schooner, running aft to be near the rest of his crew.

One of the winter sports Ceci enjoyed was rough shooting. Her uncle's estates in Argyll and Yorkshire had given her every opportunity to improve on what had turned out to be a natural skill. She had on more than one occasion bagged the most birds for a day's shooting. Picking up the heavy ancient rifle, she swung it around, picking a target on the schooner as it moved slowly past her in the confusion. This was no fleeting bird. She squeezed the trigger, and a spurt of flame left the muzzle, the weapon's recoil causing her to fall backwards against the windscreens of the cockpit. Her target slammed into the mast as the shot hit him square in the chest. Eyes wide open, he slumped, lifeless, to the deck.

Standing around the side of the same protective mast, van der Valk had seen the shot and lifted one of the grenades from his belt, tearing the pin from its locking position with his mouth. With both van der Valk's hands occupied, Kelly took the initiative and stood, for a moment balancing on his one good leg. Pushing off sideways, he crashed over the vessel's side into the ocean. Alerted by the splash, and annoyed, van der Valk turned briefly, firing his pistol at the swimming Kelly, to no avail. Then, turning back instantly, he raised his good arm to throw the grenade at the aircraft.

Watching him intently, Ceci noticed that the grenade appeared to slip from his fingers as he threw, aiming at the cockpit. Instead, it flew slightly sideways, hitting the cabane struts supporting the engine behind the cockpit. It fell onto the wing below, before detonating. There was a huge flash of orange as aircraft and fuel ignited. Ceci and Wills, standing in their respective cockpits, were blown yards from the fiercely burning Walrus.

Penetrated by dozens of shrapnel holes, the machine very quickly filled and sank. Kildonan, sitting in the cockpit as the machine exploded behind him, was knocked out as the blast wave passed over him. Coming to as sea water washed over his face, he kicked and struggled across the remains of the sinking cockpit, managing to leave through the opening where Wills had been standing only brief seconds before.

Surfacing, shocked and coughing, all three swam away from the remains of the burning aircraft. There was a torn, bloody body in the water near the schooner's side bobbing about among bits of wood and oil that littered the disturbed surface. It appeared to have been stripped naked by the blast and looked little better than a side of bloodied meat at a slaughterhouse. Around its neck a stained white sling carried an arm. Pieces of burning aircraft, wood and fabric bobbed in the breeze towards the shore. The schooner was dead in the water with no sign of the remaining raider. Wills made it first, managing to climb, exhausted, from the filthy, flame- and oil-covered water, then helping Ceci and Kildonan aboard.

Under the influence of the onshore breeze the schooner drifted ashore along the beach. Penrose, Rawlinson and Deverall had watched the unexpected turn of events, horror-struck and helpless. They ran along the shoreline ready for further action until it became clear that the schooner's surviving raider had surrendered to Snell. He had come carefully up and onto the deck after the aircraft explosion.

The two escaping swimmers were helped ashore, the Malay crewman apologising profusely for leaving Captain Kelly behind. Laughing between deep intakes of air, Kelly said he might just have done the same in the circumstances. Ceci, Wills and Kildonan had been extremely lucky, remarked Deverall; they'd all escaped with only minor cuts and abrasions. Ceci and her ex-beau Harvey Wills had had some hair singed away.

❖ ❖ ❖

The days were hot, almost windless as the schooner with the high red prow drifted, rather than sailed, finally making it back to Dumai. The dead captain's brother told his story to a small crowd of family and onlookers who gathered round quickly as word spread. The cruel deaths hit the community hard; loss of breadwinners would create even greater problems for their families, who were already living barely above subsistence. Albert Cox and Yoshi gathered their cargo from the hold of the schooner. To the captain's bereaved mother and her youngest son they gave a single ingot in a private ceremony away from prying eyes – but insisting to them that all those affected should benefit. They knew somewhat guiltily that it was not theirs to give, but the prospect of leaving the families with no income or means of raising income brought on a sudden attack of morals that seemed to leave them no alternative.

Feeling better, they hired a man with a small, fast sailing boat to take them north-east across the Malacca strait to the port of Kelang in Malaya. From there they would travel the few miles by road to the capital, Kuala Lumpur, and deliver the stolen bullion to the British authorities. Cox still hoped for forgiveness for his earlier misdemeanour, and Koya Yoshi for help in getting home to Nara, intending then to immigrate to Hawaii.

❖ ❖ ❖

Five months later there was a small reception at the offices of Empress Airways in London's Berkeley Square. It was followed by a private dinner at the Savoy. The directors of the airline, along with Cornucopia's survivors and Harold Penrose, Cecilia Grosvenor-Ffoulkes and her mother, as well as two senior civil servants from the foreign affairs department and the treasury, were present. Over afternoon tea the two civil servants spent an hour or more explaining as much as they could to the assembled company about what had been discovered about the events surrounding the loss of Cornucopia.

Over the intervening five months facts had emerged as to why Cornucopia had ditched in the sea so far off her prescribed course to Rangoon. The investigation, and the piecing together of bits of evidence, had revealed that Oliver Stoneman and Claude Pardoe had formed a strong friendship through their tennis activities in Singapore.

Stoneman had somehow learnt of the bullion shipment schedules and hatched a plot with Pardoe to steal it. It was thought likely that Stoneman may have picked up the airline's schedule information from correspondence left carelessly about at the Empress offices in Singapore. Cyril Porter had since been fired from Empress, as had his deputy Lee Chi Kwan, both for dereliction of duty. Porter was pleased to be back in a temperate climate.

Imperial's Singapore station manager, Claude Pardoe, had been arrested while trying to leave the island by passenger boat one evening. He was awaiting trial as an accomplice to attempted robbery and manslaughter in Changi Gaol. Under interrogation by local police and the military he admitted that when Imperial's engineers had undertaken some work on Cornucopia's cockpit instruments just prior to her last flight, Stoneman had arranged for Pardoe to personally attach the magnet to the captain's directional compass, deflecting it ninety degrees off true.

In accordance with company operating procedures, prior to any take-off, Captain Kelly should have asked First Officer Stoneman to confirm that his compass heading was aligned with the captain's, which Stoneman would have done, knowing full well that there was a difference of ninety degrees between his correctly indicating instrument and his captain's sabotaged compass. A moment of doubt surrounded whether Michael Kelly had actually carried out that particular check.

However, the civil servants went on, what had come to light much more recently from Dutch police investigations in the Netherlands and Java, was that Henrik van der Valk had known Stoneman for some years. As a youth van der Valk had stayed at the Stoneman household in England and at Batavia during summer holidays – Stoneman and van der Valk seniors were colleagues working for a Dutch oil company. Having later learnt to fly, the younger van der Valk set up an air charter company with some help from his father. He was well placed to win charter contracts from his father's employers and their clients, carrying equipment and exploration personnel around the Asia region. Later, while on holiday in England, he encouraged Stoneman junior to take up flying.

It also emerged from other bits of information, including the single page from a letter found in the floating tennis bag picked up at sea by Wills and Kildonan, that their plan was for Stoneman to force Kelly at gunpoint to land the machine in the sea near Aceh on the northern tip of Sumatra. They had to assume that Stoneman had the weapon on him when he was ejected through the flying boat's windscreens on ditching – no gun had been found in the aircraft. Pardoe had admitted during early questioning after his arrest that the letter had been written by him to Stoneman and that reference to radio courses and locations were actually codes for locations and times for their proposed aerial hijack and robbery. It seemed van der Valk knew of a small airstrip at Aceh where they would have been able to transfer the bullion to the DC-2. From there the trail had gone cold; no one knew where they would have flown to with the booty, but they would almost certainly have had accomplices in Aceh to help in moving the load from sea to airstrip.

What neither van der Valk nor Stoneman had allowed for in their plan was the ferocious, unpredicted storm. Its occurrence out of season, and from an unusual direction, threw their grand plan out of the window – literally for Stoneman, Michael Kelly had remarked with black humour. Cornucopia's real emergency landing so far off course meant that van der Valk had to find some legitimate reason for pursuing Cornucopia. The Japanese Trade delegation charter, led by Hyami, had proved to be a Godsend, playing right into his hands, until the killing began.

But there had been a twist in the situation. What was unknown to Hyami was that his agent in Penang had worked with van der Valk senior for some years before the latter was based in Batavia, looking after the interests of his oil-company employers.

The surviving raider captured by Snell turned out to be none other than Hyami's Penang agent, well known to the young van der Valk. He had agreed to talk after his arrest, hoping to mitigate any future sentence he was expected to receive. It appeared the agent had recognised van der Valk once when they had met at Penang during the search for Cornucopia and a brief discussion took place. His evidence proved vital.

Van der Valk's subsequent appearance to Krishnan at South Andaman, after his escape from death at Hyami's hands, had proved to be a vital coincidence, said the Dutch Colonial Police report. Instinctively, he knew that he needed to be further south if he was to have even the remotest chance of catching up with the bullion. Krishnan had innocently made it possible for him to travel and eventually to link up with Ceci and Penrose, who, he was further amazed to discover, were also looking for the missing flying boat. He had managed to fool everyone until those last moments when he had declared his colours and joined the black ship's raiding crew, whose second-in-command had turned out to be Hyami's Penang agent.

Nothing was ever found of Colonel Hyami. Information had been signalled from the Singapore authorities to London over the past few days indicating that more of the bullion had been recovered from an English civil servant and a young Japanese airman under rather peculiar circumstances.

Recovery of the main cargo of bullion was undertaken using Krishnan's brother's schooner to Singapore, under the firm command of Colonel Deverall, accompanied by the surviving passengers and crew from Cornucopia, together with Squadron Leader Wills and his naval co-pilot, David Kildonan.

Ceci and Harold had been berated strongly and at length by

her father for two hours on arrival in Singapore; her mother just clung happily to her. Harvey Wills was quickly cleared by a court martial of all responsibility for the loss of the borrowed Fleet Air Arm Walrus. He subsequently made clear his intention to the brigadier that he now wished to withdraw from his engagement with his daughter, preferring to take up a new appointment, after promotion to Wing Commander, at Kai Tak airfield at Kowloon, opposite Hong Kong Island.

Ceci and Harold Penrose, Krishnan and his crew all received a significant reward from His Majesty's Treasury for their initiative and in being instrumental in recovering the bullion. The insurance company eventually paid out for a new Tiger Moth for Ceci to replace her lost Gypsy Moth. The Air Ministry commandeered the machine two weeks after it was delivered. It was required for training pilots who would be needed for the predicted war with Germany. Ceci and Harold were planning to marry, with Ceci's parents' blessing, as soon as Harold had finished his initial flying training in the Royal Air Force. Krishnan was able to replace his lost boat with a larger vessel from his reward.

Since returning home to England aboard an Imperial Airways flying boat, Michael Kelly had spent a good deal of time at a specialist hospital at Chessington in Surrey. He had a new prosthesis fitted in place of his missing lower right leg and was pleased to see a number of other crash-damaged pilots there including one of the RAF's star aerobatic pilots, Douglas Bader. It gave him real hope that he would fly again.

To prove the point to himself, he had eventually taken up an invitation from one of his Empress pilot friends to fly a Miles Hawk two-seat aircraft from Woodley aerodrome near Reading. It was a bright, cold February afternoon in 1939. Growing in confidence once he'd got used to positioning his right aluminium foot onto the rudder pedal, and getting the knack of pushing from his knee and hip, he had managed an exciting, if slightly erratic aerobatic performance for his pregnant wife-to-be; watching with her heart in her mouth below. His co-pilot had been suitably impressed and said so over hot drinks in the club house.

Like Wing Commander Wills, Captain Kelly was cleared of all responsibility for any loss of life and for the loss of Cornucopia. He proudly received during the evening at the Savoy a certificate from the company in appreciation of his skill and dedication, together with a large, and, it was gently made clear, final cheque. Others in his crew were also recognised by the company, and were rewarded accordingly.

Sarah Gregson's husband, still in Delhi, finally instituted divorce proceedings against his wife, citing Michael Kelly as correspondent. Despite the scandal, they were now living very happily together in a large flat in a quiet part of Belgravia. Beth had settled well after her experiences and was attending a local school. Sarah's new baby was due in four weeks. Michael Kelly had bet her that it would be a boy. He won, much to both their delight.

After the dinner at the Savoy, the ladies retired to a private lounge and the two civil servants politely left, allowing the men their brandy in privacy. The atmosphere relaxed and talk turned to the likelihood of a war in Europe, and what were they going to do if it came.

If you have enjoyed 'Cornucopia' you may like to follow the lives of its key characters through the challenges and risks of unconventional wartime service in Part Two of the Trilogy:

'Azzaro'

By way of an 'appetiser' Chapter One follows.

ONE

Take-off had been five hours ago. A cluster of chilled, hunched figures had waved encouragingly from the lee side of the temporary control tower as the aircraft lined up in turn, facing down the slush-covered runway. Once airborne, they gathered, a small, tight flock of five, setting course eastwards as the pale, winter light was slowly extinguished behind them.

Nine hundred miles on, and nearing the point of no return, Michael Kelly looked around from the cockpit of his lead aircraft. The ruby-red pinpoints of navigation lights of two other machines held station in the darkness far below, way out on their starboard side. But where were the other two? The weather had not been kind, despite the Met man's promises. Hopefully the crews of the absent aircraft had remembered the detailed procedures he'd set out during their briefing and were safe, although not in touch.

He was concerned. Had he done and said everything he could to help? But they were all highly experienced and knew the risks of flying the route in an unforgiving northern winter. He also knew too well that any serious failure of man or machine would almost certainly lead to a solitary end in the heaving wastes below.

He'd spoken to Sarah, his new wife, briefly the previous afternoon over a crackly transatlantic telephone line that had taken almost three days to arrange. Her voice was tense at the prospect of his long flight at this time of year.

Since returning to London from Singapore in the final cold, grey and depressing days of November 1938 there had been many issues for Michael Kelly to resolve, not least of which was learning to walk again after the crude but vital emergency amputation of his lower right leg, following the enforced ditching of the Empress Airways flying boat Cornucopia in the storm-tossed Bay of Bengal. Sarah's divorce had finally come through from her husband, who was in the army in India, and she and Michael had married at Westminster's Caxton Hall in a civil ceremony, after Alistair's birth. He was a sturdy eight-and-a-half-pound boy, who had inherited his mother's classic looks – blue eyes and tufts of curly blond hair. Alistair was not Michael's but he loved him as he would his own. Michael was out of work and they were living off the remains of his final cheque of appreciation from Empress Airways. Trying not to plunder Sarah's fortune, they had moved from her comfortable apartment in a quiet part of Belgravia in West London to less extravagant accommodation: a Victorian farmhouse with a few acres of land, set in the rolling Hampshire countryside north of Winchester.

The phone call and the opportunity to fly again was a gift, and he volunteered immediately. To his surprise, he was accepted without qualms.

❖ ❖ ❖

Bitter, damp cold penetrated his bones. The draughty wooden hut barely kept the freezing wind at bay. With his back to an ancient cast-iron pot-bellied stove – a permanent cherry-red, day and night – he scanned the leaden skies. An uncontrolled shiver went through him at the prospect of nine or ten hours up there. The rotting windows rattled noisily as each blast struck their grimy panes. The scene beyond was a bleak monochrome of grubby whiteness scattered with stark black hangars and wooden accommodation huts.

He thought himself lucky. Some of their flight and ground crews were really suffering; sleeping and eating in ancient unheated railway carriages brought in especially by the Newfoundland Railway Company while proper accommodation was hastily erected in the heavy earth under wet snow. But the priority had always been the airfield; far off to his left he could see dark outlines of monster bulldozers and trucks moving jerkily in the embryonic landscape and chugging palls of black smoke into the icy air.

Kelly remembered reading somewhere in a rare idle moment that construction had actually begun in 1936; a year later there were no less than nine hundred men working in this God-forsaken spot to build what would finally be four long paved runways. In one of the dilapidated wooden offices a simple placard celebrated the fact that in January 1938 Gander was officially opened for operations when a tiny de Havilland Fox Moth aircraft operated by Imperial Airways had landed there; an understated precursor of what was to come. Pulling his collar up and his heavy dark-blue uniform coat tightly around him, Michael Kelly yanked open the warped wooden door and stepped out into Gander's seasonal sub-zero temperatures.

Known until quite recently as Hattie's Camp and literally carved out of the raw muskeg, the new aerodrome had been rechristened Gander, taking its new name from a nearby lake. Now, apart from the growing runways, there were hard aircraft dispersals, taxiways and aprons well under way or completed. Lying on a remote tract of once-heavily forested land in Newfoundland off Canada's eastern seaboard, the new Gander airport had become the final jumping-off point for aircraft bound for deprived and depraved wartime Europe. And a place of plenty, safety and temporary relaxation for tired crews battling from the east against prevailing weather systems, onward bound for Montreal and all points in luxurious North America.

Compacted stained snow and ice lay rutted on the well-trodden path that lay between his spartan quarters and the flight operations hangar six hundred yards away. It was an exposed and windswept route. They were the sorts of conditions that he detested on the ground. His 'tinny' leg, as his five-year-old step-daughter Beth had christened it, had already proved to be a liability on such a surface – his rump and elbows bore recent and bruised testament to that.

A few flakes of new snow swirled around him as he faced into the cutting north-west wind. He briefly contrasted his new situation with the warmth and humidity of his previous position, based in Singapore, as a senior captain of a huge 'C' Class flying boat with Empress Airways. That was, until the unheralded storm and their forced ditching in enormous curling seas in the Bay of Bengal. It had caused the loss of passengers' lives – and his lower right leg – with, ultimately, no blame ascribed to him. His shortened limb had now been supplemented with a cleverly constructed aluminium prosthesis that under normal conditions was highly satisfactory, but his tinny leg was unreliable on these treacherous winter surfaces.

Out of a job after his employers, Empress Airways, had had all of their aircraft requisitioned by the Air Ministry just before the outbreak of hostilities with Germany, Kelly had been invited by an old BOAC contact to join the crews that were flying vital military aircraft from America and Canada to England, so saving dangerous weeks at sea – and the need to reassemble and test machines that had been dismantled and crated for the ocean-crossing. Michael's contact explained the background: the Atlantic

Ferry Organisation, quickly put together by Lord Beaverbrook, Churchill's Minister for Aircraft Production, had been rapidly created so that no time should be lost in delivering new machines to help fight the Nazi threat. This bold and dangerous venture was being led by ex-RAF and former Imperial Airways captain Don Bennett, who had been appointed as Flying Superintendent for the whole complex transatlantic ferry operation.

❖ ❖ ❖

Despite the fact that Australia was the land of their births, separated by just two years, Michael Kelly and Don Bennett had never met, though there were many parallels in their early-life experiences.

Both learned to fly with the RAAF at Point Cook, and both later sailed from Australia to England to fly with the RAF. Both had learnt to operate flying boats from Pembroke Dock in south-west Wales and later at Calshot in the protected waters of the Solent, between the Isle of Wight and Southampton. However, severely disillusioned with peacetime flying in the RAF, and the pedantic and short-sighted nature of some of its commanders, Michael Kelly left the service with some regrets in 1933.

Bennett followed, resigning his commission in 1935 but not before he had gained a sound reputation for his navigational skills and flying training expertise, largely on flying boats. He enjoyed some early fame in 1934 while still serving with the RAF through entering the MacRobertson Air Race, from England to Melbourne. Starting from Mildenhall in Suffolk on England's east coast in late October, Bennett and his navigator made good time as far as Aleppo in northern Syria, where their aircraft, a single-engine Lockheed Vega, overturned on landing while being flown by his co-pilot, Woods. Depressed, and after a trip back home to

Australia, Bennett joined Imperial Airways flying their European, Middle East and South African routes.

Out of the RAF, and despite being keen to continue flying in his new civilian life, Michael Kelly spent time in various non-flying jobs, working for brief periods in shipping and in the oil industry – he found most of it, stuck at a viewless desk in central London, soul-destroying and was seriously contemplating a return to his native Perth in Western Australia. Lunch with some business colleagues of his managing director led, some days later, to an evening telephone call and an early-morning meeting with Sir Claude Vickers, chairman of the embryonic airline Empress Airways. The new airline were intending to take delivery of five new four-engined flying boats after Imperial Airways had received all of their order for twenty-eight type S.23 Empire Flying Boats, or 'C' Class boats, as they became known, from Short's, the builders, at their Rochester factory in north Kent, flying them finally off the River Medway. It was a calculated risk; competing with the State-supported Imperial Airways, but Sir Claude and the new Empress Board, including Michael Kelly, enjoyed and were prepared for a challenge. Joining as their senior pilot, Michael Kelly led the pioneering mail and passenger routes to Darwin for Empress, operating from a new flying-boat base at Sandbanks, near Poole, in Dorset, on England's south coast.

Arriving intact, and slightly relieved, at the substantial wooden extension built onto the rear of one black hangar, he made his way gingerly towards the entrance door feeling cold but safe. Pushing the heavy door open, he was enveloped by a fug of tobacco, wood smoke and damp humanity as he climbed the three gritted steps into a large well-lit room. Inside were dozens of pilots, radio operators and navigators, all chattering noisily nineteen to the dozen: American, English, French, Poles and Czechs, and some of indeterminate nationality; all with a diverse mix of valuable, and sometimes hair-raising, flying experience.

Turning as the open door unleashed untainted blasts of arctic air through the gathering, they quietened momentarily. Some shouted greetings of recognition; others looked on, assessing the man now taking off his heavy coat and shaking the snow from it. Some were to be his men for the next twelve hours, and they were a truly mixed bunch.

Before his pioneering first flight of seven Lockheed Hudson bombers across the North Atlantic in November 1940, Don Bennett had established a set of routines and standard procedures for ferrying much-needed aircraft to the Royal Air Force and Royal Navy's Fleet Air Arm. The Hudson was a welcome and necessary replacement for the RAF's Avro Anson, which had eventually proved less than suitable for the hazardous wartime roles assigned to it, including patrolling the unforgiving seas around Britain as part of the RAF's Coastal Command.

Successfully developed as a military version of the Lockheed Company's twin-engine Super Electra passenger airliner, the Hudson had been flown briefly by Michael Kelly while he had been attached for three short weeks to the government's purchasing commission in Washington DC. He'd been impressed with its speed, equipment and handling.

Half a dozen of the men now watching Kelly had been on Don Bennett's inaugural flight; the first non-stop delivery across the Atlantic in early winter. Other successful crossings had been undertaken since, and now, three months later, Michael Kelly was going to lead a smaller but equally valuable formation into the coming night skies aiming to arrive on Prestwick's new tarmac runways on Scotland's Ayrshire coast in about nine or ten hours – if the meteorological people had got their forecast of tailwinds right – he'd spent some time with them and their spidery synoptic charts immediately before lunch.

Ensconced in a wooden box-like extension to the new control tower and huddled around a brightly glowing stove like a coven, the Met men's view, with all of their inevitable caveats, mumbo-jumbo and hieroglyphics, was that the weather now casting its depressing spell over Newfoundland would move swiftly off into the North Atlantic, leaving them almost-clear skies during the early evening and the first part of their transatlantic flight. Three days earlier, the initial leg of their long journey had begun at Dorval airport, just outside Montreal, where the Atlantic Ferry Organisation HQ was located; from there they had flown in safe company and clear, bright weather along the well-established Canadian airways following a regular series of radio navigation beacons; it had been a piece of cake, they all agreed. Beyond Newfoundland's eastern shores no navigation beacons existed to provide easy step-by-step guidance to far-off Europe; it was more akin to flying by Braille, as one of his captains had pointed out, looking concerned at the stark emptiness of the landless charts in front of them.

Michael Kelly moved carefully through the hubbub of mingling men, smiling, exchanging greetings and occasionally shaking hands or thumping someone on the back, before relaxing on a tall stool set against a wall supporting a huge map of the North Atlantic. Eastern Canada and Western Europe formed its extreme left and right margins. He began the briefing. He was going to lead five Hudsons in loose formation nearly two thousand miles across an empty, inhospitable, winter ocean. Empty, save for U-boats and their prey: vital convoys of deeply laden ships with their crucial supplies of military equipment, food and oil for an isolated but increasingly defiant Britain.

The next hour and forty-five minutes were spent briefing the crews: the route, what action to take if separated from the group, engine revolutions to maximise range, and the need to maintain radio silence except in an emergency, particularly as they came within range of enemy ships and aircraft approaching Europe. Kelly had opted for the classic great-circle route to Prestwick – the shortest distance across – instead of breaking the journey and calling at either Goose Bay in Labrador or the new American-built Bluie West 1 airfield on Greenland's south-eastern coast – at the end of a long and dangerously fog-prone fiord.

He knew that the airfields in Greenland and Iceland were popular, and they were often included by some crews in their flight plans, depending on their experience and the forecast weather, and also, crucially, their need for cheap and tax-free booze and nylons. But each of his five aircraft would have two highly experienced pilots on board, one of whom was fully qualified and licensed as a navigator able to take astro sightings of the stars and other heavenly bodies en route, to complement their dead-reckoning and radio navigation. The third member of each crew was the wireless operator/gunner, able to report their advancing position from radio bearings on distant navigation beacons, complementing the pilot navigator's sextant skills as they approached blacked-out Europe.

There were questions and some lengthy discussion about altitudes to be flown to avoid the sometimes-catastrophic results of airframe and engine icing. During winter in particular it was of real concern to his pilots, particularly as later that night the small formation would catch up with frozen air captive in the depression that was wending its way slowly across the Atlantic ahead of them. Finally satisfied, the five crews went to the mess for their last unrationed meal. Just over an hour later a battered and muddy American-built five-ton truck with a ripped and flapping canvas cover picked the airmen up from their various accommodations, transporting them out to their aircraft, which were standing remote and inert in wet snow and treacly, dark earth.

Arriving at their individual machines, they jumped from the battered truck carrying charts, bulky flying clothing and precious boxes of rations including Thermos flasks. They laughed and joked with forced bonhomie, wishing each other luck and the promise of haggis and beer in Scotland tomorrow. Most of them hadn't a clue what a haggis was. Michael Kelly's crew was the last to be dropped. It was just before two-thirty in the afternoon, and the daylight had almost run its course.

Their Hudson bomber sat lifeless, cold, its metal freezing the hands of those foolish enough to let them linger too long on its exposed camouflaged surfaces. The ground crews had been motivated by the cold to keep busy, warmed by sweeping wet snow off the wings and tailplanes and applying thick, sticky anti-icing paste to the machine's propellers and wing's leading edges. It was a time-consuming and laborious activity on the exposed airfield, some doubting its efficacy. Finally settled into the left-hand seat, Kelly commenced his pre-start checks for the twin-engined machine.

Sitting alongside him, his co-pilot, Paul Mossman, a Canadian, called the list of items. Kelly undertook the checks carefully; the machine had to be one hundred per cent for this long and potentially dangerous sortie. Mossman was a young man, late twenties, Kelly guessed. Paul had learned to fly with his father around the wastes of north-western Canada and Alaska and in doing so had acquired rare skills and an instinctive understanding of his chosen craft. He'd volunteered for Atlantic Ferry just after his father's death; his mother had died some years earlier, so now there was nothing tying him to the coastal town of Prince Rupert, north-west of Vancouver. He'd never been too far from Canada's beautifully rugged western seaboard; a chance to go east and to see England tickled his fancy and innate sense of adventure. Mossman didn't say much, but Kelly instinctively knew he was a man he could trust, both on the ground and in the air. Typical outback Canadian, he was tough, above average height, and well built, a reflection of one or two years spent logging instead of at university. He had a well-deserved reputation for being able to drink most men under the table, and with a wide, open smile below unkempt dark hair, was immediately loved by any woman that came within his orbit.

Three minutes later Kelly opened the side window to signal to the relieved ground crew that they were ready to start. Making a circular motion with a finger, he pushed the starter button, and the propeller on the port engine turned slowly, its oil, cold and viscous, making difficult work for the straining starter motor. Eventually, after some stuttering, the Wright Cyclone settled into a regular beat, followed by its identical twin on the starboard side. The machine was alive, vibrating; even beginning to warm slightly as limited hot air was ducted into the tight cockpit. Behind, in the empty fuselage, a temporary additional fuel tank had been fitted at the Lockheed factory in Burbank, California. They would need all the available fuel for their long ocean-crossing.

Looking around the crescent of parked aircraft, Kelly noted

with satisfaction the shimmering discs of their spinning propellers in the harsh, white light from lamps placed around the remote aircraft dispersals. Behind their windscreens they watched, waiting for him to make his move. Thumbing the radio transmit button on the control wheel, he advised the air-traffic controller that they were ready. Waving 'chocks away' to the shivering and hunched ground crew, he released the brakes. Opening the throttles gently and taxiing clear of the dispersal, they turned left onto the slush-carpeted taxiway passing in front of Kelly's gently growling flock. The surface was unfinished in places, and he and Mossman watched carefully, avoiding areas where the machine might become bogged down.

Just short of the long runway Kelly carried out final checks on the health of the machine in general – its engines in particular – temperature one hundred and twenty degrees, oil pressure sixty-five pounds per square inch, all magnetos on, OK. With all other checks completed, Mossman confirmed, after twisting right around in his seat, that the rest of their small air fleet were behind them, lined up and waiting.

"Seems no problems during the taxi, Skipper." Kelly nodded and grunted an acknowledgement into his face-mike.

Their noisy rush down the runway was punctuated by sharp decelerations as the wheels cut through piles of slush or huge puddles of icy water that had failed to drain off the near-freezing concrete surfaces. Despite this, the main wheels lifted clear well before the runway's end and they drew away from the land with twenty-three hundred revolutions showing for both engines, and a speed of one hundred and twenty miles per hour.

Climbing steadily and turning the aircraft gently to the left, Kelly allowed the undercarriage to remain down for a few minutes, encouraging the speeding air to blow icy water off its streaming-wet mechanisms – it could freeze at altitude and give problems when they eventually selected 'down' for landing. Turning to look over his left shoulder, he could just see that the second aircraft was airborne behind them, the twin beams from its yellow wavering landing lamps like probing fingers piercing the dense, cold air; the third aircraft, he noticed, had now commenced its take-off roll. They made a wide orbit of the darkening airfield, allowing the remaining four Hudsons to climb and formate on them in a wide 'V' before setting an easterly course out over the black ocean. Minutes later the lights of Newtown and Wesleyville sparkled invitingly up at them as they left the coast over Cape Freels at one hundred and forty-five miles per hour and climbing slowly into clear, star-spangled indigo.

The depression that had inflicted so much cold and wet on Gander over the previous two days had departed North America to the east, as forecast by the Met men. What these same weather wizards had not fully predicted was that the depression would finally stall as it butted up against a newly developing area of high pressure drifting lazily south from the Arctic and Greenland's high frozen tundra. The widely spaced 'V' formation of five Hudsons soon reached the near-stationary weather system, plunging headlong into its heavy mass of dark, swirling stratus from behind. Instinctively, the pilots of the five aircraft separated further, the danger of collision uppermost in their minds as they entered the ragged, wet cloud. Every so often they emerged briefly from its folds as they continued east, eyes alert, each crew counting their fellow travellers and their relative positions before they plunged again into roiling grey vapour.

Then, for a while, they were able to fly with their special station-keeping lights clearly visible to each other, a formation spread wide in the clear, freezing air, sandwiched between two opaque layers of dark grey murk. Now and again there would be a clunk or bang from somewhere behind them as pieces of melting ice detached from wing or propeller. It had been quietly accumulating like some insidious disease in the dark as the machines had driven up through clouds of freezing moisture. The noise was felt as much as heard. Chunks struck the fuselage side or tailplane, shattering, then arcing down thousands of feet to the ocean.

After four and a half hours their sandwich of clear air was consumed, the two levels merging in the darkness into a single dense, unstable mass. They droned on, now and again the aircraft lurching unpredictably and violently in the system's turbulence. Working quietly behind the two pilots, Peter Gaul, the radio operator, spent his time taking radio navigation bearings on any of the few available powerful radio beacons within range: Bermuda, way to the south, Bluie West 1, Largens in the Azores, and much later he would hear Prestwick itself. There had been no opportunity to use the sextant for star shots over the last hours, the sky above them completely obscured by hundreds, possibly thousands of feet of turbulent, icy water molecules.

Mossman was now in control. Michael Kelly had left his seat, stretching his legs and taking time to look at his charts and the radio plots gathered by their wireless operator/gunner, Peter Gaul. Together they studied the information, holding firmly onto the aircraft as it bounced and lurched unpredictably across the sky. Kelly's thoughts returned continually to his co-flyers, out there somewhere in the heaving darkness. The hot coffee from the Thermos was seriously welcome. Now, at nine thousand feet, the outside air was well below freezing and inside he doubted that the temperature inside was much above that. Their bulky, sometimes awkward Sidcot flying suits were fully vindicated in the conditions.

Mossman called Kelly back to the cockpit; he was experiencing difficulty in maintaining height, and the machine was handling sluggishly. The next two hours had them worried and fighting to keep the Hudson free of accumulating ice. They descended every so often to the marginally warmer air near the surface of the sea, where it might be persuaded to melt and break free. There was the ever-present risk of damage should large chunks strike some vital area such as the elevators, stuck out at the tail extremities of the aircraft.

On one occasion they flew so low in their desperate attempt to dump the weighing ice that as they fell out of the lowering cloud base they found themselves barely two hundred feet above the Atlantic's heaving, white-scored surface.

As they maintained a great-circle course to faraway Prestwick, the cloud base sank lower until it almost merged with the sea; forward visibility at times became nil in the cloud and near-darkness. This was highly dangerous instrument flying, with no real reference points to allow them to gauge their height accurately, so they were forced to rely on their two altimeters, whose sensitivity in indicating proximity to the sea was normally considered dubious at such low levels. Climbing the machine again, Kelly decided to look for clear air away from the maw of the ocean. The Hudson rocked and rolled violently as it clawed up through the increasingly turbulent mass, engines roaring solidly and comfortingly either side them.

Later, safe on the ground, coffee and cigarette in hand, they talked light-heartedly and with ill-disguised relief about those worrying couple of hours as they had sought the safety of clear air away from unpredictable turbulence and the freezing moisture quietly accumulating on their aircraft, weighing them down.

Eventually it was past; after a final bout of severe turbulence they had finally overtaken the intense weather system and were now cruising comfortably at five thousand feet in smoother, brighter air. Glancing around the horizon, Mossman saw them first; way off to the right and some way below. Two aircraft loosely formating on each other were heading in the same direction as themselves. They still had their navigation lights illuminated despite orders, two pinpoint red jewels dancing in the gloom. It had to be two of his flock; who else would be wandering about mid-ocean on a night like this, Kelly surmised with some relief. Peter Gaul focused the aircraft's powerful Aldis lamp on the two machines sending a short burst of white Morse to confirm their identity. A minute later both aircraft acknowledged – it was them.

He was tired. He'd managed to snatch a star shot of Betelgeuse with the sextant through the gunner's Perspex-covered turret as the upper layers of cloud had thinned and broken open for a few brief miles. Ten minutes later, after laborious calculations with a cold-dulled brain that seemed unable to engage fully with the problem, the outcome from his single star sighting was a general confirmation that they were roughly where he had anticipated they would be, with some six hundred miles still to run. With help from a strengthening tailwind and the two roaring Wright Cyclones, they should be settling onto Prestwick's new hard runway in just over three hours.

They kept looking, scanning the sky around every one of three hundred and sixty degrees. Where were the other two Hudsons? Pale shafts of daylight were beginning to penetrate the layers of cloud ahead, and despite his worries Kelly decided to doze, slumped uncomfortably in the cabin behind the radio operator's position. Soon he would need all his faculties about him as full daylight, hastened by their flight eastwards, brought increased dangers from lurking enemy aircraft.

The need to be alert and prepared for a landing at what would be a new airfield for them was vital. Fifty minutes passed before Paul Mossman's nasal Canadian twang cut in over the intercom. Kelly awoke with a start, uncomfortable and stiff; it was almost full daylight; the soft grey light cast a metallic sheen on the sea thousands of feet below. They were closing the west coast of the Irish Republic, he knew; occasional fishing boats began to appear plunging south-east on their way home in an unremarkable dawn.

Mossman was pointing out to his right, quietly commenting over the intercom that he'd seen something three or four miles away to the south of their position at about the same height. He thought he'd seen the brief silhouette of a large four-engine aircraft weaving stealthily downwards through layers of broken cloud. Kelly took control while his co-pilot and radio operator watched the southern skies intently where the aircraft had been spotted.

"Perhaps its one of the Hudsons," articulated Gaul over the intercom.

Mossman shook his head and grunted emphatically into the mike in his facemask.

"Uh-huh. Four engines, definitely."

Their first clue came from somewhere else. Unusual movement in the wave patterns below them began to show on the sea's face – a series of merging 'V's etched for a few minutes on its long, rolling surface. Broken cloud a thousand feet or so below them precluded their sighting of the cause, but from experience both pilots suspected a large ship or ships. Then it was exposed, ploughing a determined course just north of east: a convoy of ships, eight long lines of deeply laden vessels, each line set up for twelve plodding transports of one sort or another. Here and there, cutting a white swathe through the grey seas, the dark shape of a grey-blue camouflaged naval vessel turned and metaphorically prodded some of the slower or out-of-station merchantmen onwards. It was noticeable that most of the lines were incomplete – empty spaces – mute evidence of recent death and deep, crushing destruction, no doubt delivered after dark by a deceitful hidden enemy.

Not wanting to be fired on by the convoy's naval escort, Kelly, in control, climbed the Hudson, banking sharply away from the lines of ships towards the south. From their present course he guessed that the depleted convoy was headed for either Liverpool or Glasgow intending to round Malin Head, which jutted out from Northern Ireland's welcoming coast, promising safety and the delight of sleep in warm, dry beds for those who eventually made it.

The two Hudsons they had seen earlier during the night had now closed with Kelly's machine, once again in a loose 'V' formation, rocking their wings gesturing 'Hello' in the daylight – still no sight or sound from the two missing aircraft. Just fifty miles or so off Ireland's west coast the cloud was broken, the air becoming unstable as they caught up with the tail of another intense winter depression that was presently dumping its cargo of cold rain onto the partially neutral island ahead.

Its plan silhouette was visible for barely a split second as the large aircraft turned, steeply banking downwards across their path, right to left, about a mile or so ahead, sliding from one thin cloud layer into another below. In the instant available they could discern that its dark shape bore the faint white outlines of German markings on its exposed undersides, and it had four engines.

"Jeez!" Mossman breathed. Kelly had seen it too and pulled the Hudson sharply around, hoping that the two following machines in their loose formation were sufficiently awake to his manoeuvring. He guessed that the German machine they had just spotted was descending through the cloud, hoping to report accurately on the convoy they had seen a few minutes earlier.

"Wireless! Man the turret – quick!" Kelly barked urgently through the intercom.

Pushing his charts away, Peter Gaul moved quickly down the fuselage towards the Perspex-shrouded mid-upper turret with its two .303 machine-guns. Then he remembered: they were not carrying ammunition, in the interests of weight-saving, allowing for more precious fuel to carry them across the Atlantic. Plugging in his intercom, Kelly swore silently as Gaul's comments crackled in his headphones.

They could not attack what they had now identified as a large Luftwaffe four-engine Focke-Wulf Condor; but they would certainly attempt to upset its reporting activities, shouted Kelly above the increasing engine roar. Kelly was familiar with the machine: the Germans had developed their four-engine Condor from a pre-war civil airliner. With a range of over two thousand miles it could easily patrol Britain's Western Approaches, leaving from their base at Merignac, near Bordeaux, in western France, curving north-westwards out into the Atlantic around Britain, before final landing at Kjeller in southern Norway, a few kilometres from occupied Oslo.

Mossman glanced quickly around at Peter Gaul, who was

standing behind his seat, his eyes grimacing above his facemask. They had strict instructions from Atlantic Ferry Command not to attack or become involved with any enemy aircraft en route, giving away their presence in a place where the enemy would not normally expect to find them. It would not take the German intelligence people too long to make a reasonable guess at why such types of aircraft were somehow way out in the empty ocean. And there was always the chance that the enemy, aware of regular movements of aircraft, could arrange a well-timed ambush in future, a waste of experienced crews and a vitally needed aircraft. They all knew that the Condor was armed; intelligence passed to all military aviators was that the machine was fitted with a twenty-millimetre cannon plus four or five machine-guns, and also carried bombs. Mossman turned towards Kelly, his eyes now wide above his facemask.

"You do know the bloody thing's armed, don't you, Skipper?" Michael Kelly glanced pointedly across at his co-pilot,

"Yes. I do know."

Throttles open, the Hudson plunged noisily down through broken cloud. Kelly intended to make for sea level, hoping to see the silhouette of the reconnoitring Condor etched clearly against the cloud base above them. With no ammunition for their guns he really had little idea how he was going to take any disruptive action against the huge, well-equipped German machine. Emerging from the lowest layer of cloud at two thousand feet, still plummeting seawards, Mossman and Gaul glanced about urgently, looking up for the big machine, which the Germans regularly employed to stalk and spy on vital convoys as they approached Britain's shores. Out of range of the guarding naval escort's anti-aircraft guns, the Condors would circle the convoy safely for hours, radioing its position, course and speed back to their base. Grateful U-boat commanders would position themselves, lying in wait as a wolf pack across the convoy's reported path, receiving crucial information that would enable them to plan concerted attacks. Recent months had been nothing short of disastrous for the merchant marine in terms of vital tonnage and men lost in the deep.

"Seems like we've lost him, Skipper," grumbled Mossman through his mike, looking, eyebrows raised, across at his captain. Thin-lipped behind his facemask, Kelly nodded, still looking avidly about hoping to see something of the machine and its crew of armed spies. Circling a couple of times between the sea and cloud base brought no sighting.

"OK, we'll resume our course and climb back; I hope the other two haven't lost their way." He opened the two throttles and boost controls to climb power. The cloud became more broken as they climbed eastwards. Once settled on top of a scattered white layer, they caught sight of two moving dots towards the far south-east horizon, which seemed to be performing some odd antics.

Minutes later they could see their own two Hudson bombers performing an unusual aerial waltz with the apparent agility of fighters; now and again one would dive into the thin cloud layer then re-emerge seconds later, climbing hard. The second aircraft would then cut in on the gyrating performance, undertaking a similarly risky manoeuvre. Within a few minutes they were at the same location, a couple of thousand feet above their waltzing colleagues. Circling, they watched below, worried. Gaul shouted something almost unintelligible over the intercom.

"The bastard's there, Skipper, look, at three o'clock. See the shadow, just in the cloud?"

Looking off to his right and pushing both throttles almost fully open; Kelly banked the machine hard to starboard looking down through the cockpit's right-side screens. Both he and Mossman saw it together: the dark-grey outline of a large four-engine aircraft just below the surface of the cloud, like some predatory shark cruising shallow waters. Now and again they could see bursts of fire from the Condor, its machine guns sparking anger at the two cavorting Hudsons.

"The buggers are teasing it, look, stopping it from turning south!" shouted Mossman, gesticulating towards the whirling machines. It was true; Kelly could see that each time the Condor attempted to turn south, presumably to make its escape towards its home base near Bordeaux, the two Hudsons performed some highly dangerous and risky flying for such large aircraft – finishing with a steep pull-up through the translucent cloud just ahead of the Condor's nose.

"Stupid buggers; it's those two bloody Poles, isn't it?"

The Condor's attackers were like small birds mobbing a larger bird of prey that was intent on stealing their young, thought Kelly. The two young Polish captains had also received the same instructions about interaction with enemy aircraft as had Kelly. Since the Nazi invasion of Poland, the vengeful bravery of Polish pilots was well known, as was their ignoring of orders and their excitable, heroic indiscipline at certain times.

At their level, in the thin cloud, the two Condor pilots would not have been able to see the cavorting of the two Hudsons once they had dived and were submerged in thin surrounding cloud, but the Hudson crews could see the Condor's sinister shadow against the lighter sky as they pulled up almost under its nose.

"It must be most disconcerting for them," said Kelly with deliberate understatement, smiling slightly; still turning the

Hudson in a steep bank, watching.

"I wonder how long he's been out on patrol. He might be short of fuel, could be desperate to get home." He looked at his own fuel gauges. They did not have the luxury of loitering too long either, and he hoped the other two Hudson captains were conscious of their fuel situation.

Another five minutes saw all three aircraft back in loose formation droning eastwards; ahead a thin solid line sat on the ocean's horizon, visible through the thinning cloud. Its image slowly resolved into cliffs then emerald-green fields and brown earth, with groups of dwellings and barns clustered together here and there as the aircraft closed on the Six Counties coast. They took great care not to infringe the neutrality of its southern, Republican neighbour.

Within an hour of passing Ireland they had all made a good landing at Prestwick and were handing kit and their remaining rations to a pretty and petite young WAAF driver who was steadily loading them into the back of an ancient squadron-blue Morris van. Looking keenly about him, Kelly was partly relieved to see the missing fourth aircraft of his flight parked close to one of the camouflaged hangars, with its engine cowlings swung open and mechanics on ladders peering inside. The smiling WAAF driver said that it had landed alone forty minutes earlier; its crew had reported to the duty officer and were now having a cup of tea in the operations block. It would appear that the aircraft's young and extrovert French captain had made a favourable impression on the girl.

After completing delivery formalities and a debriefing by the unit intelligence officer over their meeting with the Luftwaffe Condor, all four crews were taken to the officers' mess, fed and then allowed to sleep – Kelly for fourteen straight hours after managing to wangle a priority call to Sarah. On waking, he contacted operations and spoke to the duty officer; there had been no news yet of the fifth Hudson. They'd tried ringing around other likely airfields for news but there had been nothing to report so far. The officer did mention, however, that they had just received a report concerning a wireless intercept, seemingly from a German aircraft. The story was that the aircraft had sent out a message en-clair reporting they were almost out of fuel and were preparing to ditch. A rough-and-ready fix on the transmission suggested a position seventy miles south-west of Cape Clear, off the south-east coast of the Irish Republic. Coastal Command was going to investigate during a routine patrol. Sitting in the mess ante-room, a cup of lukewarm coffee in hand, Kelly knew that by now the missing Hudson would be long out of fuel wherever it was.

Awful, he thought, I hardly knew any of them, and now I never will. He recalled the crew's captain: an older man, English, with a large scar across his face and chin gained over Arras during the first conflict in 1916. He became conscious of a mess steward standing by his chair as he dwelt unwisely on their probable experiences as they tried to save the aircraft before finally ditching in the sea. The thoughts were too raw, too near his recent experiences with Cornucopia.

"Mr Kelly, Sir?" Kelly looked up, slightly surprised, and nodded. Smiling, the elderly, white-coated steward handed him a sealed envelope. It contained a request for him to visit the duty operations controller as soon as was convenient. Nodding, he thanked the steward, rose and left the mess, making his way through the bright winter sunshine among well-ordered roads and hangars to Flying Control.

A week later a Sunderland on patrol far into the Atlantic spotted a yellow dinghy with two men in it. The sea was uncharacteristically calm, just a long unbroken swell. Even as they taxied across its rolling surface they could guess at the worst. No movement from the two individuals sitting stiffly opposite each other in the half-filled boat. The two deceased airmen, one English RAF, one Norwegian, were lifted with difficulty from the bouncing craft and returned to their base near Stranraer. When identified, they turned out to be two members of the crew of Kelly's fifth Hudson and were buried with ceremony in a small churchyard looking to the hills and the sea beyond. The third crewman – the older, scar-faced pilot with the soft, west-coast Scots accent – was never found.

❖ ❖ ❖

Cecilia Grosvenor-Ffoulkes jumped down from the dull khaki-camouflaged Tiger Moth with its yellow-painted training bands and walked across the glistening dew-covered grass to the reporting office at the far end of the hangar. For about four months she'd been delivering new machines to pilot-training airfields from her base at Hamble, near Southampton. Having returned to England with her mother from Singapore in early 1939 – her Colonel father had remained there in his post under Australian Army command – she had been at a loss for something worthwhile to do. All talk was of a possible war with Germany; her fiancé, Harold Penrose, had joined the Royal Air Force, accepted for pilot training. Since learning to fly in 1936 she had accumulated a good few hours' flying her Gypsy Moth around England and the near continent followed by her flying adventures in Asia with Penrose while looking for the downed Empress Airways flying boat Cornucopia.

She had returned by car to the London Aero Club at White Waltham airfield one bright autumn afternoon some months earlier, hoping to run into some of her old friends, but she had been a little disappointed. Although it was a Saturday afternoon there appeared to be very few people about save for a couple of flying instructors she didn't recognise, and some very young mechanics. The wooden clubhouse was cool and smelt a little of damp and fresh creosote; in the fireplace a desultory fire flickered occasionally from within its tall red-brick surround. An elderly club steward hovered nearby. He was intrigued at the young woman's presence, not dressed for flying but in neat chequered skirt cut fashionably above the knee and a twin set – but no pearls. Her waterproof jacket and a bright matching chequered scarf were thrown across a nearby chair; her attractive round face was flushed pink from driving her open Riley sports car in the bracing air; which was now parked untidily outside. On one of her well-manicured fingers was a huge sapphire engagement ring; he noticed that she kept looking at it.

Relaxing in one of the tired-looking but comfortable chintz-covered armchairs facing the long windows she sipped at a warming brandy, alone, looking at the late sun and the dozens of flying machines drawn up outside. She remembered a lively time at the club during her training, four years earlier: it always seemed so full of young people laughing and enjoying the freedom of the air and the club's vibrant, sometimes risqué social life. But it had changed. The war was clouding everyone's view of the future. She saw an Avro Anson making a long, steady approach, its landing lamps glowing feebly yellow in the sunlight. After a faultless landing it taxied towards an empty space on the apron almost in front of the clubhouse. The silver-painted twin-engine machine with RAF markings lurched over the undulating turf until it came to a squeaking halt. Its two Cheetah engines ran on for about two minutes then clattered into silence, propellers jerking suddenly and awkwardly to a halt.

Ceci, as she was known to all her close friends, watched interestedly. There was movement in the cockpit, and then the cabin door at the rear of the machine popped open and the pilot jumped lightly down onto the grass, leather helmet still on, a small bag in one hand. One of the two mechanics she had seen earlier and a boyish-looking RAF officer strode out to the machine from offices further along the dispersal area. There was a brief discussion, then the pilot shook hands with the officer as he pointed to something further down the dispersal while the mechanic prepared to refuel the eight-seat communications aircraft. Although the Anson had proved inadequate as a coastal patrol aircraft, in its new communications role it had been a valuable and reliable workhorse.

She was dressed in dark-blue slacks and wearing an oversize fleece-lined leather jacket. The clubhouse door banged shut after her as she clumped in heavy flying boots towards the small bar area, throwing her leather helmet and bag onto a nearby chair.

"Hello, George, again! Seems only yesterday since you were making tea for me." A grin crossed the steward's creased and tired face.

"Hello again, Miss Helen. Didn't expect to see you back quite so soon. Another pick-up?"

"'Fraid so. Can't keep the girls waiting, you know what they're like, bloody impatient bunch." She took the freshly poured tea and walked across the threadbare patterned carpet towards the patch of late sun by the windows, gently shaking free the curls from her chestnut hair.

"May I join you?" The voice was cultured and friendly with just a trace of a foreign accent, the smile warm and infectious. She was quite short with an oval face and dark-brown eyes. Ceci smiled back.

"Of course," moving her empty glass to one side of the small table. The brandy had had the desired effect, warming and relaxing her. The girl sat down and, despite her thick boots and jacket, managed to make it an elegant exercise.

"By the way, my name's Helen Lorenzo," she held out a small, delicate hand. Ceci took it and looked into the girl's tanned, open face.

"Oh hello. Cecilia Grosvenor-Ffoulkes..."

The pilot interrupted, eyes wide.

"That's an awful mouthful, if I might say so."

It was not meant unkindly – the girl was smiling broadly, her dark-brown eyes twinkling.

"Yes, rather. All my friends call me Ceci, actually; it helps to speed things up." They both laughed.

"Are you a member here?"

"Not now," Ceci replied, "used to be, I learned to fly here and came back looking for lost friends, but as you can see, there aren't too many people about," she said with a sweep of her arm around the empty room

"Oh, so you fly, do you? Great fun – where do you fly from these days?"

"Well, nowhere now, actually. The Air Ministry commandeered my brand-new Tiger Moth almost as soon as I had collected it from de Havilland's. Anyway, I'm a bit rusty, haven't flown for about seven or eight months now. Wonder if I'm still up to it," sighed Ceci.

"That's interesting ... how many hours have you done?" Helen asked pointedly.

Ceci turned in her seat and waved to the steward.

"Can we have some more tea, please? And I'll have a cup too." Then, looking back to the pilot, "About six hundred hours now, mainly on Gypsy Moths. I learned to fly here with Paul Maddern – about four years ago – he taught my mother as well. Is he still about?"

"Paul Maddern! My dear girl, you lucky thing, he was quite a dish apparently, so I'm told by some of my girlfriends."

"Was? You mean he's no longer based here?" Ceci looked askance. There was a brief pause. Helen looked down into the steaming cup on her knee.

"Oh dear, you obviously don't know. I'm so sorry; Paul was killed about two months back. They think the young student he was with froze on the stick during instruction. Witnesses say the aircraft stalled on recovery from a spin, went straight in from three hundred feet, caught fire. Unusual. Sorry. No one survived."

Although now very happily engaged to Harold Penrose, whom she loved dearly, Ceci had very fond memories of Paul. He had been a lot older than her, an ex-RFC pilot and not only a brilliant flying instructor but also a gentleman – and a greyingly handsome one. Still in her teens and impressionable, Ceci had shared more than one late-night dinner engagement where she had fallen in love with him all over again. They had once spent an illicit weekend together in the early spring of 1936 and Ceci had had the devil of a job explaining to her mother where she had been. She'd never regretted the weekend and her gentle initiation. Annoyingly, she found out later that her mother had also had a fleeting affair with him some years earlier on his return from France.

"I'm so sorry you had to find out like this ...." Helen Lorenzo sensed that there was something meaningful in her bluntly delivered news.

Ceci's face was white. 'What a horrifying and unfair end,' she thought.

"It's alright, just a bit of a shock that's all. Poor ... dear Paul." She caught herself biting her lip, her eyes glistening slightly.

Helen changed the subject quickly.

"Listen; if you're really serious about flying again I might be able to help you. We need pilots with experience pretty urgently. I work for the new Air Transport Auxiliary, the ATA," she said, pointing at the shiny gold badge logo on her uniform jacket, "We have bases all around the country now – I'm down at Hamble, but the HQ is here at Waltham, just across the airfield. It's great fun, we're all girls at Hamble – we deliver new aircraft from factories to squadrons in the south or wherever else they're needed so that the RAF and navy don't have to use their own pilots. We've only been in existence for about a year. It was the idea of Gerard d'Erlanger, do you know him, by the way? He was a director at British Airways; a great pilot, too. Anyway, when the Munich thing happened, he had the idea and the Air Ministry thought it was a good one. So the ATA was formed. Our CO's great too; Pauline Gower, she runs the whole show as far as female pilots are concerned, over two thousand hours, flown almost everything!"

Ceci looked up at her as the girl stood looking out of the window towards the west. Perhaps this was something she could do. Just then a gaggle of six camouflaged Tiger Moths landed, taxiing into a neat row on the other side of the airfield. Ceci and Helen watched together for a few minutes, then Helen turned briskly.

"Sorry, time to go. I'm taxi driver for that lot today, got to take them back to Hamble. Listen, if you're interested, I'm sure our unit CO, Harriet Brotherton, would love to meet you, why don't you come down one day and see what we get up to?" Helen left an expensively printed personal card on the table, plucked from her jacket as she left.

"I might just do that," called Ceci, smiling after her as she clumped out of the door.

She watched a bunch of laughing girls amble across the grass airfield towards the Anson. Using her hands as imaginary aircraft, one young pilot demonstrated some quite impossible manoeuvre to her colleagues to be greeted with howls of good-natured derision. They piled into the machine in their unflattering thick Sidcot suits, their faces bright and alive. Soon both engines were turning; Ceci moved outside to watch. She could see Helen at the controls; waving briefly for a moment, she gunned one engine causing the slowly moving machine to pivot about a wheel before lurching off, rolling like some ancient dowager towards the grass take-off area. When she went inside to collect her things, the steward was clearing cups.

"She's a live wire, that Miss Helen, always full of beans."

Ceci nodded at his comment.

"Very pretty, too."

"Oh that'll be the Italian in her – dark," he added. "I think she once told me her mother is English and her father's Italian, a professor or something at a university somewhere in the north of Italy. Must be difficult for her, being at war and all that, with mixed-nationality parents."

Ceci thanked the kindly man and with a faint smile on her lips put on her jacket and scarf. Roaring off down the narrow road that led from the busy airfield, she began to think seriously.

Three weeks after her encounter with Helen Lorenzo, Ceci visited the ATA airfield at Hamble. It was a lovely location, just outside an unspoilt hamlet, evocative of a past era with traditional shops: Serpells the grocer, Spakes the butcher and small Victorian houses scattered along its narrow main street leading down to the banks of the tidal Hamble River, which emerged clear into turgid Southampton water before diluting fully in the salty, tidal Solent. The hamlet provided billets for many of the ATA's pilots and staff, and importantly for them, offered a choice of four pubs: The Victory, The King and Queen, Ye Olde White Hart and the unit's favourite, The Bugle, plus a number of still partly active sailing clubs. Ceci had lunch with some of the all-female operations staff and pilots and immediately felt at home. Harriet, the unit CO, had a long talk with her after flying had finished for the day and Ceci decided on the spot that she would like to put her past flying experience to good use.

On a damp, cold and misty February morning she reported for duty and training at the Central Flying School of the Royal Air Force at Upavon, remote on the downs in Wiltshire. Here she was to be assessed and given her ATA training before being sent to a unit for delivery duties. She would probably be flying light aircraft initially, like her Tiger Moth - collecting completed machines from the de Havilland works at Hatfield, or from Cowley, near Oxford, for example, then flying them to training airfields around the south of the country. As time went by, she was told, if she showed promise, she would undertake further training on heavier aircraft like the Spitfire and Hurricane, and be taught to fly twin-engine machines including Ansons, Hudsons or Oxfords.

❖ ❖ ❖

Prestwick's Flying Control office was flooded with light from the low afternoon sun. Smoke curled up from the duty operations officer's cigarette as he tried to make sense of a signal from the Air Ministry about conserving motor transport fuel.

"Good afternoon, I'm Michael Kelly – you sent a note?"

"Oh, Mr Kelly, of course. Please do sit down." Smiling, the elderly and bemedalled Flight Lieutenant waved him to a seat as he lifted a heap of official paper from one of the wooden chairs facing his desk, dumping it onto an adjacent desk where a bespectacled and matronly WAAF was trying to type, head barely visible above an encroaching wall of files.

"Thanks for coming in, I'll come straight to the point. We've got a problem and I wondered if you and your crews could help us out?" Kelly raised his eyebrows.

"The ATA are overwhelmed at the moment with aircraft deliveries from our own factories to the squadrons and I wondered if you could fly your four Hudsons down to White Waltham. The ATA could manage to take them to the requesting squadrons from there; it's just that they don't have the manpower or time to come all the way up here to Prestwick to collect. Kelly thought for a moment. They would have to get down to England by some means anyway. They also had to find transport of some sort back to Montreal and then Gander in readiness for the next transatlantic delivery.

"I don't think that's going to present a problem. We have to get to Liverpool somehow for a sailing back to Canada. When do you want us to leave?"

The operations officer looked relieved.

"Any possibility you could leave first thing in the morning? I can advise your people of what's happening and arrange fuel, charts and any crystals needed for the radios."

Kelly called his remaining crews together before they all set out to tackle the local Scottish hostelries.

"Sorry, chaps, early start tomorrow, and an early night tonight, I'm afraid, but I can promise you a night in London's dens of iniquity tomorrow." Faces dropped momentarily. He hoped he would be able to make just a token gesture of hospitality to them before catching a train from London's Waterloo rail station for rural Hampshire, Sarah and the two children. He wanted desperately to see her and their children before returning to the bright lights of Montreal before as brief a stay as possible in wintry, inhospitable Gander.

Just after 6 am the Hudson crews were delivered yawning and shivering to their aircraft for the two-hour flight to White Waltham, north-west of London, just off the main London–Oxford road. With just three-tenths cloud at four thousand feet the flight went without a glitch. Switching off, he and Mossman rose from their seats, grabbing their bags along the way. Out in a fresh breeze, they gazed about. The airfield seemed to be covered in aircraft of almost every description. A small crew van arrived, bumping across the grass; they piled in looking forward to a night out in London after a nap. Kelly decided not to join them in the van; he favoured a little fresh air and a walk to the flight offices.

Ahead of him a shortish, bulky figure in thick Sidcot suit and boots, leather flying-helmet in hand, walked towards the operations hut. He thought that the RAF must be letting things go a little despite it being wartime; the airman could do with a good haircut, his dark tousled hair blowing in the wind. Entering the corridor of the operations hut behind the pilot he noticed that his gait was not quite normal – couldn't quite put his finger on it.

The pilot turned, holding a door open for him. It was a girl, he realised.

There was a brief glance of recognition and developing smiles.

"Michael! My goodness, what are you doing here?"

"I might well ask you the same question! By the way, the suit doesn't do you justice!"

She grinned broadly and attempted a curtsey in the heavy flying garment.

"Michael, how lovely to see you again. Are you flying?"

"Can't do anything else, girl. Just arrived from Canada via Prestwick, its great to be warm, or, rather, warmer. I'm with the Atlantic Ferry people. Just brought five – no, sorry, four – Hudsons across the pond. Regret to say we lost one on the way."

Her smile dropped for a moment then Ceci looked at him, pleased.

"Oh, it's really good to see you again, Michael, how are Sarah and little Beth?"

"Oh they're just wonderful; we've got a little boy now: Alistair, he's growing fast, nearly two and as you'd expect, into everything – and little Beth is no longer little. We're living down in Hampshire, moved out of London before it becomes too dangerous for the family. Sarah's still beautiful and busy with the children."

"That's wonderful! I'm based at Hamble with the ATA, only Class I at the moment though. Only trusted to deliver Tigers and Magisters. Harold's just got his wings, due to join a squadron in the next few days. We must get together soon." They touched briefly on their shared Cornucopia experiences; Ceci had been largely instrumental in finding and reporting the lost flying boat and its survivors including the injured Michael Kelly, Sarah, who was now his wife, and her daughter Beth. As they completed their delivery formalities they continued their light-hearted talk until Ceci had to dash outside to catch the taxi Anson back to Hamble but not before exchanging addresses and telephone numbers.

❖ ❖ ❖

Harold Penrose had done well at flying training, starting with Tiger Moths at No. 10 Elementary Flying School at Yatesbury, in Wiltshire, followed by a period of 'square-bashing' at Uxbridge, north of London, and more advanced training on North American Harvards. He was hoping to be posted on to fighters, either Spitfires or Hurricanes. He'd missed the Battle of Britain during his training, which had been interrupted by a period of illness: scarlet fever, but it was not a fighter squadron flying the iconic eight-gun Supermarine Spitfire that he was to join, but a photo-reconnaissance squadron based at RAF Benson in Oxfordshire. Despite having his flying log book annotated: 'Exceptional' by the CO of his training unit – a comment very rarely inscribed – he was bitterly disappointed at being given second-best in his view. It was, however, a view he was soon to change once the value of his new unit's work was revealed to him during some reconnaissance flying training from a bare, freezing and windswept coastal airfield: RAF Dyce in north-east Scotland.

Ceci was secretly pleased that he was not going to join a normal combat squadron. Although, she knew of the sometimes-greater dangers and risks that existed in flying an unarmed single-seater Spitfire fighter high over enemy territory with little except speed, height and pilot skill to ensure survival. And there was the constant and vital imperative to complete the sortie, bringing back crucial images that would aid intelligence-gathering for the fight against Hitler.

❖ ❖ ❖

Michael Kelly crept up the stairs of the red-brick Victorian farmhouse, managing to avoid the squeaky third and seventh treads; it was well past two in the morning. As he passed Beth's bedroom door he peered in. In the dim night-light the little girl lay asleep facing the part-open door; he gently pushed it further. She opened her eyes briefly, then closed them, fast asleep with a slight smile on her tiny face. Sarah had just got back into bed having been up with Alistair again. He'd been crying but was now settled and sleeping deeply and gently snoring. Michael came into their bedroom. Sarah's side-table light was on.

Turning, slightly startled, "Who ... ? Darling ... why didn't you say?"

"I didn't know myself until this afternoon, didn't want to raise your hopes in case I couldn't make it." He sat on her side of the bed holding her. She was crying gently as the tension slowly ebbed away.

Four days later he was packed and ready to go again. Sarah and the two children went to the local railway station at Whitchurch to see him off on the long and arduous wartime rail journey to Liverpool where he would board a ship for Canada. It would be at least a month before there was any chance that he would return home again.

The following day Sarah went up to London to have lunch with her mother, who insisted on staying there despite the increasingly obvious dangers of remaining. The children stayed at home with their newly acquired French nanny. Patricia, a bilingual young teacher had escaped from France in an overcrowded fishing boat with her soldier father just as the Nazis started to move westwards towards their home near St Nazaire.

The wartime Empire restaurant was very crowded, the din of

knives and forks on plain white china and the hubbub of blurred conversations almost ear-splitting; it took a few moments for her to see her mother among a sea of uniforms sitting on the far side of the room at a small table. Opposite sat another, younger, woman in a light-blue uniform. A harassed and balding waiter led her over and pulled a chair out.

"Sarah! At last, I was beginning to think you weren't coming." She pecked her mother on the cheek; she was looking fit despite being plunged back into damp English weather after Singapore's humidity and sunshine.

"Darling, this is Daphne. You probably don't remember her, its years since you met, you were very young – she's your step-niece." Sarah held out her hand to a very slim, pale woman of about twenty-six with auburn hair pulled back in a rather severe style.

The handshake was warm despite first appearances.

"How nice to meet you again. I must admit I didn't remember you. You're in the RAF?" Then Sarah noticed the gold ring on Daphne's left hand.

"Yes, in the Women's Auxiliary Air Force, WAAFs in current jargon. I'm based up in Buckinghamshire at the moment; we haven't been there long, got bombed out of the last place, Heston aerodrome, in September." Ceci's mother intervened in a conspiratorial whisper.

"Daphne's engaged in some hush-hush work, top secret and all that."

Daphne smiled and her whole face lit up, totally altering her appearance. Stunning, thought Ceci.

"It's not quite as dramatic as that. I'm attached to a photographic unit. It's quite interesting at times trying to see what the enemy is up to."

446

"Oh, do you mean photographic interpretation?" nodded Sarah, "I should think it can be very interesting?"

"It is. Strictly between you and me – our problem is a shortage of people to do the interpreting at the moment; the whole operation has grown by leaps and bounds since Sid Cotton first set it up. Originally we only had two pilots before Dunkirk, 'Shorty' Longbottom and Robert Niven. You might have heard of their exploits. Now we are receiving film from a number of photo-reconnaissance ... er ... PR ... squadrons around the country. The growing insistence for more and more photo intelligence from the army and navy is creating a real problem for us." Daphne picked up her glass of water.

"How did you get involved in something like photography – were you in the business before the war, so to speak?" asked Sarah.

"Oh no, I joined the WAAF just after the outbreak of the war hoping to do something useful, duty and all that. I met this chap at the Air Ministry when I was being interviewed for a job involving translating – I speak French and German tolerably well; did modern languages at university – who said jokingly that I should stay out and become a model. I had a good figure then. Service food has seen the end of that," she grimaced. "Anyway, I laughed at such a preposterous idea and suggested that he learned to use a camera first!"

As it turned out, he could – at over three hundred miles an hour, it seems – he was a reconnaissance pilot back from France; he'd been serving in the Special Survey Flight helping the army's Expeditionary Force keep abreast of the German advances – just, by all accounts. Anyway, to cut a very long story short, he invited me to meet another chap after lunch who ran a specialist photographic unit at Heston aerodrome over in west London. He gave me some idea of what they did and how they did it, without giving any secrets away, I should add – and I was hooked. Mind you, he was very persuasive."

Sarah sat for a while picking at her food and listening to the din around her. The food was barely warm and the tiny portion of meat was tough, the dark-brown gravy congealing. She looked up.

"Do you think I could do photo interpretation?" Daphne stopped, fork midway between plate and mouth.

"Of course you could, I knew absolutely nothing to start with. We train people, you know. It's not the sort of job you can pick up in civvy street. Listen, why don't you come and talk with my boss, Peter Riddell? He could explain what's involved and I'm sure he could get you on board with minimum fuss." Sarah was excited by the idea; perhaps she should meet Daphne's boss, she pondered as her mother wittered on about the cost and rarity of fresh vegetables today.

"It sounds interesting, I'm sure I'd enjoy it once I understood what to do. I've got to do something useful, but I've two young children and my husband is often away, so it might prove to be a logistical nightmare. Still, I'd be keen to meet your man if it can be arranged."

"Let me have some dates when you could come to Danesfield, that's our new place near Medmenham in Buckinghamshire, or give me a ring later. Don't worry; meeting Squadron Leader Riddell isn't a commitment, just a way of finding out." Daphne touched her arm and smiled warmly as she spoke. Sarah was reassured.

Later, in a taxi taking her mother back to her flat in Bayswater, Sarah and her mother chatted about Daphne. Her mother warned her daughter about not putting her foot in it at some later stage; Daphne's husband was missing after an attack on some key bridges in France in an effort to hold up the German advance in May. He'd been flying with a squadron equipped with Fairey Battles; the aircraft had soon proved totally useless against the German flak and fighters and had been rapidly withdrawn from action. But not before a lot of young pilots and crews had been sacrificed, she went on. Daphne's husband had been declared killed in action only the previous month, following information from the Red Cross.

After helping her mother sort out some pieces of furniture and papers to be stored in the basement of the building where she lived, Sarah caught a bus to Waterloo station, boarding a very full train home packed with soldiers and sailors armed with large canvas kitbags and rifles. She was conscious of a number of the men looking at her admiringly. So she hadn't lost her looks and figure after the birth of Alistair, she thought, rather pleased. One very young naval officer, a schoolboy almost, offered her his seat, and gazing out at the cold countryside, she thought about Michael. Had he got away from Liverpool yet? The trains were so unreliable these days and there was always the danger of being bombed or strafed by an opportunistic German aircraft. Michael had told her of his chance meeting with Ceci at White Waltham aerodrome. It would be nice to see her and Harold again after all they had been through together; perhaps they could arrange a weekend soon. Sarah and Michael's farmhouse had plenty of room and it would give them an opportunity to catch up with all the gossip.

Five weeks later Sarah Kelly eventually made her way to Danesfield, a large sprawling country house set in acres of once-carefully tended grounds between Marlow and Henley-on-Thames which had been commandeered by the military for the period of hostilities. What had been originally set up by Sidney Cotton at the behest of the military, when they had finally recognised the gaping photo intelligence deficits in their organisations, had grown into a very large and expanding organisation. As Sarah was later to learn, just before the outbreak of war in September 1939, Ian Fleming, Assistant to the Director of Naval Intelligence, had asked Sidney Cotton, an Australian civilian at the time, to take on a secret intelligence reconnaissance job for them using his own private aircraft; a Lockheed 12A. The machine had been cleverly and secretly converted to take high-quality aerial photographs.

The story she heard was that the Admiralty was worried; the issue concerned the feasibility of German U-boats using ports or bays on the neutral Irish Republic's west coast for refuelling and support. Sid Cotton took off in his civilian Lockheed shortly after the meeting with Fleming; he and his co-pilot managed to photograph the entire Irish Republic's west coast from ten thousand feet and again later from two thousand – there were no U-boat refuelling bases evident, he was able to report to a relieved navy. A few days later Sidney Cotton had been brought into the military fold and made an acting Wing Commander with responsibility for a special RAF photographic reconnaissance unit: the Heston Flight, based at the former civil aerodrome in west London. Daphne mentioned how upset everyone had been in 'Sid Cotton's Air Force', as his growing photographic unit was called, when he had been forced to resign his commission a month or so ago.

"It appears from what has been said that there were a lot of regular officers who didn't like his go-do-it approach to problem-solving. He didn't dither about, just got on with things. He did some incredible things, you know. Once, before the war, he flew some senior German officers around Germany in his private Lockheed. What's so funny is that the aircraft's specially concealed cameras took photographs of sensitive areas of Germany while he was flying them about – they knew absolutely nothing about it. I think it's a dreadful way to have treated him. Without his ideas and energy the military would still be literally fighting blind." Sarah detected a note of outrage in Daphne's voice.

Her arrival at the newly named Photographic Reconnaissance Unit at Danesfield coincided with a new peak in photo interpretation activity and Sarah was both relieved and disappointed when met by Daphne and told that Peter Riddell was away at meetings with the Admiralty and Army Chiefs of Staff. The afternoon was spent amicably enough with various members of a relaxed but highly competent group of men and women, working very hard as part of the Special Intelligence Service, or SIS, as it was constantly referred to. As she left with Daphne that evening her mind was made up; she would do it even though it meant some weeks at Farnborough undergoing training. How would Michael take it, she wondered?